See Me, Feel Me
Laylah Jackson

Quill and Company

ISBN: 979-8-9925856-3-6

Published by: Quill & Company Publishing
thequillandcompany@gmail.com
www.quillandcompany.com

First edition, 2025
Printed in the United States of America

Contents

Dedicated to my mom, who has supported me more than I've ever supported myself.

Chapter 1

I remembered the day I was born. Even in the earlier days before taking my first breath, when I heard my real mother's voice through the muffled haze of the woman carrying me—Kelly, I believe her name was. My mother's voice was soothing, full of underlying messages, false promises, and deceit. It was a melody of beautiful lies, a lullaby of manipulation, and I loved her before I even met her, before I could even enter this world.

My real mother, the witch (as my parents would call her when she wasn't around), promised them the baby they swore they deserved. My parents, Kelly and Chad, were all looks and very little brains, loving each other only to create offspring that rivaled Greek gods. Their love was a mirror, reflecting their own vanity back at them. So when they learned that I was going to have a genetic mutation—an imperfection in their perfect lineage—and not be the flawless child they expected, my mother, the witch Priscilla, was sought out. She promised to bless me with looks that could be indescribable, envious, and unmatched, but unbeknownst to my vain parents, she also blessed me with the powers only comic books portrayed.

After agreeing to her terms, my parents offered the witch money. She refused everything, telling them that she would get her payment soon enough. They continued with the pregnancy, and I floated in the warm dark, listening. I listened to their hollow plans, to the way they spoke of me like an accessory, a future showpiece. And I listened to the other voice, the one that whispered through the veil, promising me a world of strength.

Finally, I was ready to come out and meet my *real* mother. Instead, I was only greeted with the sight of Kelly and Chad, their initial shock at the sight of me still ingrained in my memory. The sterile smell of the hospital, the bright, unforgiving lights, and their faces—a mask of horror poorly disguised as concern.

"She looks," I remembered the doctor pausing, a slight stutter in his words as he held me up. "She looks fine. Healthy weight, her lungs are clear, and her eyes," he trailed off, staring deeply into my eyes before finally forcing his gaze away, a flicker of professional fear in his expression.

"Her eyes are a little baffling for a newborn; they are usually not that alert, but after a few tests, she should be fine." He handed me over to my parents' judging faces. I heard my father mutter, "She better be, or I'll kill that witch myself."

My newborn blood boiled. A fury I didn't know I could possess surged through me, and it took everything in my tiny, uncoordinated body to force my eyes open once more and glare as strongly as I could at him. Taken aback by the sudden, intense stare from a creature that should have been barely sentient, my father's breath caught in his throat before he turned to Kelly.

She was looking at me strangely, a mix of repulsion and fear swirling in her gaze. When my new and hazy eyes met hers, she couldn't hold my look for more than a few seconds before glancing at anything else in the room. The fact that they were scared by my looks alone was satisfying, and I allowed myself to slip into the deep warmth of slumber, the world outside already a disappointment.

Early on, I knew I was different. Not necessarily special or different in a good way, but just different from other people. Humans. I don't really think I belong with them. With help from the witch that would visit only once a year, when my parents or whatever nanny they decided on for the week were distracted, she would warn me of a new power. She was my only true constant, the one who saw my darkness and called it beautiful.

At my first birthday party, the house was a storm of noise and fake laughter. My parents were having a photo op with other local influencers, their smiles as plastic as the decorations. Amidst the chaos, a woman dressed in a ridiculous and albeit pun-intended witch outfit scooped me into her arms. It was her. Priscilla. She smiled big and predatorily, her hands grazing my cheeks and dark hair. She only whispered, "*Bloodied nose,*" before setting me back down with a soft kiss to my temple and whisking away into the cold, October night. The words echoed in my mind, a seed planted.

A short while later, my father's mother—a woman whose face was a tight, unmoving mask from years of Botox—picked me up with a tight-lipped smile. She flashed her teeth brightly at me, holding my gaze steady. I looked right back at her, the whispered words of my witch mother pulsing in my head. Before I knew it, her nose twitched and crinkled. A small trickle of blood trailed thinly from one nostril, staining her upper lip before soaking into her perfect white teeth. She gasped, her composure cracking, calling my father over to clean herself up. After a while, the party had to be canceled early because it seemed like everyone was starting to get a nosebleed. I could thank my witch mother for that. I sat in my highchair, watching the chaos unfold, a quiet, cold satisfaction settling in my chest. They were all so fragile.

For my second birthday, it was another big get-together for an ungodly reason. It was all to show off the money my parents made, though nobody else but the three of us knew where that money came from. I couldn't wait to form words well enough to get them in trouble with anyone I could, just anything to get away from their conceited and selfish ways. My parties were always Halloween-themed since I was lucky enough to be born on the day. You could guess that we wore outfits every year, and they forced party guests to dress up, too. It was torture for all of us.

My witch mother once again showed up disguised in that same black pointy hat, shoes, and a hairy mole on her nose to tell me what my eyes could do this time. She only whispered, "*Head opener*," kissed my temple, set me down, and left once more. This time, a small, distant cousin of mine who couldn't be any older than ten scooped me up onto her bony hip. She was blabbering on about getting some cake, looking over at me in the process. I stared at her, the power buzzing beneath my skin, an energy I couldn't control but was morbidly curious about. She paused mid-sentence, her face paling. She groaned loudly, her hands flying to her temples. Adults came to her rescue and mine as she cried out, gripping her head as you could visibly see the veins pulsating and throbbing in her forehead. She collapsed, shivering and whimpering for the pain to go away. I could only watch from my father's arms, a silent, unnerving observer of the agony I had wrought.

My third birthday was considerably smaller than the last, but still large enough for it to be considered big. She came once more. "*Like a rabid dog*," she whispered, kissed, and disappeared into the chilled night. That one confused me, but curiosity got the best of me. I wobbled over to another cousin of mine, my age, with big blue eyes and a toothy smile. He grinned, reaching out to hug me as he stared with pure love in his eyes. This one hurt. With a sudden confused look, he coughed and fell to his knees, eyes rolling to the back of his head. His mother screamed and rushed over, holding his tiny body on her lap as he started foaming at the mouth—like a rabid dog. I didn't like that power much. The sight of his pure love curdling into terror and pain soured something inside me. It was the first time I felt a pang of something akin to guilt.

My fourth birthday consisted of just me, Kelly, and Chad. They had noticed the pattern of people getting hurt whenever I was near them at my parties. They said it ruined their reputation, that I was going to be a murderer before I even hit puberty, and that I was a sociopath at just the ripe age of four. They feared me. I kind of liked the power it gave me. I only wondered how my witch mother, Prissy, as I would call her in my head, would contact me this time and warn me of my power. This year, she didn't get the chance to.

My ugly mother, Kelly, plopped a lazily decorated cupcake in front of me. The smell soured my nose, and the candle barely held its flame. They had ordered real, professionally made cupcakes for themselves and gave me the homemade one that contained enough vinegar to kill. I don't even think cupcakes needed vinegar, but it showed their appreciation and love for me as they feasted on the good ones.

Angrily, I pushed the cupcake to the ground, uncaring of the mess I made. My parents gasped, my mother screaming at me, coming at me with her hand raised. I flinched, and then I heard a soft whisper carry through my ears, "*Going under.*"

As my mother stared at me with the fury of a thousand suns burning through her false lashes, with a sudden jolt, she fell to the ground in a heap of gangly bones and skinny limbs. My father yelped and dashed toward her limp body, screaming at me all the while, asking what I did to his wife, why had I come out like this, and what that witch did to me.

"Made me better," was all I said, my voice small but clear, before crawling out of my chair and heading to my overly priced and decorated room. I heard Kelly's voice come cracking through the walls with a wail to rival a banshee. She cried about wishing I was normal, about what was to come next, and if I would be able to kill next year. I think they both already knew the answer to that.

My parents didn't celebrate my fifth birthday. They instead locked themselves in their room and told me that I could do whatever I wanted by myself for the day. I did. I walked outside and waited for my real mother to come, scoop me in her arms, whisper whatever she blessed me with this year, kiss my head, and leave.

I was outside for only a couple of minutes before I saw her, gliding through the thick fog in the air, head down but her smile still white and wide. My heart warmed at the sight of her, and I giggled lightly.

"Mama!" I yelled, running full force toward her as she picked me up with a lighthearted laugh and spin. I hugged her neck tightly, burying my face in her loose ash-blond curls as she squeezed me back. I pulled back to look into her soft blue eyes as they crinkled at the corner at the sight of me.

"What power did you give me this year?" I asked with a toothy grin. Her smile matched mine as she set me down, holding my hand and guiding me to the large, overly expensive house. We skipped lightly as we made our way to the grand front door. My mother squatted down and grabbed both of my tiny hands in hers, a serious look on her face.

"I'm going to pack your bags and all of your essentials as you go and show your parents your last new power, okay?" Confused, I nodded but kept my feet planted on the ground as my mother tried to pull me in. Once noticing my resistance, she looked back and was at eye level with me again.

"What's wrong, baby?" she asked quietly, cupping my cheeks. I shrugged and played with the loose string on my pajama pants.

"Does this," I paused and heaved in a large breath. "Does this mean I'll never get to see my parents again?" I couldn't meet her eyes as my mother rubbed her thumb soothingly under my eyes. She kissed my forehead softly before leaning back.

"Do you really want to stay with them?" she asked, cocking her head to the side. I tried to shake my head quickly, but she cut me off. "You see how horrible people they are, don't you? They called you a sociopath all because you have these powers! These amazing powers that I have gifted you with! What kind of parents treat their children like that?" She pursed her lips disapprovingly as I glanced between her and the front door.

"If I was your mommy forever, I would *always* love you. I wouldn't give you any nasty cupcakes, or make you converse with people who are filled to the brim with plastic, or hate you like how they hate you." My ears perked up at that last comment.

"They hate me?" I asked slowly. My chest grew tight at the thought. I knew my parents were scared of me and didn't like my powers much, but it never occurred to me that they *hated* me. My eyebrows scrunched together as my bottom lip started to wobble. I could feel the mother who loved me put her hand on my shoulder and under my chin, willing me to look up at her. Once I finally met her eyes, she was smiling so softly, it looked like a halo gleamed above her head.

"Yes, but baby, I would never hate the child that I gave life to." My eyes lit up like a Christmas tree, love blooming all around me as I gazed into my mother's eyes. This was my *real* and *actual* mother! She would love me no matter what, something the people who only pushed my vessel out into the universe couldn't do. I wrapped my tiny arms around her neck as she laughed lightly and pulled me away. She gave me another serious look as she steadied me.

"Are you ready to get your last power, baby?" I nodded excitedly. My mother leaned in next to my ear, her lips brushing the shell softly. As quiet as a wisp of wind, she whispered, "*To rot.*"

It was like a fever dream, almost. We walked hand in hand throughout the house, my mother gliding through like she had been here a million times before. She kissed my cheeks one last time before pushing me to my parents' door as she slinked into my room to pack my bags. I counted to five before knocking on their door, hearing their conversation stop abruptly.

"What do you want?" I heard Kelly yell, her voice timidly shaking. "We told you that you have the whole day to yourself, Vivienne, please just leave us alone!" I could almost see her quivering. I smiled wide and put on the sweetest voice I could muster up.

"Mommy, please," I tried to hold in my snickering. "My tummy hurts, and I just want to lay down with you and Daddy." I paused once more and tried to drain all of the sweetness from my core into this last word. "Pleeeaaase?" I heard them pause before there was a slight shuffle of feet and then locks coming undone.

My father looked down at me with a wary look on his face as I batted my eyelashes up at him. I grinned cruelly as he continued to stare, body locking up on him before he stilled and crumbled to the ground. I heard Kelly scream as Daddy's mouth hung open, blood pooling from his 'O' shaped lips onto the glistening wooden floors. His body convulsed before curling in on itself and emitting an awful smell. I couldn't be bothered enough to care though as I started to make my way toward her.

She scrambled from the bed, screaming and crying and reaching for her phone as I walked closer. Her hands shook as she babbled on to the 911 operator, her words jumbled and unclear. She made the mistake of looking at me, eyes locking in on mine as my grin stretched wide like a Cheshire Cat.

Before I knew it, her body slumped the rest of the way to the ground. A soft thump on the floor, hair in disarray, blood spilling from her fake lips, her body curling in on itself, smelling like rot. Just like how my real mother wanted it. I skipped out of the room to find her sitting on the couch, two small bags beside her and a glass of wine against her lips.

Her smile matched mine as I grabbed a bag and she grabbed the other. We headed out the door, my mother throwing the rest of the wine back before carelessly dropping it on the floor. It shattered loudly in the otherwise eerily silent house and I laughed, loud and joyous. She laughed alongside me as we walked to the gray van that I don't remember being there beforehand. Throwing my bags in the seat beside me, my mother buckled me into the backseat and quickly hopped in behind the wheel as police sirens were heard not too far from us.

She pulled off quickly, glancing at me in the rearview mirror. I matched her smile as I stared at her eyes and eyebrows that were visible. I couldn't believe that she was finally taking me out of that hellhole after five years. Finally, reunited with the one person in the world that loves me. I realized that she was speaking to me and pulled myself out of my thoughts quickly.

"We're on our way to pick up your new brother, baby. Would you like a brother?" I nodded excitedly. She grinned and pursed her lips, glancing at me once more in the mirror before she dug into the bag sitting in the passenger seat. She reached back, eyes still on the road as she passed me a pair of large black-rimmed glasses and thick, black lenses. I grabbed them and eyed them quietly.

"Put those on, baby. We don't need you hurting someone on the ride over," she chuckled. I nodded and slipped the glasses on, feeling like some cool spy. I shot a couple of finger guns and blew imaginary steam from the tip of my finger as my mother laughed. She stole a couple more glances before twisting her mouth once more.

"And you know what?" she spoke sharply in the quiet car. "While we're at it, since you won't be going home again, we should give you a new name." Instantly, I perked up.

"Tionna!" I yelled excitedly, kicking my feet. "I've always loved that name."

"Hmm," my mother hummed. "I was thinking something more like," she paused before lighting up, her finger tapping the steering wheel. "I love Areya! How does that sound? Areya." My mother tasted the name on her tongue. I nodded quietly, not wanting to upset her especially after she had just saved me from those monsters who called themselves my parents.

"I like it. Areya," I repeated the name as my mother smiled happily, humming and dancing in her seat. She nodded once more, speaking more to herself as she turned onto the highway and off into the setting sun.

"Yeah, Areya Light, even through all of my darkness." I stared at her in the mirror, but she never caught my eye, too busy mumbling to herself. I wondered how long it would be before I met the boy who would become my new brother. Excited at the thought but insanely sleepy, I visualized what he would look like, what his new name would be, and how awesome it would be to meet someone like me. Before I knew it, I fell asleep, glasses barely hanging onto my nose.

I was woken by the harsh slamming of the car door. My mother was cussing and screaming and smacking the steering wheel as she started to drive off furiously. Confused and still tired, I leaned forward to grab her shoulder. Suddenly aware of my presence, she calmed slightly and I could hear the waver in her voice.

"You can't get your brother right now, Areya." My eyes grew wide as my lip wobbled, sudden disappointment flowing through me.

"Why," I swallowed, my throat dry and begging for water. "Why not, mama?" She turned quickly toward me, eyes wide as a tear rolled down her cheek. I heard honking before she swerved and focused back on the road.

"Things didn't go as planned, baby," she whispered, reaching back with one hand and grabbing onto my own. I unbuckled my seat belt and climbed into the passenger seat, clinging onto her free arm. She looked at me with watery eyes before focusing on the road once more.

"It's okay," I tried to reassure her, but sleep started to overtake me again. My eyes grew heavy as I wrapped my arms around her free arm, rubbing circles into the backs of my hand. I felt her kiss the top of my head as I whispered sleepily. "You can always try again next time," I yawned and leaned into her as much as I could. Before sleep could fully consume me, I heard my mother whisper into the rain-filled night,

"You're right. We'll try again in thirteen. Until then, it'll just be me and my Areya Light. Always me and you, baby. Always."

Chapter 2

I ignored the throbbing in my cheek, biting the split lip between my pristine white teeth. I don't remember what I did wrong this time, but I'm sure it was something minuscule. Prissy was going on another tangent again about another mistake I had made while completing a job, and at this point, I wasn't listening. The landscape outside the car window was a monotonous blur of faded greens and browns, another state I wouldn't remember, another temporary stop on our endless, frantic marathon away from consequence.

She drove like a madman down the highway, swerving with every smack upside my head and against my cheek, cussing and spitting with every name she called me. I couldn't care less anymore. I was getting tired of doing these 'jobs' for her with nothing in return, no light to look forward to.

"I have told you time and time and time again to always wear gloves and to always cover your face!" she yelled, jacking my collar and swinging my head wildly around. I sat there emotionless and waited for her rampage to be over with.

"Now, we have to move for the *third time* in only two years! Two years, Areya!" She pulled my ear as I followed her hand down to the console before she released me to hit me again. My lack of response only made her madder, but she couldn't blame anyone but herself. She broke and reprogrammed me into learning more about my primal urges, accepting the black magic and spells that bound my veins together, becoming nothing but her weapon.

The training had started when I was nine. That was the year Prissy had deemed me ready to "earn my place." We were in a damp, mildew-scented basement in some forgotten town in Ohio. She had tied a stray dog to a post. It was old, its fur matted and its eyes cloudy, but it whimpered, pulling against its rope.

"You feel for it, don't you?" Prissy had asked, her voice a soft, dangerous caress. She stood behind me, her hands on my shoulders. "You feel its pain. That's your weakness, Areya. We have to carve it out of you."

She had handed me a dull, rust-flecked knife. "You're not going to use your eyes. You're going to use your hands. You're going to feel it. Understand that life is fleeting, and you are the one who decides when it ends." I had refused, my small body shaking. The dog whined again, a sound that tore at my insides. That refusal earned me my first lesson in what she called 'recalibration'. She didn't touch the dog. She touched me. The pain was sharp, precise, and it didn't stop until I was on the floor, my own whimpers mingling with the dog's. By the time I could stand again, the knife felt heavy but necessary in my hand. She broke me down and rebuilt me in her image, a machine forged in pain and obedience.

Yet, as the years passed, she grew more and more frustrated by the second. Gods, what a joke. I couldn't wait for her to be my last job, and it didn't matter where I would end up after. I just wanted to get away from her and go far away from any place she had ever touched. Another pull to my short locks brought me back to the reality of the beat-up car and her endless tirade.

"Are you even listening?" Her crazed blue eyes darted around the car, on the lookout for any cop cars, even though we were far away from the crime scenes. I rolled my eyes at her paranoia and grunted.

"Yes, *Mother*," I sneered through clenched teeth. "I made a simple mistake, and now we have to move to the middle of *nowhere*. Like I said earlier, sorry." I rolled my eyes, smirking at her screech that rang through the beat-up trash on wheels. She pinched my cheek tightly in between her sharp claws and growled.

"Don't be cheeky, Areya. This is serious." Her voice grew low, and my smirk fell dimly. I sank deeper into the seats and glowered at the sun that shone too brightly in the gloomy car. "If you make another mistake like this in North Dakota, we *will* be caught." She paused. "And I don't think I'll be able to escape this time," she murmured under her breath.

I grumbled to myself some kind of affirmation, sneering at the spiky blue and white "Welcome to North Dakota" sign that seemed to taunt me. I knew I had screwed up my last job, but did we have to move here out of all places? I crossed my arms over my chest, blocking out the almost constant nagging from Prissy and thinking back on what got us here.

"It's just another simple job," Prissy had told me only a week ago. "Don't screw it up; it's as simple as a cakewalk." She had patted my cheek and kissed my forehead, a gesture that was meant to look motherly but felt as cold and calculating as a snake's kiss. She was wishing me luck on the latest 'job' she had assigned. She gave me at least one job a week of killing someone that she said "had to go" for a "good reason that I didn't need to concern myself with." I didn't question it, just went along with every murder. I wasn't scared of Prissy killing me if I refused, but I decided against the hassle of all the arguing and plotting. Just get it over with; these people probably deserved it in someone else's eyes.

For the final job in Arizona, she had sent me out to finish the victim at around 1 a.m. She wished me luck, smiled, and waved lovingly at the door as if she were sending me off on my first date with a boy I liked. In some parallel universe that I liked to imagine at times, I let it comfort me. It was a small, fragile daydream of a normal life, a temporary shield against the ugliness of my reality.

I think it's the way I screwed up so badly that night. I was so engulfed in this warming daydream, this fantasy of first dates and nervous laughter, that I made one of the biggest mistakes of my life. I was careless. Lazy. I left a footprint in the mud by the back door, a single strand of my short hair on the victim's carpet. Small things, but in our world, small things were catastrophic. In only a matter of hours, Prissy and I had been packed and on the road to a new state, the lingering scent of fear and anger clinging to her like cheap perfume.

"You were never one for subtleties, huh Prissy?" I asked, glaring at her from the corner of my eye as she pulled up to our new house. She grinned lazily before picking up and rolling her two bags inside the ridiculously mint-green-colored house. I rolled my eyes, heaving my duffle bag over my shoulder and slamming the car door shut. I walked through the disgustingly yellow front door and paused.

The inside of the new house surprisingly wasn't as bad as the outside. The walls were soft blue and white, and rooms were already stocked with minimal furniture. Prissy came to stand beside me in the archway, under a cheap-looking chandelier that held no real shine to it on the low ceilings.

Looking straight ahead, I was greeted by the baby-blue living room. There was a small, white leather loveseat next to a low glass coffee table that already had a couple of Prissy's books neatly stacked up. Seated in the corner, there was a ridiculously large white bean bag chair in front of a cozy-looking fireplace and a couple of fluffy grey throw pillows around it.

I shifted my eyes to the dining room, a more sophisticated look with a mahogany table and only three chairs around it. Hmm, that's kind of...odd. You would think it would either be an even two or four, but I let the number of chairs roll off of my shoulder. I turned to the small kitchen that matched the colors of the living room. The walls here, though, were painted grey with white and blue accents. It looked bare and kinda creepy. I was getting hospital vibes from it but found a warm sense of home to it all. Hopefully, we won't have to move too soon this time.

Finally, I faced Prissy who was already staring at me with a wide smile, hands cupping her cheeks excitedly. She beamed brightly and gripped my hands in hers tightly.

"So?" She asked, eyes darting around the house. "How do you like it? I used to live here years ago and decided that we should make do with this spare house! We still have the furniture and everything!" She bounced on the balls of her feet, suddenly rushing skittishly around the house to poke and dust off everything that she hadn't touched in obvious years. In all of my thirteen years of living with Prissy, we had never been to North Dakota, so I can't imagine how long it's been for her. I wondered who even kept up with the place for it to not be in a complete heap of dust and bones by now. But she had mentioned calling up an 'old friend' and getting them to turn the water and heat back on. They must have been caring for this place since then.

I walked around until I found white steps leading to the upper rooms and went in search of a bedroom to call mine. I heard Prissy yell, "The one on the left!" and pushed myself up the almost endless flight of stairs. By the time I made it to my new room, I was almost visibly taken aback. The room was hot pink and covered in rainbows and unicorns and all kinds of girly things I had never been fond of.

I crept slowly into the room, glancing around as if some creepy child that had been left for years would come emerging from the closet with a cry of "Mine!" I checked the closet first too, though just to be safe. It was empty, save for a stuffed pink bear that had a suspicious stain on its tummy. I left it alone and checked out the rest of the room.

There was a small bed in the middle with a pink canopy hanging above it and fluffy pink covers with a unicorn farting rainbows draped across the expanse of it. To the left of the bed was a white night table, void of anything on it except for an empty notebook whose pages had obviously been torn out. I checked out the empty dresser drawers and cringed at the tiny clothes and underwear still left in it. The kid couldn't have been older than seven by the sheer tininess of each neatly folded shirt. Finally, the vanity that sat primped and pretty a couple of steps in front of the bed gave me the biggest creeps. And I don't get creeped out easily.

There was a single hairbrush sitting directly in the middle of the three mirrors that faced whoever sat on the leather white bench in front of it. There was a large clump of orange hair still sitting in between the bristles. I wouldn't have minded any other time, as this wasn't the first time Prissy and I had moved into a previously owned home. But the clump of hair was thickly matted with something that couldn't be described as anything other than blood. It was dry and crumbly and I didn't want to move it, touch it, or even look at it at this point. Especially knowing that it most likely came from a child who hadn't even hit puberty yet. I was startled at the sight of Prissy in the three mirrors.

"Oh?" she asked, surprised at my wild and wide eyes. "Do I need to retrain you, Areya?"

I glanced down at the brush and quickly averted my gaze elsewhere. I shook my head and mumbled, "No, mother." I only called her mother when she 'trained' me, another term for beating me until I moved exactly how she wanted me to, reacted how she wanted me to and behaved like a dog that she had found battered and abused. I didn't even want to think about what nine-year-old me had to suffer through.

She smiled cruelly, picking up the brush and pulling the matted hair from the bristles. She sat the bloodied hair directly in front of me on the white vanity, using the hair to border the crayon drawings I hadn't noticed before. The drawings were almost indescribable, with loops and colors overlapping. I could only make out a little girl with a black and purple striped sweater and orange hair with a wide smile on her face. And red scribbles painting her hands and teeth.

"Good. All that training back then was so exhausting, don't you agree?" By the time she had finished pulling all of the hair out, Priscilla ran the brush through my head. I cringed inwardly, slightly pulling my shoulders up and biting my lip to keep from yelling at her. She studied my expressions in the mirror, and though they were minuscule, she still noticed.

My hair wasn't even long enough to comfortably run the brush through. The end of the bristles kept stabbing the tips of my ears, roughly scratching the back of my neck. She didn't stop there though; she ran the brush to the base of my spine as if it were pure muscle memory to brush this long. My hair was cut low to my head, long enough on top to cover my eyes and the bottom of my nose. I don't know why she continued to brush this far down, but I raised my shoulders higher and higher with each stroke.

By the time she finished, she simply tapped in between my shoulder blades, signaling me to relax. I let out a shuddered breath and hoped she wouldn't pop me upside the head with the brush the same way she did when I was little and didn't want to sit to get my hair done. I prepared myself for the hit but was surprised when she roughly dropped the brush down in front of me on the vanity, making the hair fly everywhere.

I sputtered and tried to peel the strays off my lips as Prissy only watched. By the time I got it all off, she was smiling widely. A smile that unnerved me to no end. We sat staring at each other in the mirror for a couple of beats longer before she clapped her hands with a squeal.

"What color do you want to paint your new room?" she asked excitedly. "I know you hate pink and everything in here, plus you need a bigger bed, and I know you hate that canopy too…" Prissy started to ramble on and on about all the changes I would want to make in the room. I tuned back in when she grabbed my shoulders and excitedly grinned at me in the mirror.

"I'm gonna get some paint and new covers and the new bed I preordered should be arriving in the next couple of hours! While I'm out, answer the door if they deliver it, will you? The shopping might take me a while. You know how much I love decorating a new house!" she squealed and skipped out of the bedroom. I sat watching the door for a couple of minutes, still slightly in a daze at her pure excitement. I could never get used to her happy outburst after seeing how quickly she could change and snap at the drop of a dime.

When I heard the door open and close, I finally moved from my spot in front of the vanity to the bed, pushing back the canopy that I needed to take down soon. Crawling up on the fluffy covers, I fell back, coughing up the dust that flew around my face. I toyed with the glasses in my hoodie pocket, thumbing the blacked-out lenses and letting my mind go where I always tried to avoid while conscious. My prison and my protection, all in one.

Chapter 3

The police had eventually tied Kelly and Chad's murder to a string of others who had died at the hands of my eyes, unbeknownst to them. The local news had dubbed the killer "The Rot," a name that was both crude and chillingly accurate. No visible cuts or bruises beforehand; a body decaying in only a matter of minutes; the smell of rot wafting through each place so heavily you couldn't ignore it. I'd seen the reports on TV in cheap motel rooms, the sensationalist headlines flashing across the screen: *MYSTERY DECAY PLAGUES MIDWEST*.

They believed it was the "person" who took me that had committed every gruesome murder. The official narrative was a tragic one: little Vivienne McDowell, snatched from her loving home, now a pawn in a monster's game. Missing-person posters with my five-year-old face—a face I no longer recognized—were probably still tacked to bulletin boards in towns I'd long since forgotten. But the police couldn't figure out *how* the victims were specifically killed and *why* they had even taken me. How could someone's body decompose so quickly with no visible evidence and nothing incriminating showing up in an autopsy?

And they just could not grasp for the life of them *why me*. Why little-old Vivienne, from a well-cared-for couple in a fancy neighborhood, had gone missing with someone that has murdered at least a hundred people by now? They believed that this kidnapper would eventually give me up, exchange me for ransom, and drop me off, dirtied and confused, in the middle of some small town. Why did they start with my parents first? There were no clear connections between them and future victims. Why did this person take me? And then the question came into play: is Vivienne even still alive?

I wished I could answer them, tell them that Vivienne has been long gone. That she has been smothered by this new name, new identity, by this new mother. I even thought about telling the police every once in a blue moon, but it was almost like Prissy knew every time. She would stare pointedly at me, bare her teeth, and push a warning snarl from her throat.

I'm unfazed by the threat now. I don't even think I want Vivienne to be found anymore. Priscilla doesn't either. She would only beat every remnant of the girl that just wanted parental love. I don't know if my body has enough room for new scars.

I popped up from my dream in a cold sweat. My hoodie stuck closely to my sticky body as I heaved in and out to catch my breath. When I finally gathered my bearings, I heard the ring of the doorbell that must have woken me. I peeled the hoodie off, the fabric clinging to my skin, and slipped on my glasses to *not* kill whoever was dropping off the mattress. I headed downstairs, my feet silent on the steps.

They rang the doorbell for the third time when I finally made it to the archway. I swung the door open wide and grunted at the guy who was standing there in a forest green uniform. I glanced over his shoulder at the truck sitting in our driveway and couldn't miss the way his eyes roamed my form. I had completely forgotten that I only wore a tank top under the hoodie despite the chill of the weather. The worker glanced around the empty house.

"Is this the," he paused to look down at a clipboard, his eyes struggling to meet mine. "Matthews residence?" he asked.

My lip twitched and I grunted again, reaching forward to sign whatever was on the clipboard. He handed it over, and I tried not to acknowledge the not-so-subtle brush of his fingers against the back of my hand that lingered a bit too long. I sloppily signed my name and handed it back to him as he stared at me with a small smirk. He glanced around the house once more before throwing a look over his shoulder at our empty driveway.

"You home alone, Ms. Matthews?" he asked, a grin splitting his pretty, handsome face, as a gleam of metal shone in his mouth. I had to admit; that he was easy on the eyes. But the last thing I was interested in was boys and dating. I would end up killing them before I even got my first kiss. I grunted again and shrugged, leaning on the doorway.

"Yes, I am. Now, can I get my mattress?" I asked, my short temper already ticking. I knew what game he was trying to play and I didn't feel like indulging in it. He quirked an eyebrow, but never let that smile fade. He shrugged and trotted back to the truck as I followed behind him. He threw a glance over his shoulder and stopped, as I almost ran into the back of him.

"You're a lady, Ms. Matthews. I got the mattress." I rolled my eyes and groaned. I had been trained by Prissy for years to not only be obedient, but how to hold my own weight as well. I could probably bench twice his weight and he wouldn't even be able to tell.

He only laughed at my groan and lifted the door to the back of the truck open. He grabbed the closest mattress and obviously struggled there for a moment. After watching him try to find a way to pull it inside by himself, I grabbed the other end of the mattress and hauled it up quickly. I heard him sputter before pulling his weight and lugging the mattress inside with me. I dropped it in front of the steps leading up to the bedrooms and turned to him, signaling his time to go. I suddenly started backing him up as he stumbled to the front door.

"Thanks for dropping it off. Goodbye, now." When he reached the door, he quickly grabbed my forearm. I paused, staring at his brown hand as it slowly started to loosen.

"Hey! I just wanted to get your name and number before I left, if you don't mind." He grinned at me, dimples piercing his cheek. "I'm Ace, by the way." He let go of my arm and shook my limp hand instead.

"And I'm not interested. Again, goodbye." I tried to close the door on him, but he quickly shoved his combat boot in the door. He peaked his head through with a frown, pushing the door open more.

"There's no need to be rude about it," he sneered. "I'm just trying to help you make a new friend in a new town and here you are being all pissy about it." He folded his strong arms against his chest, an obvious sign of him trying to show off his strength and intimidate me. In return, I did the same as I squared him off with an equally impressive strength.

"Not being pissy," I sneered. "Just not interested."

"What?" he scoffed. "You gotta thing against guys like me, or something? Against guys in general?" At that, I chuckled. My temper had reached its limit and I was ready to be done with this conversation and this scum called Ace. A scummy name for a scummy guy.

"You know what, Ace?" I hummed, a crooked, malicious smile pulling at my face, ignoring the car that was pulling up behind him. "I think it's time for you," I started to pull off my glasses, ready to send him crumbling to the ground, any neighbors that might be watching, be damned. The world narrowed, the sounds of the street faded, and the only thing that existed was the space between my eyes and his arrogant face. The familiar, cold power began to prickle at the back of my neck.

"To rot—"

"Areya!"

I paused at the sharp call of my name, glasses barely on the tip of my nose. I clenched my eyes shut and gritted my teeth, cursing at the awful but life-saving timing of Prissy. If it were nine-year-old me standing here, I would have cried and run into the darkest corner I could find merely at her stare. But instead, I kept my head down and willed myself to calm down, eyes aflame and burning.

Prissy put on a sickeningly sweet smile at Ace, who had just assumed my sexuality because I didn't accept his advances. He had basically harassed me for my name and number. Been an absolute creep with the way he'd looked at me. Yet, I'm the bad guy for almost killing him in broad daylight. I scoffed under my breath as Prissy made her way to the front door.

"And who is this handsome young man?" I could tell when she was irritated by the twitch in her eyebrow and the pseudo-sweetness dripping from her tongue. Ace glanced in between Prissy and the hand that still lingered on my glasses.

"Hello, Ms. Matthews. I was just dropping off the mattress." He tipped his hat that capped his thick curls and dyed a lighter brown at the tips. "Well, I'll be off then. Hope you enjoy the mattress." He threw me one last scornful look before smiling sweetly at Prissy who thanked him and smiled back. We watched him climb in the truck and quickly pull off. I tried not to shrink when she turned to me, her gaze dark and leering. She didn't even have to voice her implied instructions.

I briskly walked into the house, head low and ready for the beating I was about to receive. I bit my lip to muffle the cry at the punch I took in the kidney, doubling over and holding my side. Prissy punched me again on my shoulder blade and kicked my feet from under me. I landed on my face, glasses skewing to the side as I bit back a groan.

"Areya," she said calmly. "Have you lost your entire mind?" I couldn't help the flinch at the sudden crescendo in the last word. "I've been gone for five," a kick to the ribs, "hours," a kick to my arms blocking my face, "and you're already trying to kill someone. Have you not learned?" The final blow was delivered to my stomach, knocking all of the wind out of me.

I struggled to catch my breath as Prissy stood over me silently. She glowered for a couple of moments before trudging outside to get the bags she had to leave in the car to stop me.

"Come help me with the bags. After retrieving them, go to your room and start taking everything down and painting. I want the room completed by dawn. Any later and you will receive a harsher punishment than this evening. Go." I struggled to sit up, clutching my stomach as I pushed myself to stand. I left the glasses on the ground and limped out to the car as Prissy only watched me from the doorway.

By the time I brought in the last bag, I was completely beat. My legs wobbled, my arms ached and my back felt like there had been a burning hole gaping cruelly inside of it. Prissy only stared at me with cold eyes before turning to the kitchen.

"Get to it," she snapped. I moved as quickly as my sluggish body could and started taking each bag up to my room. This was going to be a long night.

*

I had been standing above countless bodies, all dead at my hands. Every corpse curled in on itself, emitting a god-awful smell that would choke any ordinary person. But not me. I had been smelling this rot for years and years now; the smell comforted me almost. It showed that I had finished yet another job for Prissy and got to live for another week.

Out of the mountains of bodies that I stood atop, I never forgot a face. From every person whose life I have taken since five, each face haunted my memory. I was confused at the sight of a new one, eyes gaping wide and confused, my mouth curled into a frown. I squatted down to look closer at the boyish face and lightly held his cheek in my hands.

I would have remembered him. He looked so familiar but I couldn't seem to place him. I haven't killed him yet if he was even a real person. In the midst of my hazy and confused thoughts, his eyes quickly scanned over my form before gripping my hand in his. I screamed as he squeezed me tighter, wrenching my arm from his face, causing me to fall from over the mountain I had been standing on.

As I fell, each body turned its rotting head to face me. They all watched me scream for help, eyes wide and curious, arms too weak from the decay to help catch me. Even if they could, I doubt they would ever save me.

I saw Kelly and Chad's faces on the way down, still judging and frightened. I reached out to them but fell even faster. I squeezed my eyes shut and whimpered, hoping that whatever I fell on impacted my fall enough to only knock the breath out of me. As I grew closer to the bottom of the mountain of corpses, the sudden stop jolted me awake.

I jumped up at the sound of a high screech carrying throughout the house. I snatched off my glasses, chest heaving as I dashed out of the room for any sight of an intruder. I fumbled down the steps and looked wildly around, only to be greeted with the sign of Prissy standing in the kitchen pouting. I briskly walked over to her, immediately checking her body for any signs of cuts or bruises as she waved me off.

"What's wrong?" I hurriedly asked. "What happened? Are you okay?" She pulled back from my grip and picked up the steaming cup of coffee on the counter to the right of her.

"I hate this stupid state and their stupid rules!" she cried like a petulant child. I grunted in confusion and quirked a brow, signaling her to finish.

"I had to jump through hoops to get to homeschool you! They're telling me to just put you in regular *public school* for the last six months of your senior year. I don't wanna!" She stomped her feet and I cocked my head at her. This was the woman who helped and coerced me into killing my parents at five, and now look at her. Acting like a child because she couldn't get her way. I had to hold back from rolling my eyes at her tantrum and sighed, pinching the bridge of my nose.

"Prissy, I don't mind." She quickly cut me off.

"But *I* do! I don't want you surrounded by those numbskulls for the next few months." She suddenly pulled me into a tight hug, bumping her head under my chin. I stood there awkwardly for a moment, unsure of what to do with my hands. We had stopped all affection after I turned nine; she said she didn't want to soften me up. She said that it would only make me weaker, have a bigger heart, and cry for the people I had to murder. This was completely out of the ordinary for us and it made me tense up.

Finally, when she pulled away, she held onto my upper arms and looked up at me with her big doe, watery eyes. Her bottom lip wobbled as she hiccuped.

"You really don't mind, Areya?" she asked softly. "If it's a problem, then I can always just fight harder. I know you've never been to a real school before, but if it's too much—"

"Prissy." I pulled her hands off of my arms and smiled awkwardly. "I promise you, it's fine. It's just the last five or six months, right? What's the harm in that?" I asked, inwardly hoping I wasn't jinxing myself.

She nodded, eyes still watery before she sniffled and pulled away, dabbing at the tears that stuck to her lashes. "Okay, I get it. I'm going back up to the school to get you registered and you'll start Monday." She picked up her worn-out purse from the hook in the archway as I followed her to the door.

"And when I come back, we have to do some serious shopping for clothes and school supplies." She turned to face me, holding my cheek in her hands. I don't know what was up with this affection today, but it was starting to make me uncomfortable.

"We'll have to discuss some rules and play-by-play on how you're going to keep up with your jobs." She paused, eyes darting across my face. "And how not to kill other students without my say so." She pinched my cheek harshly for a split second before fluttering out of the door and into the old beat-up car. I watched her leave before turning back inside the house.

I went up to my now red room with black accents—much more fitting to my taste, as Prissy knew me too well—and sat in front of the laptop she allowed me to buy for myself a couple of months ago. The laptop sat on the still white vanity, now scrubbed clean of any old crayon drawings, hair, and brushes. I positioned the mirrors to all line up in one direction instead of curving in to face me, so I could glance up and see the entire expanse of my room with ease. No more surprise scares from Prissy.

After opening it and waiting for the laptop to warm up, I typed up a quick search for the local neighborhood school. Lo and behold, one of the first news articles about the school is praising one of the many wins of the football team, glorifying one student in particular who helped drive the win home. *Ace Foster*. The jerk that almost died at my hands just two days ago.

I was going to school with *him*? Prissy just told me that I couldn't kill anyone without her say, and he was at the top of my own kill list. This is going to be a lot harder than I expected. He better tread lightly, lest he falls prey to my eyes. Prissy's permission or 'jobs' be damned.

Chapter 4

Shopping with Prissy was always awful. It wasn't merely a chore; it was a performance, a carefully choreographed dance of submission and manipulation where I was the un-willing star. She constantly wanted me to dress more to her standards—bubbly, bright, mismatched patterns and animal print. Every time she bounced around our house, a whirlwind of chaotic color, I had to shield my eyes from each god-awful outfit she had worn. She loved it though, and I didn't want to make her feel bad for it. Plus, it wasn't like I was the epitome of fashion sense anyway.

My taste was the complete opposite of hers. All I ever wore was black, on top of black, on top of black. If it was a good day, then I would throw on more monotonous colors like grey and white, but that was rare. Prissy thought it's because I'm gloomy, brooding, and want to stay incognito, but it's just because I'm lazy and matching colors takes too much work. It was a simple, stark uniform for a simple, stark existence. It was armor. Bright colors felt like a lie, a betrayal of the darkness I carried inside me. Black was honest.

We were in a generic department store, the air thick with the smell of cheap perfume and the faint, chemical scent of new clothes. Fluorescent lights hummed overhead, casting a sterile, unflattering glow on everything. Prissy flitted through the racks like a humming-bird high on nectar, her fingers dancing over fabrics, pulling out one monstrosity after another.

"What about this?" Prissy held up a rainbow dress that would've stopped about mid-thigh on me. It was a cacophony of color, an assault on the eyes. I narrowed my eyes at her and pursed my lips as she threw her head back in laughter.

"Why the face?" she giggled, putting the dress back on the rack. "You need more color in your life, Areya. All this black... it's so draining."

"I wouldn't even look right in that," I grumbled, picking up a black sweatshirt with a single, elegant blue rose embroidered on the front of it. There's that pop of color that

Prissy wanted from me so bad. It was a compromise, a tiny concession in a war of wills I was destined to lose.

"Of course you would think that because you never *tried* to wear something this colorful." She rolled her eyes, a smile still lingering on her face. "Plus, I thought it was fitting seeing as how you are," she trailed off, clearing her throat and side-eyeing me. I paused and faced her, arching my eyebrow.

"I'm what?" I asked, confused but slowly getting the hint. My mind flashed to Ace's stupid assumption at the front door. Because I wasn't interested in him, I must be interested in girls. The logic of a simple mind.

"Rainbow...? You know?" she asked lowly, her voice dropping to a conspiratorial whisper as she shifted her eyes around the quiet store. Nobody else was in sight, save for a hooded figure about two aisles over that seemed to linger, their back to us. I blew a breath from my nose and groaned, thinking back on Ace's stupid assumption all because I rejected his advances.

"I'm not gay, if that's what you're asking." Squaring her off with a pointed look, I watched the subtle play of emotions on her face. She wasn't just asking; she was probing, looking for another weakness, another angle of control.

Prissy shrugged, a gesture too casual to be believable. "Just want to make sure we're on the same page here. I need to know my daughter, right?" She continued to look through the clothing, picking up anything she assumed I'd like as I stood watching her. There was a double meaning behind what she said but I couldn't exactly put my finger on it. It felt like she was cataloging information, filing away my preferences and denials for later use.

I continued to follow behind her, my own eyes instinctively eyeing the person who had been watching me. The feeling was a cold prickle on the back of my neck, a sensation I had been trained to recognize. Danger. Or at least, observation. They turned quickly, their face obscured by the deep hood, and rushed out of the store without another glance. It was too quick, too deliberate.

I looked at Prissy, who had been watching them too, a thoughtful, almost predatory look in her eyes. I raised my eyebrow again at her, a silent question. She only hummed, a low, noncommittal sound, and stared at the door for a few beats longer before turning back to the clothes as if nothing had happened. But I saw it. The flicker of interest. The assessment. She had seen them, and she was not concerned. She was intrigued.

"What about this?" she asked, her voice once again bright and airy, the moment of tension completely erased. This time she was holding up a mini skirt with neon green and black zebra stripes. I don't even think the skirt could cover me properly. I groaned and threw my head back as her cackle carried throughout the store, the sound grating and false.

It was Monday morning. I was already dressed—a black tank top under my new hoodie with the blue rose, black jeans with holes in the knees, and black combat boots with blue laces—and waited for Priscilla to make her way downstairs. I fixed breakfast, just eggs and bacon, the simple, domestic act a stark contrast to the violence that simmered just beneath my skin. As I scrolled through more news articles about my new school, I looked up as I heard her footsteps pad into the kitchen.

"Good morning, my Light. Are you ready for school?" she asked. This all felt too mundane for me, too normal. The normalcy was a trap, a thin layer of ice over a deep, cold lake. "And don't forget the rules. Absolutely no killing whatsoever without my permission." Ah, there it is. The unordinary warnings my peers would never have to get.

I hummed, biting into the crispy bacon as I locked my phone.

"I looked up the school yesterday and I saw that that guy who had dropped off your mattress goes there." She pointedly stared at me as I averted my eyes, glancing at everything I could. Her ability to know things she shouldn't was a constant, unnerving reminder of her power.

"I want you to become his friend." My eyes shot up to hers quickly.

"But Priscilla—" her eyes went aflame, a cold fire that promised pain. I snapped my mouth shut.

"No ifs, ands, or buts about it," she snapped, her voice sharp enough to cut glass. "Become his friend because he won't let you slide through the cracks after you guys' little dispute the other day. There would be no avoiding a man like that." She picked up her purse, heading to the door that signaled me to follow. I threw back the rest of my water and picked up my book bag on the way out.

I met her in the car as she pulled out of the driveway silently. The silence was thick and heavy, charged with unspoken threats and my own simmering resentment. We were halfway down the street when she finally spoke up quietly.

"I'm serious, Areya. Either become friends with him or at least be cordial. He's linked to a new job I need you to do, but I need you to gain his trust first. *Especially* after your last slip-up." Prissy snapped, her knuckles white on the steering wheel. "If it's not a quick, passing job, I need you to be close and personal with these people. Understood?"

I nodded grimly, biting my lip to keep from snapping. So that was it. My budding, complicated connection with Ace wasn't mine at all. It was a tool. An assignment. He was a target, and I was the weapon aimed at him. A wave of nausea, cold and bitter, washed over me.

Prissy never felt the need to tell me why I had to kill these people. She always said that her say-so was a good enough reason, that she wasn't just some cruel being that killed for the fun of it. She told me that all of her jobs had some kind of special reasoning, but it was none of my business on what in particular. You would think I should be in on it, seeing as how I'm the one *killing* people that could be completely innocent, but I try to let it slide. I couldn't let it bother me, or else I'm sure I would've gone crazy and been killed by Prissy nine times over by now. The thought was a familiar cage, one I had lived in for so long I sometimes forgot the bars were there.

"I'm Sophia. You must be the new student. Areya, right?" I turned, surprised at the sight of a small girl with braids and a big smile. "I'll be your personal helper for today." I took her hand and nodded, quickly letting go. I wasn't used to much physical contact unless it was a start or end to a fight.

"Yes," I answered shortly. She stared at me for a beat more before turning away and walking quickly into the busy hallway, gesturing for me to follow her.

As the first bell rang, Sophia finally stopped in front of a mostly empty classroom. There were about five students with fifteen seats still open and a teacher who looked to be dragging, passing out a worksheet. She faced me and grinned.

"Okay! This is your first class. I'll be back a little before it's over to come pick you up and show you to your next class, lunch, and then—" she was quickly cut off by someone wrapping their arms around her form. She gasped, hands resting on the person's forearms as they met me at eye level. I practically sneered.

"Oh, hey, Soph. What are you doing with the newbie?" Ace asked, a crooked grin resting on his face as his braces shone brightly under the fluorescent light. I wanted to melt his smug grin off. Sophia swatted him off with a frown.

"Ace, don't be rude." She turned to him, giving him a side hug before facing me again. "Don't mind him. He just likes to pick on people. Thinks it's fun, or whatever." She rolled her eyes, pinching his side as he threw his head back with a laugh. His Adam's Apple bobbed, and I wanted him to choke on it.

"You know how I like to tease," he said, winking at me. I almost gagged and started to walk into the classroom. Sophia caught my arm with another smile.

"Don't forget that I'll be here right after the bell rings, okay?" Before I could answer, she was skipping away, talking to more of her friends as they all glanced back at me with hushed whispers and giggles. I rolled my eyes, ignoring Ace's stare as I stomped into the room, huffing under my breath. This first day was going to be extremely long.

****

"Now, for this project, you will be creating a brain from whatever materials your heart desires," Ms. Ross, my psychology teacher, paused, pursing her lips. "I would prefer if you guys worked together on it, but it can be solo if your heart really desires it." There were some murmured praises and other squealing as people started to choose their own partners. Ms. Ross cut her eyes at them as the room fell into a quiet lull, before making her way over to my desk. I instantly stiffened.

"Ms. Mathews?" she said gently. "I came over to say that I think that it would be best if you worked with someone else on this project, just to ease you into the new school setting." Instantly, I shook my head, ready to assure her that if I could kill people and then finish my homeschooling homework after, I could do the project by myself. Before I could get anything out, I felt a large hand slap onto my shoulder. I stiffened, ready to flip his entire body over my shoulder with one quick, solid move.

"Ms. Ross, I would love to work with Areya and help her into public school life." I could hear the wide grin in his voice as our teacher darted her eyes between the both of us. She stared at me for a few beats before shrugging and straightening her jacket.

"I guess that wouldn't be too bad of an idea, Ace." She glanced between us for a couple seconds more, leaning down closer to me and away from his prying ears. "I've known him since before he was born. He can be a lot to handle, but he's practically harmless. If he ever steps out of line, you can always just put him back in his place." She winked at me, standing up straight again as she went to pull at Ace's ear. He whined, holding onto her hand without pulling too hard away from her.

"Ace, if I hear that you pick on her too much, then you won't hear from your father, but from me instead. Understand me?" She squinted at him as he nodded frantically, pleading for her to let him go. Ms. Ross held him for a second more before releasing his ear, smiling at me and turning back to head to her desk. It was kind of satisfying to see him in pain, and I chuckled under my breath.

"Oi," he poked at my shoulder blade. "That's funny to you?" I glanced back at him over my shoulder, scoffing at his fake offended look. He couldn't wipe the smile that was still cracking his face.

"Hilarious," I muttered dryly, turning back to read over the rest of the directions. I could hear Ace's annoyingly loud laughter ring through the room, his desk shuffling as he scooted closer behind me. I unsurprisingly didn't flinch when his lips brushed my ear.

"Can't wait to work with you, partner. My house or yours?"

Chapter 5

It was Friday, back to another A day and my last class of the day, psychology with Ace. The minutes ticked by with agonizing slowness, each one a tiny, sharp stone pressing into my patience. Ms. Ross had allowed us some time to plan how we would be working on our projects and guiding us on how we should start, materials, etc. Ace had brought his chair around to share a desk with me, an invasion of my personal space that was becoming his signature move. He rested his chin in his hand, typing quickly with his other hand on his phone, a picture of effortless, infuriating confidence. The casual way he existed in the world, so open and unguarded, was a language I couldn't speak. He moved through life like he expected it to be kind, a concept so foreign to me it might as well have been from another dimension. I, on the other hand, moved through life expecting a knife in my back at any moment, often from the person standing closest to me.

"Oh, how the tables have turned," he muttered with a smile, sliding me his phone with a new contact application open. The screen glowed, a silent demand for a piece of me I wasn't willing to give. I counted to ten before picking it up, my fingers stiff. I punched my name and number in his phone angrily, the taps of my fingers against the glass sharp and aggressive. It felt like a concession, a small surrender in a war I didn't even know I was fighting. Every piece of myself I shared felt like handing someone a weapon they could later use against me. I slammed it back down on his open palm as he grinned evilly.

"Was that so hard to do the first time?" he asked, his voice laced with amusement. I gritted my teeth, biting my tongue to physically stop myself from spitting back the nastiest words I could call him. The taste of blood, coppery and familiar, filled my mouth.

"So, before I go to work this evening, I'm gonna go to the store and pick up the supplies. You don't have to worry about getting it since you'll be doing all of the work." He winked and threw his head back in laughter as I snarled at him. The sound was a low growl, a promise of violence I was struggling to keep leashed. "I'm just kidding, Areya, I'll help.

Kinda." He muttered the last part to himself as he sat back in his seat to stare at me, his eyes dancing with a light I both hated and found myself inexplicably drawn to.

"When do you want to actually work on it?" I asked, biting back all of the venom that fought its way up to the back of my throat. He pushed a strand of hair from in front of my glasses, and I slapped his hand away quickly, my reaction instantaneous and reflexive. He grinned, settling back into his chair as he cocked his head to the side.

"You're just a ray of sunshine, just like your name, huh?" he asked. His words were a playful jab, but they landed like a punch to the gut. Sunshine. Light. Everything I wasn't. "I think instead of calling you Areya, I'll call you," he trailed off, staring at me with an impish grin as I shook my head.

"Don't—"

"Bubbles!" he exclaimed, cutting me off. "I'll call you Bubbles." The nickname was so absurd, so utterly disconnected from the storm of darkness inside me, that for a second, I was just stunned. Before I could snap back at him, the bell had rung, signaling my time to go home. Ace stood quickly, towering over me with an evil look as he started to back out of the room.

"I'll text you my address and we'll meet at my place tomorrow. I'm gonna assume 3 is fine." With one last wink, he jogged out of class, dapping up and greeting his friends in the hallway. I stood there in a silent fury before forcing my legs to move me out of the classroom, building and all the way home. I decided to walk today because I think I would have physically exploded on the bus. The thought of being confined, surrounded by the noise and bodies of other students, felt like a pressure cooker with no release valve. The walk would be long, but at least it would be solitary.

When I finally made it home, Prissy's car wasn't in the driveway. A wave of relief, so profound it almost made me dizzy, washed over me. Silently thanking the universe, I pushed open the door and dropped my stuff off, making my way to the kitchen. I fluttered around, grabbing different things as I started to make a sandwich. Prissy would've slapped me at the mess I was making and the lack of plates and utensils I used, but I couldn't care less. I was alone, and for a few precious hours, the house was mine. The silence was a balm, a welcome quiet after the storm of a school day with Ace.

I made my way upstairs, brushing the crumbs off of my jeans as I pushed inside of my room and over to my laptop. I might as well finish this English project while I had this free time. Surprisingly enough, Prissy hadn't given me any job so far this week, but I think this was her way of letting me adjust to being in a public school for the first time ever. I'm not sure how quickly I would be doing the job connected to Ace, but I hoped it took some time. I didn't feel like having to sneak around and be careful to not get caught. I was getting lazy.

Holding the rest of the sandwich in my hand and typing with the other, I clicked around, opening a blank document before getting a notification of a new email. I paused, eyebrows furrowing. I never got too many emails from outside people since Prissy liked for me to stay hidden to most of the internet. I mainly used my computer for research and writing, and my phone to stay connected to Prissy. She was my only contact because nobody else wanted to get close enough to me to get my number. Nobody, but Ace.

Clicking on the email, my heart instantly dropped and my eyes widened. No way. There was no way this was happening. Nobody could have found this out; that was simply not possible. The digital walls Prissy had built around us were supposed to be impenetrable. She had boasted about it, her voice laced with smug satisfaction. "No one can find you unless I want them to, Areya. You're a ghost." But, I guess, not impossible enough. Feeling bile rise in my throat, I swallowed and scanned the rest of the email with shaky hands.

Subject: Vivienne McDowell

I hope this email finds you well, Vivienne. I know you don't go by that name anymore since Priscilla made you change it after "adopting" you. I know the truth though. I have been tracking you since you left a trail of bodies starting from the age of when we were nine.

Do you remember the first person she made you kill, beside your parents, Kelly and Chad McDowell? If your memory is as good as mine, you do.

Nobody knows the first person she made you kill, since all of your bodies rot so quickly, there is never a clear or accurate time of death. But I figured you'd know exactly what their name was, what their address was, the exact time.

Does it ever eat you alive, the guilt? Do you ever cry over a body? Are you growing tired of being her puppet? Is that why you messed up so badly in Arizona?

Was it the fact that the woman was a new mother and home alone or simply because you were tired? You still carried through, though, so it couldn't have been the latter.

I wonder if your power is the same as mine? Did Pricilla curse you the same way or does each child get something slightly different? Are we special in some way, in the sight of her eyes?

I want to know why you went with her. Why on that day you chose to kill your parents, why you chose her over them, why did you trust her? I want to know the difference between you and me.

I would like to meet you, Vivienne. Can I call you Vivienne or would you prefer the name the witch gave you?

-Judas

I was absolutely livid by the time I finished reading the email. I was shaking, eyes completely seeing red now. It took everything in my willpower to not snap the laptop in my hands, crush it into nothing but crumbs of wires and glass. Standing quickly, I paced the room that started to feel smaller and smaller by the second, taking quick, heaving breaths. The words on the screen had breached my fortress, had torn down the walls I so carefully maintained. He knew. He knew my name. He knew my history. He knew my sins.

I had to calm myself down before I gave myself a full-blown panic attack. I couldn't let Prissy see me in such a vulnerable state. The last time she found me curled in a ball in the corner of our old apartments' bathroom, she had pulled me out by the hair. Dragged me into the middle of our living room, beaten me until I was sure I was going to die. Until I couldn't catch my breath, until my eyes burned to the point where I couldn't open them, until my body was littered with bruises. I couldn't move for two days. That was the price for acting anything but the aloof, strong, and brooding warrior she raised me to be.

Counting until I was sure I could properly type without smashing the keys, I made it to 128 before taking another deep breath. The numbers were a mantra, a fragile thread of control in a world that was spinning off its axis. Slowly heading over to the computer that had dimmed in my absence, I slid onto the bench. My chest rattled with another huff, as I slowly started typing a response back to this alleged 'Judas'. By the time I finished typing, I read over my response once more, my own words a weapon I was aiming at an unseen enemy.

Subject: Re: Vivienne McDowell

I don't know who you are, or how you even know me. But I would suggest that you don't contact me anymore, lest you want Priscilla to find you. She's very savvy with tracking and locating. But I'm sure you know, since you seem to know every detail of my life.

She doesn't like it when you tamper with things you shouldn't. Stick your nose in business that doesn't concern you.

One thing though, is driving me crazy. What made you link me with the murders of Kelly and Chad McDowell? The woman in Arizona?

Are you a part of one of those conspiracy theory groups? Are you with people who dig and dig their noses into little evidence to find some kind of answer to a mystery that will never be solved?

Does it help you sleep at night, Judas?

I would prefer if you called me Areya, although this will be our last time talking through a screen. After I show Prissy your pretty accusatory email, I'm sure the next time I see you, everything will be surely cleaned up and made crystal clear.

Until we meet.

-Areya

I read the email over and over again until I felt satisfied and counted to three before hitting send. I let out a deep breath, slamming my head beside the computer on the cleared vanity. I felt so conflicted; I wanted this Judas person to respond back, snippy and smart just so I could argue back, track him down, strangle him until I let my eyes finish the job.

But on the other hand, I didn't want him to respond back at all. I wanted to delete the email thread, delete any trace of him from my computer, push his words to the back of my mind. I wanted to ignore it, hide it from Prissy. If she reads what he sent me, all she would do is delete my email, smash my laptop into a million tiny pieces, drag me by the scruff of my neck and beat me like a dog.

She would somehow blame me for everything, tell me that I led him to us, if I wasn't so sloppy in my work then we would have never been found. She would make us move again. I'd have to get adjusted again.

I think we were running out of states to move to; we would finally be forced out of the country. I'm not too sure if I would want to go sight-seeing with Prissy across the world. While she would be out and about, going to fancy restaurants and theater plays, I would be forced to roam empty, darkened streets. Like a dirty rat, scurrying under people's noses as she would somehow find people for me to murder in cold blood. I could almost hear someone pleading for their life in a language she forced me to learn. I could almost understand each cry reverberating through my skull.

I hadn't realized how wet my face was, how shallow my breaths got, or how much time had passed until I heard a familiar dinging from my laptop. I popped my head up, wiping my tears on the back of my hand as I blinked through blurry tears at the beaming screen.

Subject: Re: Vivienne McDowell

Oh wow :)

I wasn't expecting such a timely response from you, Areya. I guess you really do stick to your everyday schedule: wake up, cook breakfast for you and the witch, go to school, flirt with that dumb jock, stomp home, and eat a snack if she's not there.

Did I get it right? Down to the stomping, huh?

And I would suggest that you don't tell Prissy about our little conversation, honey bunches. This email is untraceable and your efforts would only be futile.

You sure are one tricky person, Areya. You seemed to avoid all of my hard hitting questions. Guess it was a rookie mistake to think that you would confess to murder through email, right? Eh, you can't blame me for trying.

When would you like to meet? Anytime is fine with me. I'm practically jumping with joy just thinking about finally getting to see you without having to hide in shadows. I'm surprised you never noticed me. I thought Prissy trained you better than that.

Guess you really are getting sloppy, huh, honey bunches?

-Judas

If I wasn't fuming before, I definitely was now. I shook all over, roaring in anger as I stomped over to my dresser, punching the handles and ridges until my knuckles ached and bled. Who was this guy? How long had he been watching me and how did I not notice? Was this the same person from that clothing store?

If Prissy ever found out about this and beat me, I wouldn't blame her. She wouldn't be wrong to tell me that it was all my fault. How could I be so stupid? So lazy?

I punched the drawers a few more times until the pain stung all the way to my elbow. I had to stop soon, or else I might damage a nerve, if I haven't already. Shaking the loose blood from my hand, I stomped over to the laptop and angrily started typing. There was another distant ringing from my phone on the middle of my bed, but I figured I'd finish typing before getting up. It could be Prissy, but whatever it is had to wait. As I hit send, I tried to drown out the constant beeping from my phone.

Subject: Re: Vivienne McDowell

Let's make this clear. Don't call me anything other than Areya. Not Vivienne, and especially not 'honey bunches'.

You really are a rookie. Admitting to stalking and even trespassing on school grounds on an email. How do you know that I won't take this to the police? Let them find you and arrest you, humiliate you as being some perverted stalker?

There will be no need to tell Prissy now. I am an adult and I feel as though we could handle this without her, since I am not her "puppet", as you liked to say.

We can meet up tomorrow night. Tell me a time and a place and we'll meet there. If you are even a second late, I will crack whatever code you think you've implemented that has made you untraceable and we can talk at your little hideaway. Just pick your poison, Judas.

Oh, and I do not flirt with that numbskull jock. Maybe if you actually listened instead of watching from afar like the creep you are, you would know that.

-Areya

I huffed, glaring at the phone that continued to ding with alerts. I pushed up angrily, snatching the phone up as I saw I had one notification from Prissy and six—why would he ever feel the need to text so many times instead of one long text?!—notifications from Ace.

Priscilla

2:36 pm

I will be home later. Cook something nice for the two of us. I have new info.

I read her message a few more times, trying to figure out what this news could be. She couldn't have found out about the emails already? A thought quickly hit me; she could've logged into my account and went through the messages. The thought made my blood run cold. Prissy had never done it without my knowledge before, but who's to say she's never done it at all? My heart dropped as I started to panic again.

Taking deep breaths and trying to steady myself, I plopped down on the bed, holding the phone above my head. I tried to take my mind off of the possible impending doom as I opened Ace's messages. Instantly, I rolled my eyes and saved his address in my phone.

Ace

2:48 pm

Hey Bubbles

9746 Landing Drive, Devils Lake, North Dakota
That's ^^ my address.
See you tomorrow at 3 ;)
Dress comfortably, you might be leaving kinda late
Not being creepy!!! The project will just take long, I'm guessing.

Curling my lip back in disgust, I growled and typed a quick "okay" to Prissy and a snippy "whatever" to Ace. I lay there, staring at the ceiling for a couple more seconds before one last dooming ring of a notification from my laptop. My breath quickened as I forced myself to sit up and read his last email.

Subject: Re: Vivienne McDowell

Maybe you're right in that sense, gumdrop. But you and I both know that you'd never go to the police. You don't have to admit it to me over the internet, but you know the truth as much I do.

And I wouldn't necessarily call myself a perverted stalker. That's taking it a little too far, don't you think, gumdrop? :(

Meet me twenty minutes away from Devils Lake, near the abandoned park. I'll send you the exact coordinates.

Can't wait to formally meet you, love.

-Judas

I memorized the coordinates Judas sent before deleting the entire email thread. With a sigh, I shut the laptop and rested my forehead on top of it. I had to meet Ace tomorrow at 3 and then Judas later on that night. Hopefully, I wouldn't be coming home with two extra bodies.

Pulling myself up, I changed into more comfortable wear; black biker shorts and a black sports bra. Simple and easy, although I already knew I'd dirty it from cooking. The fabric was a second skin, offering no comfort, only utility. I couldn't care less, though. My mind was a chaotic storm, and the only anchor I could find was a singular, desperate mission: I would have to fix the best dinner I could think of, anything to beg for the mercy of Prissy if she had found the emails before I deleted them. It was a pathetic, groveling sort of plan, but it was the only one I had. Appeasement was a language Prissy understood, even if she rarely accepted it as payment.

I padded down the steps on shaky legs, each footfall a soft thud of dread on the wood. The house was too quiet, the silence amplifying the frantic beating of my heart. I began to get to work on fixing all of Prissy's favorite foods. It was a frantic, clumsy ballet in the kitchen. I pulled out pans with trembling hands, the clang of metal against the stove top sounding like a gunshot in the stillness. I worked from memory, a mental checklist of Prissy's culinary whims. She liked her Alfredo sauce with extra garlic and a hint of nutmeg; her baked potatoes had to be fluffy on the inside with skin so crispy it crackled under the fork, loaded with an obscene amount of bacon, cheese, and sour cream. Every chop of a chive, every stir of the sauce, was a prayer. *Please don't know. Please don't know.*

I was sweating, the kitchen smelling of different flavors, spices, and seasonings. The air was thick with the aroma of garlic, melting cheese, and baking biscuits—a scent that should have been comforting but instead felt like the cloying perfume of a funeral home. Fluttering around as I finished cooking the favorite foods compiled of what we had in the fridge, I wiped my hands on the navy-blue apron. My knuckles, still tender and scabbed from punching my dresser, scraped against the rough fabric.

It was now 6:09. Prissy would be home any minute now, and I only grew more and more nervous by the second. My stomach was a tight knot of anxiety. Would she immediately come in and hit me? Would the first sound I hear be the sharp slap of her hand against my face, or would she be silent, her disappointment a cold, heavy blanket that suffocated everything? Instead of coming home with hugs and kisses, will her hands only be full of knives and a sickening hatred?

I started to feel sick as I heard her car pulling up in the driveway. The sound of tires on gravel was like a death sentence. My hands shook so violently I nearly dropped the bowl of salad. With a surge of adrenaline, I started to stack the food on the dining room table as quickly as I could. I set out the last plate just as I heard her open the door. The click of the lock turning was the sound of my cage being secured.

Freezing in my spot, my shoulders hiked up to my ears as I heard Prissy's footsteps getting closer and closer. The deliberate, unhurried pace of her heels on the hardwood floor was a form of torture in itself. She was in no rush. She was in control.

I tried not to flinch as she rested her chin on my shoulder, her presence a sudden, chilling weight behind me. I held my breath in anticipation, my entire body rigid. I almost cried when her arms circled my waist, squeezing tight as she whispered in my ear, her breath a cool wisp against my skin.

"Hello, my Light. How was your day?"

I paused, completely surprised at the quiet cheerfulness in her voice. It was disarming, more terrifying than any scream. She nuzzled my cheek softly, a gesture so foreign and unsettling that I had to fight the urge to recoil. Then she pulled away and gasped at the arrangement on the table, her performance of surprise flawless.

"Oh, Areya!" She smiled, turning toward me brightly. "Is all of this for me?" Prissy clasped her hands together as she started flitting around the room, smelling everything on the table as she stripped off of her shoes and jacket. She moved with a practiced grace, her delight a little too theatrical, her eyes a little too sharp.

"Is there any special reason why you made all of this?" she asked, almost innocently. I couldn't tell if she was playing me, being coy to catch me off guard and make my pain last even longer than necessary, or if she really didn't know about the emails. I gulped and shrugged, wiping the sweat off of my brow with my pained knuckles.

"No reason," I mumbled, wiping my sweaty palms on my shorts as we sat across from each other at the table. "Just figured I'd make your favorites since I haven't cooked them in a while." I gave a forced grin, mostly just a show of teeth, awkwardly. Prissy examined me for a few moments, cocking her head to the side as her large, jangly earrings clattered noisily. She only smiled lazily, before picking up a fork and a plate, digging into everything that I made. Her gaze was analytical, dissecting my every twitch, my every nervous glance.

"Good enough reason for me." She winked and immediately began to stack her plate. Almost deflating, I sighed in relief before starting to fill up my own plate. The food on my fork felt like lead, but I forced myself to lift it. I had cooked chicken Alfredo with this special sauce she seemed to die for, loaded baked potatoes with bacon bits, cheese, sour cream, and tiny green chives, a large healthy salad with an unhealthy amount of dressing that seemed to spill over onto the table, and a can of biscuits I found in a lone drawer in the fridge. I mixed up some sweet tea and lemonade, more sugar than Arnold Palmer, that Prissy adored.

Safe to say, I was definitely sucking up to her, if she had found the emails. It was a feast of appeasement, a banquet of fear.

But instead, we ate mostly in silence, save for the hums and praises Prissy muttered through a mouth full of food. Her compliments were hollow, each one a carefully placed stone in the wall of deception she was building around me. I poked around, too nervous to eat, feeling as though as soon as I swallowed, the food would only come back up. My throat was tight, my stomach a churning sea of dread. I quickly looked up as Prissy called my name.

"Areya," she hummed, picking up her drink to wash her food down. I watched her with slitted, curious eyes. When she finally put the glass down, she smiled at me, bright and wide and forced. The smile didn't reach her eyes; they were as cold and clear as ice.

"That news I mentioned earlier, through text." She nodded to her phone, though never taking her eyes off of mine to gauge any kind of reaction. I relaxed my shoulders, just a fraction, shoving a forkful of salad into my mouth as I cocked my eyebrow in question. The pretense of normalcy was suffocating.

"I have a job for you, connected to that boy, right?" She placed her fork down to rest her chin in her hands. Her movements were slow, deliberate, each one designed to heighten the tension. I lowered my eyes, stuffing my face with as much food as I could to avoid saying any thing, fighting against the nausea at the pit of my stomach. The taste of the dressing was acidic, burning the back of my throat.

"I want you, Areya, to kill his father."

My eyes shot up to hers quickly. The room seemed to tilt, the air growing thick and heavy. His father. Ace's father. The man from the store, the man whose name I didn't even know. She leveled me off with a look as I mulled it over in my head. Her expression was flat, devoid of any emotion, as if she had just asked me to pass the salt. It was just another task, another name on a list. But this was different. This wasn't some random person. This was Ace. This was a line I hadn't realized existed until this very moment.

Well, this was going to get complicated.

Chapter 6

I struggled to sleep the entire night, following Prissy's news. Now, I wasn't bothered by the fact that I had to kill a man in cold blood for reasons that I am forbidden to know. No, it was the fact that I was at said man's house to complete a mundane school project with his son. Now, *that* was a little cruel—to know that I'll be spending the day with him before having to kill his father in the following week.

And then to still see Ace at school for the next few months. Prissy sure did know how to put me in an awkward situation.

I stood outside Ace's door; a huge, brown door that was double the size of me. The house itself was huge, with an obvious two-story build to it. The outside was a beige color with bright green leaves and plants snaking around and even up the side of the house. There were only two cars in the driveway, and they both looked expensive.

And they were just supposed to be mattress sellers? I was starting to get the feeling that maybe there was something else going on under everyone's noses in this town. That, or everyone knew and just didn't seem to care if they were profiting, too.

Whenever Prissy assigned me a job, she would never give me a reason why. Just a name, address, and time. No questions asked or hesitations, lest things would only get worse for me. I made a game with myself when I was younger, though: try to connect any and all dots to just get some kind of reason, some kind of justification, on why I had to kill these people.

If they had a mug and a smart mouth, I'd tell myself that they had been rude to Prissy, so of course, I had to kill them. If they owned just one too many cars by just selling vacuums for a living, they were drug dealers—of course, I had to kill them. If they were new mothers and presumed to be home alone, begging for their life—of course—

Before I could get lost in my thoughts, the door swung open and there he stood. Ace, in nothing but an old, ratty jersey that showed off the brownness of his arms, rippling biceps that flexed as he leaned in the doorway, loose-fitting black sweatpants, and beat-up sneakers. He looked as comfortable as me in my near-matching outfit. Looking me up and down with a grin, Ace started to quickly back me up with his body.

"Okay, so, here's the plan for today, Bubbles," he started as I growled at the nickname. He quickly put his hands up in defense. "I got pretty caught up earlier when I was practicing with the team, sooooo..." he drawled, grabbing his nape as he stared abashedly through his thick lashes that fanned his cheekbones.

"We have to go to the store together to pick up some supplies." I glared at him as he grinned crookedly. "And by some, I mean *all*." I could only stare at him, quietly fuming as my fists clenched and unclenched quickly. Ace's eyes dragged up and down my body, making note of my flexing hands before smirking and grabbing my shoulder. He turned me around and softly pushed me toward a large truck I had surveyed as I walked up, sitting prettily in the driveway.

The windows were rolled down, the gray gleam shining brightly from the reflection of the sun as Ace practically shoved me into it.

"It'll be quick. I promise." We climbed in the huge truck together, and I was surprised at how clean the inside was. Save for a couple of books and a football in the backseat, the interior was close to being perfect. I turned around and was greeted by the sight of his outstretched pinky. I glared at it before shifting my eyes to his.

"What's this?" I grumbled, ignoring his hand as I buckled my seatbelt. Ace scoffed as he turned to completely face me in his seat, a shocked expression adorning his face.

"What, have you never heard of a pinky promise?" he asked exasperatedly. I rolled my eyes and ignored him, sitting back in my seat as I waited for him to pull off. After we sat in silence for a couple of beats, I glanced over at Ace, who still sat there with his pinky out, eyebrows raised expectedly. I sighed, pinching his finger tightly in between mine before shoving his hand away. He hummed, turning the car on as he grinned to himself happily.

"Now, was that so hard to do?" he mumbled under his breath, putting his large hand behind the passenger's headrest, shooting me a wink as he began to back out of the driveway. I groaned, turning to face the window as Ace's laugh filled the car. This was going to take a lot longer than expected.

We were in the middle of some crafts store as Ace rambled on and on about something I couldn't bring myself to listen to. When he started getting louder and more exaggerated with his waving hands and arms, people around us giving him nasty glares, I held my hand up. His mouth closed abruptly as he frowned.

"What is it?" he asked, picking up a bouquet of fake flowers and burying his nose into it with a deep inhale.

"What are we even looking for?" I asked lazily, snatching the flowers from his hands and throwing them back haphazardly. Ace sputtered as he went to pick up another flower, a blue-colored rose. "What supplies do we need to start?" I glanced around the store, just trying to find anything to make this go by quicker.

"Don't these smell just lovely, Bubbles?" Ace grinned, pushing the flowers under my nose. I snarled and swatted them away.

"They're fake, you birdbrain." He shrugged, placing them back softly before he briskly walked away into another aisle.

"No need for name-calling, Bubbles," he threw over his shoulder as I struggled to keep up with his fast pace, zigzagging through the aisles until he quickly stopped.

"Here." Ace gestured to the colorful clay stacked up. "We need this clay stuff, glue, styrofoam, and..." he paused, scratching the back of his head. "I guess I should've made a list. Oh well, we can come back if we're missing something." He shrugged again, grabbing a bunch of clay before he realized he didn't have enough hands. He looked up sheepishly as I rolled my eyes.

"I'll go get a cart. You pick the colors." I huffed, turning from his cheesing face to stomp down the aisles and try to find my way to the front of the store. I heard Ace laugh airily from behind me, and I tried to ignore the shiver up my spine.

Yeah, Ace was handsome. And had a nice laugh. And was built. But I couldn't let my eyes stray from my true goal: killing his father. Suddenly, the shiver turned into cold goosebumps running up and down my exposed arms, more so with the winter chill of the store.

I was pushing the cart through the store, getting lost a couple of times before I heard Ace's booming laughter carry, bellowing over the quiet music playing from the weak speakers hanging overhead. I followed his laughter, already getting irritated when I heard him conversing with other people. I really didn't feel like being friendly to more than one person in a day. Ace was already pushing past my limit.

I turned into the aisle with a frown, eyes immediately locking on the three other guys that stood around Ace, all wearing matching jerseys. Even worse, they were his football buddies. I could feel the headache already pulsating above my eyebrow.

"Bubbles!" Ace called with a smile, taking a few long steps to dump all of the clay into the basket. I could feel my lip twitch as all three of his friends' eyebrows raised as they shared knowing looks.

"These are my friends," he introduced them all, and I quickly zoned out on what their names were. Couldn't care less; if I ever had to know their names, I could always learn them later. And they didn't *want* me to know their names. I nodded at them but stayed silent. The three of them looked at each other again as Ace only grinned brightly at me, completely unaware of the judging and confused faces behind him.

"Hey bro," one whispered, stepping up behind him slowly. "Is she blind? What's with the glasses?" he asked, voice squeaky and barely able to maintain a whisper. Ace frowned and opened his mouth to speak before shutting it quickly.

"No," I interjected before any of them could say anything as stupid as they looked. "Not blind." I turned to face Ace. "Let's get the styrofoam and glue so we can go already," I snapped, quickly grabbing the cart and turning around. From over my shoulder, I heard a low whistle. I froze, shoulders tensing.

"A blind girl shaped that good, bro?" another one said with an obnoxious laugh. "I didn't think your standards went that low, Foster. You surprise me every day." There were three different sets of laughter.

Okay. So, if I were to take off my glasses and kill all three of them, and maybe Ace too just as collateral, then I wouldn't be wrong, right? Prissy would find it reasonable, right? The way that these stupid pinheads looked at me, sized me up like a piece of meat, talked about me as if I wasn't standing here. I wouldn't be wrong to just *kill* them, right? I could feel my fingertips twitching, nose itching as the glasses slid lower and lower on my bridge. If anyone walked in front of me right now, they would drop dead, body stinking up the store with rot. But I couldn't bring myself to care right now. The intense fury ripped through my body as I slowly started to turn from the waist up.

"Hey," Ace suddenly interjected, turning to them with a frown as he suddenly stepped in front of me. His broad back cut off my line of vision as he held his hands up.

"I already told you creeps that she's just a friend, and *she* already told *you* that she's not blind," he snapped, placing his hand on his hip like he was scolding a child. I couldn't see the three of them over his broad stature.

"I'll see you guys Monday." Ace's voice held a sense of finality before turning, eyes aflame as he glanced down at me. He placed one of his warm hands on the small of my back, turning me before gently pushing me forward and grabbed the cart in the other hand. In this position, I was trapped between his chest and the handle of the cart. His friends called after him, but he only continued to push us forward.

I let him guide me throughout the store, unthinking of our current position as I talked myself down again. I fiddled with my fingers, picking at the still-new scabs on my knuckles as I chewed my lip harshly.

How could I be so stupid? Almost killing four guys in a store just because they were being creeps? I was starting to lose control of my anger more and more, and it was becoming lethal by the second. I have to ask Prissy when I go home if we can build a workout room in the basement. Maybe blowing off physical steam could do the job for me, instead of resorting to killing everyone that slightly pisses me off. If I used my power on every man that has ever catcalled me, then half of the world would be dead right now. And that is *more* than suspicious.

I was brought back from my seething when a familiar and comforting warmth detached itself from my back. I stopped chewing my lip and turned around to Ace, his eyebrows furrowed and his mouth curled down.

"I'm..." he started, eyes searching the bottles of glue before meeting mine. "I'm sorry about what they said, Areya," he whispered, searching my face as I stood there, unsure of what to say exactly. Finally, his eyes stopped on my glasses, eyes bouncing from lens to lens, trying to find any kind of direct contact. I turned to the glue, nodding my head.

"It's fine, Ace. Boys will be boys, right?" I whispered, picking up the stick, liquid, and a hot glue gun. I showed him the three options as he frowned deeper.

"Which one?" I asked. He only stared at me for a couple more seconds before grabbing them all from my hands and throwing them noisily in the cart. I cringed from the sound, quickly straightening my back as his large hands suddenly engulfed mine. On instinct, I pulled away, but Ace held on tighter.

"Boys will be boys, but Areya, these are *men*. That doesn't excuse it." He bent slightly at the waist to face me at eye level. Even though he couldn't see directly, his gaze still bored into mine. I turned my face away slightly and nodded, cheeks heating up in embarrassment.

"Whatever," I mumbled, still pulling away from his grasp as it felt like he was only getting closer. I snapped back to face him as he straightened his back, a large smile cracking his face as he let my hand go to instead pinch my cheeks in calloused fingers.

"You're cute when you blush, Bubbles," Ace hummed. I growled, digging my nails into the backs of his hands as he threw his head back and laughed. He turned around, looking at me over his shoulder.

"C'mon," he grinned. "Let's go get this styrofoam so we can head back to my place already." Ace nodded his head in the direction of another aisle as he started walking, checking behind him every few steps to make sure I was following him. I grumbled under my breath the entire time as he only hummed happily, stopping as he found what we needed.

"Okay, so," he surveyed the styrofoam in front of us. "We need to find two halves since the brain has to open to show the left and right side. We're probably going to have to cut it, in order to get the correct shape of the brain stem and the medulla and pons, and all that other good stuff," he muttered to himself, rubbing his hands together as he eyed the different options in front of us. I was stunned, looking at the side of his serious expression, before he noticed my shocked look. He raised an eyebrow.

"What is it? Do I need to say it again?" he asked innocently. I huffed a quiet chuckle, mouth quirking up to the side as I found exactly what we were looking for.

"No, I heard you," I said, tossing the styrofoam in the cart. "I just wasn't expecting for a jock to know so much about the human brain," I snipped sarcastically, pushing the cart out of the aisle. I could hear Ace sputter and laugh as he jogged to catch up with me.

"Just because I'm a jock doesn't mean I have a birdbrain, as you like to say." He stuck his tongue out at me. I plucked it quickly as he gasped and instantly grabbed his mouth with a whine.

"Keep your tongue in your mouth and pay for this stuff. I'm ready to go," I said, pushing our cart to the self-checkout as Ace frowned beside me.

"You're so mean, Bubbles," he grumbled, pulling out his black leather wallet and swiping his card.

"Yeah, yeah, yeah. Let's go." With our bags in tow, Ace and I headed toward his car in the busy parking lot.

On the ride to his house, we were fairly quiet, but I kept seeing his eyes linger over to me. I stayed silent, though, not knowing what he wanted to say and, fairly, not caring. Finally, when we stopped at a red light, Ace shifted in his seat to look at me.

"Can I ask a possibly very personal question?" he asked, fingers tapping at the steering wheel as his eyes grew wide and curious. I groaned, throwing my head back on the headrest and rubbed my temples.

"If it's about my eyes, no," I snapped. The light turned green, and Ace sat there, staring for another few moments before the car behind us honked. He flipped the person off, tearing his eyes off of me as he pulled off. He shifted in his seat a couple of times as we grew closer, obviously still wanting to ask. I sighed loudly and spoke under my breath.

"I wear these glasses because I have to. Can we leave it at that?" I asked, turning my head to face him as his surprised eyes met mine. Suddenly they narrowed, shifting between me and the road as his mouth twisted.

"The first time I met you," he started, pulling up in his driveway and parking perfectly. The doors were still locked as he unbuckled his seatbelt so he could face me head-on. "You said something about *rot*, or whatever, and started to take off your glasses. Why?" he questioned, hands fiddling with the hem of his jersey, but never taking his eyes from mine. I stiffened in my seat before slowly relaxing, grabbing our bags and settling my hand on the door handle.

"Just wanted to freak you out, is all," I mumbled, unlocking the door with a flip of my finger as I quickly hopped out before Ace could stop me. "People say my eyes are creepy enough to kill," I whispered at him, twiddling my fingers under my chin with an otherwise bored expression. Ace paused for a second before throwing his head back in laughter, Adam's apple bobbing as he trudged out of the driver's seat.

"Good one there, Bubbles." He snorted, patting my shoulder as he unlocked the front door. He grabbed the bags from my hand and directed me to take my shoes off as he started toward a large, circular table in what I assumed was a living room. Everything in this house was just too big and open, with little furniture and other details.

There were barely any pictures hanging up, save for a few of Ace in his uniform and on the football field. There were a few chairs here and there; I spotted a couch, widescreen TV, and a fake plant in the living room. Other than that, it was empty and boring. If Prissy saw this, she would be absolutely livid and on the way to a furniture store in no time. Ace snapped his fingers in front of my face suddenly as I whipped my head around to look at him.

"Earth to Bubbles," he whispered. I glanced down and saw that everything was already set up in front of me. I needed to get out of my head; I can't seem to get enough of my own thoughts lately. Tired of hearing myself think, I nodded and started picking up the materials.

"Do you have a box cutter? We have to cut out the shape of the brain stem," I said sternly, immediately jumping into work. Ace raised an eyebrow but nodded silently, getting up and jogging into a nearby room. I tried not to stare at the way his shoulder blades flexed with every swing of his arms on the way out. I had to stay focused. Prissy told me to canvas the house like it was any other job. Right.

The first floor obviously had one door: the front door. There was a small white box hooked up by the doorknob, after entering on the left with a numerical keypad, which I was guessing was the alarm system. One camera focused on the front doorstep outside of the house. One round alarm chip was set up in almost every room. One door in the kitchen, as I leaned up to see Ace digging through the drawers beside the oven. Two windows above the stove. A large, almost ceiling-to-floor window in the living room that was covered in a blacked-out curtain. If I leaned back far enough in my chair, I could see what I was guessing was either a basement or a bathroom door. That was all I could get to in my seat without looking suspicious by walking around and being caught red-handed.

My eyes snapped up as Ace walked back into the room with a grin, wielding two open box cutters. He waved them around in his hand as he sat beside me, placing the sharp tools down on the table as he picked up one-half of the styrofoam and a pencil.

"I'll mark the placing on both so we can cut them, and it'll be—"

"Ace!" There was a sharp yell of his name as Ace suddenly tensed, his shoulders coming up to his ears. His eyes grew cloudy as I saw a large, burly man stomping inside from the kitchen door. The man paused at the sight of me before smiling softly, stepping up behind Ace and smacking his hands on his already tensed shoulders. My eyes jumped between them as Ace suddenly grew quiet, his mouth drawing into a firm line as he kept his eyes cast down.

"And who might this young lady be?" the man asked, an obvious forced smile on his face. I kept my mouth shut, scanning Ace's face the entire time as he forced his lips to move.

"This is the girl that I have to work with on a project in Ms. Ross' class, remember?" Ace asked quietly. In the few days that I had known him, I had never heard the loud jock become so meek. Instantly, my guard was up. I tried not to snip and be rude for Ace's sake, but I could tell what kind of man his father was. I put my hand out stiffly.

"Areya Matthews," was all I said. Ace's father stared at my hand for a moment, eyes glancing up to my glasses before shaking it tightly, gripping my palm in both of his. He gave me a beaming smile, eyes squinting as he ruffled Ace's hair when he pulled away. Ace tensed again, biting his lip as his hands started to twitch in his lap.

"Oh! My boy told me about you a couple of days ago. Forgive an old man for his elderly memory, won't you?" He laughed loudly, grabbing his belly as he trotted back into the kitchen. "I'm Mr. Foster, Ace's dad, if you hadn't figured it out already," I heard him call.

With his back turned, I faced Ace again, who sat there stiffly. He couldn't meet my eyes, and as I tried to slide my hand to his, he quickly pulled away. Almost as if he were snapped out of a trance, Ace picked up the pencil he hadn't seemed to notice that he dropped and began outlining where we would cut.

I glanced back to his father, who seemed to float around the kitchen without a care in the world. He wore the same forest green uniform Ace did the day I first met him. I picked up the name tag of "Manager - Ben" when he first introduced himself, when it finally hit me.

This was the man that I would be killing soon. Sitting right in his face, beside his son who seemed to shake at every word he said, tense whenever his own father touched him. Prissy had made me study body language like it was a college course, growing up. I know pain, abuse, when I see it.

Maybe this wouldn't get so complicated after all.

"I just ran home to get some documents for the store. I should be back later, Ace," Mr. Foster called from the kitchen before slamming the door shut. And almost like a trance, Ace was back to his normal, smiling self. Albeit a little forced, but he tried. The sight of his tired smile made me loosen up slightly.

"You ready to start?" he asked, voice sounding drained and exhausted. I nodded and picked up the styrofoam, ready to start before I heard a sharp gasp. I looked up quickly at Ace, who was staring at my hands.

"What is it?" I asked, as he turned them over as he grabbed them in his. My hands looked like a child's compared to his large, brown ones. Ace flipped them over to survey my knuckles with a frown.

"What happened?" he asked, eyes curious and sincere. His gaze was so intense, so honest, I had to turn away and bite the insides of my cheeks. I don't know why I always grew embarrassed whenever someone saw my scars.

"I punched a dresser once or twice," I lied, shrugging. Ace narrowed his eyes and pursed his lips.

"This doesn't look like a once or twice hit, Bubbles." He sounded almost disappointed. Mulling it over in his head, Ace twisted his mouth before pulling me up to stand, my head coming directly under his chin.

"Come on," he murmured, pulling me throughout the house. I know I should've been surveying everything I saw, but I couldn't seem to pull my eyes away from where our hands were interlocked and the muscles in his lower back pulling with every step. By the time I was focused on my surroundings, I found myself in what was seemingly his room.

The room was painted a navy blue and black, with white and gray accents. His bed sat in the middle, stuffed between a small night table and two curving lamps that faced outward from each other. There was one window, covered by gray curtains, and a small desk under it. There sat our psychology textbook and other books, papers, pencils, and a laptop. He had two large dressers with lotion, deodorant, jewelry, and a football sitting atop it. There were a couple of movie posters, some that I recognized from being from the '80s. I think I spotted a gaming system underneath the TV plastered on the wall. It was all surprisingly clean. Ace seemed to keep everything he owned organized, and I could come to appreciate that.

I was suddenly pulled into an even cleaner bathroom attached to his room. Ace pushed me on top of a closed toilet seat.

"Sit," he simply said as he started to rummage around the cabinet above the sink. I watched him silently as he murmured under his breath the entire time. When he found what he was looking for, he quickly pulled it out and sat in on the sink. A first aid kit. I raised my eyebrow in question as he grabbed my left hand in his, kneeling in front of me.

"You wanna tell me what really happened?" he asked quietly under his breath. I rolled my eyes, sighing as he started to slowly clean out some of the still-open wounds on my knuckles. I ignored his glance up at me.

"I told you what happened. I punched a dresser," I said shortly, hissing when he cleaned out a deeper cut. He hushed me quietly, eyes focused on the task at hand as he went to my other set of knuckles.

"Once or twice?" he whispered into the quiet bathroom, stilling as he stared up at me from the floor. I twisted my mouth, turning my head to study his blue and white shower curtains instead. Ace continued to watch me before he started rubbing some type of cooling gel over the now-cleaned wounds.

"How do you even know how to do this? So well, at that," I grumbled. Ace laughed softly, picking up some gauze from the kit as he carefully started to wrap my hands. He shrugged halfheartedly, his warm grip tightening on my fingers.

"I've had to clean up my hands after punching a dresser, once or twice," he said softly, eyes betraying the closed-off hurt as he smiled up at me weakly. I chewed my bottom lip, eyes searching his face as he glanced down at my fully wrapped knuckles. Ace patted my knee before standing, completely towering over me. He pulled me from the toilet seat with a crooked grin.

"Let's go finish this project, yeah?" he asked. I don't think I could ever understand how he could be so obviously hurt, so obviously reliving trauma that he's had to go through, most likely alone, and still smile at me. It would take me days to even open my mouth after Prissy would beat me. I told myself that a smile after a punishment only goes to show that

I hadn't really learned from it. I guess Ace had a different idea than me, and I think I liked his better. I nodded at him, forcing the corner of my lip to curve up.

"Yeah."

Chapter 7

"This is stupid," Ace grumbled for the nth time today. I rolled my eyes.

"Stop your whining. It's only making this take longer than it has to," I snapped, struggling to get this stupid clay to look like brain matter. This was proving to be more difficult than I expected it to be, and it was frustrating the both of us.

"C'mon, Bubbles," Ace whined, pushing the half-glued clay and styrofoam across the table and nearly knocking it on the floor. With my quick reflexes, I caught it at the last minute. I heard him whistle lowly as I raised my gaze to his. He sat back astonished, a smirk resting on his lips as he crossed his arms.

"Quicker than I thought," Ace winked. I snarled at him, baring my teeth as I set everything back up nicely.

"We should just stop here for now, and maybe finish sometime next week. I'm getting tired." He yawned, leaning back in his chair as he stretched languidly. I tried to move my head to the side to signal that I wasn't looking at him, but my eyes betrayed me. Luckily, Ace couldn't see where my gaze lingered, or that would be something else he would tease me about.

"Plus," he stood from his chair to stand in front of me. Ace rested on the back of the chair beside me, staring down at me with a smile as he cocked his head to the side. "Isn't it past your bedtime? I don't think your mom would want you to be out this late with me." He faux frowned, reaching out to pinch my cheek. I swatted his hand away and growled.

"It's literally only 8:03," I snapped, but slowly started to put the materials away. Our brain was barely halfway completed; we still needed the cerebral cortex, brain stem, and the inside matter. We also had to label it and explain each function on a separate sheet of paper. Yeah, this was taking a lot longer than expected.

"Still," Ace shrugged, yawning again as he started to neatly place everything on the corner of the table. "So, does your mom always let you come over a guy's house to do projects, or am I—"

"No, you're not special," I cut him off before he could finish that cheesy line. He only grinned, braces flashing, a dimple deepening as a chuckle escaped his lips.

"Worth a try," he mumbled, scratching his nape sheepishly as he stared at me through his lashes. I turned away and swallowed thickly.

"So, what do you want me to take home and finish?" I asked quietly, fiddling with the clay and styrofoam. I could hear Ace shuffle in the kitchen before coming back with his car keys in his hand. He shoved them in his pocket as he leaned against the doorway, taking up the entire space as he folded his arms over his chest.

"Nothing," he said simply.

"Nothing?" I asked, quirking an eyebrow at him.

"Nothing," he repeated. "This is a group assignment, Bubbles. Every part of this project will be completed *together*." Ace smiled devilishly. I only rolled my eyes, turned on my heel, and headed for the door. I could hear him splutter behind me, jogging to catch up to my quick pace.

By the time I made it to the car door, it was already unlocked as I hopped in. I watched as Ace exited the house, slamming the grand door shut behind him as he briskly walked to the driver's side. He climbed in hastily, rambling about him needing my address again, since it would be weird to remember it clearly from when he first visited me. I ignored his blabbering as it finally hit me.

Judas. I was meeting with Judas for the first time tonight. And I almost completely forgot! While he didn't give me a specific time, I figured any time after dark was appropriate for what we would be discussing. And in an abandoned park, no less.

"Wait!" I snapped, cutting Ace off quickly. He startled, shoulders jumping to his ears as he looked over at me incredulously.

"Jesus, Bubbles, you scared me half to death. I almost hit the gas, you—"

"Can you take me to that abandoned park twenty minutes away?" I cut him off, turning to look at his baffled gaze. At the sound of the location, his eyes almost bulged out of his head.

"Excuse me?" he whispered, eyes suddenly squinted and accusatory. "Who are you meeting there, 'cause I'm sure you wouldn't wanna go swinging by yourself this late." Ace pursed his lips, then paused in thought.

"Well, at the looks of you, I wouldn't be surprised." At that, I reached back and punched his bicep. We both hissed in pain; him at my sheer strength and the pain that shot through my still-sore knuckles. Not my smartest move, but it shut him up. I yelped when I felt him punch me back, not very hard, but enough to leave a frog.

Growling, I pulled my fist back to punch Ace again, but he quickly dodged it, swerving as much as he could in his seat. He grabbed my hand quickly, and when I reached back with my leftie, he grabbed that one too. He huffed, leveling me off with a serious look.

"Stop playing get-back and tell me who you're meeting," he whispered lowly, pulling my hands closer as he yanked me forward. My elbows fell roughly against the middle console, and I hissed again.

"You started playing get-back, you overgrown—"

"Who are you meeting?" Ace snapped loudly, his grip tightening enough on my wrists to bruise. I knew a couple of ways to get out of this position, but they mostly ended with me snapping his wrist. And now *that* was going too far. I still needed him to finish his load of the project.

We sat in silence for a few moments, his eyes boring into my glasses as I kept my mouth in a straight line. After realizing that he wasn't budging any time soon, I huffed and rolled my eyes.

"What's it to you?" I asked quietly, looking at anything but him. "Why can't you just take me?" His grip was still unrelenting, no matter how hard I struggled.

"Oh God, Bubbles," he groaned, rolling his eyes dramatically as he finally let me go. I snatched my arms back, rubbing my sore wrists as Ace turned in his seat. He stared out of the front window for a few seconds.

"I forgot how new you are to Devils Lake," he sighed, rubbing a hand over his face before turning to me. "Nobody ever goes to that creepy park unless they're looking for trouble." He gave me a slow glance over before finally resting his gaze on my face.

"And by the looks of it, trouble is definitely following you. Or maybe you *are* the trouble," he shrugged. I reared back to punch him again, but he put his defenses up. We watched each other in tense silence before slowly putting our fists down.

"I'm just," I shifted uncomfortably in my seat. "Meeting a friend there. He said he wanted to talk about—"

"He?" Ace snapped. I lifted an eyebrow at him and nodded slowly. Quickly, he shook his head and backed out of his driveway.

"Nope." Was all he said as he started his way to my house. I thought he didn't remember where I lived because it was creepy. Slitting my eyes at him, I sneered, "Just take me to the park or I'll walk there myself." I gritted my teeth, waiting for Ace to respond. He flipped the radio on and pretended not to hear me. After two minutes of me staring holes into his head, and him completely ignoring me, I shrugged. Before he could stop me, I unlocked my door and prepared to open it, even with him flying down the street.

"Hey!" he snapped, slamming on the brakes. I'm glad there weren't too many cars around, or else we would have surely gotten into an accident. "Are you crazy?" Ace yelled, gripping my upper arm as I still tried to escape the car.

"Apparently I am to you," I said, digging my nails into the back of his hand. He growled, letting me go, but reaching over me to slam my door shut. As I went to protest, he locked it on his side of the car, immobilizing me. I could always break the window if I wanted, but that was too much work.

We sat there, quietly huffing before Ace decided to break the silence. He stared forward the entire time, the red of the stop light casting a soft glow on his skin since we were still so far away.

"Have you known him long?" he asked suddenly. I rolled my eyes.

"Yes." I lied straight through my teeth. Lying was like a second language to me, the only language that I couldn't speak as fluently to Prissy. The thought made me shiver.

The car fell silent again as Ace chewed his lip, lost in thought. I didn't understand his protests against me going to meet a stranger for the first time, unbeknownst to him. Yeah, he should be worried about a new girl in town suddenly having a 'friend' that I mentionably haven't named yet, past eight pm by herself. In his eyes, he was the closest and only friend I had so far. And that said a lot.

I guess he would have to worry about any other girl, but not me. My eyes were all the protection I needed. One look at Judas, and this would all end tonight. I could hide his body somewhere in the woods and trek home right to Prissy. I doubt she cooked anything for me, so I could grab a snack, maybe just some apple slices, shower off today and go to sleep. Yeah, it would be that simple, right?

I didn't even believe myself. If this Judas person knew about Kelly and Chad, the origin of my powers linking to Prissy, and pretty much everything else about me, I couldn't downplay the situation. It would take a lot to kill me, but who's to say it won't be the same for him?

Suddenly, the thought hit me hard. Pieces of his email lingering behind my eyes as I started to put the puzzle pieces together.

His question of, "Were we cursed in the same way?" The mention of my memory is as good as his—with my power, not only were my eyes cursed to kill, but my mind was forced to remember every vivid detail I wished to repress.

Are we special in some way, in the sight of her eyes?

I was brought back down to reality with a sharp gasp. Ace pinched my upper arm as I slapped his hand harshly. He frowned at me.

"I said, how long have you known him?" Ace asked. I hadn't even realized that he turned around and started heading out of Devils Lake. I'm pretty sure that the ride would take a little longer since we were coming from his house, but that helped me gather my thoughts more.

"A while," I said shortly. Ace sighed, clicking his tongue as he started to slow the car.

"I know we've only known each other for barely a week now, but my mom always told me to look out for women, whether I knew them personally or not." He shifted in his seat, the memory obviously being a painful one. I could read him like an open book.

"It's just kinda weird meeting up with a guy. In an abandoned park. This late. By yourself." He punctuated every sentence, tone turning sour as he slunk lower in his seat. "Especially one that you don't know," he snapped, glancing at me from the corner of his eye.

"I told you he's a—"

"And you lied." He was sharp-tongued and snippy. I slightly recoiled at the aggravated look on his face. "You're not as passive as you think you are," he mumbled, making a sharp left. I grabbed onto the door handle for support as my weight was thrown around. There were a couple of minutes of silence as we slowly neared the edge of Devils Lake.

I wondered if Judas would attack me. He didn't sound too threatening in those emails, but I couldn't base his actions on measly words to persuade me out of the house. I'm sure he would say anything to get me to meet up with him.

I wondered what he looked like. Would he tower over me like Ace? Broad shoulders that could trap me, hands big enough to wrap fully around my throat. Would his eyes be like mine? Gray, feral, and deadly? Would his mouth close off secrets that he had to protect? Would he have scars like me, from beatings and trainings, littering his body? Would he be destroyed goods, just like me?

I could feel the bile rise in my throat at the thought of it. What if he was raised by a witch as well, pushed and taught to rival me? To beat me? To *kill* me?

As I opened my mouth to tell Ace to just turn around, we arrived. They weren't lying when they said it was abandoned. It looked like something out of a stereotypical horror film. I could almost hear the gothic, creepy music wafting from invisible speakers.

Everything had a draft of fog over it. There was a large, paint-chipped slide that looked too dangerous to go down. A set of monkey bars that I'm sure could cause a bitten-off tongue when falling from the rusted metal. There were different kinds of contraptions that just looked downright dangerous if touched. Like the whole park could crumble, bury itself into the sand, swallowed whole in one bite.

And finally, a swing set. One seat was slowly being pushed by the wind while the other was occupied. I couldn't see his face, but I knew it was him. It *had* to be him. The only visible thing about the boy swinging was the hoodie pulled over his head and gloved hands that held loosely onto the chains holding his seat up. He didn't lift his head as we pulled up, but I know he heard us, with how his feet softly dug into the ground below him. He didn't stop swinging, just slowed his pace ever so slightly. I could feel a shiver going down my spine.

"That him?" Ace grumbled, eyeing the man who sat silently in the cold night. I nodded, wetting my suddenly dry lips. I was practically vibrating in anticipation.

"Yeah," I murmured. We both sat in the car for a few more moments, waiting for any of us to make the first move.

It was Judas. He lifted his head slowly and turned. His face was covered by a mass of dirty blonde curls, but I could see the distinctive cock of his head. He let go of the chains and lifted his hand, waving it once before turning to stare down at his feet again.

"I'm taking you home," Ace snapped, already shifting gears. I reached out quickly to stop him.

"No, let me just," I stammered, starting to unlock the door again.

"Bubbles, this doesn't feel right," he whispered, eyebrows drawing in as he grabbed my elbow. I didn't fight as hard as I did earlier to make him let go of me. A part of me wished that he wouldn't. Wished that he'd trap me in his car, drive off, take me straight home to Prissy, and scold me before wishing me a sweet goodnight. But this wasn't some romance novel that I'd self-indulge in before Prissy got her hands on it and ripped it up. If I wasn't learning explicitly, then there was no need for any other kind of book, she'd drill into me after beating my spine with the spine of the book. *No need. No need. No need to love anyone but me.*

"Ace," I whispered, turning to Judas who continued to swing slowly, head facing our direction again. "Just let me do this." My mouth pulled into a frown as I slowly pulled away from his grip. He let me go hesitantly, eyes darting between me and Judas.

"I'll wait here for you, okay?" he said so quietly I wanted to scream. Wanted to punch him square in his jaw, wrap my hands around his neck, look deep into his eyes, and watch him crumble. Because why did he care about my safety so much? Why did he want me to make it home alive? Does he even know what home is like? Does he even know that the scar above my eyebrow was from Prissy slamming it into a mirror after accusing me of being so vain? Does he know that I've split my knuckles more times than I can count after punching harder things than my dresser? Does he know that I've killed before? Does he know that I'm supposed to kill his father? Does he even know about that stupid lady, still soft after birth, who I could've sworn was home alone—

I was wrenched out of my thoughts at the sudden tap at the window. I yelped, hands poised on my glasses, ready to pull them down and kill whoever got this close to me without me even realizing it.

It was Judas. He stood there, gloved hand still resting against the glass. His eyes were covered by his hair, but I could see the curving of his mouth, a small smile. It didn't look mischievous, but only eyes could give true intent. I heard Ace growl behind me as he cracked the window slightly.

"Piss off, creep. I'm taking her home," he snarled. Judas smiled even wider.

"But we have some things to discuss." His voice was soft, honey-like. It sounded comforting, save for the way he turned to me eerily, teeth too bright and straight in the darkness of the night.

"Isn't that right, love?" Judas cocked his head to the side, a glimmer of blue eyes glinting in the moonlight. Another shiver went up my spine.

I turned back to Ace, who looked just about ready to pounce. I placed a hand on his warm arm and stared at him until he finally broke his staring contest with Judas.

"I'll be fine, I promise. Just go home, okay?" I whispered, squeezing his arm, trying to talk him off of a ledge. Instantly he shook his head.

"Bubbles, I can't just *leave* you with him." His eyes shot accusatory looks at Judas, who only smiled again.

"I don't bite," he said softly, sincerity dripping in his voice. Ace, on the other hand, seemed to only get riled up more. He growled, foot ready on the gas, but I gripped his arm tighter.

"I'm serious, Ace." I leveled him off with a look as he kept glancing between the two of us. Finally, he threw his hands up and slouched back in his seat. I heard my door unlock, trying to ignore the burning of my cheeks as Judas opened the door for me. I wasn't sure if he was doing it to be chivalrous or if he was leading me right into the lion's den. Either way, I went in blind and almost uncaring. *Almost.*

"Call me if you need anything," he leaned over his console to throw out the window. "And I mean *anything*," he snapped, staring pointedly at Judas, who only seemed to smile wider, but I could see the way his shoulders tensed.

I nodded, feeling like my mouth was glued shut. Ace watched us for a few more seconds before sighing dramatically and pulling off. As we watched his silvery truck slip into the darkness of the trees leering overhead, I heard a laugh beside me.

"Wow, that guy's tense, isn't he?" Judas chuckled, turning fully to face me. He stuck out a hand and beamed.

"I'm Judas." Staring down at his hand, I took it gently in my right hand. Before he knew it, I pulled his wrist toward my chest, pushing my other forearm into his sternum as my right leg hooked behind his left, unbalancing him. He fell onto the soft ground with a grunt as I clambered on top of him quickly, pinning one arm under my knee as I held the other tightly in my grip.

"You're an idiot, you know that?" I snarled, shaking immensely above him. I wasn't sure if it was the guilty excitement of having my "own" kill without being ordered to do so or the thought that he could be just as strong as me. *If not stronger.* Either way, I was practically vibrating as I grinned down at him, teeth biting into my lower lip as I felt it snag and rip. I could taste warm copper in my mouth, but I ignored it in favor of reaching for my glasses.

"Thinking you could intimidate me with a couple of theories you just pieced together. Idiot," I snapped. I leaned back slightly at his relaxed smile. He didn't struggle or strain to get up as he shrugged.

"Try me." He nodded toward the hand that stilled on my glasses. I gaped at him for a minute before snarling again, snatching them off quickly and staring into his eyes.

"Now *rot*," I leered, waiting for him to crumble at any minute. It was...weird. Whenever I had someone in a position that immobilized them, they always struggled, bucked their hips up, twisted in my grip, thrashed their heads around to resist the temptation to just *look*. But Judas did none of that.

Shaking off the eeriness of it all, I counted slowly in my head. After just five seconds, he'd be gone. Dust and wind swallowed by whatever lingered in this creepy park. Three more seconds. He grinned at me. One.

Chapter 8

I counted again in my head. And again. And again until I was sure that five seconds had flown by, by now. Judas grinned up at me, wide and proud.

"Cool, right?" he whispered, cocking his head to the side as his hair fell back so I could get an even better look at his face. Piercing, deep blue eyes framed by thin-wired, golden glasses, a smatter of freckles dotting along his nose and cheeks, lips round and chapped from the cold wind. I wanted to break every bone in his face.

"Who are you?" I mumbled, slightly astonished. I've never...not been able to kill someone. No matter how much of a struggle or fight that they'd put up, I always gained my kill. So why was he...different? Tightening my grip on his hand and digging my knee further into his arm, he winced slightly.

"You know, Bright Eyes," he croaked out, shifting underneath me but never making a move to get up. "It's kind of hard to explain everything with you crushing my hand. And knee. And chest." His eyes glanced down to where I rested most of my weight on his sternum as I leaned back slightly to knock more wind out of him.

"You calling me fat?" I snarled. Judas chuckled and shook his head as much as he could as he peered up at me. His laugh was soft, a little strained, and I wanted to hear it again. Just once more before I could properly kill him. I was going to find a way, somehow.

I watched Judas for a few more seconds before slowly releasing my grip on him. I stood quickly, still poised and ready if he were to attack. He only shakily got up, brushing the dirt from his hair and the back of his pants with a grimace.

"I really liked these pants," he frowned, trying to get as much off as he could. I examined his outfit and almost gagged at how much his style resembled Prissy's. He wore a black poncho with red, green, and yellow stripes, obviously a bit too small for him as a sliver of pale skin peeked between the bottom of it and the waistband of his pants. Now his pants—they were an eyesore. Bright red with green and white stripes running along the length, form-fitting, and hugging him tightly. He wore simple black shoes with yellow and green stripes that looked old and beat up.

But what caught my eyes in his bright outfit were the gloves. They were thin, black and simple, stopping shortly at his wrists. I hadn't even paid the thin barrier any mind as I held him down earlier, but I could recall the fabric being soft, feeling like it was handcrafted from cheap scarves, patchy but smooth.

"They're ugly," I commented simply. Once he felt like he had brushed as much dirt off as he could, Judas glared up at me with no real hurt behind his eyes. He frowned deeper as he shook the dirt out of his hair more.

"That's rude," he muttered. I shrugged and watched him. The silence was quickly growing tense as we both waited for the other to make the first move. Again, it was him.

"Well, let me introduce myself again," Judas said, a shy smile gracing his face. "I'm Judas." This time when he held his hand out, I took it. I didn't flip or pin him, or try to do any funny business. He breathed out a sigh of relief when I released him.

"And again, who are you?" I asked, short and ready to get to the point. He seemed to perk up at that, cocking his head again and letting those stupid curls rest on his glasses.

"Right." He mumbled, scratching his nape. "Let's go sit down so I can explain." Judas nodded toward the still-swinging seats, waiting for my response. I cocked an eyebrow but trudged over to the swings in front of him. I could hear his steady footsteps behind me as I tensed, waiting for him to make the wrong move so I could finally end this and go home. But as we both sat down, I realized that I would be here for a lot longer than expected.

Judas pushed himself up slightly, so his feet still brushed the ground. I sat watching him, wondering how this man-child could know so much about me but look as soft as butter. The thought made me grit my lip and curl my hands into the chains holding the seat up. I needed to calm down, lest I cut myself on this rust and get a nasty infection.

Maybe, that wouldn't be so bad. The pain could give me a wakeup call.

"Do you remember hearing your parents' voice, even before you were born?" Judas asked softly, gazing up at the moon. "Or is her voice, the first one you remember ever hearing?" He cut me off before I could even answer. Still, his eyes were locked above as I watched his slowly swinging form. I chewed my lip for a few minutes before I decided to answer.

"I don't remember," I lied. Judas snorted, looking over at me with a lopsided grin.

"We're not going to get anywhere if you keep lying, Bright Eyes," he said before staring back up at the moon. Not one, but two guys in one night could call me on my bluff. Prissy was right; I was getting lazy. Puffing up my shoulders, I squared him off with a look I was hoping was intimidating.

"Are you going to tell me how you know so much about me, or what?" I snapped. "Because I could be home right now, and in bed sleep." I went to stand, but Judas only chuckled again.

"In bed sleep, or out killing as many people as you can for Priscilla?" he asked nonchalantly. I stilled, hands digging deeper into the chains.

"What's your body count now?" he asked, his pace slowing as he stared up the entire time.

"Has it surpassed a hundred, or do you have some sick goal of killing—" Before I could stop myself, I was on him again. Fingers digging into his collar as I pulled his face closer to mine, feeling my eye twitch with the burn of just wanting to kill.

"What do you want?" I snarled, feeling absolutely livid. I was starting to go off of the deep end again; could feel the rage bubbling over again; could feel the itch in the bridge of my nose again. I couldn't tell if I was angry because he knew so much or downright fearful on how this strange boy, who couldn't crumble over and die at the sight of my eyes, knew so much about me.

Or was this some setup, made by Prissy? Some trick, some test, to prove my loyalty to her? This wouldn't be the first time, but I'm sure it would be the last after I stopped denying the allegations of being a killer.

Shaking, I gripped him tighter, could feel the well of tears in my eyes from the absolute fear that coursed through me. I couldn't die tonight. I couldn't. I still had so much I wanted to do, even with Prissy breathing down my neck constantly. I had a life to live when she would finally be dead and gone; I had to outlive her. I had to.

Judas noticed my shaking and wobbling lower lip. Slow and cautious, as if I were some bomb set to go off any minute now, he wrapped his gloved hands around mine. He stared at me the entire time, never breaking eye contact as he nodded lightly. He squeezed my hand in his gently, anything to coax me down, keep me from snapping his dainty neck, not add another body to the list that seemed to go on forever.

"I'm not here to hurt you, Areya," Judas spoke calmly. He finally broke eye contact to follow the tear that ran down my cheek from under my glasses. Quickly, I pulled away from him to wipe it. I still stood too close for comfort, but Judas held my other hand in a vice-like grip.

"I just want to talk," he reassured me.

"Then talk!" I snapped, wrenching my hand away, my finger hovering dangerously close in front of his nose. "All you're doing is bringing up kill counts! What do you want?" I practically screamed. I could feel the sudden rush of a panic attack as I tried to gulp in air quickly. I paced around the swings, trying to calm down, trying to breathe. Nothing was working.

I dug my fingers into my short hair, pulling until I felt a few strands ripping from my scalp. The pain burned so good as I panted, pulling and pulling with one hand, pinching any piece of skin I could until I broke through, until blood stained my nails. I needed this pain to bring me down, as I muttered to myself, "She knows, Rey, she knows. There's no backing out now, she knows. Just get up and leave, yeah, just leave. Just go and run until she can't find you." I reassured myself before a full-blown panic started to overtake me again.

"Of course she'll find you, idiot! You can't go anywhere without her finding you! You're so stupid, just give up, just roll over and die, just—" I cut myself off quickly, eyes wide and frantic. I stomped over to the sides of the swings and got an awfully painful idea in my scattered mind.

And as I reared my hand back to punch the pole that held up the swing set, begging for the pain that I knew would really ground me, my wrist was quickly caught. I snarled, ready to attack whoever interrupted my plans of leveling myself out, but was brought back down to reality as Judas jumped in front of me, bringing me in to meet his eyes with mine. He grabbed my other hand and brought me close to him, as I slightly leaned back to meet his eyes.

Judas scanned me over, his gaze lingering on the bandages wrapped around my knuckles, the panic strewn across my face, erratic breathing, tears still steadily leaking from under my glasses. He sucked in a shaky breath as his eyebrows creased.

"What has she done to you?" he muttered. I froze, body locking up at his words. Prissy hadn't done anything wrong, had she? Everything I got beaten, berated, burned, marked, scarred for; it was all for a good cause, right? It was to make me stronger. Make me a better warrior, make me the machine she needed in this world to rid of all the people she deemed as being bad.

"The only thing she's done," I panted, snatching my wrists from his grip, stumbling back slightly. "Is make me stronger." I snarled and pointed an accusatory finger in his direction.

"You," I said, practically bordering on delirium now. "You're the one who's weak. You can't even fight me properly; you just lie there like some," I stammered, pulling at my hair again. "Like some—"

"Fighting a person back who is terrified on whether or not I'll report them to their witch caregiver isn't moral to me," Judas said softly, shoving his hands in his pockets as he shrugged. I sneered.

"Prissy isn't just some caregiver, she's my mother," I growled, posed for a fight once more, uncaring if he would fight back this time.

"So what about Kelly?" Judas said coolly, cocking his head to the side as those stupid glasses seemed to gleam in the moonlight. At the very mention of that woman's name, I lunged for him before he could brace himself.

We fell back on the ground, knocking the wind out of Judas as he caught the brunt of the fall. Before he could catch his breath, I reared my fist back and struck him as hard as I could across his cheek. His head whipped to the left as he gasped, a split already cutting across his smooth skin. I wanted to see more; more cuts, more blood. I wanted to see him in as much pain as I felt.

As I pulled my arm back to strike him again, he looked up at me with soft eyes. Not pleading, but quiet, understanding. Like he was silently convincing me that it was okay for him to be my punching bag, after being one myself for so long. I pulled back once more, this time punching the earth next to his head. He flinched anyway, but quickly opened his eyes to meet mine.

"She was never my mother," I muttered, leaning over him as my breath started to slow shallowly. "She never loved me. He didn't either. Only Prissy loves me." And with that, I stood. I started to trek away from the swings, determined to wander around until I eventually found my way home, right into her arms, confess everything I did, and be slain where I stood. I had to prepare myself for it all.

"Areya, wait," I heard Judas's soft voice call out, a sudden cold hand wrapping around my wrist. I gasped at the cool contact and tried wrenching away as I turned to look back at him, but his eyes seemed to glaze over.

After another second, Judas let my arm go slowly. He looked confused, eyebrows furrowed as he worried his bottom lip. With curiosity getting the best of me, I asked him tiredly, "What is it?" My voice sounded hoarse and scratchy in my own ears. It sounded almost completely unrecognizable. Just like how my body and face would be in a couple of hours, after I arrived home to Prissy.

"I knew I wouldn't be able to kill you with our powers, but," he shook his head, hair falling in his face as he slowly put his glove back on. "I can't even see. Everything is blurry and dark, like I can barely open my eyes," he murmured, gaze going unfocused again as he started muttering to himself.

"Can't see what?" I asked, befuddled. Judas whipped his eyes to me, almost as if he completely forgot that I was still standing there. He looked away sheepishly as he smiled.

"That was one thing I wanted to talk about," he murmured as he rubbed his nape. I gaped at him.

"So you start the conversation off about my kill count?" I asked incredulously. Judas flinched, holding his hands up in defense as he stared off to the side.

"I'm sorry, I just really didn't think that you'd show up, and after finally seeing you up close, I just..." he trailed off, looking at anything but me. Quickly, he shook his head and another bright grin adorned his face.

"Anyway, can we start over?" He paused. "Again?"

I mulled it over in my head, pulling out my phone to check the time and see if I had any missed calls or texts from Prissy. It was pushing 9 PM. I was surprised she hadn't said anything, but I guess she wanted me to get as close and spend as much time as I could with Ace. With zero interruptions. I shivered and turned back to Judas, whose eyes were dancing between me and the phone.

"What, did your jock boyfriend text you?" he asked, slightly snippy as he blew the hair out of his face. I raised an eyebrow at him.

"Told you he's not my boyfriend," I mumbled, trekking over to the swing set one last time. I heard him grumble behind me as he plopped down on the seat to the left of me.

"Sorry, I meant guard dog." He breathed out, slowly starting to push himself forward and back. I rolled my eyes at his childishness.

"Whatever, let's just get started, yeah?" I asked, nerves already starting to return to me. He nodded, huffing out a breath before he slowly began.

"Remember that little brother you were supposed to be getting?" he murmured, and I immediately stiffened. Oh God, I thought, don't tell me—

"I didn't go with you guys that day, obviously." Judas' swinging slowed considerably as he started toeing at the dirt below us. "Maybe that's where we both went on separate journeys. I wanted to stay with my mom and dad, and you..." he trailed off, eyes searching the trees not too far away. I stared at my bandaged hands that laid in my lap, barely strong enough to tighten them into fists. It was a lot harder when you weren't high on a panic rush.

"Can I ask why?" he whispered, still unable to face me.

"Why what?" I snapped, feeling the shake of my bones. Of course he wanted to know; the day they died, everyone wanted to know. Judas cleared his throat, tugging uncomfortably at the collar of his poncho.

"Why did you kill them? What made you choose her over your parents?" His voice sounded desperate, confused, and even hurt. How could he feel empathy for those two monsters that he had never even met? How could he grieve parents that weren't his, especially knowing that he had his own? Knowing that he most likely loved him, even with his curse? Why did he grieve over the loss of the monsters who birthed me and not the death of Vivienne?

"You didn't even know them," I grated through my teeth, trying to keep my composure for the last time tonight. Judas suddenly turned to me, his eyebrows furrowed as I met him in an equally intensive stare behind my glasses.

"I don't have to know them to feel bad for two innocent people who were brutally—"

"Brutally?" I snapped, leaning forward to grip his collar tightly. "You think that was brutal?" I let him go, pushing him back and hoping he would lose his balance and topple out of the swing. He didn't.

"You obviously don't know me like how you thought you did, idiot," I snarled, crossing my arms and staring out at the leaves that blew silently on the ground. Judas sat quietly for a minute, trying to gather his thoughts as I could practically see the gears shifting in his mind.

"How do you become so brutal if you have the gift of not even having to touch someone?" he asked slowly. "You could just look at someone; why do you need to," he stuttered, face scrunching up as I imagined he was thinking about my uglier kills.

"Does it bother you that bad?" I asked lowly, staring down at the hands that have torn people apart too many times to count. I could almost hear Prissy's words ringing throughout my head.

"This job; slit his throat first. He deserves to suffer a little. Don't ask why."

"This job; disembowel after. I don't care if you can't stand the smell. Rot is just as bad. Don't ask why."

"This job; torture him until your knuckles bleed. Until you cannot tell his blood from your own. Don't ask why."

"This job; break as many bones as possible. Why do you need a reason? Are you defying me? Haven't I told you not to ask why?"

"Don't ask why. Is something the matter? Do I have to remind you that you are mine? My machine, my monster? Do I have to retrain you, Areya?"

Shaking the thoughts from my head, I glanced back over at Judas, who had been silently watching me. Looking back down at my hands, I huffed.

"If it bothers you, then why did you meet me?" I asked.

"I said it doesn't bother me." Instantly, my head swiveled to look over at Judas. He was staring forward, starting to slowly push himself up and down. He shrugged as I made a noncommittal noise in confusion.

"I know you don't want to do more than you have to," he murmured, twisting his mouth in thought. "It was written all over your face," he said, almost sadly. He turned with a forced smile, I'm guessing to try and comfort me. It only made me feel worse. My throat tightened, quickly looking away and over to the entrance of the park.

"How did you find me?" I muttered quietly, ready to change the subject. This weirdo studied me too well, and I didn't like it. Usually, no one could see through my facade unless they were a trained professional. If we were around the same age, then he couldn't be one, but still, it unnerved me.

"I was actually just trying to find Prissy first." He shrugged. "I wanted to make her pay for cursing me with this," his head nodded to his gloved hands. "So I got into a lotta tech stuff to find out about tracking, and then I remembered you," he said. I arched my eyebrow.

"Me?" I asked. "We never met before this. I would've remembered." I tried to rack my brain of all the memories of his face, only coming up with the hazy figure that was stalking Prissy and I in the store that day. Other than that, I don't think that I have ever seen him.

"Yeah," he nodded. "But, on your birthday, when she came to get me, she mentioned you. How you had the same gifts as me, how we could be the best brother-sister duo to ever grace the universe." He looked up at me shyly as red dusted his cheeks.

"You know, we're not really," he trailed off, rubbing his eyebrows as his eyes darted around me. I snorted.

"Yeah, I know, idiot." Judas nodded quickly, muttering something under his breath as he tried to fan the warmth from his face.

"But, yeah, I remembered her mentioning you, and then a couple of years later when I was searching for her, I came across a news article online. It was something like, 'eleven different bodies found scattered in West Virginia. All with no visible marks, all unable to calculate the time of deaths. All smelling of rot.'" I could see a shiver pass up his spine, and deep down inside of me, it gave me a sick sense of satisfaction. Knowing that someone was that disgusted, that troubled with the jobs Prissy gave me. Shaking the thought off, I tuned back in so I could keep listening.

"Immediately, I knew it was you," Judas murmured, staring off into the distance as he pushed his thin glasses up his nose. "And after that, I followed your trail of bodies from city to city, state to state. I always was a step behind until Arizona," he said, glancing over at me as I stiffened. Just the sound of the state left me feeling icky, all gloating and prideful thoughts from earlier quickly draining as it was only replaced by nausea and dread. Judas must have noticed as he suddenly perked up.

"You don't wanna know anything about me?" Judas suddenly asked, pouting in mock hurt as he tried to divert the conversation somewhere else. He probably figured that I would attack him again. I rolled my eyes, letting out a small snort as I shrugged.

"Who was the first person you killed?" I asked, straightforward and upfront. He winced, hands gripping the chains tightly as he slowly curled in on himself.

"I don't really wanna talk about it." I gaped at him, turning quickly as I jabbed a finger in his chest. He frowned, rubbing the spot with a quiet whimper.

"You can ask me about why I killed my parents, why I have to slaughter people for a living, but I can't ask about the first person you, I'm guessing, killed on accident for the first time?" I snapped. Judas looked down abashedly, rubbing his nape as his lips pursed. I stared at him for a few more seconds as he sat there, pushing himself forward and backward until the creak from the old swing started to drive me up the wall. With a scoff, I stood, shoving my hands in my pockets.

"Whatever," I grumbled, starting my long trek home. "I don't care anyway. Bye, Judas." As I started to stalk closer and closer to the entrance, I could hear him call something out. I paused, turning slightly to look at him over my shoulder. He sat in the same position as when Ace and I first arrived.

"It was my older sister," he said again as I strained to hear his soft voice. "I had just turned five, Prissy hadn't gotten there, I didn't know—" He abruptly cut himself off.

I waited another minute to see if he was going to continue, but he only pushed his legs backward to propel higher in the air. His head was down, dirty blonde curls spilling under his hood. I could practically see the tight hold on the chains that threatened to crack any minute now. But he never looked back up. Turning again, I made my way out of the creepy, abandoned park that seemed to whisper my name in the wind and the soft cry of an unfamiliar name under it. Shuddering, I murmured into the collar of my thin jacket, "Goodbye, Judas."

Chapter 9

I was surprised, to say the least, to see Ace's shiny silver car sitting a couple of feet away from the entrance of the park, shrouded by overgrown bushes. Instantly fuming, I stomped up to his window and knocked harshly, ignoring the throb in my knuckles.

Ace didn't look startled at all. I figured he saw my furious face stomping up to him in the rearview mirror. He grinned, rolling his window down as he leaned out, his face inching closer to mine as he cocked his head to the side.

"Need a ride?" he winked. Cocking my hand back to punch him, he quickly caught it, bellowing out a laugh.

"Oh, calm down, Bubbles, and get in the car." He brushed me off and rolled his window back up.

I had to count to ten in my head to get my life and fists together before rounding the front of the truck and hopping in the passenger seat. Before I could say anything, Ace rubbed the top of my head roughly, like I was a puppy. I snarled, smacking his hand away as he beamed at me.

"I saw you tackle that dude like two or three times. I'm glad you know how to stick up for yourself, Bubs!" he said excitedly, and if he were a dog, I could see his tail wagging. Growling, I folded my arms and faced the front window.

"Shut up," I muttered. Ace ignored me, starting to ramble on as he pulled off. As curiosity got the best of me, I looked into the passenger's rearview mirror. Judas stood there a few feet behind the car, hands in his pockets, the glint of his glasses shining in the moonlight, body stiff and rigid. He grew smaller and smaller as we drove away, Ace too busy rejoicing and amazed at my strength to even notice Judas. I pulled my eyes away when I couldn't see him anymore.

"Why did you stay?" I asked Ace, cutting his loud voice off in the quiet car. His mouth snapped shut audibly as he looked over at me, a small smile gracing his face.

"I already told you why I didn't want to leave you alone with him. So I pulled my car up a little, where you guys couldn't see me but I could kinda see you, and stayed." He winked at me again as I rolled my eyes.

"Told you I could handle myself," I grumbled under my breath. "You didn't have to stay; it's been almost a full hour. You should've gone home, I'm sure it's past your curfew." I pushed him, trying my best to make him slam on the gas and get me home as quickly as possible. I was ready to just crash in my bed, not have to think about everything that went on today—this awfully long day—and sleep for the next sixteen hours.

"I don't really mind. Plus, my curfew isn't until one." He shrugged, getting a little quieter at the mention of his home life. Right; trashy father. I almost forgot. I felt kinda bad about bringing it up, but I quickly brushed the feeling off.

"Still, next time you don't have to," I said, picking at my nails. The car quickly grew silent.

"Next time?" Ace asked, a low undertone of his voice that sent a shiver down my spine. I glanced at him in the corner of my eye as his grip on the steering wheel tightened.

"Yeah, I think I want to ask him more questions, learn more about him," I mumbled, scratching at my chin in thought. This thing between Judas and I wasn't over. It was still so much I wanted, needed, to know.

"So, did you just have me dropping you off on a date, or what?" Ace chuckled with no real humor. He rubbed the scruff of hair on his jaw as he turned the corner sharply. I rolled my eyes at his obvious jealousy. He didn't even know me. Stupid oaf.

"And if I did?" I challenged, turning in my seat to face him. He looked over at me with a malicious grin as he shrugged. Before he could speak, I quickly cut him off.

"I already told you that it wasn't a date, Ace." I rolled my eyes again, huffing out a breath as I folded my arms again. "Get over yourself," I added quietly, relieved to see my stupidly bright-colored house sitting at the end of the cul-de-sac, sticking out like a sore thumb. I jumped slightly at Ace's loud, boisterous laugh that shook the car.

"Cute." Was all he said as he smoothly pulled into the driveway. I cut my eyes at him, lip curling back in a snarl.

"And what does that mean?" I snarled. Ace parked, letting go of the steering wheel and unbuckling his seat to fully face me. He rested his chin in his hand as his eyelids drooped, giving me a dopey smile.

"Your attitude, your snarky remarks, you." He breathed, eyes scanning my face. In the corner of my eye, I could see the light in the living room turn on, and I prayed that Prissy wouldn't come out here in just her bathrobe, pounding on Ace's window. Come to think of it, she didn't care much about how I could handle situations that could go bad in an instant, especially seeing how close she wanted me to get to Ace.

"You're cute," Ace said simply, wrapping a lock of my hair around his finger and tugging playfully. Instantly, I could feel my face get hot, my mouth dropping open as I fought to find something smart to say. I couldn't. Guys had never complimented me much; I was always too aggressive or too standoffish, and they were always intimidated by me.

Either that, or they went straight into catcalls and sexual harassment. To be so blatantly called cute by a guy that I had been nothing but snippy to was a little overwhelming. Finally snapping my mouth shut, I grabbed my bag and fumbled with the door handle.

"Shut up," I grumbled, trying to claw my way out of his car. Chancing a glance back at Ace, he still sat there watching me with a small smirk. I wanted to punch the look right off of his face.

"Are you going to let me out of this stupid car, or are you trying to hold me hostage?" I snapped. "You know I could take you, just like I did with my friend." I tried to appear bigger than I was, intimidate him as much as I could. It didn't have much effect though. Ace only sized me up once more with a predatory grin.

"I bet you could, Bubbles." He winked, finally unlocking the doors. I groaned, mentally smacking myself as hard as I could as I hopped out of the car. Stupid Ace, stupid boys, stupid cars, stupid, stupid, stupid. My head whipped up as I heard his car door close as well.

"What are doing?" I snapped, coming around to his side to stop him. I held my hand against his chest to keep him back, but he merely looked down at me, smiling even wider. His canines seemed to shine brighter in the moonlight, like a silent promise to tear me apart with one wrong move.

"Walking a lady to her door," Ace said simply, grabbing my wrist so he could walk around me and drag me behind him. "I know you could," he cleared his throat, "take me, but it's still the proper thing to do." I could hear the smile in his voice. Too stunned to rip my hand from his, I walked numbly to the front door. He stopped, waiting for me to open it with watchful eyes.

"You know you're not coming in," I snapped, still trying to find a bite in my voice that shook slightly. Ace noticed as he grinned wider with a shrug.

"Didn't expect to." Before I could comment back, the front door was swinging open. There Prissy stood, in that stupid lavender bathrobe with yellow ducks on it, with a smile adorning her seemingly never-aging face.

"Areya!" she cried, pulling me into a tight hug. Instantly, I froze, hands limp at my sides. Was I supposed to...hug her back? Did she expect me to? Oh God, I wish she would just pull away already.

After a moment, she did but still held on tightly to my upper arms. She examined my face quickly before looking over at Ace, who stood beside me quietly.

"And who might you be?" she asked, finally letting me go. "Are you my sweet Areya's project partner?" Prissy said so innocently, she almost made me believe that she really didn't know who Ace was and that I was her sweet. He smiled brightly, rubbing his nape.

"Yes, I am, ma'am." He held out a large brown hand. "I'm Ace. I dropped off Areya's mattress not too long ago, so we've met briefly before." Prissy nodded, feigning an 'ohh that's right!' as she shook his hand that seemed to dwarf her own.

I stood there awkwardly, ready to just go in the house and face-plant onto my pillows. I guess they both could sense how uncomfortable I was getting. Before long, Ace finally spoke up as he gestured to his truck.

"Well, I'll get out of you ladies' hair." He nodded, a crooked smile adorning his face as he turned to Prissy. "It was nice seeing you again, Ms. Matthews." Finally, he turned to me, an even wider grin plastered brightly.

"And I'll text you for the next time we can meet up and finish, okay?" He cocked his head to the side, curls spilling over. I nodded mutely and waved at him, pressing my way into the house as I heard him laugh and trek over to his car, pulling out of the driveway quickly.

I watched him go through a crack in the blinds, sighing in relief. I could finally just get a moment to breathe. Or so I thought.

"He's nice," Prissy said simply. I cut my eyes over at her as she started to boil some water in a kettle. I shrugged, trying to slyly find my way upstairs.

"Yeah, he's fine," I dismissed. Before I could make my way to the steps, Prissy held a hand up.

"How much of the project did you finish?" she murmured, back turned to me. Her body was lax, seemingly unbothered, but she always appeared like that. Especially when she was ready to attack and wanted my guard to be down. I felt myself tense.

"About half," I struggled to push out without stuttering. She hummed.

"You only finished half and it's pushing 10?" Prissy asked, looking at me over her shoulder. I swallowed and tried to appear nonchalant.

"The big idiot didn't even have the supplies," I waved off. "And we had to keep taking breaks to figure out how we wanted to set it up and eat and his father came and—" Crap. I was rambling and let too much spill out. Prissy's eyebrows raised, and she finally turned to fully look at me.

"Oh?" she asked, eyebrow quirked. "Did you speak with him?"

"Yeah," I shrugged again, trying to inch my way over to the steps again. "He's not that good of a person, that much I can tell," I murmured, thinking back on how Ace had completely frozen and tensed up when the man came around. I was broken out of my stupor at Prissy's hum.

"He's not." Was all she provided, turning her back on me to finish making her drink. I took that as my cue to leave, squeaking out a meek 'goodnight' as I scurried up the steps. When I finally made it to my bed, I plopped my bag down and fell face first. God, this day felt so long. I didn't think I could miss a bed so much. Before I knew it, my eyes started to fall shut as sleep overtook me.

It was hot. Burning almost. As I finally fought to open heavy eyelids, I quickly realized that it was burning. Smoky ashes falling against my lashes, red and orange flames licking every crevice of the house. On high alert, I tried to jump out of bed, call Prissy, and dash to the door, but my entire body was heavy and lax.

"Prissss," I gurgled out, tongue too heavy for my wickedly dry mouth. I limped over to the door, dragging my numb legs to push me out. In the blink of an eye, as soon as I exited my room, I was standing in the middle of the living room, facing the front door, a few feet away from it. There was a muffled cry behind me, seemingly from a child. I turned slowly, too afraid to see whose body would be writhing in pain.

It was a small girl, cowering on the ground, covered in blood red and singed yellow, with burnt orange hair curled and matted around her face. She shook, mouth moving, desperately trying to form words, but all that came out were bone-chilling screams. Prissy stood above her, that same look on her face for the entirety of my training. Lax, mouth set in a deep line, her eyes harsh and analyzing every single move I made. Seeing her like that made my blood turn to ice.

"Prissy, who is that?" I managed to get out. It all sounded garbled in my ears like I had cotton shoved down my throat. They both turned to me, the girl's screaming eerily ceasing with an abrupt cut-off as she smiled weakly at me.

"Mine." The little girl hissed through blood-soaked teeth. She grinned wide, red dripping down her chin as her small tongue slithered out to lick it up. I cringed, eyes darting from her to Prissy, who only frowned. She shook her head, clicking her tongue as she bent over to whisper something in the girl's hair.

"We have to go," I panted, my body starting to sag as the smoke began to pile up in my lungs and cloud my vision. "Do you not see the smoke?" I cried, words slurring beyond recognition. I went to turn away, bolt out of the door, and leave Prissy and the girl to burn because, damn them, if they wanted to stay in a melting house then there was nothing I could do to save them.

"Mine!" The sudden cry rooted me in place. My eyes went wide as the little girl came dashing at me at an impossibly fast speed, knife in hand, poised to gut me. I screamed, trying to move, fight back, tackle her, just something, but my feet stayed rooted to the spot. I closed my eyes, whimpering in pain as the knife slid through my stomach, the tip soaked in blood pointing out of my back. The blade didn't even look that long.

I blinked away tears, a gasp caught in my throat at the sight before me. It was Ace. Standing tall and broad, his cheeks wet with salty tears as he bit his bottom lip to keep from wobbling.

"Bubbles," he whispered exasperatedly, eyes flicking to over my shoulder. "Watch out." I tried to turn, but the knife was still sunk deep in the abyss of my belly. I gasped from the pain and cried out, hands grabbing onto Ace's shoulder as another sharp sting shot through the middle of my chest. I looked down, horrified to see yet another blade piercing through my flesh, the tip dripping onto the burning hardwood floor below us.

Before I could turn to see who was stabbing me in the back, I could feel angelically soft lips brushing against the shell of my ear. He nuzzled his nose against my nape as they both gripped my waist to keep me up. Ace leaned down to my other ear as they whispered simultaneously, "Stay. Repent. Don't leave us. Please. Mine." Judas and Ace repeated over and over until I thrashed from their holds, ignoring the blades ripping through my skin in the most personal way imaginable.

In unison, they released me. I was falling onto the floor in a heap of blood and melting bones as the house around me burned. I could barely make out three silhouettes and one tiny body with hair that blended with the flames. They walked quickly out of the door as I struggled to crawl over, crying out, "Please!" I could taste smoke in my lungs, blood licking my teeth. "Please, help me!"

The three bodies walked out quickly, leaving the orange-haired girl to close the door. She turned to me, the skin on her hand melting from the intensity of the fire that shot through the doorknob. She looked unbothered by the pain, especially if the scar running from the outer corner of her eye to her chin were anything to go by. The girl sneered down at me.

"Why didn't you help her?" I was too terrified to look back, trying to figure out which victim she could be talking about now. I garbled another plea as the door slammed in my face. I clawed at it, uncaring as my nails bent back and plucked out of their beds, palms and fists sizzling as I tried to bang my way out.

"Mommy?" a tiny—so, so tiny—voice called from behind me. I stiffened for a moment before banging on the door with renewed vigor. Pleading, crying, begging anyone or anything to let me out of this hellscape. With one last cry, the house crumbled with a resounding, "Mommy!" echoing throughout the burnt rubble and ashes.

I bolted up, gasping, face and pillow soaked with tears. I felt like I couldn't catch my breath as I panted, hands finding purchase in my hair as I pulled harshly. After a couple of minutes of rough breathing, it finally slowed as I started to catch my breath. Looking around the room, I detected that there were no flames, no signs of Ace or Judas, and definitely no kids. I ran a hand down my face as I laid back down, chest tight as the tears still spilled over loosely.

I don't think that I'll be sleeping for the next couple of nights. A sudden dinging from my phone caught my attention. I slipped it out of the hoodie's pocket I fell asleep in, grimacing at the bright light that momentarily blinded me. As my eyes adjusted, I noticed I had six texts from Ace—seriously, why couldn't the guy just type one long message?—and one single text from an unknown number. I answered Ace's first.

Ace
12:08 AM

Hey Bubbles! I had a lotta fun hanging out with you today
The project is due next Friday, but nothing is wrong with getting things done a little early right?
We can meet up again this Wednesday, after my practice since I don't work that day either
We can go to your house this time, if you want
Oh and your mom is kinda scary lol intense but pretty sweet
I see where you get it from ;)

Rolling my eyes with a scoff, I texted back a quick "whatever, fine with me" and scrolled over to the other text from an unknown number. I didn't get too many of those, seeing as how Prissy typically had the latest technology on how to keep us safe from hackers and trackers, so I was surprised to see who it was from.

Unknown: Possible Scam
12:17 AM

Hey, Bright Eyes. This is Judas. I think we got off on the wrong foot tonight. That wasn't at all how I expected for our first time meeting to go. Can we have a do over this time? I promise I'll try not to bring up anything that might trigger another panic attack from you. Hope you get back to me, gem. Sorry again if I caused you any added stress.

I couldn't help but chuckle at his last line. Sly boy, I thought. His wording was so slick I almost missed it. Rolling my eyes, I replied to his message quickly and saved his number in my phone under a simple J.

Bright Eyes
12:19 AM
Yes, we can meet again. Wednesday at 11:30. I'll send the address. And I don't even wanna know how you got my number, creep.

And with that, I sent the message and turned my phone off. I didn't feel like arguing back and forth with his choice of words. I would pretend to play dumb for the time being, let him think that Prissy was the root of all my problems until I was in person to correct him again. Now that would take the stress off.

Since it was a little past midnight and I didn't plan to go to sleep any time soon, I decided to finish up that English project that we had to turn in sometime next week. Ace wasn't wrong about trying to get things done early.

I padded over quietly to the other side of my room, shuffling through my book bag and folders to grab the assignment details. As I went to go sit down at the vanity, I felt a shiver creep up my spine. Snatching my laptop from the top of it, I slumped back over on the bed and started to read over what we had to do specifically.

Write a 500 to 1000 word essay ... should be 3-5 pages ... must have a clear beginning, middle, and ending ... do not plagiarize under any means ... any genre ... romance or horror is recommended ... no inappropriate language ...

A short horror story it is then. And with that, I tapped away at my laptop until the sun rose.

Chapter 10

It was a quiet night. The house completely silent, save for the quiet hum of the little girls' shared TV. Their mother had chastised them on multiple occasions to turn it off at night; they always refused, told their mother that the quiet made their ears ring. Or if they weren't ringing, the creaking from the steps always woke the twin girls.

"The steps only creak when someone is using them, my loves," their father would always say gently, bringing the girls to his side and kissing their cheeks. That did nothing to calm their hearts. They knew that the stairs groaned with every step, so the question became: who is always using them at 3 am, every night?

The girls continued to leave the TV on. Much rather comforted by children's laughter and silly sound effects from the cartoons blaring from the screen. It was either that or staying up until it was time for school, shivering and terrified at who always seemed to be standing right on that top step at night.

At first, the girls thought that it was their older brother playing tricks on them. Trying to scare them, make them wet the bed at night just for the fun of it. But after shakily walking to his room hand in hand one night after the creaking got louder, they were surprised to see him sleeping soundly, mouth agape with a line of drool falling onto the pillow.

So what was that creaking? Who was constantly running up and down the steps every night that the girls could not see?

After finally becoming fed up with the constant groaning of the stairs, the girls set up a plan. They would sleep, set quiet alarms on their phones to wake half past three, stand beside their door, and peer out of the crack. Any other time, the girls would snatch open the door, quietly demanding to know who it was that kept waking them. But this time, this plan would be silently fulfilled.

They were already awake before the alarm set off. Too hyped on their nerves and excitement to finally catch whatever it was on the steps, they slipped out of bed silently. Feet bare and clammy from sweat as they interlocked hands, tiptoeing over to their door. And when they cracked it open, it took everything in them not to scream in fright.

There, standing in the doorway of their older brother's room, was some humanoid, hybrid figure. Its back was hunched, spiked brown fur running along its flank and hips, each and every bone in its body poking out through the skin, some tearing through its leather-like flesh. Its head oval-shaped and bare, hanging knuckles scraping the ground. The girls couldn't see its face yet, but nothing could prepare them for when it turned its owl-like stare at them.

Its eyes were hollowed out, nothing but blank sockets, two small circles for nostrils, a gaping hole for a mouth. But the thing that terrified them the most was the front of its body coated and covered in blood. Their family's blood.

Hanging from one of the large, scarred hands were bones, guts, and gore, smattered in the red, inky liquid as it pattered quietly onto the floor. They could see their parents' faces, mangled and torn from their bodies, sitting at its feet. Their brother's body sprung along the floor—and was that his spine the thing was holding?

Broken from their stupor, the girls screamed. The thing growled, dropping the bones and turning its body to them. The twins slammed the door shut, hearts palpitating wildly in their tiny chests at the sight they had just laid eyes on. They could hear the thing moving quietly at first, scraping its knuckles across the door before all movement ceased.

The girls listened with rapt attention, trying to calm their fast-beating hearts with no success. And almost like it was its routine, the scratching stopped, turned its feet to the stairs, and began to climb them. Up and down, the steps creaked and groaned, over and over again until it hit four AM.

Like clockwork, the creaking stopped. The girls sat huddled in the corner, arms full of each other as they waited a couple more minutes. Once they were sure that the thing was gone, the girls took a deep breath and peered through the crack in the door once more, to be met with—

Nothing. Absolutely nothing. No blood, no bodies, no gore. Confused, they shared twinning looks, carefully stepping out into the hallway to peer into both rooms of their brother and parents. They were fine. Everything was perfectly intact, like there hadn't just been a massacre in front of them. With tears rolling down their faces, the girls slipped into one bed, holding each other tight and letting their cries lull them to sleep.

The next morning, the girls tried to explain what they saw. Obviously, they got smacked down, told to be quiet, that they both just shared one awful dream, eat their breakfast, and just go to school. So they did. And the monster followed them in their minds the entire day.

That night, it happened all over again. The monster, the blood, the bodies, the skinless spine. It happened over and over again until they couldn't take it anymore. On the fifth and final night of this torture, the girls did not close the door when the monster walked up. Instead, they welcomed it with shaking knees, quivering hearts, and wobbling bottom lips.

"What do you want?" one twin asked.

"Why do you keep killing them?" the other cried. The thing only cocked its head, a wry smile pulling at its lipless mouth as more blood poured from it. Raising a heavy, red-soaked claw, he brought it down to cover both of their faces. With a rumbling breath, it spoke.

"Go to sleep, my loves," and the voice sounded awfully like their father's. Like a spell, both girls dropped and were sound asleep. And the cycle continued every night after that, but this time, the only bloodied bodies they found were of their mother and brother.

Soon enough, the twins' bodies were matching the disfigured corpses in this recycling nightmare until the end of time, their father's voice ringing sweetly in their head every night.

"Goodnight, my loves. Go to sleep."

I could feel the ache in my back as I finally finished typing up this story for English. Yeah, it was a little over a thousand words, sue me. I wasn't an overachiever, but there was nothing wrong with adding a little more to the story. I wanted to add anything I could to give it a little zest, since creative writer wasn't in my job description, alongside being a killer. Hopefully, though, this would manage.

I yawned, rubbing my eye as I hopped out of bed and prepared to make breakfast. It was a little after 7 AM, so Prissy was still snoring loudly in her room. I trotted down the steps, ignoring the shiver tingling up my spine at the thought of my dream last night as I passed the front door. Slipping into the kitchen, I instantly went into work mode, grabbing everything I could to make us simple bacon, egg, and cheese sandwiches.

After stuffing my face, I climbed up the steps two at a time and swung into the bathroom. Taking a quick shower, I peaked in Prissy's room and saw that she was still sound asleep. This lady could sleep for hours on end, something I could never understand. The buzzing of my phone in my pocket caught my attention as I reached down to check it. Plopping down on my bed and towel-drying my hair, I rolled my eyes at who it was from again.

Ace
7:59
Hey Bubbles!!! Have you finished your English project yet?
I think I need help with mine.

Growling under my breath, I rolled my eyes. How could I possibly help him with his story, other than writing it myself? Or maybe, the big oaf just wanted to hang out and work together again. Any excuse to come and annoy me, I was guessing. With an exasperated huff, I texted him back.

Bubbles
8:01
I just finished this morning. How would I be able to help you? Do you just want me to write it for you, you cheater?

Ace
8:02
Lol no!!! Don't write it for me. Just wanted to hear some ideas from you. Suggestions on how to transition, and what ending sounds better. All of that good stuff.
So could you help me, Bub?

Ace's response was instantaneous. I had barely put down my phone when he was sending something back. Mulling it over in my head, I chewed my lip in thought. There would be nothing wrong with just aiding in his writing process, right? Just me reading over it, giving him tips on how to improve. Shrugging to myself, I replied again.

Bubbles
8:04
Sure. I guess I can help a poor birdbrain jock write his story. Do you want to meet up again or what?

We weren't supposed to be meeting up again until later this week, since we just decided this at midnight, but I couldn't see any other way to help him. Although, I secretly hoped that he wouldn't bring the brain with him. It was too much to work on this early, and my Sundays were for resting, or working if Prissy required it of me. Other than that, I planned to just laze around the house all day if I could. The vibration from my phone brought me back to my senses again.

Ace
8:06
Just checked the schedule and I have to go into work at 11 so can I come now?
I can write it there really fast and just clean it up when I get home.
That okay with you and Ma?

My eyebrows furrowed in confusion. Ma? Was he referring to Prissy? If she were to hear him calling her that, she would give the brightest smile she could before cursing him under her breath. I could practically see her sneer now.

Almost as if my thoughts had conjured her up, there was a rap on my door, signaling her presence. My head snapped up to give her my full attention, phone held tightly in my hand, almost as if I were a child caught stealing a cookie from the cookie jar. She leaned against the doorway, arms crossed over her curvy frame as she glanced from my pinched expression to the phone in my hand.

"Who are you talking to that's making you make that face?" she asked softly, her eyes glinting with mischief. I furrowed my eyebrows more, my mouth pulling down into a frown.

"What face?" I asked, darting my eyes across the floor. I could hear her huff out a laugh as she smiled at me softly, cocking her head to the side.

"Who are you texting?" she repeated, a bit more sternly this time. I shrugged, trying to act nonchalant as I waved the phone around.

"Ace. He asked if he could come over and get some help with an English project that we have to work on," I said, heart racing as one of her thin, blonde eyebrows lifted. Half of her mouth pulled up as she huffed again quietly, unfolding her arms to place them on her hip instead.

"He wants to come over here?" Prissy asked before I nodded. "Now?" I nodded again, subconsciously cracking my toe knuckles against the cold floor, a nervous tick she always hated.

She glanced down at my feet, lazily dragging her eyes up to my face as her eyebrow arched higher. She stared at me for another moment before shrugging, shuffling out of the doorway and to the steps. She waved a careless hand behind her as her voice grew quieter with distance.

"I don't care. Just stay out of my way by staying in your room." I nodded, even though she couldn't see me.

"Thanks, mom!" I called out, trying to suck up to her as much as I could. I heard her snort, feet lightly padding down the stairs as I let out a breath I didn't realize I was holding. I quickly picked up the phone to text Ace back with an affirmative.

Bubbles
8:11
Yes you can come now.

Ace

8:12

Great, should be there in ten.

Ten? As in ten minutes? He didn't even live that close! So did this mean that he was just hanging around my neighborhood, waiting for me to say yes so he could sweep in as quick as he could? Shaking it off, I padded around my room, pulling out something to wear other than the clothes that I had crashed in last night. It wouldn't be a good look for him to find me still lazing around in the outfit that I had worn literally all day yesterday.

I found a gray tank top, black stretchy leggings, and colorful socks that Prissy had insisted that I wore to bring my monochrome outfits some pizzazz, as she liked to say. I was pulling the longer pieces of my hair into a small bun on the top of my head when the doorbell rang. Pulling up the covers of my bed and kicking any stray clothing laying around into my closet, I bounded down the steps to see Ace already standing in the entryway.

Prissy was smiling up at him, hips leaning against the kitchen doorway as she murmured something with a wink, before sipping from her mug. Ace laughed softly, a breathy sound as his eyes crinkled, dimple sinking deeper into the brown skin of his cheeks, his large hand rubbing his nape abashedly. They hadn't seen me until I cleared my throat, eyes bouncing between the both of them. Prissy perked up as she pulled her cup away to gesture at Ace with excited eyes.

"Oh! Areya, honey, did you know that Ace gets up early every Sunday to help and volunteer his services for our neighbors?" She cocked her head to the side as he laughed again with a shrug.

"You know that old senile lady a couple of doors down? The blind one with the nurse?" she asked. I nodded slowly—I had no idea who she was talking about. I didn't care about knowing my neighbors, but Prissy liked to keep up the facade every time we moved. She always made it seem as though she was a doting mother with a rebellious teenage daughter to keep her busy. She liked to go over to their houses, collect as much information as she could about the city and town that we lived in, gossip all day long, and then send me out for another kill whenever she gathered enough for a job that night. I didn't really understand how much information you could get from a barely-alive old lady, but I didn't question it.

"Well, every Sunday, Ace here comes along and mows her lawn, trims her hedges, dusts around the house, and the like. Isn't that sweet, honey?" Prissy asked, cocking her head to the side as Ace grew more and more bashful. He was stuttering, holding his hands up as he spluttered, obviously just ready to go and start this English project. I exhaled through my nose, slowly dragging my eyes over his form with a smirk.

"Yeah. So sweet," I sneered, watching the look on his face darken. He slitted his eyes at me, mouth pulling up in a curve as Prissy looked in between us with a knowing look on her face. Obviously sensing the tension, she looked back into the kitchen.

"Oh! Let me finish cutting up this fruit. I'll bring some up to you guys later on, okay?" She cocked her head to the side again, a subtle way of saying just get out of here already. Tight-lipped, I nodded, turning on my heels to indicate for Ace to follow. I could hear his heavy footsteps behind me on the steps as he called out a thanks to Prissy for her hospitality.

As we made it to my room, I let him in before closing the door behind him. Ace did not fit in my room. With the red and black walls, dark furniture, and low lighting, he looked out of place. Not to mention the fact that he towered over pretty much everything in my small room. He was almost eye level with the bulb hanging from the ceiling fan.

Nevertheless, he looked around quietly, a small smirk on his face. He stepped up to my dresser, glancing at me over his shoulder at the small splatter of blood that darkened the wood of it. I shrugged, body practically radiating a told you so energy as he shook his head at me. He continued to canvas my room before finally plopping down on my bed, pulling out a laptop from an old book bag that I hadn't noticed before. He glanced up at me.

"Cute," he muttered, his smirk morphing into a smile as I growled, stomping my foot petulantly.

"Stop calling me cute, you oaf," I snapped, folding my arms. Ace placed the laptop beside him, leaning back on the bed as he cocked his head to the side, curls falling in front of his eyes.

"I actually meant your room, but you're cute too, ya know. Especially when you puff your chest up and extend your claws like some feral cat." He grinned, blowing the curls from his face with a wispy breath. I narrowed my eyes at him, face burning in embarrassment. I hoped he couldn't see how red I had gotten under the lights of my room, but when he grinned even wider, crinkling his nose, I could tell he saw it. I rolled my eyes, pointing to the empty vanity seat.

"Shut up and get off my bed. I don't want your sweat tainting my sheets," I snapped, much less venom than I had wanted in my tone. Ace laughed, throwing his head back as his Adam's Apple bobbed, bringing a hand to his chest as he slowly got up.

"Oh, stop being so dramatic, Bubbles. I didn't even have to break a sweat today." He smiled, brushing past me to plop down at my vanity. I cut my eyes at him, the skin on my arm warm from his soft touch as he rested his cheek in his hand.

"I thought you had to mow her lawn today." After examining him though, he was as fresh and clean as ever. His tight, black V-neck and black and orange basketball shorts looked straight from the dryer. Ace noticed my staring as I brought the plush chair in the corner over to the vanity. With the round back and curve of the chair, it made me feel even smaller than him. I hated it. Hated how I had to look up at him through my glasses, how he smiled down at me so softly.

"I ended up just reading to her today. Her lawn wasn't too bad, so I decided to just give her some company instead." He shrugged, tapping away onto his laptop as it booted up. I snorted at him, reaching over to tug my own laptop into my lap.

"Reading to the elderly. Grade A guy, huh?" I teased, snickering softly. Ace snorted, reaching down to pinch at my cheeks as I swatted at his hand.

"Shut up," he murmured with a small smile. We fell into a comfortable silence as he waited for everything to load.

"So," Ace asked, eyes scanning the screen as he starts pecking away at the keys again. "What genre did you write?" He shifted his eyes over at me as I pulled up my own assignment.

"Horror," I shrugged, passing him my laptop as he passed me his own. He snorted, settling back into the chair with a grin.

"Figures," he murmured, shooting me a smile. I slitted my eyes at him, punching his calf as hard as I could. He yelped, glaring down at me as he shoved my shoulder, almost sending me toppling back. I grabbed his basketball shorts to steady myself as he snickered.

"Just shut up and read it, idiot," I grumbled, face red as I puffed my cheeks in irritation. I heard Ace chuckle softly, staring down at me for a moment before turning to the screen with a soft smile. With a roll of my eyes, I huffed and began reading his stupid story. It was only a paragraph in length but wasn't bad in the slightest.

"They were star-crossed lovers...or whatever that meant. In every lifetime they lived, they always found each other. Both spirits connected, bones pulling to finally become whole, veins tugged through their skin to intertwine and tangle. Their souls cried for the other. Every life they lived, they always found each other. No matter the distance, the barriers, and the dangers of loving each other; they always ended up in each other's arms.
Until they didn't."

I glanced up at Ace to see him already staring down at me, a fingernail being gnawed in between white teeth. I glared up at him, pushing the laptop back to him as he smiled sheepishly. His eyes darted around the room as he pushed my laptop over to make room for his own.

"So?" he asked. "What did you think? I kind of don't know where to go after this, and I was hoping that you could kind of direct me. If that makes sense," he muttered, biting more incessantly at his nails now. I softly hit his knee with another roll of my eyes.

"I thought you were going to read mine," I grumbled with a frown. Ace rolled his eyes, that cunning smile plastered once again.

"I didn't want to keep stopping and starting, so I figured that I could just read it after I finish mine," he said, shrugging as his eyes started scanning his writing once more.

"Makes sense," I said. We sat in silence for another second before Ace stared down again at me expectedly. I rolled my eyes, tucking a loose strand of hair behind my ears and pushing up my glasses.

"I like it," I shrugged. "What did you want it to be about? Reincarnation is what I'm getting."

"Something like that," Ace responded nonchalantly as he started slowly pecking at the keys again. "I just want to write something kind of sappy and sad, you know? I just don't know what kind of direction I would want to take, or how to spin this." He started muttering to himself again, moving to bite on his thumbnail after chewing off all of the others. I rested my hand on his knee to gain his attention. He glanced down at me, eyes slightly widened as he pulled his thumb back, a thin trail of saliva connecting them.

"Just write what you think the characters would benefit from best. Use old language and references from old books without stealing, make it rough around the edges. Write about what you would want from a star-crossed lover, turned violent," I provided, racking my brain on whatever it could weakly throw at me. I wasn't an expert writer, so this was kind of hard to even think of, but I tried to be as helpful as I could. And I guess I was, seeing the gentle smile Ace gave me.

"Thanks, Bubbles. That was very insightful." His tone dripped sarcasm. I groaned, punching his calf again as he threw his head back and laughed.

"Ugh, get out!" I yelled, shoving at his legs that didn't even budge. "You ask for my help and then laugh, you jackass!" I continued with my tirade as Ace only blocked my shots with a large hand.

"Okay, okay! I'm sorry, I am!" He continued on with his laughing as he tried to calm himself, a large grin still spread across his face. I eyed him, crossing my arms over my chest as his eyes drooped, leaning in closer to me so his face hovered inches above mine.

"Just didn't know you could be such a good teacher. It's just kind of cute, is all." Ace pulled back before my punch could land on his jaw, another bellowing laugh following. I grumbled, muttering under my breath as I started to question why I even let him come over. He patted my cheeks softly as I bit at him, cooing at me all the while.

"Aww, it's okay to be embarrassed. Just not used to it, huh?" he asked, cocking his head to the side. I saw complete red, standing up to really punch him this time and not miss, but he held his hands up in mock surrender.

"Okay, I'm done messing with you. It's just fun, is all." He snickered, turning back to his laptop. I flipped him the bird, which he only interlocked with his own finger, typing with one hand to hold the position. I growled, snatching my hand back and watching that smile light up his face once more before a more concentrated one adorned it.

I sat watching him as he typed. The way a peak of his pink tongue would slip past his lips as he paused in concentration; his thick, arched eyebrows furrowing; the way his lips would curve as he mouthed whatever he was typing; the slight nod after a moment's hesitation in typing. I hadn't realized that I had been staring for so long until his eyes met mine.

"It's rude to stare, you know," he whispered, winking at me and turning back to the screen. I scoffed, face heating up the same way it always did whenever he said something cheeky. I stared intently at the side of my bed, trying to keep from looking at him as he typed away in the silent room.

"I don't mind it, though," Ace nudged me with the toe of his shoe, gaining my attention. "It just reminds me of how pretty I am." He smiled cheekily, wincing slightly at the hit I landed on his thigh. I arched an eyebrow at him in slight confusion.

"Pretty?" I asked. "You call yourself pretty?" In all of my secondhand experiences, every time I saw or heard a boy being called pretty, they always immediately took offense to it. To hear Ace refer to himself as pretty was baffling. He shrugged, slowing his typing but never fully stopping.

"Yeah. An ex used to call me pretty all the time, and at first I would be offended, you know? Like, I'm a man. I'm handsome, sexy, even cute. But pretty?" His face scrunched up for a moment before relaxing, his shoulders dropping as he pecked away quicker now.

"But she eventually just chalked it up to me having a toxic sense of masculinity, or whatever that means." He shrugged again. "Told me that it's okay to use soft words to describe myself, that I didn't have to be all straight lines and hard edges all the time." His voice grew softer as his typing slowed this time. He paused, scanning the screen before darting down to me. His eyes were round, soft, holding so much of a person whose story I wouldn't even dream of knowing after only meeting a week or so ago.

"Why did you break up?" I asked, voice soft and slightly confused on why he was sharing this with me. He only snorted, resuming his rightful place at tapping away at the keys.

"Just fell out of love, or whatever," he said, trying to sound indifferent, but I could see the subtle way he swallowed. I figured I'd leave the issue alone for now and let him continue writing so he could finally leave.

He did just that. After sitting in silence for another fifteen minutes, he sighed, leaning back in the chair to yawn obnoxiously loud. I rolled my eyes, trying to ignore the sliver of skin as he scratched at his belly and a purpling bruise near his right hip. His shirt was pushed back down before I could fully register it, tongue suddenly felt too heavy in my mouth.

"Okay, I finished. I'll read yours, and you can read mine," Ace said, another small yawn coming from his lips as he passed me his laptop. Immediately, he threw himself into the two-and-a-half pages of work, and I quickly followed suit.

"They were star-crossed lovers...or whatever that meant. In every lifetime they lived, they always found each other. Both spirits connected, bones pulling to finally become whole, veins tugged through their skin to intertwine and tangle. Their souls cried for the other. Every life they lived, they always found each other. No matter the distance, the barriers, and the dangers of loving each other; they always ended up in each other's arms.

Until they didn't.

Life was completely thrown, the perfect balance that they held for centuries tipped to one side. Blood, tears, and kisses all poured grotesquely everywhere it could reach. The pull apart was painful; every being in the universe felt the unwinding of one connected soul being brutally split into two.

When they came together in the next lifetime, it was all wrong. There was no accidental brush of hands, no shy first kisses, no childhood best friend turned high school sweetheart, no adoration, no genuine love. No, it was all painful.

Meeting each other with fists and blood, knocks of teeth, and scraped bottom lips. They were volatile, two explosions that set the other off packed too closely together in an unsuspecting warehouse. They exploded every chance they got, lighting forest fires and winter storms at every opportunity, taking down any and everything in their paths.

They were toxicity in its finest form, its rarest and most dangerous form. Nothing but hot and cold clashing and fighting for dominance. When one didn't win, the people surrounding them always took the brunt of the damage. It wasn't until they were adults when everyone was sick of being victims to their terror acts of what they deemed as love.

They were forced away from each other. Pulled their aching hands away from the other, their hair grasped in bruising grips to tear their lips away. They loved the fight, no matter the cost. Loved being covered in blood, as long as it was the others. This was their love language; the hostility, the fight, the taste of copper soaking their tongues, the apologies afterward, the lingering thoughts of wanting to do it all over again.

They were told that this wasn't normal, wasn't healthy. No one should love their partner with fists and gunshots, broken bones and whittled marrow, bites and wounds that would never heal properly.

The lovers knew that this wasn't anyone else's normal but their own. They couldn't explain it; couldn't comprehend why their fingers itched to wrap around the other's throat instead of their hand; couldn't comprehend why every kiss turned into who could bite the other hardest; couldn't comprehend why they craved the taste of the other's blood; couldn't comprehend why they desired so strongly to bathe in it.

This was love, wasn't it? Wanting to tear your partner apart, let them pull you from your skeleton, crawl into your skin? It was the most basic way to become whole again. With their souls severed, they had to find one way to belong to each other once more.

One day, they finally did. Fought the other until the bloodbath became too much to handle. Too volatile for anyone to break up. Everyone realized that, in order for them to stop, this had to happen. Had to let them tear into each other and build themselves anew. Pick away at each other's skin until it intertwined once more, let their souls sing in harmony at finally being attached again, no matter how violent the nature.

Mangled and bloodied fingertips sought the other. Bound by dripping copper and an infinite amount of lifetimes shared, this was what they had wished for. Had craved and cried and sought for so long. Sobbed into the other's arms, asking, questioning, why does it feel so right to be with you? Why do I like the pain of burnt fingertips? Why do I cherish the scars? Why does breathing the same air as you feel so natural? Why can't I bring myself to hate you? Why do I love you, the ache of being in your arms, the breath escaping my lungs whenever you kiss me quietly?

And when they are gone, it is peaceful. Quiet. No more explosions, no more bombs, no more clashing of teeth and tongue and fists. When their lips seal with one last final kiss, one last breath pressed into the other's mouth, the world is once again, balanced."

By the time I finished reading, Ace was already looking at me, nails back in between his lips. We sat there staring for a few more moments before I rolled my eyes, shoving his laptop back on his lap with an exasperated sigh.

"Okay, I liked it," I said. "It was just sad. Like, depressing as hell, kind of sad. Very well written, though." I hated to admit it, but his story wasn't half bad; it was great, actually. The pure, raw, and emotional pain of wanting to be with someone but the universe saying otherwise. Knowing that you belong in the other's arms but never being able to fit quite right. This was what Prissy always hated whenever I snagged a romantic book like this. Hated the way the characters would inevitably make me think, what they would make me feel. Like an addict with an itch, I wanted to just keep reading more and more.

"Thanks, Bubbles!" Ace smiled brightly. "I wrote it with a certain girl in mind, ya know?" He winked, leaning lower so I had to sit back slightly to look at him evenly. His eyes slowly raked over my face before quickly darting over to my bedroom door. I glanced back too, wondering if Prissy came in and I hadn't heard her, but the door was still shut. With a confused grunt, I faced Ace again, only to be met with him leaning even closer to me.

"Does your mom always let guys come into your room, or am I just special?" he asked, breath husky and his voice low as his lips curled into a lazy grin. Narrowing my eyes at that line he's used twice already in only one day, I spat,

"Not special. Just desperate for my help."

Ace chuckled at that, eyes darting to my mouth. Before he could lean any closer, I planted my palms smack on his face. He grunted, leaning back with a slight shove of my hands. I shook my head as he whined against my palm like some mangy mutt.

"Nope." Was all I said with another push. Ace sat back in the seat with a frown, obviously disappointed at being rejected. I don't know how they do things here in North Dakota, but I was not going to have my first kiss stolen by a guy who I had only known for barely two weeks and whose father I had to kill soon. Nope, not happening.

"I liked your story too, by the way," Ace cleared his throat, sliding his gaze over my dimmed screen. I perked up, raising an eyebrow as a small smile grew.

"Yeah?" I asked. He nodded, any previous awkwardness melting away as he grinned back at me.

"Yeah. Really creepy, Bubs. How did you come up with it?" Ace asked, turning to shut his computer off. A tiny piece of me wanted to think of any reason to make him stay longer, but I beat those thoughts with a crowbar until they silenced.

"Had a bad dream last night, and scary fictional things usually help ground me," I shrugged, standing from my seat and stretching my legs. Ace glanced over at me, his brows furrowed as his eyes searched my face.

"Really? What was the dream about?" At his concerned tone, I paused. I almost forgot that he was in it, warning me of Judas, stabbing me, holding me, whispering in my ear. A shiver crept up my spine as I shuffled over to my bed to set my laptop back down. I tried to shrug as nonchalant as possible, but I could tell that he could see straight through my weak facade.

"The house was on fire. You stabbed me. My friend stabbed me. Lots and lots of smoke." I tried to tiptoe around the rest of the dream. Tried to forget about the little girl with orange hair who mysteriously looked like the drawn picture from the vanity before I cleaned it. Tried to forget about Ace's tears as he warned me of the knife slicing through my back. Tried to forget about his pleas to repent. Tried to forget about that desperate cry from the day that everything went further downhill—lower than I even imagined possible.

"I stabbed you?" Ace asked incredulously, crossing the small space of my vanity and bed to sit down beside me. "You haven't known me long, but I would never hurt you like that. I wouldn't ever try to hurt you in general. Promise." His eyes were soft and sincere, darting between my lenses as I lowered my head.

"Everyone always says they won't hurt you, Ace," I mumbled quietly, just ready to get this conversation over with and have him out of my house already. I looked up at the soft feeling of his warm hand on the crook of my shoulder, his thumb rubbing soothing circles onto the underside of my jaw. His eyes were serious, searching for any kind of humanity in mine, something he would never get.

"I'm not everyone, Bubbles," Ace said softly, bringing up his other hand to brush away the stray hairs that fell from my bun. We sat there staring at each other until I broke first, slightly pulling away from his soft hands—seriously, how could someone who has played football for God knows how long have such soft hands?!—and leaned into my pillows.

"It's whatever, Ace," I said, looking at anything but him. He slowly retracted his warmth from my body, and my shoulder suddenly felt chilled in the stuffy room. We sat in silence for a minute before his eyes shone with mirth and a crooked grin.

"So, were the twins dead the whole time?" Ace asked suddenly. It took me a minute to figure out what he was talking about before it hit me. I laughed through my nose, leaning more onto the pillows so that my legs were drawn up on the bed to face him fully.

"Yeah," I laughed. "They were just, like, spirits or whatever, figuring out how they died and having to go through it for the rest of eternity." I shrugged, picking at the edges of my covers. Ace winced, his smile never faltering.

"Ouch. Sounds terrifying," he said, lightly smacking my exposed ankle as my leggings bunched up. I nodded, before he started another influx of questions again.

"And it was their father, who was the creature thing?" I nodded. "How did he become the creature? And why did he climb steps? I didn't understand that part. And did the brother and mother have to go through the same thing, when they died?" Ace was rambling now, his fingers combing through the scruff of his short beard as he started going over the events of the story in his head again.

I waved my hands, huffing and shaking my head. He looked over at me, eyebrows raised as I started to shove him off of the bed with my feet.

"Okay, now you're just overthinking it. Get out already!" I snapped with no real venom. Ace laughed, throwing his head back and letting my weak pushes at his hip guide him into a standing position. He held his hands up, shrugging, and picking up his backpack with a grin that never seemed to leave his face whenever I pushed him around.

"Okay, okay, I'm leaving!" Ace pulled out his phone from his shorts pocket, smile slightly faltering as he tutted. "I should've left twenty minutes ago, anyway. Thanks for keeping me past my time, Bubbles. You sure know how to keep me entertained." He winked, laughing again and ducking as I threw a small throw pillow at his head. He easily dodged it, ruffling my hair and stalking over to the door. Ace opened it, glancing back at me with the softest smile he could muster.

"Thanks for helping me. See you tomorrow. And don't forget about us meeting up at my house again on Wednesday!" He called the last part over his shoulder as he made his way out the door. I yelled an affirmation, thinking back on how we never really agreed on whose house we would be meeting at, but thinking better of it to say anything. Snuggling deep into the covers, I slid my glasses off, ready to nap away the rest of my Sunday morning and prepare myself for another grueling week of school and midterm testings.

Chapter 11

"Put your pencils down." The drag of my English teacher's voice called to the class. I had finished only a few minutes into the test since it was so simple. I couldn't believe that this was what I heard the other students crying and freaked out over. This test was based on things that I had learned at the ages of thirteen and fourteen with no difficulty.

Ace seemed to be in the same boat though, judging by how he laid his pencil on the desk and rested his head in his arms only minutes after I had finished my own test. He would peek his eyes from under his arms, make faces at me, and stick out his tongue until I sneered and faced away from him.

Our teacher came around and collected our tests, dragging on and on about how we still had one more test to finish Friday before they let us go early to prepare for some midyear pep rally. He mentioned something about how it would have a battle of the classes, games and tournaments, and a small football game between the under and upperclassmen on the team. At the mention of it, everyone started quietly guessing who would win, sending glances back at Ace and patting him on the back. He would shrug, trying to play humble, and swatted everyone away to prepare for the bell to ring.

I would be going home with him today since it was Wednesday. He seemed to be bouncing on the balls of his feet as he stood beside my chair, chattering excitedly about everything and nothing. He got my attention with a tap on the arms of my glasses.

"Hey Bubbles, you coming Friday?" he asked, cocking his head to the side innocently. I raised an eyebrow, picking up my book bag as the bell rang.

"Why would I want to go to that?" I spat, body suddenly propelled forward as Ace grabbed my arm and started pulling me every which way throughout the crowded hallway. He spoke and dapped up people who called out to him, all of them sending a confused look at where we were connected. I sneered at them all, shoving my way through the massive crowd and ignoring any complaints.

"Why wouldn't you go?" Ace called back, looking at me over his shoulder with a wide grin. The students started dispersing, returning to the last two classes of the day while Ace and I got to leave early because of our half days. I shot him a confused look as we neared the front exit.

"What would I gain from going to an overcrowded school event, where I know only one person, who will most likely be busy throwing a ball around the entire time?" I asked, pulling my arm back from his grip. He didn't need to hold me anymore since there wasn't anyone outside or a crowd for me to get lost in. Ace frowned at me but continued leading me to where his truck sat on the other side of the parking lot.

"You could always make friends, you know," he muttered, rubbing his nape. "I could introduce you to some of my friends," he suggested, looking at me in the corner of his eye. I wrinkled my nose, shaking my head slightly as we neared his car, whose lights lit up when he unlocked the doors.

"I'm not here to make friends. Just here to get my degree, and go," I said, finality laced in my tone.

"Well, you made one friend." Ace snorted, bumping his elbow into my shoulder. I paused in my tracks, turning to face him and shifting my weight to my back foot. With as little strength I could muster that wouldn't be overkill, I shoved his side roughly. He yelped, quickly losing his balance and barely catching himself on his hands, knees not touching the ground but extremely close to.

"Seems more like a puppy that can't seem to leave me alone," I snipped, no real venom in my words as I stared down at him with a smirk. To see his shocked face glaring up at me almost sent me howling with laughter. I quickly choked on my own laugh as he suddenly launched at me, gripping me around the middle. He tackled me onto the nearby grass but twisted his body so he caught most of the brunt of the fall. We landed on our sides, panting and out of breath as giggles flowed from his mouth. I snarled, trying to twist out of his grasp as he only held me closer.

"Let me go, you stupid birdbrained—"

"Pet?" Ace cut me off, more laughter bubbling out of him. He held both of my arms at my sides, rendering me useless. I started kicking at his shins, thrashing my head from side to side as Ace wheezed from the assault to his shins.

Finally releasing me, he pushed me slightly to send me sprawled on my back. I quickly flipped over, reaching for his throat, but he grabbed my hands in his own. I grew closer and closer to his Adam's Apple as his laughing made him grow weaker, tears springing into his eyes as he tried to keep me off of him.

"Let go of me!" I snapped, trying to wring my hands from his as he shook his head quickly.

"So you can choke me?" he asked, eyes squinted in mirth as his teeth shone brightly in the blinding sunlight.

"Exactly!" I yelled, which earned another bout of laughter. Our tussle was quickly cut off when someone yelled at me to stop from in front of the building. With a slight hesitance, I stopped my goal from wrapping my hands around his neck and slowly pulled away. Ace watched me intently, that stupid smile still bright on his face as he released me just as slowly. We sat there staring at each other for another moment, his smile turning lazy as he glanced at his car.

"Can we go finish this project now, or are you still on a mission to kill me?" Ace asked, an eyebrow raised as one side of his mouth lifted. I crossed my arms over my chest and puffed my cheeks in mock irritation, still slightly giddy from getting him down earlier. I nodded, standing to my feet and picking up my backpack that I had dropped during our tussle.

I heard Ace behind me, still softly snickering to himself as we padded to the car. I glanced over my shoulder when he was standing at the passenger's side, opening the door wide for me.

"Do you want me to drive?" I asked incredulously. His eyes almost bulged from his head as he quickly whipped his head back and forth.

"Good God, no," he said, pulling my straps from my shoulders and chucking my bag in his back seat. "Do you even know how to drive?" he asked as I turned to face him.

"No, I don't need to drive if I have you and my mom," I said, serious as ever. There was no point. Prissy and I moved like crazy, so the only car we needed was her own. And now with Ace around, I'm sure I could snag a few rides out of him whenever I wanted to go to the store or pick something up that I didn't want to walk or ride the bus to.

"Are you serious?" he asked, eyebrows shooting up into his hairline. "You don't want that independence of taking yourself wherever you want to go, whenever?" He sounded so disbelieving, resting his elbow on the top of the still-open car door. I shrugged, shaking my head as I finally slid into the seat. I waited until he rounded the front of the car and hopped in behind the wheel to answer him.

"I mean, there aren't a lot of places that I would want to go, that I can't just get a ride, walk, or ride the bus or train to," I answered, hearing the car roar to life as Ace still looked over at me with curious eyes. He let the car warm up, leaning against the driver's door to fully take me in.

"I don't understand you, Bubbles," he said quietly, his lips tilting up into a smile as I shrugged again, reaching for my seatbelt.

"I'd rather just stay in the house and keep to myself," I answered truthfully. Ace raised a single eyebrow, shifting in his seat to pull out of the parking spot as he huffed under his breath.

"Except for when you want to meet random guys in the middle of the night, right?" he asked, glancing at me from the corner of his eye as I rolled my own. I didn't answer him, instead checking my phone for any messages and slightly relieved to see that I had none. We were on the road for a few minutes before I spoke up again.

"Why did you open my door anyway?" I asked curiously. Ace furrowed his eyebrows, looking at me quickly before darting his eyes the other way to make a left turn.

"Because it's gentlemanly?" he asked more than stated, sending me another confused look as we eased onto the road leading up to his quaint neighborhood.

I had read that once in a book before Prissy took it and smacked me across the face with the hardened spine of the lengthy book. I could still feel the dull ache in my cheekbone after she fractured it, the purpling bruise that covered my entire left cheek for weeks on end. The guy in the book had wanted to woo and impress a girl that he liked, always did things that she would classify as "gentlemanly." I didn't really understand it, albeit, I read the book when I was eight, but still.

I remembered Prissy yelling at me as she tore the pages from the spine of it, slicing my skin with each rip that stung a thousand times over. She yelled that I could never be interested in boys, that they would only hurt me, betray me, wouldn't understand my powers, and would use it against me. At one point, I believed her, killing every man that looked at me wrong after I started developing. I didn't get punished as much in those instances for killing without permission.

I was ripped from my thoughts when I felt Ace tap my thigh twice. I swiveled my head in his direction, not noticing that we had pulled up to his house already. He cocked his head, eyes scanning my face before settling on the blacked-out lenses of my glasses.

"You okay, Bubbles?" he asked quietly, pushing a lock of hair that stuck to my lips behind my ear. I swatted his hand away and nodded wordlessly, opening the door and hopping out as quickly as I could. I was starting to feel like I was getting stuffy in the car, like it was closing in on me faster than I could handle. Sucking in a deep breath, I nodded again to myself before pushing my heavy legs to the front door where Ace waited for me.

He sized me up once more before turning his key in the lock and opening the door. He let me go in first, shutting and locking the door behind me as I took the familiar path to the living room. The supplies were already laid out, and I instantly got to work.

"I'm gonna go change and get my laptop, okay? I'll be right back," Ace called from the bottom of the steps, not waiting to hear a confirmation before he made his way to his room. I nodded anyway, muttering a quiet okay as I started shaping the clay into the perfect mold to resemble brain matter.

I had already glued it on the backside of both halves of the brain, working on another part of it when Ace had finally come back down. He was wearing a white tank top and gray shorts, his feet clad in socks and black slides. He tapped away concentratedly on his laptop with one hand, resting it on his opposite forearm as he approached the table. He glanced over to what I was doing around the screen as his eyebrows shot up in astonishment.

"Oh wow, we're almost finished, huh?" he asked, sliding into the seat across from me as he went back to typing. I gave him an unamused glare as he furrowed his eyebrows in confusion.

"Yeah, because you finished the rest of the top of the brain yourself," I said lazily, finally finishing up the top layer of the brain. He ducked his head behind the screen, wide shoulders hiked up to his ears.

"I don't know what you're talking about, Bubbles," he said softly, typing even faster now. I couldn't help the small smile that eased its way onto my face as I rolled my eyes.

"I thought we were supposed to be working on this together, Ace," I said, tone fitting like a disappointed mother scolding her child. He grumbled under his breath, eyes catching mine over the top of his laptop as he pouted.

"I know, but I couldn't help myself," he muttered. "One side was uneven, so I went to fix it and then found myself just finishing the tops of the brain." He brought a hand up to chew his nail, still pecking away with one hand on the keys.

"It's fine. I'll just do the underside of both halves and the inside of the right hemisphere. You got the inside of the left and written descriptions?" I asked, a small chuckle escaping me. Ace's eyes seemed to light up like the stars, perking up and moving his computer over so he could grab my hand in a rough shake.

"Deal." We agreed and immediately jumped into work. There weren't many words exchanged after that; both of us were preoccupied with finishing this project so we could lie down in our beds and sleep away the rest of the day.

I had finished the underside of the brain and was almost finished with the right hemisphere when I found myself struggling. With the shape of this side, we hadn't cut the styrofoam enough to fit everything on there. An idea came to mind, and I perked up, catching Ace's attention as he paused in his typing.

"Do you guys have any styrofoam cups? I need to cut it to make the right shape for the brain stem," I said, planning out the idea in my head all the while. Ace nodded wordlessly, standing and stretching his muscles at the same time.

That's when it caught my attention. A bruise, another one that was next to the smaller bruise that I had seen days before. This one was large, purpling, and turning blue and black against his brown skin at the corners of it. The bruise was so big that it dipped into the waistband of his shorts, curling up the left side of his ribs and spattering into tinier bruises that slipped further under his tank. Now that I had seen it without the fabric layer, you could almost completely make out the grotesque form of it through the whiteness of the shirt.

Before I could stop myself, I reached out to caress my fingers alongside it, skimming more than actually pressing down. Ace gasped and jerked, catching my hand in a menacing pull as my shoulder quickly ached uncomfortably in its socket at the sudden motion. My eyes shot up to him, as he stared down at me with wide, panicked eyes.

"What are you doing?" he hissed, searching my face as he moved his body to keep the bruise from view. I tilted my head slightly.

"Where did you get that from?" I asked innocently enough. Since the football season was over, I knew it couldn't have been from that. Well, he did still practice and do conditioning with his friends, but I doubted any of them would've caused this much damage to him, even if it was on accident. Plus, he hadn't had any practice since I saw the first bruise Sunday, so where else could it have come from?

"It's none of your business, Bubbles." The nickname lacked the same playfulness as it usually did whenever he threw it at me. Turning stiffly, Ace let go of my wrist and stalked into the kitchen, shoulders tensed, and his fists curled up. As he returned with a styrofoam cup, he looked like someone else, someone—

My eyebrows shot up in realization before an ugly hatred started simmering low in my gut. Oh, I thought. The reason why all the color drained in his face that day, why he couldn't seem to relax whenever that voice yelled just a bit too loudly, why he stiffened when those hands gripped his shoulders.

Those hands weren't loving, gentle hands of a proud father. They parallel those of a parent who cried, "*this is for your own good*" whenever they beat you. Who cried "*I'm doing this because you must learn*" whenever their knuckles were ingrained into your skin, marred your bones and marrow to fit and become accustomed to its shape, press back painfully when another punch came. Who cried "*I'm doing this because I love you*" whenever they smacked you hard enough to spit up blood and baby teeth. Who cried "*why won't you just listen to me?*" Whenever their hands scarred your flesh, shifting bones under their knuckles like some dance only my cheeks could find the rhythm in.

Before I could stop myself, I stood in front of Ace. I snatched the cup from his hand and, raising my own shirt along the left side, pressed his cold fingertips gently to my skin. It was tender there, still sensitive, and the feeling of him touching it made me wince slightly.

These were the bruises I got two weeks ago, coincidentally after trying to kill the very man I was sharing my scars with. They were a little lighter now, dimming in color, but still just as noticeable. They ran from across my back to my ribs, paralleling Ace who stood stock-still. He tried to retract his hand, but I kept him there, still staring up to him. I was glad that he couldn't see my eyes, couldn't see the vulnerability that lay within.

If you asked me why I let him touch the bruises Prissy inflicted upon me, I wouldn't be able to answer you. I couldn't explain why I shared such an intimate amount of pain with someone that I had only known for two weeks. I couldn't comprehend why, but all I knew was that at this exact moment, it was the only thing that felt right.

Ace's eyes softened, glancing down at the smattering of bruises and scars littering my sides and the sliver of stomach—the bruises that he could see. His face fell, meeting my lens as I couldn't seem to let go of his wrists, grip becoming tighter and tighter by the second as my breathing picked up. Softly, as if handling a dandelion, his hands gripped my own, prying away my death grip on him.

Ace wrapped my arms around his neck, pressing my body against his own as he wrapped his bulging arms around my frame. He dwarfed me completely, large body fully encompassing my own as he squeezed me tightly. We didn't say anything while we hugged. He just snuggled his face into the crook of my neck, mine in his chest as we took shuddering breaths to calm ourselves. His scent was grounding, smelling of cinnamon and caramel as I breathed in another shaky breath.

Ace pulled me impossibly closer, his soft breaths fanning over my neck as his arms wrapped even tighter around my waist, mindful of the bruises still scattered along my body. We stood there for what felt like hours before he pulled away slightly to whisper into my ear, "Do you want to take a break and just finish tomorrow?" he asked softly, not wanting to disrupt the peace we had created. I thought about it for another second before shaking my head, pulling away from the hug to look at him fully. He still kept his arms wrapped around me as I stared up at him.

"No, let's just finish today so we can rest," I whispered. "Is that okay?" I asked, pulling my lip between my teeth as his face softened. The corner of his lips pulled up weakly as he finally released me, stepping back slightly to let me breathe in the air that didn't smell of him.

We sat back down in our respective seats, his foot brushing mine occasionally, and I let it. I usually hated any kind of physical reassurances. Prissy had ruined it so many times with false hugs and kisses, turned what was supposed to be a comfortable embrace into a bruising death grip that left my throat feeling raw and scratchy after releasing me. I didn't even liked to be touched, didn't like the feeling of someone brushing against me, didn't like hugs that could be turned into a headlock, kisses against my cheek that turned into bites to gnaw my skin open and leave prints embedded deep into the flesh.

But with Ace, I hadn't rejected it. Didn't push him away when the hug went from thirty seconds to a full three minutes. Didn't try to pry my way from his grip when he inhaled my scent with a shuddering breath. No, I had embraced it fully. I wasn't even sure if I wanted him to let me go, at one point. I perked up when Ace ran his foot up and down my leg to catch my attention, a lazy smile on his face.

"So, are you coming to the game Friday?" he asked. I couldn't help the roll of my eyes, smiling either way.

"I told you I wasn't," I said. Ace pouted, twisting his mouth as he looked at me through his lashes.

"The football game should only last a little over an hour, since it's not a full, blown-out game." He shrugged. "It's the last activity of the festival, so before that, maybe we could," he trailed off, gluing on different pieces of clay to the inside of the left hemisphere. I stared at him for a long while, watching him shift under the intensity of my glare, even if he couldn't see my eyes.

"Are you asking me to go to the festival with you, Ace?" I asked, innocently enough. He grinned, smacking on the last piece of the clay before leaning forward slightly in his seat, resting his chin on his palms.

"Well, that, and I wanted to know if you could cheer for the star quarterback on the sidelines too?" He waggled his eyebrows. "Maybe I could get you to wear one of my old jerseys with my number on it, so everyone knows who you're cheering for?" Ace suggested, his grin turning into a predatory smirk.

And, just like that, the soft and nurturing atmosphere was gone. I sneered at him, reaching out to softly smack him upside the head. He caught my wrist though, turning my hand over and pressing a kiss to my palm. I faux gagged, pulling my hand away to cradle it against my chest as he threw his head back and laughed obnoxiously.

"You're literally disgusting," I grumbled, wiping my hand on my pants leg. "I'm pretty sure I had glue on my palms, you weirdo," I called out over his dying laughter. Ace sat watching me for a moment, his eyes softening as he scanned my face and shifting body.

"Seriously though," he said, tilting his head and smiling again, nothing playful lurking behind his eyes this time. "Go with me Friday. I'm guaranteeing that you're going to have fun. Promise you." Ace's face held an abundant amount of seriousness, eyes pleading as his foot continued to rub against my own.

I sat there contemplating it for a moment before shrugging and nodding. He smiled wide, pushing his chair back as he came to stand beside me. He ruffled my hair before shoving both halves of the brain in my hands quickly. I sputtered, barely holding on to them at the surprising amount of heaviness that weighed them down in my palms.

"What are you doing?" I snapped, struggling to hold them up at the same time. He grumbled, reaching into his pocket to pull out his phone and aiming it at me.

"Hold still, I wanna get a picture of you holding the brain we worked so hard to make," he drawled, snapping multiple pics before I could protest.

"Why do I have to be in the pics?" I snapped, quickly setting the offending objects down with a huff. Ace snickered, ruffling my hair once more as I swatted his hand away this time. He shrugged, going to pick up his keys and head toward the door as I followed.

"Because," he snipped childishly, guiding me out the door quickly. I glanced back at the mess still sprawled over the table.

"Don't you want me to help clean that up with you?" I asked curiously. Ace only snorted, squeezing my shoulder as he once again rounded the car to open the door for me.

"Nah, I got it," he answered simply. The car ride back home was mostly in silence, save for the quiet radio playing as background music. When Ace finally arrived at my house, he grabbed my arm softly before I could get out.

"I'll pick you up Friday before the festival, okay? Make sure you change into something comfortable and warm," he said. I nodded and went to get out of the car again, only to be pulled back once more. I went to protest, but quickly quieted when I was forced into another embrace. This one wasn't as long or as soft as the first one, but I still appreciated the warmth of it. We sat there hugging for another few seconds before Ace pulled away with a soft smile.

"See you tomorrow, Bubbles." I nodded, mouth feeling like I had shoved cotton inside of it, throat constricted and tight.

"Yeah, see you."

Chapter 12

"God, you suck at this game," I muttered under my breath as Ace missed one of the clown heads he had to throw a ball at. It was the first time he had missed so far, but only because I had purposefully bumped him. He slitted his eyes at me as I covered a smile with the back of my hand.

"Oh yeah?" Ace challenged, handing over a ticket to the bored-looking student behind the stand. "How about you give it a go?" he smirked. I shrugged casually, picking up the balls the concessions guy handed to me after dragging on about the rules. I waved him off, grunting as I lined my vision up with the clown furthest to the left.

With a deep inhale and intense focus, I threw the balls one after the other. They each hit the clown heads in quick succession; you would've missed it in the blink of an eye. The guy's eyebrows raised as he whistled low under his breath with an impressed grin. I turned to face Ace, who was still staring at the lowered heads, his own eyebrows hidden under his draping curls.

"What prize do you want?" I asked condescendingly. He sputtered for a second, whipping his head back and forth as the guy went to stand beside the hanging stuffed animals.

"What—no I'm the one—wait," Ace stuttered, eyes bouncing from me to the stuffed animals as he started to pout.

"I'm the one who's supposed to be winning you prizes! Not the other way around." He pointed an accusatory finger at me as I shrugged, stuffing my hands into my pockets.

"Just pick one, you overgrown baby." I sighed, looking around at all the other students walking around the busy festival. With another huff, Ace looked over the prizes and muttered which one he wanted. It was a brown teddy bear, about the same size as my torso, sitting in a gold and black jersey of our school colors and a matching helmet with a green stripe running horizontally on the sides of it. Ace grabbed it begrudgingly, tucking the bear under his arm as he quickly turned away, not waiting to make sure I was following him.

It was comical, almost. Seeing this strong football player whose shoulders practically tripled the width of my waist, his body nothing but lean muscle and strength, carry a teddy bear that matched the jersey he wore under his jacket. It was like he was holding a mini version of himself that I started to quickly grow fond of.

Catching up to him, we strolled side by side throughout the festival. We had already played a load of games beforehand, any and everything that was competitive. Ace quickly grew to realize that I equaled his strength and agility, if not surpassed him. This only pushed him to play more challenging games, dragging me along to everything he could before the football game started.

If I thought about it, I was having fun. Seeing the way he would poke his tongue out of the corner of his mouth in concentration, the way his eyes would light up whenever he'd beat me, the cries and cheers of students who surrounded us whenever I beat him. I was enjoying myself more than I believed that I deserved, but I continued to bathe in the moonlit night with an idiot jock that didn't know personal space.

We had been walking around having small conversations when we weren't engaged in any games. We talked about everything and nothing, with Ace leading most of the conversation. We strayed away from topics about our home life and parents and focused solely on what made us our own person.

"You want a funnel cake?" Ace bumped me with the overgrown teddy to get my attention. I furrowed my eyebrows in confusion as I looked up at him.

"A funnel cake?" I asked. Ace's face fell as he stopped walking abruptly, squeezing my upper arm to stop me.

"Bubbles, I don't think I can handle you not knowing what a funnel cake is. I really don't," he said, as serious as ever. I huffed, rolling my eyes as I shifted my weight from one foot to the other.

"Stop being overdramatic and just tell me, Ace." I sighed, ignoring the stares people were giving us as his hand went from my upper arm to rest on my shoulder. He closed his eyes, sucking in a shaky breath before popping them back open.

"Let's just get one and see how you feel about it," he said as if talking to a small child who asked for another boatload of candy. I frowned, being forced to move from my spot as Ace dragged me to another small stand with a line. It looked to be serving foods of all kinds that I had never seen before.

Prissy hadn't allowed me to eat much junk food growing up. She told me that sweets only made me too hyper, too unaware of my surroundings because I would only be focused on getting another sugar high. She would say that I needed to stay on guard, protect her from any evil of the world, and I couldn't do that if I was hyped up on sugar.

I was ten when I finally got my hands on a piece of candy that some worker had given me in the middle of the mall. Prissy had told me to stay put while she went into a store to get something, and the worker was giving out free samples. It was a sour gummy worm that made my face crinkle in disgust. Prissy caught me red-handed, yelled at the worker and accused him of being a pedophile for giving me candy, and stomped out of the store. She drove us around the back of the mall, tugging my hair up and forced her fingers down my throat to make me throw it back up.

I haven't had anything relatively sweet since then.

"Can I get a funnel cake with cookies and cream topping and, um," Ace's loud voice cut through the haze of my mind. "Can I get one pink cotton candy too, please? Thanks." He was handing over money from his wallet before I could offer up my own.

The girl who worked behind the cash register smiled brightly, eyes slightly lowered whenever she focused them on Ace. He didn't seem to notice, but by the way he shuffled closer to me, hands ruffling my hair, I could tell that he saw her. He must be used to it, judging by the way he completely ignored her hungry gaze.

"I'm guessing you never had cotton candy either, huh?" His face was suddenly in front of mine, bending down at the waist to look at me evenly. He still couldn't get much with the glasses, but he tapped one lens anyway.

"Earth to Bubbles," he called out. I smacked his hand away and grumbled, wrapping my arms around my waist to bat off the cold wind sweeping through. Ace had told me to dress warm and comfortably, but I didn't think that I would be this cold.

"I don't even know what cotton candy is," I snipped, pulling my thin layer over my shivering frame. I had only worn a black hoodie with a green sniveling snake—and again, no shirt underneath because shirts under hoodies always felt constricting—black sweat-leggings with a navy green stripe up the side, thick-soled black combat boots, and green socks peeking from the top of the tongue. This was practically the warmest outfit I had.

"Bubbles, that's awful," he groaned, shaking his head as he shucked out of his jacket, revealing the skin-tight jersey underneath. I cocked an eyebrow as he wordlessly draped it over my shoulders, turning back to get our food and forks from the girl who narrowed her eyes at me. I stood there stiffly as he nudged his head to one empty corner of the festival.

"C'mon, let's see how your body reacts to nothing but sugar and dough," he smirked. I followed him, peering over his forearm to look at the red and white carton filled to the brim with what looked like gunk and a stomach ache. In his other hand, he held a fluffy pink ball of, what I'm assuming too, was even more flavored sugar.

We leaned against an empty stand, sitting on the top of the placeholder for your bags, and made ourselves comfortable. Ace set the funnel cake between us, handing me a fork with a smile as he picked up his own.

"Ladies first." He grinned, tucking a curl behind his ear, a small diamond earring glinting in the night. I mumbled incoherently under my breath about being forced to eat trash but stabbed my fork into a small piece anyway. Before I could bring it to my mouth, Ace grabbed my wrist.

"No! You have to get some cookies and cream and sugar with that. You can't just eat the dough by itself, Bubbles," Ace chided as if I was his dumb kid. With a determined expression, he took my fork from me and scraped up as much cookies and sugar and dough that he could. He held his hand under the fork, crumbs falling into his palm as he held it up to my face. With a grimace, I leaned back and shook my head. It looked disgusting and sloppy and like I would be sick with just one bite.

"Open up, Bubs, c'mon. I promise it's good!" Ace said excitedly, more crumbs falling as he pressed it to my closed lips. I squeezed my eyes shut, opening my mouth the tiniest bit that I could, allowing him to shove the forkful in. After chewing for a minute, Ace watched me with wide eyes, brushing his hands off with a hopeful look. I swallowed and blanched, immediately feeling my stomach churn after it settled.

"You shouldn't break promises, you know," I grimaced, wiping my mouth with the back of my hand as Ace frowned.

"It's just because you haven't grown up with the luxuries of having funnel cakes during Devil Lake's yearlong festivities." He frowned, shoving his own forkful into his mouth. He still held the cotton candy in one hand as he pushed it toward me.

"Well, try this at least," Ace said around a mouthful. "It's not overloaded with too many toppings. Just flavored sugar." He grinned, chocolate coating his bottom lip. I gagged, whipping my head back and forth quickly.

"That sounds even worse," I said, clutching my stomach. Ace shoved it under my nose with a grumble, forcing my hand to wrap around the paper cylinder holding the cotton candy up.

"Just try it, Bubbles!" He looked hopeful again, sure that I would like this treat better than the last. With one last deafening sigh, I took a small bite out of it. The cotton candy instantly melted on my tongue, tasting of nothing but plain sugar, that I actually enjoyed. My eyebrows raised slightly as I tilted my head, taking another bite, a little bigger this time, and hummed. Okay, now that was amazing. As quick as ever, I started devouring the cotton candy like a madman. I was broken out of my momentary sugar haze at Ace's boisterous laughter.

"Whoa, slow down there, Bub! You're gonna be sick," he snickered, trying to pry it away from my hands. I bit at him, jaws snapping as I held the treat against my chest defensively. Ace only laughed harder, shoving another bite of the funnel cake into his mouth.

"You better not projectile vomit when I'm playing," he laughed. I hit his shoulder softly, not having it in me to deliver a real punch. A sudden vibration came from his pocket, breaking through our comfortable little bubble as he pulled his phone out. His eyebrows furrowed as he frowned slightly, looking up at me quickly.

"Speaking of that, it looks like we're about to start." Ace stood, pulling me up with him as I finished the last of the cotton candy. He still had half of the large funnel cake but threw the rest of it in a nearby trashcan. He paused for a second, holding his stomach as his face contorted.

"Maybe I shouldn't have eaten that before I have to be tackled by freshmen that are eye level to my stomach," he mumbled, as I snickered under my breath. He was so worried about me throwing up everywhere; it looked like the tables have started to turn.

Ace smiled down at me, pinching my cheeks and pushing me forward with a hand at the center of my back. We started our way to the football field as the crowd started to gather, all heading in the same direction. Ace kept his hand on me the entire time, ignoring the passing glances of his teammates that slapped him on his back. I heard a couple whispering about me, to which he sneered at them and shooed them off as they laughed. He glanced down at me with a small frown.

"Sorry about them," he whispered, so only I could hear. "I just haven't been close to a girl in a while, and you're still relatively new so," he trailed off, eyes shifting over the field as the bright lights shone down on the clean-cut grass. I waved him off as he guided me to the bleachers.

"It's whatever," I mumbled, suddenly feeling too small in his overgrown hoodie still draped over my shoulders. His hand slid from the small of my back to my shoulder, squeezing it reassuringly as he led me to the very edge of the left side of the bleachers. It wasn't too many people down here, mostly just parents with small children who came out to support the school's midyear activities and mini-football game. They were all huddled up, close-knit, and sharing breaths as they all leaned in to get warmer. I cast my eyes away, a hole filled with dread starting to eat away at my chest. Ace must have sensed how my shoulders tensed as his hand went from my shoulder to rest on my waist.

"Hey," he called softly as he guided me to the empty first row, closest to the field. "You okay?" His thick eyebrows drew together in concern. I glanced over at the families who paid us no mind, the leering eyes of female students who gossiped under their breaths at the sight of Ace's hand, the males who made crude jokes and motions behind Ace's head.

I wanted to rip all of them apart, crack these glasses over my knees and let loose all of the fury inside of me. I could feel my breathing pick up, fists clenching as I got that overwhelming itch in my nose. I need to get out of here.

"If you want to leave, we can." Ace bent over to become face to face with me, eyes laced with concern. "I don't really care about this game if there isn't going to be any scouts here. I can drop you straight off at your house if this is too much for you." He brought his other hand to rest on my waist as he squeezed me gently.

Looking at him for a moment, it grounded me. Helped me to realize that none of these other people mattered, what they said and thought didn't matter. Ace was becoming my first friend in Devil's Lake, even if I had to become his friend in Prissy's eyes, but I quickly was starting to appreciate his presence. Even his concern of me having to be somewhere so crowded, somewhere that I didn't even want to be in the first place, without him was...nice. I liked the feeling of him expressing genuine concern over my wellbeing. I liked him not telling me to get over it because it was something that I had to do, a place that I had to be.

With one shaky inhale, everything but Ace became background noise. The call of his friends for him to hurry up and stop messing with the blind girl, the overly bright lights of the field, the shouts of me to stop hogging all of his attention. It all became distant as I focused on soft eyes and the sweet scent of cinnamon.

"No, we can stay," I reassured him with a tiny nod. "I'm sure." Ace looked unconvinced for a moment but stood to his full height. He opened his mouth to speak when someone clamped a large hand on his shoulder.

"C'mon man, we don't have all night for you to be flirting with the blind girl." As quick as a drop of a dime, the trance was broken. The itch came back tenfold as I shook all over, barely contained rage warming my shivering body. Just like the instance when we were in the store, Ace spoke up before I could.

"Don't rush me," he snapped, roughly smacking the hand away. The guy winced as he frowned at Ace, who met him with an equally as aggressive stare as I was giving him.

"And don't interrupt me." Ace turned to him, hand perched on his hip as he stuck a finger out to jab into the guy's sternum. "And better yet, why are you even worried about me? Does the team suck that bad that they can't even go against freshmen that are half their size, without me?" he growled. The guy sucked his teeth, rolling his eyes, and opened his mouth to continue, but Ace cut him off quickly.

"I don't know how many times I have to tell you halfwits that she isn't blind, and I would appreciate it if you got the rest of those idiots over there to stop hounding us. Now leave, before we go home. Got it?" He didn't give the guy any time to respond back as he turned to face me. Ace went to speak once more but paused as he glanced over his shoulder as the football player still stood there, mouth agape and angry.

"Do I have to repeat myself, Reynolds? Go!" Ace bellowed, gaining the attention of a few other people as his voice reverberated throughout the stands. The guy muttered something under his breath but quickly scurried along to the rest of the group. They all yelled at him, smacking him upside the head as he tried to defend himself. I looked back over at Ace, who rubbed his temples in irritation.

"I'm sorry, Bubbles, if you wanna go—"

"It's fine, Ace. Just go out there and throw a stupid ball around." My tone was bored, but I couldn't help the small smile that graced my face. Ace snapped his head up to look at me, ready to insist on taking me home, but he paused once he saw the smile. He chuckled, resting his hands on his hips once more as he took me in fully.

"What am I going to do with you?" he whispered under his breath, taking a step forward to reach down and zip his large jacket over my form. He zipped it all the way up to my neck, pulled the hoodie on my head, and tied the string to keep it in place. By the time he was finished, only my nose, glasses, and fingertips were visible. Ace laughed breathily at the sight of me as I flipped him the bird, one that he could barely see over the large sleeves.

"Don't forget to cheer for number 21, Bub." He winked, finally taking his leave as he trotted down the bleacher's steps. I huffed, not wanting to admit how much warmer I felt already with the jacket that smelled of him. Plopping down, I sat quietly and waited for the game to start.

I tried to keep my eye on a head full of dark curls that were quickly lost when he slipped on his helmet. He sent me one last wink before he put it on, turning his back as he gathered with his team in a small huddle. I could only keep track of him by the green-outlined number on his back as all the players got into position.

I didn't know what was going on for a long while. Just cheered quietly when everyone else cheered, or when I saw his number running with the ball. Truthfully, I was as lost as I had ever felt, but quickly tore my eyes away at the sudden buzzing coming from my pocket. I checked it, surprised that it wasn't Prissy, but someone else.

J
9:32
Hey there, Bright Eyes. Can we talk?

My heart dropped. I had forgotten all about talking to Judas again, seeing as how it had almost been a full week since I last saw him. As I went to type out a "no, I'm busy," my attention was quickly grabbed by someone settling beside me on the bleachers.

"It'll be quick, I promise." Judas' soft voice muttered into my ear. I stiffened in my seat, turning slightly to glare at him. I lowered my glasses a fraction, eyes gleaming eerily as he only smiled back at me, shifting his body in case someone saw me. Would that count as being gentlemanly, too?

"You really are a stalker," I groused, sliding away from him on the bench. It wasn't really anywhere I could go, seeing as how I sat on the very end. Judas just turned to face me, hair spilling out under a bright red hoodie as he pushed his glasses up on his nose.

"Not stalking, just going to school events," he leveled with a shrug.

"Yeah, but you don't go here," I sneered at him, suddenly feeling like a cornered cat. I looked back out at the field to try and find #21, but I couldn't seem to place Ace with all of the other numbers running around.

"Says who?" Judas asked playfully, a smile hinting at his lips. Before I could speak up, he snickered and stood.

"I'm joking. I got my degree at 16," he said halfheartedly as he held a hand out to me. "Now, can we talk? I promise I won't bring up anything like last time," he said, voice low and hushed so no nosy parents or gossiping girls could overhear. I smacked his hand away with a growl.

"What more do you want me to say?" I asked, glancing back quickly at the field. I finally spotted Ace, who was in another huddle, but his head was raised in our direction. I couldn't see his face, but I already knew he was fuming. I turned back at the sound of Judas clearing his throat.

"I just want to make some comparisons, ask a few more questions. I want to know what my life would've been like if I had chosen her that day," he muttered, tucking his reddened fingertips into his pockets. I glared up at him a moment longer, glancing back at Ace, who still had his sharp gaze on us, even as his friends yelled in his ear. With a huffing breath, I nodded, tearing my eyes from Ace and standing in front of Judas.

He sized me up slowly, taking in the too-big jacket before lazily sliding his eyes over to Ace. Watching the both of them, you couldn't cut the tension with a knife, even with the few hundred feet distance between them.

"Let's just go," I mumbled, pushing softly at his shoulder to turn him. He followed wordlessly, stalking down the bleachers with a practiced coolness. His shoulders were back and relaxed, head held high as he lazily kept his hands in his pockets while we crossed in front of the people who sat watching the game. A few girls made more noise and commotion, crying about how hot he was, wondering if he was the new kid, and how I was so lucky to be surrounded by all the cute dudes in the school. I wanted to gag.

Throughout all of the chattering and gossiping, I couldn't bring myself to look back at Ace. I could feel him staring holes into the back of my head. I almost felt guilty. Being brought here by Ace and Ace alone, letting him drag me around the park to show me all of the things he swore I had been missing out on, filling me up with sugar that I could only dream to have, lending me his hoodie after I had ignored his warning of dressing warm. Now, I was walking out of his football game, a game that I was supposed to be cheering him on, with a guy that I knew he didn't really like—even if he didn't know him. A guy that I knew that he felt uncomfortable over. A guy that always seemed to get me alone at night. I understood his concerns, but Ace would never fully understand the fact that any kind of conversation Judas and I had would be too much and too open to have for any daylight to bear witness to.

Pushing any slight guilt to the back of my mind, I tugged Ace's jacket closer over my torso and headed out to the empty parking lot after Judas.

Chapter 13

"Out with the questions." I snapped at Judas the moment we were alone and away from any prying ears. He raised his eyebrows in question, a small smile pulling his lips up as he guided me to an empty bench with the school's color paint chipping off of it. He pursed his lips, eyes lost in thought as he breathed in quietly through his nose.

"First and foremost, I wanted to say that I'm sorry." Judas turned to me, eyes bright as they bounced between my lens. I reeled back slightly, nose scrunching in disdain.

"For what?" I snapped. He shrugged, leaning back on the bench as he started to survey the empty parking lot.

"Making our first time meeting feel almost like an ambush, or an interrogation. I didn't mean for it to go in that direction, so I wanted to apologize for triggering a panic attack." His voice held all the sincerity in the world, eyes sharp and focused when he finally looked at me. His gaze was too intense, even with the blacked-out barrier of my glasses between us, so I averted my gaze to stare over at the cars as well. I could see Ace's silver truck not too far from where we were sitting, and fought to look somewhere else too. Everything was too suffocating tonight; I felt as though I was bound to explode any minute now.

"What's a panic attack?" I asked quietly instead, anything to avoid acknowledging his apology. I could see Judas' eyebrows shoot up as he turned his body to face me.

"You don't know?" he asked softly. I sneered, turning to face him now, as my lip twitched in disdain.

"Obviously not, if I'm asking you, idiot," I snapped. Judas stared at me for a moment, eyes scanning and analyzing my face before he shrugged again.

"Sorry, I just assumed you did, since it seems like you get them a lot," he said quietly, toeing the dirt under his shoe. "A panic attack is like, your body's response when it thinks there's something wrong and has a strong physical reaction to it. It feels like you're about to die almost, even though you're not." He started rattling off facts, almost as if this was something that he had rehearsed for years now.

"Sometimes, they make you detach and dissociate from reality, which happened to you last time. That's why you tried to punch the railing, to gain that sense of reality that you felt like you were losing," Judas said coolly, almost as if he wasn't psychoanalyzing me on the spot. I arched an eyebrow, mouth curling down into a frown as I poked a finger into his chest.

"You don't know that," I mumbled petulantly, poking him again just to hear him wince. He did, rubbing his chest before a small chuckle rumbled from his throat.

"I do," Judas said simply. Silence fell over us, cool on his part, as the hair on the back of my neck started to rise. We sat quietly for a moment before he opened his mouth once more.

"Tell me about them," he whispered, eyes roaming over the expanse of the parking lot. He zeroed in on a few teens who were giggling and walking over to a car not too far away from Ace's. I glanced over at him, shivering as the cold wind swept sharply through the air.

"Who?" I asked.

"Kelly and Chad," Judas said softly, glancing over at me as I visibly stiffened. "I don't want to pity them if you claim that they were monsters to you. So change my perspective, and tell me about them."

I could hear my heart pounding loudly in my ears, the blood rushing through as everything sounded so distant. Felt like I had drifted off to another planet, the sounds of cheering coming from the football field, the raucous laughter of teens who smelled suspiciously of smoke wafting through the parking lot, Judas' ever-kind voice, sounded so far off.

I didn't want to think about them. Didn't even want to utter the names of Kelly and Chad. Didn't want to remember cruel things spat to a child who could barely form two words from a mouth that could barely hold two teeth. Didn't want to remember that day, the look on Chad's face when he opened the door. So blissfully, ignorantly, painfully unaware of what loomed in front of him in the form of a child that he was supposed to love. Didn't want to remember the sick glee when I finally got Kelly down. Didn't want to relish in the way her screams gave me chills as the operator's voice from her phone repeatedly asked what was wrong.

But I did. If this was to help show Judas that these people were monsters who had never loved me, then I would force myself to remember the wicked details that I wanted so painfully to forget.

"There was a chance that something would have been 'wrong' with me," I started slowly, hunching over as I tried to slyly breathe in Ace's lingering scent from his collar. "They were seen as the most perfect couple since high school; they couldn't have a child with a disability," I said, snorting softly, though it held no amusement.

"I read about that when I looked them up. I couldn't tell if they were vain, or if everyone just loved them that much," Judas interrupted quietly. I cut my eyes at him and barked out a loud laugh. I could see the way his shoulders tensed, eyes bulging momentarily at my sudden outburst.

"Loved them?" I chuckled. "Everyone hated them. People were only around them because fame, money, and attention followed them. No one liked Kelly and Chad because they were two successful and beautiful people in love. No, they liked them just so they could get a come up," I snapped, all laughing ceased as Judas watched me quietly. I collected my breathing for a minute, surprised at how I didn't even notice when it had substantially picked up. Sitting back quietly, I rested my shoulders on the bench and kicked my feet out, twiddling the string holding the hoodie tucked under my chin between scarred fingers.

"I could hear them before I was born," I said quietly. Judas had asked me that when we had first met just last week but had continued to bombard me with questions before I could fully answer.

"They were always just so nasty to everyone. So mean, hateful. They didn't love anyone beside themselves. I thought that once I was born, then I would get that same love and attention, but I got treated even worse than their enemies." I laughed again dryly, eyes unfocused as I sat stiffly. Judas listened quietly, matching my stance so he wouldn't be watching me so closely, to help make me more comfortable in talking about the first two people that I killed.

"They knew that something was wrong with me when I was first born," I murmured under the loud cheering coming not too far off from the field. "They knew that I was different, but as long as my face didn't ruin their reputation, everything was fine. As long as their firstborn looked pretty, that was all that mattered to them." My voice started to taper off toward the end, that empty feeling in my chest starting to fill with hatred that I had long ignored.

"They didn't love me; they were scared of me. They knew that, while I looked good, there was something about me that wasn't normal. They pretty much dreaded my birthday after the first three years," I muttered, wiping my nose as the cold wind started to freeze it.

"When I turned five, they didn't even come out of their rooms to give their one and only child a happy birthday kiss." I smiled, a show of teeth really, as I turned to Judas. He was already looking over at me, his mouth set in a thin line as he breathed in deeply. I turned away first, peering over the hood of cars, trying to see if I could get a glimpse of the field from where I was sitting. I already knew that Ace would be fuming by now, knocking over freshmen like they were bowling pins compared to his frame.

"You don't seem like the type to like pity, so I'm going to save my apology," Judas said dryly, pushing up his glasses with one finger as he glanced at me from the corner of his eye. I snorted and nodded in thanks. We fell into silence again, just enjoying the cries and cheers coming from the game, faint cheering sounds of the number twenty-one ringing through all of the chaos.

"You've known him for, what, two weeks now?" Judas asked quietly, eyes shifting over to land on Ace's car. "You're already wearing his hoodies, huh?" I could see the small tilt of his lips as he looked over at me, eyes scanning the hoodie still sitting atop of my head. I rolled my eyes and shrugged, shoving my hands into the front pockets.

"It's cold out," I said simply, not offering more of an explanation. Judas smiled brighter, leaning over to bump his shoulder with mine. I grimaced, pushing back with more force than necessary, just to see him struggle to find his balance with his own hands in his pockets.

"So if I gave you my jacket, would you take it?" Judas smirked over at me as my head whipped to the side to face him. He was leaning back in his seat, one arm thrown behind the back of the bench as he left the other in his lap.

"I already have one on," I scoffed. Judas rolled his eyes, smirk dropping to a genuine smile as he snorted.

"That's not what I mean," he said, arching an eyebrow. I shrugged, still offering no clear answer and tried to ignore his beaming smile that grew wider and wider.

"So when did you two start dating? The day after you first met or the weekend after, when he rescued you from his friends?" Judas asked, eyes sharpened knowingly. I sat there stiff for a second, quietly beating myself up for not noticing his presence in the store again that day. If Prissy knew, I would have been beaten ten times over now. Stuffing my clenched fists even deeper into my pockets, I hiked my shoulders up to my ears and tried to drown myself in the too-big hoodie.

"You brag and boast about stalking me as if it were normal," I snapped, muffled with how deep my mouth was being covered. He huffed, shrugging as he finally turned back toward the parking lot, sharp gaze finally focused somewhere else.

"Not bragging. I just so happened to be in the area," Judas lied. I scoffed, glaring over at him as he couldn't seem to meet my eyes. The small smile on his pink lips gave away his cool facade.

"Oh yeah? In the neighborhood?" I asked. "Where do you live then, if you're just so conveniently in the same place where I am, all the time?" I cocked my head to the side, watching the smile on his face grow. He glanced over at me, running his tongue on his bottom lip before staring up at the dark sky with a fond smile. Watching him was peaceful, his whole aura and demeanor nothing but the epitome of relaxed, calm, and chill. Judging by his looks alone, nobody would ever be able to tell that he could end a life in a second by merely slipping his satin gloves off. Nobody but me.

"I just moved to Devils Lake not too long ago," Judas offered. There was obviously more, and I wanted to pry until I could strip back every layer of truth he tried to hide.

"Let me guess; about two and a half weeks ago?" I slit my eyes at him, sneering at the wide smile on his face. He chuckled, looking over at me from the corner of his eyes as a red tint hinted at his pale, freckled cheeks.

"Wow, you're really good at this guessing stuff, huh, Bright Eyes?" he asked, white teeth flashing in the night light. It reminded me of when we had first met last week, his mouth too wide, teeth too bright, eyes shining ominously in the darkness. But now, the look suited him. Didn't make him look like a predator on the prowl, trying to coax its dinner into its mouth instead of the infamous hunt.

Rolling my eyes again, I scoffed, crossing my legs over each other and watched as a few people started to exit from the football field. The game must be about to end soon, which means our conversation should be dying out now. Especially if I didn't want Ace to try pummeling Judas into the ground from brute strength alone.

"You moved by yourself? What about your parents?" I asked, innocently enough. He never mentioned anything about his parents in the present tense the last time we talked. Only talked about why it was the right decision to choose them over Priscilla. I could see the way Judas stiffened beside me, shoulders hunching slightly as he pressed his circular glasses up the bridge of his freckled nose.

"They're gone," he said, tight-lipped, body rigid and looking ready to flee. I raised an eyebrow, ready for him to continue speaking, but he didn't offer up anything more. Even though I figured I shouldn't pry, he didn't give me that same courtesy last time. Why should I grant him the chance to become silent about issues that I knew poked at sensitive places he didn't even want to think about?

"What happened to them?" I couldn't help but ask. Judas blew a loose curl from his forehead, watching as the people now started to pour out into the parking lot, loud laughter and cheers ringing throughout our previous quietness.

"I don't want to talk about it," he spoke quietly, voice firm and leaving no room for argument. Well, he left a little wiggle room for me as I continued to press on, leaning more into his space so he could properly hear me without someone eavesdropping.

"And I didn't want to talk about feeling as though I had to kill Kelly and Chad at five years old because they didn't love me. But I did." I gave him a pointed look as he turned to face me. His eyes were sad, low and droopy as they started to shine with unshed tears. Completely taken aback by his sudden teariness, I reared back, tucking my chin into my neck as my eyes widened.

"What, did they die or something?" I barked, not meaning to sound so harsh. I cringed at his slight flinch of my tone, eyes darting over the field to make sure that no one had heard me. I didn't really know how to respond back to such blatant displays of emotions like this. A hug from Ace earlier this week was as much as I could deal with for the next month. Tears from a guy that I tried to kill last week were on a whole new level that I had yet to unlock.

Judas turned, eyes cast downward as I watched the way his chin started to slightly tremble. I stared him silently, scanning over his form, when the dots all started to connect in my mind. Prissy had made me study body language so much growing up, taught me the importance of studying people, as if they were all just test subjects to me. Taught me the way a guilty form would tremble, shy away from prying eyes, keep their gazes lowered, avoid any and all contact, deflect, deny, sometimes run if it became too much.

Judas stood abruptly.

"The game is over," he said, eyes scanning the filling parking lot. "You should go back to your boyfriend slash guard dog before he tries to rip my throat out." Judas attempted to walk away, but I was faster, standing and grabbing his elbow quickly. He stiffened, tried to shake out of my grasp, but I wouldn't let go. I narrowed my eyes at the back of his head, silently willing him to look at me.

"You killed them," I stated, voice cold as the realization hit me like a ton of bricks. I could feel the familiar anger starting to broil over inside of me at just the mere thought of it. This man who had made me feel so bad about killing my own—at the age of five, for goodness sake. I was a child, and could even go as far as to say that I was coerced by a witch convincing me that this was the right thing to do. The man that made me rethink if killing the people who never loved me, would have never loved me, deserved to be graced with my presence in this world for even a moment longer. The man that tried to guilt trip me, throw the death of my parents back in my face when he had done the same thing?

"Let me go, Areya." Judas' voice was cold, dead of emotion as he attempted to yank his arm out of my grip once more. I held on tighter, feeling my lips pulling back into a sneer as the itching in my nose started to grow. As I opened my mouth to speak, I heard the sharp call of my name ring over the background noise of other teens that flitted amongst us.

"Areya!" Ace's voice rang deep and commanding that momentarily made me pause. I turned stiffly to face him, nose twitching and ignoring the way his eyes lingered on where Judas and I were still connected. By the time he had finally made his way over to us, his eyes were aflame, light beads of sweat still glistening his eyebrows as they curved down in disdain.

"It's late. We have to go," Ace said shortly, sharp gaze piercing over at Judas who still had his back toward us. I could see the way his shoulders hiked up even more at Ace's proximity as I shook my head.

"I'm not done here," I snapped, looking back over at Judas, who suddenly twisted out of my grip before I could stop him. He glanced over at us, eyes sizing up both of our forms as I could see the irritated breath leave Ace's huffing chest.

"Just go, Bright Eyes. We can talk later." Before I could protest, Judas was briskly walking off into the night, quickly disappearing into the crowd before I could stop him. As I went to follow after him, my own elbow was caught in Ace's tight grasp. Before I could stop him, I was being pulled toward the crowd, kept close to his body as people bustled and moved all around us.

"I wasn't finished!" I snapped angrily, trying to claw my way out of Ace's tight grip. He didn't answer me, only led me to his car before pulling me to the passenger's side and opening the door for me. I stared up at him, crossing my arms petulantly as I stood outside. Ace was eerily quiet, still holding the door open as he stared down at me expectedly.

After another minute-long stare down, I grumbled under my breath but still climbed into his stupidly clean car. He slammed the door after I was fully situated, stomping over to the other side as I watched him ignore people who were congratulating him on the good game. Once inside, he slammed his door shut and silently took off into the night.

We rode in silence for a few minutes, the only noise coming from the quiet stereo and his occasional huffing. I kept my arms crossed, eyes glaring at the window in frustration at how I was cut off both times tonight. I jumped slightly when Ace suddenly spoke.

"I don't like him," he said, voice strong and lilted angrily. I rolled my eyes, scoffing under my breath as I shoved my glasses up higher on my nose.

"And why should I care about who you do and don't like?" I snapped, glaring over at his face even though he couldn't properly see it. His top lip twitched, hands gripping the steering wheel tightly as he slightly pressed on the accelerator.

"Because that guy is weird, Bubbles," Ace growled out, knuckles cracking under how hard he was pressing down.

"Weird how?" I cocked an eyebrow at that as I let out an unamused chuckle. Ace frowned, eyes darting over the empty streets as he struggled to find a valid reason to dislike Judas.

"He just keeps popping up. Always tries to get you alone at night. Both times I've seen him, he's wearing those weirdo gloves." I couldn't help the snort that escaped me, failing to cover my mouth in time.

"Because he wears gloves, he's a weirdo?" I asked incredulously as Ace smiled sheepishly, finally releasing his tight grip to scratch at his chin hair.

"You know what I mean," he mumbled, easing up on the gas pedal now, the closer we got to Prissy's house.

"I don't. Does this mean I'm a weirdo for wearing these glasses all the time?" I asked innocently enough as I turned to face him. The question made Ace get serious, his grin pulling down once more as he shot a soft look over to me.

"Nah, they just make you look even more mysterious and badass," he said quietly, making me snort again before the car fell silent.

"I know you're not mine yet, but—" Ace started.

"Yet?" I asked exasperatedly, eyebrow cocked as I looked him up and down in his seat. Ace only smirked, slowing slightly as we turned the corner onto my street.

"I said what I said." He looked over at me, that playful look he always adorned, fully covering his face now as the tension started to melt from his shoulders.

"I know you're not mine, yet, but I still think you should just be more careful," he said seriously now, that crease forming in between his eyebrows again. I couldn't help but appreciate the genuine concern he had over me, a complete turnaround of how it angered me only last week. This boy was growing on me too fast for my liking.

"Whatever," I mumbled, starting to toy with the strings of his hoodie again before I perked up. "Oh, let me give you your hoodie back," I said, ready to slip out of it, but stopped when he rested his hand on my knee. I looked over at him, completely unaware of when he had pulled up and parked in my driveway. Ace was smiling again, eyes looking over at me before he reached up and ruffled my hair. I growled, smacking his hand away, to which he only chuckled at.

"Nah, you can keep it. Just give it back to me Monday, yeah?" he asked. I wanted to oppose, but being wrapped up in this caramel and cinnamon scent was really appealing, and the thought of even sleeping in this warmth sounded even better. I nodded quietly, trying to smile at him graciously, a smile that didn't look like I was only showing off sharp canines and bloody fangs.

Ace smiled either way before pulling away and hopping out. He made his way over to my side and opened the door faster than I could move. He held his hand out to help me out; even though I didn't really need it, I still took his extended offer.

Walking over to my door, I pulled out my key from my back pocket, trying to ignore the light that flickered on in the archway. Hurriedly shoving my key in the hole, I turned to tell Ace goodnight, and before I knew it, I was being embraced again by him. I stood stiffly in his arms, silently coaching myself to lift my own arms and halfheartedly wrap them around his thick middle section. He chuckled at my awkwardness, letting me go and pressing a chaste kiss to the top of my head, more so on the top of the hoodie. Again, I stiffened and turned to look up at him. Ace smiled softly, a certain fondness grazing behind his eyes as he looked back down at me.

"I'll text you, yeah?" he said quietly, starting to back away from the doorstep. I wrinkled my nose and waved a hand in his direction.

"Don't," I snapped back with no real venom. Ace threw his head back with an obnoxious laugh, starting to climb into the car. He paused, one foot sitting inside as he rested his chin on the arm sitting on top of the door.

"I can't wait to go home and blow your phone up. I might even start texting you when I'm on the road." He smiled lazily, eyes drooping as sleepiness started to obviously slip in. I snorted, turning my back to him as I made my way inside.

"If you crash, it's not on me," I waved, shutting the door behind me. I could hear his boisterous laughter ringing through the door as I stood quietly, eyes closed, to hear it carry into the house. When I finally opened them with a smile, I jumped at Prissy's proximity.

She stood in the kitchen's doorway, only a couple of feet away from the front door, in that stupid purple bathrobe. She held a mug in her hand, sipping quietly as she sized me up and down with a look of disgust. We stood watching each other for a moment before she took one last gulp and dropped the cup onto the floor with a crash. I tried not to flinch at the loud sound, stepping back slightly to avoid the sharp and jagged pieces scattered beside my boots.

"Funny," she said simply as I waited for her to continue. "That you're wearing his son's hoodie. The man you're about to kill in cold blood, right after spending the night with his son. Funny, right?" Even as she spoke, no hint of amusement laced her tone. Her face was rigid, devoid of any emotion as she sized me up. I tried not to visibly stiffen, feeling my stomach churn at the simple thought of what was about to go down.

"Shower. Change your clothes. You know the drill," Prissy said monotonously, stepping over the broken glass, the crunching under her feet sounding unacceptably loud in the silent house.

"I want him dead by sunrise," Prissy gave me a pointed look.

"Clean," she added as an afterthought. "Got that?" She paused her walking to stare me down, eyes serious as she scanned my body for any signs of rejection. I nodded once, feeling the sudden rush of another kill streaming through my body, zings of electricity starting to run rampant as I tried not to bounce on the balls of my feet.

"Got it, mother."

Chapter 14

There was the buzz that I always secretly craved, coursing through my veins. It ignited a fire that I had been ignoring for weeks now.

After Prissy told me that it was time to eradicate Ace's Dad, was it wrong to be so giddy? I don't think I've moved this fast to get ready to kill someone in a long time.

I was never usually one to be necessarily excited whenever I had to use the powers that Prissy gifted me, but this one time was an exception. I usually just wanted it to be over with, bask in the chase for a moment, but return home as quick as I could. This time though, I wanted to cherish every single second, ingrain every sound, every cry, every footstep, from this night. I knew I would never be able to forget any of this, so I wanted to make it all count.

I walked upstairs as fast as I could without looking too suspicious, too giddy and excitable. I stripped of my clothing, tossed Ace's hoodie on my bed, and hopped in the shower as quick as possible.

After emerging, I pulled out a blank, thick black sweatshirt, black leggings for more range of movement, dark running shoes, a beanie, a face mask, and finally some black gloves. I usually didn't need all of this whenever Prissy instructed me that she wanted a clean kill, but something told me that Mr. Foster would put up quite a fight.

(Or was I just hoping for one?)

I could always tell her he attacked me, so brute force was necessary, right?

(Even if it wasn't, brute force was going to be used.)

I announced my exit to Prissy and made my way to the location she had grunted to me before I left. It seemed to be the mattress supply store Ace's father owned. It was halfway across town, and I was forced to walk there. Prissy always said something about not taking the car, no matter what the weather condition was like. Something about a car being too identifiable, and it being easier to just sneak around in the darkness.

I think it's more her ability to keep me leashed, know that I could never get too far on foot without her being able to catch me in a car. Something to keep me tethered to her, gain more power over me.

Shaking those thoughts from my head, I focused on the mission at hand and couldn't help the smile that pulled my lips up. It was more of a sneer, sick satisfaction coursing through my veins as I neared closer to the store with every silent step. This is it. This is the moment where I free Ace from the binds, the constrictive rope, the vice of the person who was supposed to be his loving father.

I duck into the shadows when I see someone walking toward me. They pass by without a glance my way, eyes glued to their phone as I watch them with my own keen ones. Once I deem them a safe enough distance away, I continue onto my path to the mattress store. To my new victim. To the man who gave Ace a bruise that traveled from his hip bone and up into his ribs, a bruise that could only be forced into the skin and muscle from pure hatred.

I keep telling myself not to dwell in the badness of the man, but how else can I find his death easier to chew and swallow with my own bloody teeth, than to force myself to realize his misdeeds? This man deserves no pity. Deserves no hesitation, no second thoughts, no clean and easy kill.

He deserves to suffer for his actions.

I arrive at the mattress store quicker than I had anticipated. The surrounding stores were closed, dark and shut down, save for the one dim light that came from a small corner in the mattress store. The name Foster's Mattresses still flashed brightly, outdoing any of the other store lights, flashy and just—just too much to be a mattress store. The rest of the parking lot was empty, save for three other unoccupied cars.

Darting my eyes around to the other stores, I counted at least six surveillance cameras, meaning at least one of them actually worked. I couldn't take the chance. Sticking close to dark buildings, I eased my way around to the back of the mattress store. Taking a halfheartedly stuck bobby pin from under my beanie to pick the lock at the door but, surprisingly enough, it's already open. The moment I feel the heat being pushed into the cold night air, I instantly feel the zing in my bones lighting up.

The thrill of the kill. The chase. The fight. I could hear him screaming for mercy already. Licking my lips, I enter without a second thought, without hesitation, without any lingering preamble or guilt or anything I had felt before. This needed to be done. To protect Ace. To get rid of another scummy abuser pretending to be a parent.

Finding Ben Foster was easy. He sat in a lonesome office, feet kicked up on his desk, a cut-open mattress leaning against the wall adjacent to him. He didn't see me at first. Eyes closed in bliss, the familiar white powder that sat in lines on the desk now dusted right under his brown nose, filtering in with the hairs above his lip. There was a smile on his face, contented and easy, the smile of someone who knew that they would always get off scot-free if his "mattress business" was anything to go by. I knocked on his door as I pulled my face mask down.

"So that's why your business is so popular with everyone in town?" He jumped at the sound of me, eyes wide and panicked for a moment before they narrowed. Ben slowly wiped the white dust from under his nose, a shaky smile on his lips as he mentally tried to read the situation at hand. He smiled.

"You're Ace's little friend, aren't you?" he asked, wiping his hand clean with the other slowly. "The blind one with the glasses."

Ah, that makes sense. He thinks he's off scot-free yet again because he believes I'm blind. Believes I can't see the lines he's got in front of him, or the mattress that bleeds little baggies of other goodies I'm sure he sells to other people. I cocked my head when he stood from his chair.

"Let's get you home, missy. How'd you wander over here anyway?" He still sounded panicked, guilty eyes darting from the pills that lay not too far away from the white lines placed neatly on his desk. He paused in his haste to get over to me when I held a hand up to him.

"Never said I was blind." I could see the way his entire body locked up, eyes bouncing in between my lenses, searching, searching, trying to find a lie in my correction.

"I saw what you did to Ace. It wasn't a first-time thing, and I doubt that would be the last."

"You must be mistaken, little girl," Ben snapped, all teeth and irritation as he slowly began to round his desk. I didn't waver, instead feeling the rush of wanting to charge and attack and make him feel the pain that he had put Ace through for God knows how long.

"He got that bruise from football." Ben smiled, face changing quickly, his teeth sharp and predatory. His eyes were bloodshot, pupils large and dilated, darting over from my form to different things around the room. Most likely looking for a weapon, as if he could even land a hit on me.

"I have never understood abusers," I whispered, mind reeling on every abuser I've ever met, the one I lived with. "Why hurt someone, just to hide in the end? Why be ashamed of it?" I taunted, taking a step toward him, grinning at how he paused in his steps.

"Why do you always back down to those who hit back?" I asked, head cocked to the side as we stood only a few feet apart. His breathing became erratic, hands shaking by his sides, sweat dripping in lines down his forehead as he bared his gums in a growl. I took a final step forward, my own smile blinding as the zing of the kill started to pump my blood with adrenaline.

"I hit back."

While finding Ben Foster was easy, getting him down—not so much. I wanted the fight though. I didn't want to just slip my glasses off, whisper some cheesy line, no. I wanted to go home bloody, covered in his own bitter copper, walk the streets with the evidence that I had helped the world out by ridding it of someone who beat their own child like he hated him, like he was trying to kill him.

I did, kill him, that is. He put up quite the fight, though. Lunged at me, too quick and erratic to get any special moves or hits on me. I kicked him down, surprised though when the burly man had quickly popped back up. It must've been the inane amount of substances in his system.

But no problem for me. It just gave me that much more incentive, by pumping my mind up with thoughts that, he must've beaten Ace while high on this stuff, huh? Must've been numb to the way his knuckles split and bled onto his son's crying form. Must have tuned out the cries for him to stop, the begging for mercy, the questions as to why he hated him so much.

In all actuality, getting Ben Foster down was quite easy. Just the simple imagery of Ace silently crying, forced to clean his wounds and bandage himself up while having to go straight to football practice only a few days later was enough. Enough to send my knuckles flying into the bones of his face. Enough to block out the pain when he kicked me in the rib, nothing but a push to fight harder, get him down faster.

Ben Foster cried when I finally pinned him. Cried and begged the same way I bet his son did when he beat him black and blue. There was no hesitation when I slipped my glasses off, no sinking feeling of regret. Nothing but the pure satisfaction that Ace will finally be free.

The walk home felt as if I was floating. I had almost been caught too many times by random people walking, too lost in my head at the realization that Ace was finally free.

Finally making my way into the house, I peeked into Prissy's room to find her already asleep. Breathing out a sigh of relief, I stripped out of the bloody clothes, soaking it like the hundreds of times I had done beforehand to get the stains out. I showered, changed into comfortable pajamas, and lay down, ready to sleep the night away when a thought hit me.

Glancing over to the piece of clothing that lay sprawled overtop of my pillows, I slipped on the hoodie Ace left me, still smelling of caramel and cinnamon. The scent sent me slipping into the softest dream yet, with nothing but braces-filled smiles, pretty eyes, curly hair, and a bruise-less torso. But even as I sank into slumber, there is one, tiny little guilty thought that nagged at the back of my mind.

Is it wrong to relish and find comfort in the scent of a man whose father I just killed in cold blood?

I don't think I have ever felt so fully refreshed after a night of sleep. I usually find myself tossing and turning throughout the nights, haunted by decaying faces and new screams from a red-headed child, but not last night, no. I slept peacefully, soothed by the smell of caramel and cinnamon, pretty pictures of a pretty face dancing behind my eyelids and rocking me into slumber.

When I woke up, it felt as if I had slept for a full day. Completely energized, I was ready to start the day with a smile and a rejuvenated prance in my walk. I showered again, threw on sweats and an old tee shirt, before I made my way downstairs to where the smell of bacon greeted me.

As I rounded the corner, I saw Prissy. She's standing there with her back turned to me, a large cup of coffee in her hands, her thumb hovering over her screen as a full plate of breakfast sat in front of her. I strode over to her quickly, kissing her cheek as I went to reach for the plate of food waiting for me.

"Good morning, m—" I lost my breath though, my words cut off from the brutal and sudden punch to my gut. I gasped, feeling bile start to rise in my throat as I hurried to swallow it back down, tears springing to my eyes. Prissy held me up by my upper arm, the other still fisted in my shirt, her breath cool and soft against my ear.

"What," she spat harshly, pulling her hand back to land another rough punch to the gut, making me cry out. "Did I tell you, huh?"

She didn't let me answer before she pulled me up by the back of my hair, a wince pulling at my face. Prissy only sneered at me, no remorse for the way my cheeks turned green in nausea from being punched twice in the stomach. Instead, she looked disgusted, looked plagued with the fact that I even had the audacity to be in pain during one of her teaching lessons. She hit me again, in the face this time, before I could even answer.

I could hear the crunch of my nose before I felt it, a delayed cry ripping from my throat as I fell to the floor, landing on my hip and shoulder as I forwent catching myself to instead grip at my bleeding nose.

"What did I tell you, huh?" she repeated in a scream, rearing her leg back to kick at my thigh, the pain muted from how her fuzzy slippers made contact with my own thick sweats. When she didn't get the desired effect of me screeching, she pulled at my hair again, yanking enough that I couldn't fully stand, but high enough that it made my neck stretch and some roots tear from my scalp.

"I don't know!" I gritted my teeth at her, trying to hold back the tears, tasting blood on my tongue now. I swallowed the bitterness quickly, peeling my eyes open, but it's hard when my nose felt like it's going to fall off any minute now.

"Oh?" Prissy cocked her head to the side. "You don't know?" She pulled away from me for a moment, still holding my hair in a death grip as she reached for the phone she had previously dropped on the counter. She opened it quickly, her hands shaking from pure rage, missing what she was trying to get a couple of times before she landed on it. She shoved the phone in my face, my eyes watering as I tried to focus my blurry vision on what she's trying to show me.

"You don't know that I told you to be clean?" she snapped, pulling the phone back so I could focus on it.

Oh. Oh no.

On the screen, it's a local newscaster, and he's standing in front of Ben Foster's store. There's police surrounding the area, caution tape in front of the old building, the headline above the paused video: "Gruesome Murder of Local Businessman—Or A Secret Drug Exchange Gone Wrong?"

"You don't listen, Areya," Prissy snapped, spittle hurdling toward my face as her voice rose again. She reared her hand back once more to land another hit close to my throbbing nose, a cry tearing from my lips as I tried not to sob. I had to bite my lip to keep my noises at bay, knowing that if any of my pained sounds escaped my mouth, if they interrupted her lessons of my disobedience, then she'd only hurt me more.

"I give you one simple task, the easiest task, and this is what you do? Create a bigger problem for me? Why?" The last word was ground out through her clenched teeth, her breath heaving heavy in her chest as she kept from hitting me again. I could tell the urge was overbearing, as she smacked me again before I could even answer. I whimpered, head feeling dizzy from all of the hits I've taken in just a matter of seconds, and swallowed as I opened my mouth to finally answer her.

"B-Ben Foster," I murmured, having to swallow again the blood that stained my mouth now. But Prissy only backhanded me, finally letting go of my hair just so she could watch me fall to the ground again.

"What about Ben Foster?" she screeched, pacing the kitchen now as she rubbed idly at her temples, as if she's the one who's hurting. If she let me get it out, then I could tell her, damnit.

"He was abusing his s-son, and—and he had bruises everywhere and—"

"You're not a social worker, Areya. You're not the police or his guardian or his savior. You are mine, you hear me?" She stood above me as she screamed, making me feel even smaller than I did now with blood dripping from my nose and staining the back of my throat. I flinched when she came closer, and the reaction seemed to satisfy her, as she leaned back with a huff.

"You are my weapon of destruction, not some guardian angel for a random boy that means nothing to you." I wanted to tell her that Ace meant so much more to me than she realized. He was someone who I had found comfort in once I realized that we weren't too different, someone who hugged me even when I wanted to pull away, someone who bandaged my hands and understood that opening up about abusive households is something that isn't easily shared. He was so much more to me than she realized, but if I would've voiced that to her, then I feared that she would make me go after him next.

So I lay with my mouth shut, my eyes cast low to the ground, a look of indifference passing my face, anything to not give away just how much I cared for him. She huffed again before she turned her back to me, picking up her phone that she had dropped and a plate of breakfast from off of the counter. She didn't spare me a second glance as she walked by me, only spitting to the ground.

"I don't want to see your face for the rest of the day. Stay out of my way." She's gone before I could even think of a response, up the stairs and into her room where I heard the door slam shut. I fully lay on the floor of the kitchen now, on my back, as I tried to hold back tears. Tears won't do anything, won't clean up this blood, or wrap me in warm arms, or shove my nose back into place. But they're persistent, so hard to hold back as I let a few slip from the corners of my eyes and mingle in with my hairline.

This whole situation makes no sense to me. I did the right thing, didn't I? By killing the man who abused his son? Were all abusers not deserving of this same fate that met Ben Foster? Did abusers really deserve mercy when they had so little care for human life, especially the life of someone they vowed to love?

I saved those questions for another day though, as I pushed myself up and off of the floor, groaning under my breath the entire time, knowing that if I'm too loud then Prissy will come back down for round two. So I stepped quietly up the stairs, kept the wood from groaning, much like my own bones and muscles did with every step I took. I walked into the bathroom, grabbing a rag on the way there to bite down on when I had to clean my face, silently glad that she hadn't hit me so hard that she knocked my nose out of place again.

I couldn't bring myself to look in the mirror though, to look at my own eyes in the reflection. I focused solely on the swelling and the bruises and the blood, the sink a cherry red from where I bled over it to maintain the mess. It's all cleaned away though by the time I finished, knowing Prissy hated it when I left any of my awful presence around her perfection of a life.

Slinking into my room, I threw myself down on the bed. I couldn't help but scoot closer to the hoodie that I left draped on the other side of the bed, curling into myself as I fought back tears once more. I knew I didn't follow directions, but was it really that bad? Ben Foster deserved to be put on blast for the things he had done, even if it did tarnish his reputation in death. He obviously didn't care much about the life he was living when he was here, so why should I be precarious with his name in death?

I'm brought out of my sulking thoughts though, when I get a text message notification dinging from my phone. I fished it out of the hoodie's pockets, a little surprised to see who it was from.

Ace
9:59
Hey Bubs. Can I come pick you up really quick?

My heart shouldn't have dropped to the pit of my stomach like it did by reading his text. Did he know what I did last night? It doesn't sound like it, but a person can only decipher so much through a single text message. I hesitated for a moment before texting him back, swallowing thickly.

Bubbles
10:02
Sure.

I felt a little stupid, waiting a whole three minutes just to give him a one-word response, but what else could I say? I couldn't question him and ask if he knew, if he knew what I did, if his father was dead if they found any traces of me there. What could I say to him—what was I going to say to him when he finally arrived? I was always good at lying. Prissy taught me how to be a good liar in case we ever got caught, but I had never lied to someone that I cared about before. Would it be the same? Would I still feel remorseless for not giving a desperate person the truth? Would he know that I was nothing but a stone-cold killer, a liar, deceiver, selfish, idiotic—

Ace
10:04
Okay, I should be there in fifteen mins.

His text message pulled me from the overwhelming thoughts that crowded my head. It felt all too stuffy in here, too tight, too cramped and full. But I pulled myself out of it, slowed my quickening breaths, and forced myself out of bed so I could get dressed. Prissy said she didn't want to see my face for the rest of the day, so I guessed that going out would be okay. I was too afraid to ask if it was, and decided that sneaking out of my window would be the best option so she wouldn't have to hear the front door close. It might irk her even more to hear me leave.

So when Ace texted me that he's outside, I climbed down the two-story house, scaling it like a precise expert trained by the best of the best. I watched Ace's face once my boots hit the ground from the windshield of his car, his eyes wide in amazement from just how quick and agile I was—or maybe he looked like that because I had slipped his hoodie back on and was wearing it like it was my own? I couldn't really tell, but he didn't mention it when I hopped in the car.

"Hey." Was all he said, his usual playfulness gone from his voice. But he still smiled at me, like it was something natural, something he couldn't control when he saw me. I glanced over at him as I buckled my seatbelt, leaning back into my seat, trying to beat down the smile that wanted to pull at my lips.

"Hey," I repeated back to him. His smile widened slightly before it fell into a neutral line, his dimples disappearing as he looked over his shoulder to back out of the driveway. I spared a glance at the house, to the window that oversaw Prissy's room, heart quickening behind its confinement of my skin when I saw her already staring down at us from the window. She didn't mouth anything, didn't pick up her phone to tell me to come back in the house. She only stood there with her arms folded, watching as we rolled out of the driveway and down the road, her form never betraying what thoughts lay behind her wicked eyes.

Ace drove in silence the entire time, which was unusual for him. He usually turned up the radio and blasted some '90s rap that he swore I didn't know anything about! Or he filled the car up with his own words and ramblings, poking at me and pinching my cheeks just so my voice could carry through the car with his. But he's quiet, silent, save for the deep sighs he let out in minute-long intervals. I'm not sure if I should ask him what's wrong, but I'm not sure if I should bring up his father's death at all. Would it be appropriate for the killer to ask the killed's own flesh and blood what happened? Would it be okay if I pretended not to know?

Ace sighed again as we suddenly pulled up to a football field. It's a few minutes out of town, nothing too far, and big and wide and lush and green like it's still regularly managed. He parked the car in the closest spot to the field, but he didn't care to sit neatly in between the white lines of the parking spot. He pulled in lazily, turned the car off, and signaled for me to get out without a word. This was weird; this isn't the Ace that I have grown to know and care about.

Does death really hit a person this hard? Does it really make them this silent? I rejoiced when Kelly and Chad were dead, and they weren't even the physically abusive type like Ben Foster was. Was Ace really that upset about it?

I followed him as we walked onto the empty field, the wind blowing a little harder, making the air a little cooler outside. I folded myself into his oversized hoodie, tucking my hands inside the warm pockets as I strayed a couple of feet behind Ace. He stopped abruptly in the middle of the field, suddenly folding his legs in as he plopped down onto the soft grass. I followed him, scooting up a few inches so that we sat side by side, gasping a little when he hooked his hand around my thigh and pulled me so that our knees were bumping each other's. He kept his hand there though, and rested his head on top of mine lightly.

"How'd you get those bruises on your face?" Ace suddenly asked, his voice quiet under the soft howling of the whipping wind around us. He felt me stiffen but didn't let go of me when I tried to pull away from him. Only held me tighter as I kept my mouth shut, tight, firm, scared that if I opened it even the slightest bit, then my hidden woes would come spilling out onto the neat and fresh grass beneath me, staining the softness of the earth.

We sat in silence for a few minutes, and he didn't pry. Obviously, the bruises weren't there last night when I hung out with him at the school festival. I hoped he didn't connect the dots that I was fine last night, and his father was also fine last night, but come morning time, and his father was dead and my jaw was blooming a blueing bruise. Ace sighed shakily after a minute of more silence though, suddenly burying his face deeper into the top of my head.

"My father is dead." He whispered for the wind to carry through the trees, a delicate sound filling the woods that sat behind the field. I stiffened once more in his arms, eyes going a little wide, glad he couldn't see me, couldn't see the admission of guilt that bled from behind my irises.

"They found his body in our store. He was murdered, the police said, but they don't know how." Ace didn't sound like he's crying, but his voice was getting thicker by the minute. I'm not sure what he wanted me to do or say—do I comfort him? How would I even do that? I was so used to always being the one to have slain those that Prissy told me to, never the one to clean up the mess afterward. Never the one to hold up the bodies of loved ones once they smelled the rot. I was never the one to let their sons hold me while detailing the murder I had just committed mere hours ago.

"He used to take me to this field when I was little." He murmured into my hair, squeezing me a little tighter as he turned his head to look out at the green field. "Me, him, and my mom would come out here. He taught me how to play football, while my mom cheered us on. She was my biggest cheerleader, and he used to love me."

I was fighting back the tears that welled up on my waterline, sniffling slightly under my breath. Did he have to tell me this? Did he have to think back on the good times with the man who now hated him? He squeezed me even tighter though as his voice grew thicker, and I felt a wetness seeping into my hair.

"It was my fault, you know?" he sniffled, and I definitely couldn't hold the tears back now. "When my mother died. I pressed her out to take me to get more stupid shit I didn't even need, Areya. And she crashed, right into a pole." I wiped away my tears with my right hand, cupped his jaw in my left. It's soaked with tears, muddling in between the lines of my palm as Ace openly started to sob, holding onto me so tight, I feared that I would dissipate into the swirls of wind around us.

"I understand that it was my fault, but I don't think I deserved to be hit all the time, you know?" he cried, voice wobbling and heavy as I hung my head between my shoulders. This was too much, the guilt too heavy. I made him an orphan. This was all my fault, because I was nothing but destruction and chaos all mixed into one, and yet I was the one Ace came to. I was the one he opened up to, the one he found comfort in.

I think I'm going to be sick.

We didn't speak for a while, as we both released the tears we've been holding in for God knows how long. I composed myself quicker than he could, bottling everything back up because right now wasn't my moment to be upset, was it? Not when I was the sole reasoning behind why Ace was bawling like a newborn into my shoulder. I didn't deserve to cry, or to feel bad about myself. I had to focus on him, had to pat his back, had to make sure that he was okay.

He stopped crying after a few minutes, as he only sniffled from beside me every few seconds. I patted his knee softly, and he squeezed my thigh again in response. He lay back into the grass, and I followed him, our shoulders pressed together, his hand finding mine in between us.

"Damn, I haven't cried like that since I broke my wrist," Ace suddenly snorted, a small smile breaking his face. I looked over at him, watched how his braces peaked from between his soft-looking lips and how they hid again when he sighed from his nose. He looked over at me, eyes red and puffy as they surveyed my face, taking in all my features and the new additions that adorned my cheeks, nose, and jaw. I broke the silence before he could.

"Why are you crying, anyway? You just said yourself that you didn't deserve to be hit." The question fell from my lips before I could stop it. It's genuine though, as my confusion bled in through my words. I knew if Prissy were to keel over right now, I would rejoice and be the happiest I think I would ever be in my entire life. The same happiness that flowed through me when she picked me up from my house on my fifth birthday; the same happiness to be with her as it would also be to part from her. Ace's face fell though, his thick eyebrows drawing in slightly as he narrowed his eyes at me and pulled his hand away from mine.

"Areya, my father was just killed in cold blood last night. Yeah, he was abusive, but he's still my dad." There's an iciness to his voice that chilled me, made me frown, and get defensive. He's never really spoken like that to me before, even when I would be mean and nasty to him. The way it made me feel was something I didn't like—felt like something I should be ashamed of, should crawl and hide away, should cower and apologize for. But I've never been one to stray from what I said or how I felt, so I met his tone with my own.

"Yeah, well he didn't act like much of a dad, did he?" I snapped, looking away from him to keep from seeing the way his pretty face fell. I never knew when to stop, so I kept going with a shrug. "If I were you, I'd be relieved he's dead. Won't have to be somebody's punching bag anymore."

I jumped a little when Ace suddenly sat up. He scoffed quietly under his breath, shaking his head, his curls bouncing in place. I watched him heave in a deep sigh before he glared at me over his shoulder, his entire body tense from what I could see under the jacket he wore.

"I understand that you didn't like him, and that he's done some bad shit. But I thought that you at least had a little bit of compassion in that empty space where your heart should be." Ace snapped at me hard enough that I felt myself cringing back a little. I didn't meet his eye, purposefully turning my head all the way to the right so that he got the message that I'm refusing to look at him.

I had compassion, alright.

There was compassion for him when I killed his father, compassion bleeding into every punch I pummeled into the man, compassion when I didn't grant Ben the same mercy his son had begged him for. But I was the one without a heart? This same heart that bled for him enough to defy Prissy and her rules to make sure Ace got the revenge he needed through my hands and my eyes and my kicking feet? The same heart that tugged my insides into tight knots when I found out that we were more alike than anyone would ever realize? The same heart that realized I could help him be free in a way that I wished I could be? I couldn't voice any of this to him though; he wouldn't understand, wouldn't be able to handle that my compassion was thick and heavy enough to kill for the ones I cared for. He took my silence and turned head as ignoring him and scoffed again as he looked forward to the swaying trees.

"I don't know why I even felt like you could be a safe place for me," Ace whispered under his breath. We sat there in silence for a few beats before he brought himself to stand, brushing off the back of his pants as he faced away from me. He spoke into the open air, "I'm leaving. If you want a ride back, then come on. If not, I'm gone." He waited for only a second, before trudging off toward his car when I didn't make a move. I didn't need him and his ungratefulness. I killed Ben Foster for him, not for Prissy. Not for anyone else. And this is how he reacted? By grieving the same man who apparently blamed his own son for the death of his wife? By beating it into him that his own mother's death was his fault? This was the man he wanted to cry for? Grieve over?

I scoffed as I heard his car pull off after a few minutes. He still gave me enough time to change my mind and follow him into the car, but I was stubborn. I wasn't wrong for killing Ben Foster, and Ace would come to soon realize that when he didn't have to walk around in fear in his own house, in fear in the locker rooms that everyone will see his bruises. I saved him, and he's going to realize that soon enough.

Chapter 15

I can't say that I'm too surprised when I hear someone settle in the grass beside me. I groaned, covering my hands with my face as I slipped off my glasses and lay them beside me in the grass.

"You're such a weirdo stalker," I murmured into my palm, an airy laugh bellowing beside me.

"Can you blame me? You're quite the interesting person, Bright Eyes," Judas said, looking over at me, his gap peeking through his grinning lips when he caught sight of my eyes through the spaces between my fingers.

"Hanging out with your guard dog all evening, and then wearing his hoodie again the next day while you tell him his father deserved to be killed." His grin faltered slightly at that, a look that passed over his face as quickly as a graying cloud does in the sky. I narrowed my eyes at him, rolling on my side to sit up as I crossed my legs beneath me. Judas followed my position, slipping off black lace gloves so that he could start plucking at the grass beneath us as he glanced over at me.

"Shut up." Is all I had to offer, tired and weary and drained after pouring so much energy into my conversation with Ace. Judas was silent for a minute, letting the grass he tore up float away in the wind, pushing his thin-framed glasses up the soft slope of his nose as he twisted his mouth to the side.

"Did you kill that guy last night? Ben Foster?" he asked quietly, still tugging at the grass, picking away at the dirt that sneaked under his nails when it started to cake up. I shouldn't stiffen the way I did, an obvious sign of my guiltiness, and let my shoulders sag where I sat.

"You already know the answer to that, Judas. She made me do it." He didn't respond back, despite his obvious interest in knowing what I did last night. Who else could it be, though? Who else had the power to make someone's body rot and decay in just a matter of minutes? Why even ask me if he already knew the answer?

"What'll happen if you don't do it?" Judas's voice was so quiet, raspy, under the wind that started to pick up again. I almost didn't hear him. I blinked a couple of times, feeling the sting of my throbbing nose and swelling cheek.

"I'm scared to find out," I confessed, voice so hushed that it barely even squeezed past the tight confinement of my lips. Judas looked over at me, his eyebrows creased in silent worry, but he didn't say anything to me for a long while. We only sat there, as I started to pick at the grass as well, defiling the place that was once so sacred to Ace in retaliation for him making me feel so many things at one time.

"Did she give you those bruises, too?" He's always full of questions, but always empty of his answers whenever I reverse the roles. I don't feel like arguing with him though, and can only find the energy to nod silently. I didn't have it in me to cry anymore, a certain type of numbness that I haven't experienced since our last move. Was I really wrong for killing Ben? If I refused to, then Prissy might have my head, snuff me out with a quickness before I could even fight back. But I didn't want to refuse, I wanted to rid the world of another abuser, and what was the harm in that?

"Do you feel guilty for killing him?" Judas asked softly, eyes cast low as he started fiddling with a loose piece of fabric from the too-big poncho he wore. It's ugly, too bright and colorful, but it seemed to suit him in a way. I glared over at him before rolling my eyes with a sigh, shrugging loosely.

"I mean, should I? He beat Ace every chance he got. He was a drug dealer—who knows how many people have been messed up or even overdosed because of him? I was doing the world a favor." My words became snippy toward the end, so much that it made Judas look over at me. I knew he could see the fire in my eyes, as his own eyes widened before he glanced over at the trees a few feet away from us.

"A favor like that last time in Arizona? The reason why you guys had to move again?" He had a tone that made my hackles rise, glaring over at him as he only spared me a short glance thrown my way. What did he know about that? How could he know about that, that one mistake, that one hiccup in Prissy's plans that made us uproot yet again?

"You don't know that. You don't know anything," I snarled at him, whipping around to grab him tightly by the collar. He slunk out of my grip though, gracefully standing with only a push of strong legs, his hands still preoccupied with fiddling around stray pieces of his clothes. He stretched like a big cat, mouth dropping in a yawn as I sat there, at the edge of my seat, wondering what else could he know about Arizona. Because what he figured out could be something the police figured out, or even the CIA, and I couldn't let that happen.

"Bright Eyes, all you have to do is your research, and everything will make sense eventually." Judas shrugged, looking down at me once more before he started to trudge off into the opposite direction. His words plagued me, made bile rise to the back of my throat, trying to figure out what he might know, how he found out, if anyone else knew too. If anyone else knew of my biggest regret, of my one true admittance of guilt that haunted me, even in my dreams.

"What does that even mean?!" I yelled out to him. But Judas was already gone, disappearing into the woods as my screeching words echoed throughout the empty field. It disturbed the birds up on their high perches in the trees, but I can't care about them right now. I can't care or worry about anything or anyone else, when I had to worry about and save the skin on my own teeth. What did Judas really know about the situation? Did he know that that was the only thing I had ever regretted in my life? Was that why he asked about Ben Foster, about my remorse, or lack thereof, for killing him? He didn't know about my remorse for that last time in Arizona—how could he? But when I thought about it, everyone knew of my remorse, of my guilt, of my anxiety, with the evidence I left outside of my last victim's backdoor. As I lay back in the grass with a frustrated huff, all I could think about was my last night in Arizona, and how I screwed everything up by simply having a conscious.

I never necessarily had any preferences as to who I had to kill, never really had a say in the matter in the first place. It was always a different person every time, obviously. Different race, age, culture, ethnicity. It never seemed as though Prissy wanted a certain group of people eliminated from this world; it was like everyone was always chosen randomly. I knew she had her reasonings, but my guess for what these people did to earn this fate was as good as none.

But after years of doing Prissy's bidding, I came to the realization that she never really killed any children, incredibly older people, or the disabled. I didn't know if it was some moral compass that she halfheartedly followed, but I appreciated it the older I got.

The thought of having to take such a young life, a life that was still so clean and inexperienced with the world, made me sick to my stomach. Using my eyes on anyone that was that defenseless made me sick.

The whole point of the kill was the chase. The thrill. The euphoria of seeing the life drain, of hearing the heaving breaths, the stuttered pleas for their lives, the useless fighting. If I didn't get any of this, then it only made me feel weird inside. Incomplete. Almost made me feel like what I was doing was wrong, that Prissy had chosen the wrong person for me to kill.

Prissy never chooses the wrong person for me to kill.

Yeah, there have been a few instances where I couldn't necessarily gain any satisfaction with who I had to use my gifted sight on, but there has never been a time where I was so uncomfortable that I almost fled.

Well, not until now.

I tried not to play cat and mouse with this lady, I really did, especially after seeing the tiny, precious child wrapped in a carrier against her chest. The baby couldn't have been more than a month old. I had pleaded to Prissy as she sent me over to my latest victim's house, almost demanded to know the reasonings on why I had to kill someone who was just now bringing new life into this world. This was basically the same as me killing something precious; a defenseless person whose chase brought me nothing but nausea.

Prissy had screamed at me, accused me of being defiant and opposing her rules and demands. I only asked her, pleaded with her, just tell me what she did so I won't feel as sick for killing her, mother, please.

After digging a knife to my throat, had I left. Dragged my feet through back alleys and shaded lampposts the whole way there. Slunk drearily by strangers in the night, strangers that would never understand the weight that I was carrying on my shoulders.

By the time I had shown up, it made me even sicker to see that the lady was still bustling around in her house at this ungodly hour of the night, baby crying against her chest. Just watching her still-swollen and tired body made me feel sick to my stomach, a type of nausea that made my jaw burn.

Breaking in was the easy part. It was always the easy part. The chase was the fun part. It was supposed to always be the fun part.

This time it only brought me dread.

As I crept closer to the lady, in my distracted haze, had I bumped into a lamp that sat dim on a nearby table. The lady whipped her head around at the crash, eyes wide in fear and surprise to see my form. I had stiffened, cursing myself for being so careless, could practically feel the lashing that I would get from Prissy for making this job take much too long.

She had asked me in a shaky voice who I was. I couldn't bring myself to answer, too afraid that I would sob instead. I only took a step toward her before she bolted up the steps as quick as she could.

Stunned, I stood there in shock for a moment. I wanted to scream out, tell her to stop running, that this wasn't healthy, all this shaking around the baby or for her, but the words felt too heavy on my tongue. Who was I to tell her what was healthy, as if I hadn't snuck in in the night with the intention to harm her and subsequently her baby in the process?

So instead, I gave heed. Chased her through the house, breaths falling heavily out of my mouth from the chase. This wasn't the same thrill that I usually got, no. This one was filled with dread, anxiety, impatience to get it all over with.

By the time I made it upstairs, there was a heavy slam of a door at the end of the hallway on the right. I could hear a resounding click. That just made my heart drop further. She was only making this harder for herself.

Cursing under my breath, I reached inside of my pockets and pulled out the bobby pin Prissy always made me carry if it ever came down to situations like this. I could hear the muffled whispers and cries as I fiddled with the lock, and the sudden intake of breath as I finally pushed the door open.

The lady was backing up from the small bed in the corner. It didn't look like her room, since it seemed to be decorated for a child. I noted that there was a crib in the other corner, but I tried to avoid any of that and set my eyes only on hers, ignoring the swirling head of hair attached to her that screamed incessantly. I tried not to look below her chin, not even at her still-spread nose and chubby cheeks, to convince myself that this was only a regular kill. My eyes snapped to her mouth though, at the sudden crying and hiccuping.

"Please don't do this," the lady sobbed, eyes bouncing from me to the bed. "Please, my kids need me," she said, eyes overflowing as she grasped her hands together tightly over her the baby still crying, sensing their mother's fear and adrenaline.

I looked away, chewing at my bottom lip, fists shaking at my sides as I tried to tune out all of the crying. This was starting to become too much. I clenched my eyes shut, hiked my shoulders to my ears, shook out all of the crying that spilled from their mouths as she started crying too, and permeated the tense air. With one last heaving breath, I spoke quietly, cutting her off in her rambling.

"I have to do this. I have to, I have to, I have to. She'll kill me if I don't, I have to, please stop struggling. I don't want to make this harder than it already is, please, lady, just—" I couldn't stop the punches I delivered to my own forehead, frustrated and angry at how everything was about to go down.

I yelled out a defeated scream, pounding my hands against my forehead and cheeks, stomped around in circles, trying to convince myself that I absolutely had to do this. Prissy wouldn't just make me kill innocent women who were obvious doting mothers, right? This was all for a good reason, right? I was just eliminating all of the bad from the world. I was just helping Prissy wipe the world clean, do her bidding to keep people in check so they knew not to do wrong in life. This was all for a good purpose, this was Prissy's plan! Who was I to question it?

Snapping back in focus, I stopped my muttering and musing to myself and turned to the woman. She had fallen to her knees, full-body shakes and stammers running through her as she whimpered more pleads, shakily unwrapping the baby from her form as she set them gently on the floor. When she heard me silence, she glanced up at me. And God, that was her biggest mistake.

I slipped my glasses off with practiced precision, securing eye contact that she wouldn't be able to break away from. And only in a matter of seconds, did she crumble.

My body felt heavy, like there was lead embedded into the soles of my shoes, when the gravity of the situation came crashing down. The smell of rot had never bothered me before, but something about the stench today made me even sicker.

I turned slowly, not even realizing how deep I was into the room, and pushed my glasses back up on the bridge of my nose. It was only six steps to get me to the door, six steps that felt like they took an hour every time I lifted my foot.

It wasn't until I stood in the doorway, when I heard it under the raucous infant cries. The smallest whimper, sniffle, and whisper. I could feel my whole body freeze, lock up on me as an onslaught of tears that I wasn't accustomed to suddenly flooded my eyes.

Craning my neck back slowly, I looked back over the body and baby. It was in the same position, the baby still kicking from its blanket roll. Everything was in the same position from only seconds ago, except—except the tiny peek from under the covers with rounded, glossy eyes that stared right back at me.

It was another whimper, another cry of that same word, sniffles, and tears and snot pooling from the tiniest face that made me bolt. I crashed into the walls, heard pictures fall and break on the hardwood floor, threw myself down the steps, bruised my shoulder and ankle, and barely made it out the backdoor when my stomach suddenly expelled everything it had to offer.

I heaved, spitting out the small contents of what I had called dinner only hours before. The vomit mostly consisted of my stomach lining, acidic and sharp in the back of my throat as I willed myself to get up and away from this house. As I stumbled onto the darkened street, I could still hear that sharp cry that would forever haunt my dreams.

"Mommy!"

Ace didn't come to school that following week. Our psychology teacher, Ms. Ross, had us all make cards for him, giving us a few psych puns to write down for him on the colored construction paper. She said, knowing his humor, it would at least make him chuckle. All I did for my own card was write a simple "sorry for your loss" with a sign of my name on the bottom. Ms. Ross' face had fallen when she opened it, knowing how close she had seen us become in her class, and yet this was all I could produce for a grieving friend. I couldn't meet her eye when she collected the card from me.

As much as he annoyed me, I couldn't help but miss his presence. I missed his aggravating whispers in my ear, his stupid pokes in my sides, the caramel smell that lingered on him whenever he wrapped me up in a bear hug I swore I wanted to get out of. But, without that, without him here to annoy me, I have to say that this is the first time since we moved to Devils Lake where I felt lonely.

I've always been alone. I never got along much with the kids in my neighborhood when-ever we moved, always annoyed by the bubbly girls who wanted to make friends with me, and the guys who only wanted to make a move on me. I never really accepted anyone, and I saw no point in doing so when we moved around so often. But Ace clung to me, and I couldn't help but cling back. He was an anchor almost for me, a constant in my life, someone that I knew would always be beside me, no matter how much I pushed him away.

On the walk home from school, I couldn't help but replay the hurt look on his face when I saw him last Saturday at the football field he took me to. Kept seeing how his soft mouth had fallen, how his thick brows had screwed up, as the hurt that swarmed in his pretty brown eyes. As much as I called him names and jabbed at him, he had never looked so hurt before. I wanted to ask myself why I even cared about how he felt, but I knew the reason why. Ace had become my first friend ever in life, and I hurt him in a way that I thought was helping him.

I really do have a stupid big mouth on me, don't I?

As I neared my house, I pulled out my phone, not even having to scroll down, only having three message threads open in my entire phone: Prissy, Ace, and Judas. I clicked on the second name, slowing down on the sidewalk so I could type out just what I wanted to say to him. I found myself deleting my words every time I thought I got the right thing I wanted to say down. Nothing sounded right, everything sounded too fake and like I'm trying too hard. So all I sent was a simple, I'm sorry.

I continued walking, chest getting a little tighter the closer I got to the house. He's spoiled me in these past few weeks, always the one to respond back as soon as I sent something, like he's always waiting beside his phone for me to text him. I'm in the house, showered, and laying in bed when he finally did respond back

Ace

1:19

Aren't you supposed to be in fourth period right now?

I snorted, rolling my eyes at his text. Always one to be playful, isn't he? I found myself cuddling his hoodie that I couldn't seem to let go of or wash or return back to him. I responded back to him with the smallest smile I could barely control.

Bubbles
1:20
You know today's my half day.

Ace
1:22
Yeah I know

Wanna come over?

So you can apologize to my face and so I can see your stupid face in the process.

Bubbles
1:23
Yeah, sure. I'll catch the bus over there so you don't have to unroll from the blanket cocoon I know you've rolled yourself in.

I could almost hear his laugh when he responded back with a few laughing emojis, and it made me smile a little harder than I wanted to, really. He kept making me have these stupid reactions that I'm so used to controlling. I've been changing so much because of him recently, and I can't tell if it's a good thing, or not. It's been beaten into me to be controlled, to be stable, to have complete and utter autonomy over myself and everything that surrounded me. But there's something different about Ace, something about him and being around him that made me feel just a little bit sweeter, a little uncontrolled and uncontrollable, a little more free.

I can't tell if that's a good thing, or something that will eventually be the end of me.

Inhaling deeply, I tried to find the courage within myself to ask Prissy if I could go over to his house. She might snap at me, tell me there's no point in befriending Ace anymore; I already got close enough to him to kill his dad. What was the point in hanging around him anymore?

But she also might not care, might just dismiss me with a wave of her hand, anything to get my disgusting self out of her face and out of her beloved house. At times, I wondered if she cherished this house more than me with the way I found her cooing over broken furniture and staring forlorn at the pieces of the house that were already here when we moved in. It made me wonder if there was already a life she's lived here before, if the memories were just too great for her to forget and cherish the living, breathing person right in front of her.

When I knocked on her closed door, she only grunted. I took it as an invitation to open the door, but not to come in—never to come in. I stood at the entrance, unsure, shuffling, and I could tell my uncertainty annoyed her from where she sat at her vanity, spreading lotion over her hands and cheeks.

"What?" Prissy snapped, her eyes crystal and sharp as they surveyed me in the mirror. I peeked around to look at her too, but her gaze was too intense and made my stomach churn, so I focused my eyes on the ground in front of me instead.

"Can I," my voice cracked and shook first, so I cleared it and started again. "Can I go over to a friend's house? I'll be back before midnight." She only sat there and stared at me for entirely too long, her thin lips set in a firm line, her face emotionless and cold, stony and hard, unwavering and tight. I felt sick to my stomach again, and she hadn't even said anything yet nor raised her fists.

"Does that friend so happen to be Ace?" she murmured before she focused on herself in the mirror to watch the lotion melt into the thin skin under her eyes. "Because you're not sociable enough to have anybody else but him, and I'm sure he'll be out of your life soon enough."

Now what did that mean? Was that some sort of threat? Prissy was always full of those, and I could typically let them roll off of my back like running water, but this time—this time it made me uneasy. Prissy had threatened me more times in my life than I honestly cared to count, but she's never threatened me about a friend. Maybe because I never had any, never wanted to get close to anyone to try to form any kind of bond, and maybe that's what helped her. Maybe that's what aided in her fuel, what gas filled her tank, what fire and explosion she had packed into her missiles. She knew I had always been alone, that I had only had her before, and maybe, maybe this new incomer who was only supposed to be a stepping stone in her secretive mission to help cleanse the world was threatening that? Was throwing a monkey wrench in her plan of making me some emotionless machinery that only ever catered to her? Could she not handle me being an individual, a person with full autonomy, to make my own decisions and have my own friends and smile without having being told to?

I snapped out of my thoughts when she cleared her throat loudly. I startled more than I would like to, but shifted my eyes to hers instead. She's staring at me like she could hear everything I said in my own mind, and sometimes I believed that she really could. Or maybe she was just that good at programming me to be able to read every single expression I could ever make?

"You can go. Be back by eleven, no later than." Her voice was icy, like she really didn't want to let me go, and I bolted out of there before she had the chance to try and change her mind. I threw a thanks to her over my shoulder before I'm bounding down the steps and out of the house.

I found myself hesitating a little when I got to Ace's doorstep. Was the door always this big, this daunting? I think this was the first time I've been here without him being beside me and opening the door with the loud jangle of his keys. It felt lonely to be on the outside, lifting my scarred hand up to knock instead of already heading inside with a warm, large hand guiding me in on my lower back.

It only took a few seconds before the door swung open and—wow. Okay, wow again, because he looked like shit. Ace didn't look like he's slept in days, or maybe that he's even gotten too much sleep. Dark and heavy bags lined underneath his soft eyes, his hair was frizzier than his usual neatly done braids, he's not standing as tall or as cocky but, his smile was the same. Maybe even a little smaller than what I'm used to; I couldn't really see the shine of metal in his mouth, but it's there, glinting, winking at me when he saw me. The brackets were a light blue color, that much I could tell, and he smiled even wider when he noticed how hard I'm staring at him.

"I'm sorry," I blurted out to him before I could stop myself. What for? Honestly, I couldn't even tell. Sorry for having a big stupid mouth that never knew when to stop. Sorry for being so nasty about his father's murder because of an underlying jealousy of wanting to be the one without a parent to hit me anymore. Sorry for just not being able to listen, to appreciate the fact that he took me somewhere sacred to him and that I tarnished it because I'm selfish and stupid and mean and—

"Yeah, yeah. Just get in here, Bubs." He's smiling again, with a roll of his eyes. I stumbled before I could catch myself, falling into his warm chest when he brought me into a hug. That's it? No making me grovel at his feet and beg for his forgiveness? No explanation of what I'm sorry for? Nothing but...a hug?

I found myself wrapping my arms around him numbly, and he snuggled even closer to me. I could feel him sniffing at my hair and inhaling, melting into my arms as he sighed softly, like this was something he's been needing for a while. Could hugging me really mean that much, even after I've caused him so much pain?

"I missed you," Ace whispered against my hairline, and I had to hold back tears. I've never been one to cry so freely, but hell, he kept bringing out a lot of locked-away pieces inside of me. How could he miss me? Hug me? Embrace me and tug me into his home and onto his couch and against his side? How could he still stand the sight of me, even when I didn't know how to shut my big fat, stupid mouth?

I enjoyed it, though. I embraced it; every laugh that bubbled out of him from a stupid comedy movie he turned on, every snort, every rub against my flank as he held me on sadder scenes, every sigh into the air when the main characters of the next movie kissed. I'm not used to being forgiven so easily, so used to having to beg for Prissy to even look at me whenever I made a mistake in her eyes, as she still hadn't forgiven me for messing up Ben Foster's death, even after a week of groveling. So this was an adjustment, was something I knew I should appreciate, even if it did only last for a fleeting moment.

"Can I be honest here?" Ace suddenly asked as the last romance movie he put on started to roll the credits. I yawned, glancing at the time from across the room and knew that I should be getting home in a few hours. It's not enough, though, not enough time spent with him, snuggled together, silent, and forgiven.

"When aren't you honest?" I asked him through another yawn, stretching my limbs before he laughed and pulled me back to his side when I cracked enough of my joints. He rested his head against mine, his frizz scratching against my skin in a way that made me want to rub against it like some jungle cat.

"I'm not honest a lot of the times, Bubbles," he admitted quietly, and the room fell silent as the credits stopped and suggested another romcom. I couldn't think of a time I had ever caught Ace lying, and he's either really good at it, or his version of honesty was completely different to mine.

"You know, the reason why I got so mad at you the other day was because I felt really conflicted," he murmured, eyes cast low as I looked up at him through my lashes. All he saw were the glasses though, a barrier between us that would forever be the reasoning on why I couldn't be his safe space, just like he had said the other day. It made me glance away though when he looked down at me, a sad smile on his face as he couldn't help but tap my lens to watch me effortlessly slap his hand away.

"Because you were right." Okay, curveball from the left field. Excuse me? He was mad because I was right in telling him that he shouldn't grieve over his father? I guessed he could read all of my confusion written across my face because he chuckled humorlessly before his eyes drifted back up to the still television screen.

"I shouldn't grieve the person that has basically dragged me through hell and back but—but he was my dad. I should feel bad, shouldn't I? Because if I don't, then I'm some sort of monster, right?" I could see his chin tremble before his jaw clenched and unclenched a few times, a method to help him hold the tears back. I patted my hand against his chest where it lay, felt the unsteadiness of his heartbeat against my palm with every unsure breath he took.

"You're not a monster for not grieving him the same way a child grieves a parent that didn't abuse them," I told him, my words soft, floating through the air as he slowly shook his head at nothing in particular.

"Sure." He chuckled again, but there's no humor in it. How did I tell him that I had experienced the same? That I felt nothing against the people that had brought me into this world after they died at my hands? How did I tell him that not feeling bad for the people who had hurt you didn't make you a bad person? That not grieving a parent that you had long since lost, even when they were still roaming the earth, did not put him on the same level as them? That forgiveness came in slow waves and time, not at the sudden hands of death knocking at your door? How did I tell him that he couldn't just forgive his father's actions just because he's growing cold in the morgue?

But I found myself saying nothing instead. What was there to say that wouldn't make me incriminate myself, make him run for the hills away from me, once he found out who and what I truly was? We're silent for a while as he scrolled through the TV options and finally decided on a new romantic cheesy movie that he knew I'm going to hate, before I found myself speaking up.

"His death does not automatically erase all the bad that he has done. You can still be angry. You can still be resentful for being treated the way you were, but you can't beat yourself up for not grieving normally when your situation wasn't normal to begin with." I spoke slow, concise, hoping that my words came across with the same meaning that I had intended. Ace didn't say anything for a long while, and I'm scared that maybe I screwed up again.

But when I looked up at him, I saw the tears rolling from his eyes, as one dripped onto my glasses.

I couldn't find it in myself to care, as I immediately started to wrap my arms around him. He cried outwardly this time, even if he was quieter than he was last time. He wrapped himself around me too, and I tried to pretend that the tears that slipped from beneath my glasses aren't actually mine.

Ace didn't deserve this. And if I knew that killing his father would cause this much pain, I don't think I would've had the guts to do it. But how could I just let him continue to get beat? Continue to be his father's victim instead of his father's successful and happy and sweet and loving son? How could I continuously let his father deprive him of that joy of being Ace for any longer?

"Damn, did you become a therapist over this past week or what?" Ace suddenly laughed through a sniffle. I laughed with him, wiping my eyes with the backs of my hands, making sure to look away from him so he wouldn't catch my stare.

"Yeah, I learned so much in my week-long psychology school. I even know what a medulla oblongata is now." I said with so much seriousness it made Ace throw his head back and cackle louder than what I've heard in this past week. And it's...it's a good sound. Hearty and full, genuine and joyous, and I missed it. I found myself looking up at him as he laughed, watched how his Adam's apple bobbed and, how pretty his teeth were and, how his long lashes framed his face, and how soft his lips were—

He's looking down at me, caught me staring. He couldn't see at what though, but I thought he had a good guess, since he started leaning down toward me. Before I knew it, I'm leaning in, too, eyes unsure, mouth parting softly in an inhale. Ace paused before our lips touched, his eyes bouncing between the lens, hoping, wishing, that he could get a peek of what lay behind them.

"Is this okay?" Ace whispered, voice unsure, but his eyes were. He knew what he wanted, but he's hesitant on taking it. I liked the look on him.

"More than okay," I whispered back, finally making the first move as I slid my lips against his. It's a simple brush first, his top lip skidding in between my own, the feather-soft feeling of his mustache tickling my top lip. It got heated fast though after we've finally had one taste of the other. He pulled me closer than I thought humanly possible, one hand gently holding my jaw, the other tightening around my middle section. I carded my fingers into the softness of his hair at his nape, the other holding his face firm in my hands as my lips molded against his.

Why didn't anyone tell me that kissing felt this good? Maybe this was why Prissy had always forbidden me from indulging into romance and love—this felt all-consuming. It felt both fast and slow, too much but not enough, it felt both warm and soft yet cold and chilling. All in all, it felt good, felt addicting. And if Ace's mouth were a drug, I'm sure I would feen for it the same way I feened for his mouth when he pulled away for a breath.

I could get used to this.

Chapter 16

The next morning was Ben Foster's funeral. It was an awkward affair, to say the least, as being the killer of the man of the hour.

The church was cold, even if it was filled with people, bursting through and flooding out of the room and into the halls. Most were quiet, all wore black, some with tissues gripped loosely in their fingers as they viewed over the body. Ace didn't go up though, told me last night that he wouldn't, that he's seen his body enough in the morgue and after the funeral home dressed him.

I'm not sure if I should say anything to him, really. We kissed last night, but was that even on his mind? Or was it filled with the past thoughts of his father, both good and bad times? Who would I be to intrude on his thoughts like this, his grief? So instead, I only squeezed his shoulder once to let him know that I'm sitting behind him in the second row, and I didn't say anything to him. He looked at me over his shoulder, and he didn't look as tired as he did last night when I saw him for the first time in a while. The bags under his eyes were still there, but they're not as prominent, and his smile isn't big enough for me to see his braces, but he did smile at me nonetheless.

When Ace had asked me to come to the funeral last night, I had paused, hesitated. He's been able to tell when something was wrong with me since the first day he met me, really, and he could instantly tell that something was up. He had reassured me that I didn't have to come, that if I was too uncomfortable then I could just stay home and meet him at his house again afterwards if that was better for me.

But...I panicked. I had never been to a funeral before, never got close enough to anybody to grieve their loss, especially when I was usually the cause of death in the first place. Prissy had never taken me to one—and why would she? Why would she smile in the face of the stricken mother that had lost her daughter, her body already decayed minutes before the police arrived? She was evil, but not stupid enough to show her face in a place where everyone already suspected her and her troubled daughter had something to do with it.

But how could I tell him no with the way he was looking at me right now? With the way his eyes had softened and his hands had loosened their grips on my side? How could I tell him no when he started to pull away from me, disappointed but reserved with the fact that I would never truly be his safe space?

So I pulled him close and told him yes—yes, I could come and yes, I'll be there to greet him at his house afterwards too. The way his face lit up shouldn't warm me the way it did, and I shouldn't bask in his lightness the way I did, but I told myself that I deserved this. I helped him by freeing him of the man who was supposed to be a loving father, so the least that I could do was hold his shoulders and wipe his tears when he had to put on the performance tomorrow of grieving his abuser.

When he told me that it would be at the church, I gave pause to that, too. I had never been in a church before, never set foot in a place so holy. Prissy once told me that I would burn, burst into flames at my first step in, because I was nothing but a killing little devil, she had called me. She had said it as a joke, but it made me wonder if I would have ever been a killer if I hadn't had her in my ear since before I was born. She didn't like when I wondered though, and I proceeded to get a beating after that for questioning her "grand plans for the new world."

Ace had seen the look on my face again, and I was reassuring him that I would be fine once more. That I had been to many funerals and many churches, maybe with a smile too wide and unconvincing, and managed to change the subject before he could dwell on it.

But now, I'm eating my words. Everything in here was so stiff, so melancholy and chilling. I was more than uncomfortable, and had to bite my words when people started going up to the podium to speak on what a good man Ben Foster was.

"He was a loving father."

"A good man with a heart of gold."

"He gave back to the community, someone we could always count on."

Yeah, right. The only thing he loved were the bruises he would practically imbed into his son's skin, and the only thing he gave to the community were the drugs he laundered in his mattresses. Would Ace get upset if I hollered that out right now? He was upset enough when I told him that he shouldn't grieve Ben, so I thought it's best to keep my truth to myself.

I strayed a little behind Ace as the pallbearers walked out with Ben Foster's body on their shoulders. His body looked tired, his gait heavy and slow, his shoulders rolled forward as if he's curling in on himself. They loaded the body in the hearse, and I trailed behind Ace as he walked over to his car, waving people off and hugging the more persistent ones. Once they all finally left, I walked up to him, looking up at him through the darkened lens of my glasses as he stared down at me with a soft frown.

"You don't have to go to the gravesite if you don't wanna," he told me quietly, shuffling on his feet as he shoved his hands in his slacks pockets. I looked around the filled parking lot though, seeing more people here in this small town than I thought even occupied the place, before looking back up at him with a shrug.

"It's okay." Ace nodded at that, the tiniest smile pulling at the sides of his lips before he gestured me to get into his truck. Followed me around the front to open the door before he rounded back to hop into the driver's seat. We sat there for a while, as the hearse got ready to pull out and for the town to follow, all the cars adorning bright orange tags that sat in their windshields. I found myself speaking before I could stop it from spilling out.

"Do you think he deserved it?" I asked quietly, eyes darting to watch Ace as his face slowly morphed into something ugly. "Knowing what he's been doing to you for all these years? Do you think he had it coming, Ace?"

He's fuming, I could tell, his thick eyebrows knitted down, his mouth forming a thin line, as he turned slowly to watch me. I only blinked back at him—not like he could see it—but I didn't retract my words. After a long pause, he faced forward again, pulling off slowly to follow the hearse as it pulled in front of the church, gathering everyone in the parking lot before we set off to the gravesite.

"Nobody deserves to be killed, Areya," Ace said, his voice carrying a finality tone, making me flinch slightly in my seat. He used my first name, and why did it hurt this much? I hated whenever he would use those stupid nicknames like Bubbles and Bubs—so why did I miss hearing it so much? Why did Ace calling me by the name Prissy had given me hurt so bad?

"Not even the bad people?" I asked him, my voice a whisper as his words finally settled in. I was so focused on him not calling me Bubbles that his words took a few seconds to sink in. How could no one deserve to be killed? Did he not know of the wicked people that roamed this earth? The one he lived with? How could he be on the side of compliance, of just letting these people live and hurt others?

What would he think of me if he found out that I—

"Not even the bad people, Areya." His voice was tired now, his eyes heavy again as he slumped in his seat. Ace followed the hearse out of the parking lot now, mouth tight and thin, signaling that he's done speaking for now. I didn't press him, only sank down further into my own seat, wishing that I had learned the first time to just shut my big, fat mouth.

There's more singing at the gravesite, and I wished I could blow my ears off of my head. I'm tired of hearing it at this point, the graveling voices and the croaky tones. I don't think I could handle another tune about sending him off somewhere high, when I knew that he should be down, somewhere burning. I stayed silent though, lingering in the back as Ace stood in the front row, beside the casket, eyes looking as dead as ever.

After a few more minutes and a few more speeches, did they finally lower the body down into the ground. Some people still cried and wept, holding on to each other as they watched Ben Foster go one last time, but Ace didn't change. Just stood there, hands in his pockets, his lids low, jaw clenching and unclenching, as he watched everything past by him. He flickered his eyes up to meet my own from where I stood practically hidden across the open grave from him, but he didn't say anything, didn't motion for me to come beside him, only stared. I shuffled a little on my feet from the intensity of his soft brown stare and his twitching lips, before he finally looked away.

He stalked off when the body was finally lowered and the preacher dipped his head at everybody, only spared me a glance before he walked away into the fogginess that always seemed to lie over cemeteries. I could see him stop a few feet away though, leaning against a withering willow tree's bark, head hanging low, as he must be waiting for me, I assumed.

I started to walk off, but then an idea hit me. Glancing around, everyone seemingly turning away, their backs to me, the people there to throw dirt over the body occupied with talking to the preacher as they leaned against their shovels. No one seemed to be looking my way, and so I did what I knew best with scum of the earth.

I leaned over the open grave and spat in it, before flipping the gold and white casket the bird. I wiped the back of my mouth quickly and looked around again, seeing nobody looking at me—except for Ace. I paused where I stood, wondering if he's caught me, if he's going to curse me to hell and back and condemn me for the disgusting sin I've just committed against the dead, but he must not have seen, as he only opened his arms out for me.

I welcomed his warm embrace with a few quick strides, burying my face into his unsteady chest, and wrapped my arms around his thick frame, as if he's too weary to stand up on his own. He gave me his weight though, leaned into me, and we stood there, under the deadening tree that seemed to wrap its arms around us and pull us in even tighter.

I wondered if things would get better for Ace. I hoped they did, even if he wouldn't hug me as tight after this.

The weeks passed quickly after Ace's dad's funeral, and he seemed to be on an uphill, which was nice to witness. He still sometimes had his moments when he realized just how alone he was now in his house by himself, but he also used that as an excuse to invite me over as much as Prissy would allow, which was actually a concerning amount. I tried not to dwell on it though, tried to take this little taste of freedom and run with it, even if I did get beat for coming home a minute too late.

The school year was also almost over for us seniors, just a few more weeks left before we got to go to prom and graduation and leave this hellhole called high school in the past. Ace had been talking nonstop about prom, about his friends pressing him to run for prom king, about what he's going to wear, but he didn't know if he even wanted to go at all. The way he talked about the dance made me wonder if he's only saying it, putting on a show, for me, if he thought that it's what I wanted, to not go and talk about how stupid dances were.

But honestly, I thought quite the opposite.

"You'd really wanna go?" Ace asked me one night as we sat in a tattoo shop a few minutes out of town. He's already eighteen, so he just walked right in, and was seated after giving his tattoo idea to the artist. It's a scorpion with some random roman numerals over top and underneath the stinging creature, shaded in black and white and gray, and I'm glad we came early because I thought we'll be here for a while.

"Yeah," I shrugged, voice quiet under the loud buzzing of the machine. I sat in the chair in the corner of the small room, knees to my chest as Ace looked at me funny in the leathered tattoo chair. I tried not to stare at him too much with his shirt off, but it's hard and he's a little distracting. I could tell he was muscular from how much we've been hugging lately and with how many play fights we got into, but to see him like this, made my cheeks burn and my eyes cast away from him. His skin just looked so soft, despite the hard muscles, and I liked the fact that his bruises on his ribs had started to fade into something barely there.

"I didn't think you would." Ace chuckled under his breath, tried to bite back the hiss coming up from his throat when the needle started to hurt. I shrugged at him again and rested my chin on my knees, wrapped my arms around my shins.

"I figured you would think that," I grinned at him. "But I was never allowed to read romance books, or even indulge in anything that dealt with romance. Everything I consumed had to be logical, fact-based evidence, and too-thick textbooks."

"About what?" Ace asked quietly with a furrow of his brow.

"Everything," I whispered, eyes far off as I thought about all the things Prissy had forced me to adapt to and learn. "Teen novels were out of the question—it was all too emotionally based. She wanted me to know everything, to be smarter than everybody, to be able to spit facts like some robot. I couldn't indulge in romantic things because to her, romance was all about feelings and I shouldn't be feeling-based. I had to only act on logistics, and she still expected me to."

The room went silent for a while as I thought about my past, thought about the bruises on my spine from when Prissy would beat me with the spines of books that she had found hidden under my bed. Books that I had stolen from libraries, books that girls in my school would lend me, books that were all about defeating bad witches and getting a prince in the end.

She didn't like that. Didn't like the fact that I was trying to defy her. That I had a vision, a plan, against her, that would drive me away from her and straight into someone else's arms. I remembered her telling me that I was hers, only hers, that she would never let another get in between the two of us. And even though I tried to reason with her, tell her that me falling in love with another wouldn't get in the way of her being my mother, she didn't listen to me. Just told that there was only one type of love, and that love that I would experience, would only come from her.

That was the first time she had broken my nose. She had hit me so hard in a fit of rage that she had broken the bone clean. She was crying the entire time, something I didn't think she was capable of, but she did. Cried that I would never leave her, could never leave her.

Cried that romance was something curated through filth and lies and cruelty. Cried that I would learn that no one could love a monster like me the way she did. Cried and cried and cried, so much for the both of us, that I could only stand there in silent shock at the excruciating pain that radiated from the middle of my face.

She made me sleep on the broken nose before fixing it in the morning. She called it love, nurturing me after hurting me so badly, showcasing the power that love had over another, kissing the now fully healed nose with her witch potions all better. And for a moment there, I believed that she did love me, just maybe in her own way.

"I'm sorry." Is all Ace whispered under the buzzing of the tattoo machine. I swiveled my head up from where I had glanced off to the side, frowning at him as I waved a hand in his direction.

"Don't apologize for something someone else has done. It's stupid." I scoffed, to which him and the tattoo artist both chuckled under their breaths. The male artist pulled away from Ace's chest with a shake of his head and laugh, wiping down the section he's working on, as Ace took the quick reprieve to shrug.

"You're right." He smiled softly, staring at me for a few seconds before his eyes fluttered a little in pain when the artist started again. We sat in silence for a while, as I watched the tattoo start to come to life before a thought struck me.

"What do those roman numerals stand for?" I asked, jerking my chin in his direction. Ace's eyes fluttered open, eyebrows raised before he smiled softly.

"The numbers on the bottom are my birthday, November 19," he answered quietly, paused as he looked around the room for a moment. The other set of numbers must be something important as he hesitated to share the answer, but he opened his mouth after a few beats of silence.

"The top numbers are for my mom's birthday," Ace finally told me, a sad smile on his face. I knew his mother was gone, but I never asked or pried on what gone really meant. He didn't share and I didn't press, as it wasn't my place to do so, not until he shared with me when he was ready. It must be significant to him though, as his lids instantly lowered and his jaw started to clench and unclench quickly. I tried to lighten the mood though, as I've never dealt well with the aftermath of death, and shrugged at him.

"Getting your mother's birthday tattooed on you after your abusive father croaks is a real boss move, Ace," I said nonchalantly, jumping a little at Ace's suddenly loud laugh. It made the artist pull back, shaking his head again, as he pinched the bridge of his nose and couldn't help but laugh himself.

"You kids are really screwed in the head, huh?" the man asked, glancing at both of us before he smiled and went back to tattooing. We sat in silence again, Ace staring at me with the dopiest of grins, and the almost lovesick stare made me squirm a little, before I finally broke the silence that had fallen over us again.

"Tell me about her," I said with a subtle nod in his direction. His eyebrows shot up again before they relaxed, his smile fading the tiniest bit at the corners.

"My mom?" Ace asked, and I hummed in confirmation. "She was a great woman. So pretty too; I always get told I was her twin, and when I look back on pictures of the two of us, I can see it." His eyes got a far-away look, and I could tell that he's about to go on a tangent, but I'm happy to listen.

"I think she made my dad a better person, mainly because of how kind and amazing she was herself. She just had an energy around her like that, made you want to be better, do better." I could see him blinking back a few tears, and if it's from the pain of the tattoo gun digging into his skin, or from talking about his mother, I couldn't really tell.

"I was so hurt when she died, you know?" Ace sniffled as he looked over at me, smile a little wobblier than what I'm used to seeing. "I mean, obviously, I was like six, and all, but I was heartbroken."

"Can I ask how?" I asked him quietly, wondering if it's rude to inquire, hoping it won't make him shut down and flee from me again. But Ace only nodded and wiped at his face with his palm, glancing down to see how far along the tattoo was before he flitted his eyes back up to meet mine again.

"Car accident." Is the only thing he said for a long while, letting the words hang in the air as he obviously struggled with spitting out everything else that he wanted to share with me. "I asked her if she could take me to get a new toy, something I didn't really need. And on the way there, she looked back at me for just a split second, and accidentally steered off too far."

Ace quieted, his voice trailing off, and I could paint enough of a picture to understand what happened. I didn't say anything for a long while, and neither did he. What do you say after sharing your trauma? After expressing an underlying sense of guilt about asking for a toy as a child? For being the distraction that made your mother get into her accident? Did I comfort him? Combat his guilt and try to rewire years' worth of ingrained self-abuse? I'm not too sure what to say anymore as the minutes passed on and his words still hung above our heads with their weight, but I finally found something in me to spit out.

"I'm sorry." It felt like that's all I'm good at saying at this point to him, felt so weak and not as impactful as I was hoping it would be. But Ace smiled at me anyway, kind and small, its enough for me to see a glimmer of bright orange brace brackets, and the sight made me shuffle a little in my seat. He didn't respond for a while, and the sound of the buzzing gun comforted us for the time being.

The artist announced that he's going to go over a few more sections of the piece until he's finished, and I could see Ace perking up, finally ready to get out of the chair and move around again. I huffed a laugh through my nose at the way his entire body started to shuffle in anticipation, when he ducked his head between his shoulders when the artist asked him to sit still again. Ace shot me a look, narrowing his eyes at me playfully before he laughed himself, head rolling until it rested back on the chair, and he looked down his nose at me with a grin.

"You really wanna go to prom?" he suddenly blurted out, baritone voice ringing throughout the room. I looked at him for a while as I thought it over, thought about how much I would dread having people fussing over me getting ready for prom if my life were normal. How, if Prissy loved me, she would probably hire someone fancy to come drench my face in a pound of makeup, how she'd probably curl my hair herself and stick some homemade hair decorative pieces in until they pinched at my scalp. How she'd go out and buy a dumb expensive dress, even if I told her I wouldn't mind something cheap but pretty. How she'd fawn over me, dote on me, look at me with love and tell me that I was beautiful.

I'd never get that though, but it didn't hurt to dream. Well, it did, but I couldn't dwell on it too long, lest I got too many ideas in my head, and Prissy found it necessary to beat it out of me again. I realized that I've left Ace hanging for entirely too long, and I nodded once with a shrug.

"Yeah," was all I answered him. He looked at me funny for a while before he hummed under his breath, eyes fluttering closed as he sat out the remaining time of getting his tattoo touched up and finished.

After what felt like forever, the artist finally announced that he's done, and wiped down the fresh ink a few times before he backed off and let Ace get up from the chair. He nodded his head to me as he stalked to the mirror on the other side of the room, grinning the entire time he made his way over. As I walked behind him, I couldn't help but to admire the muscles that rippled in his back with every stretch he made from sitting for so long, how his shoulder blades moved and rolled with every crack of his spine, how his back dimples deepened with every step he took.

"This looks so sick." I could hear Ace muttering to himself, big hand reaching up to trace the still-untouched skin around the new tattoo as he admired himself in the mirror. I sneaked up beside him, leaned against his arm to get a look at the new ink, eyes tracing every line and curve and letter that made up the newness of it. The tattoo was pretty, simple in design but visually appealing; a scorpion with its stinger curled in front of its face took up the majority of his left pec, the roman numerals above and below the shaded-in creature. Numbers that suddenly had such a deeper meaning to it now when I thought about how at peace he looked when talking about his mom.

My attention was grabbed when there's suddenly two fingers under my chin, lifting my head until Ace made me crane my neck up to face him. He stared at me for a few seconds, his breathing calm and steady, his eyes soft and round, as he exhaled slowly, skin warm against my own where we touched. Without a word, he leaned down and pulled me up until our lips brushed, until I could feel the featherlight kiss of his mustache against my skin, until he hummed into my mouth and wrapped me up tight against him.

The kiss didn't last long or get as heated as it did the first time, but it's still just as electrifying, still made my body feel loose and light, like I could float away into thin air with Ace's mouth still against mine. When he pulled away, I felt like it should be considered a heinous crime, to gift me with something so sweet, so loving and tender, and take it all away with only a smile to follow.

"Would you like to go with me to prom, Areya?" Ace asked softly into the air shared between us. He couldn't see it, but I could feel my eyes widen, lips parting slightly in an 'O' as his words sank in to me. Ace wanted to go to prom with me? That thing that he just deemed as stupid and pompous and useless? Was he asking just because he knew it's a distant dream of mine to have any experience with romance, or because my love for wanting to be loved was enough to sway him? I tried not to think about the reasoning too much, and finally answered when I felt like I've left him waiting long enough.

"I'll go if you're that desperate for a date, Foster." I spat his last name out on my tongue, shrugging, unable to help the chuckle that spilled from my mouth. Ace threw his head back and laughed then, fingers falling from my chin as he instead went to wrap his entire thick arm around me and pulled me in, hissing though when the fabric of my shirt met his fresh tattoo.

He pulled back then, but still smiled at me, still laughed, and threw his head back until he could look at me again. Ace pulled me into another kiss after that, something to keep my stupid big mouth quiet, I'm guessing, but I guessed it's not that bad to be silenced in a way that's so sweet, it made me want to be good for once.

Chapter 17

Ace has felt the need to send me a picture everyday of his new tattoo. Feels the need to show me the healing and peeling process of it all, even though I keep threatening to block him if he doesn't stop. Maybe he doesn't quit it because he knows I won't block him, but I'm seriously considering it. We lay in bed, texting back and forth for a while before I get a new message from someone else, and my mood instantly sours.

Judas
12:37 pm
Hey, Bright Eyes. Can you meet me here in an hour, please?
Promise this isn't an attack.
0170 Gorgon Ave, Devils Lake, North Dakota

Bright Eyes
12:37 pm
No.

Judas
12:38 pm
Please? I want to do more of the talking this time. Figured I could start to share more stuff with you since we've been getting closer.

Instinctively, I roll my eyes at his last message, huffing under my breath. Closer, my ass. He says that every time, that he'll talk more when all he ever does is load questions as ammo into his never-ending firing gun poised at my temples. As I go to message him back with another simple 'no,' Prissy is suddenly standing at my doorway, her hip cocked and a hand resting on it. She eyes my phone for a long while before she speaks, and it takes everything in me to not lock the device and hide it somewhere safe from her prying hands.

"I'm going out today," she tells me, her voice steady and hard, feels like a snap against my jugular from its sharpness. I swallow, eyes bouncing between her own cerulean ones and the simple outfit she wears: a black dress shirt, black and gray striped linen pants, a thick chocolate brown sweater thrown over top, and her favorite black wedge heels. She must be going to one of those business meetings she never wants to full-on tell me about but likes to hint around. She always has at least one of these meetings every time we move states with these so-called people that she never seems to name. I've learned the hard way to not ask questions about it and simply nod at her.

"Okay. I hope it goes well," I tell her, trying to keep my voice as firm and leveled as she taught me. I'm vague in my well-wishing, too used to her flipping out about the idea of me overstepping my place by questioning her moves and what she decides to do with her life. Completely unacceptable for me, but she's allowed to pry into every single aspect of my life. I try not to frown at the double standard. She stands there staring at me for a bit, still looking between me and my phone before she hums, sticking her nose up in the air as she steps back from my open door.

"It will." She nods, about to turn away, before she suddenly stops herself, pokes her head back inside to narrow her eyes at me. "If you would like to go out and hang with your little," she pauses, damn near has to spit the word out, "friend, then I'll allow that. Just be home before midnight," she says, finality lacing her tone. I try not to perk up too much, try not to show so much emotion, so much excitement.

"Thank you, Mother," I tell her with a nod, pulling up the corners of my lips in the best smile that I can manage for her. She can tell that it's strained with how her eyes take in every little aspect of my face before she hums and backs away from the door again.

"Don't mention it." Her tone is snappy, but what I did to upset her, I don't know. I also can't be bothered to care, especially if me thanking her gets this kind of reaction. I roll my eyes when she turns away, perking up when she calls over her shoulder as she marches down the hall in her too-loud heels.

"Don't forget to use a condom, either!" she says cheerily, all irritation from her voice completely evaporated as I splutter and choke on my own spit. "Or don't, I can't control your every move." And just like that, her tone is icy again, that sweetness melted from its previous sentence like warm butter under hot radiation.

Why the hell would she say something like that? We never even...discussed those kinds of things together, her and I. She would always beat down my curiosity, quite literally, and would even go as far as ripping out all of the pages in my textbooks about such matters. Why would she think something like that would be going on between me and Ace? And why tell me not to use one either, all in the same breath?

Is it jealousy? Of my relationship with Ace, a relationship she never thought could come to such fruition as it did, as it has now? Is she that unused to sharing me that she lashes out with such pettiness, if only to make me uncomfortable? Is she that cruel, that she has to play these kinds of games that I'm really starting to tire of?

My thoughts are ripped away as another chime of my phone dings in the emptiness of the house after Prissy has slammed the door shut. My eyes dart to it quickly, picking the device up, hoping that it's from Ace, wishing that it's not from her, somewhat surprised that it's Judas.

Judas
12:47 pm
I promise I'll be on my best behavior. At least consider it.

I toggle his words around in my head for a little while, biting on the insides of my cheek until it stings, trying to sort my mind out. On one hand, I could text Ace and ask if he'd like to come hang out over here, if we could watch more movies and maybe end the night the way it did last time. But also, what if Judas did actually have something to say, to tell me about? As much as I don't want to think about it, I'm still quite curious about his intentions, who he is, how he came to be, why he and I are so different. As I ponder, my curiosity gets the best of me, and I find myself answering as I stand to get dressed.

Bright Eyes
12:49 pm
If you say anything stupid, I'm leaving.

Judas
12:49 pm
Lol. I'll try not to say anything stupid, then.

I walk to Judas' house, surprised that the creep only lives thirty minutes away, walking distance, from my house. I narrow my eyes at the blandly painted brick house, rectangular and long all over with squared windows and chipping paint on the windowsill. It's not much, wildly separated from the other similarly styled houses I saw while walking up, some with built-in garages and sharp-topped with smoking chimneys. He has a little porch in the front of the cream-colored house, and I find myself ascending up the old rickety steps, taking everything in. He doesn't have much outside to decorate, save for a stray tabby cat that hunches its back and yowls at me when I step up to the front door.

"Shut up," I mutter to the animal, frowning when it hisses at me and scatters when I knock a little too harshly on the door. I only stand there for a few seconds before I hear the door unlocking, and out pokes a dirty blond head of hair and a small smile.

"You came," Judas says, his little gap peeking through the rosiness of his lips. I survey him and his plethora of freckles, thin eyebrows, and stupidly big golden glasses. I cock an eyebrow at him though, the longer he keeps me out here to grin at me.

"I told you I'd come, didn't I?" I frown at him, looking around his untamed mass of hair into the house behind him. "You gonna let me in, or do you want me to freeze to death out here?" Even in late March, it's still too cold in North Dakota for my liking. Judas nods quickly, stepping back and swinging the door open quickly as I trudge inside. I shed my thicker layers as he closes the door behind me, placing them on a coat rack and swatting him away when he tries to do it for me.

I take in his living room, and honestly, it's hard to do so when it's so barren, so desolate. He has muted gray curtains that cover the front window that would oversee the porch, a single couch in the middle of the room, a dingy green that makes me recoil a little at the worn look of it. There's a pair of shoes by the front door, and if I peek my head around, I can look into the kitchen. But Judas doesn't let me, as he starts taking off on the steps behind the ugly couch.

"We're gonna be in my room, if that's okay? Feels more lived in than down here."

"I hope your definition of lived in is the same as mine," I mutter under my breath, ignoring Judas' tiny chuckle under his breath. There aren't any frames on the walls, just more cracked paint and disappointment.

His room is on the right as we venture off the stairs, the hallway empty, and the rest of the doors closed. I should look around in those later, but for now, as I enter his room, I'm pleasantly surprised. It does look a little more lived in than any other part of the house—he has a twin bed pushed against the corner, navy blue sheets tucked in neatly on the sides, two pillows decorated in yellow cases sitting against the gray headboard. He has a few posters on his walls of things and movies I don't recognize, but I think they're all album covers, maybe, from different eras. He has a chestnut-colored dresser pushed against the opposite wall of his bed, with only a few pieces of jewelry in an open black velvet box, lotion, and a jangle of keys strewn about the top of it, the only messy part of his room. Where a TV would typically be is instead hosted by a light blue night table, a big opened box sitting atop it, a few thin slips sitting underneath that are stacked up nearly to the top.

"That's my vinyl collection," Judas offers when he sees me looking long enough. I raise an eyebrow at him, but don't ask what a vinyl is, too afraid that he might nerd out and never shut up. I take another look around the room before I hum, leaning on the wall in between his dresser and bed as I cock my head to the side, blinking a few times behind my glasses.

"I didn't know you had a job to be able to afford this kinda place on your own," I murmur, glancing at the posters as he chuckles, turning his back on me. He doesn't answer for a few beats, and I guess it's because he starts up the vinyl. A quiet and jazzy song starts to play around the room, the beat of it smooth and gently flows into the atmosphere, making Judas look extremely dorky when he turns on his heels to look at me, grinning, his shoulder shrugging noncommittally.

"Yeah, well, North Dakota is known for having affordable housing," Judas answers coolly, winking at me before he darts out of the room quickly to return with a rolling chair that he offers me. I take it, back against his dresser as he sits on his bed, patting at the sheets a few times as the silence drags on.

"So affordable that you don't even need a job?" I pry, resting my cheek in my palm as I eye him with boredom. Judas only smiles at that, leans back far enough until he rests against the wall behind him, placing his hands in his sweatshirt's pocket.

"What did you want, Judas? Why am I here?" I sigh, tired, and the memory of our last run-in fresh on my mind. He always seemed to trudge up a lot of memories and feelings that I wanted to oppress, a lot of commands ingrained into me that I know I should rebel against. Me and him were like ticking time bombs together, and it could only take a single flicker of fire to light me ablaze and take down this entire neighborhood.

Judas shuffles a bit where he sits, his mouth twisting this way and that, his eyes suddenly unsure. He glances up at me once, twice, a little smile playing at his mouth as he jerks his chin in my direction.

"Can you take your glasses off?" Before I can protest, and he can tell by the way my face immediately screws up, he continues. "I wanna share some stuff with you so we can get a better understanding of everything, and I would like to see your eyes while we talk."

Shut up, I think to myself, rolling my eyes as I huff under my breath and fold my arms over my chest. I stare at him for a while, and he at me with that same smile that I want to rip off of his face. We're in a deadlock for a while before I give in, ready to get this forest fire that will become of our conversation over with already. With a sigh and grumble under my breath, I snatch my glasses off, blinking a few times before I level him off with a glare, tucking the spectacles into my own hoodie's pocket. He smiles even wider at that and nods once at me.

"Time before last when we talked, I got really defensive over my parents and what happened to them," Judas starts quietly, his smile suddenly fading at that as he glances past me and toward the squared window across the room.

"You killed them," I state blankly, watching the way he winces and frowns a little at my words, but he doesn't deny them.

"Yeah," he mutters, chin suddenly tucked into his chest. "My sister too." My eyebrows raise in surprise at that, before I think back to his vague words the first time we met. That must've been who he was talking about. I nod though, letting him continue as he struggles to find the right words. I don't rush him, and I count it as positive progress in my personality that I have learned from Ace, because a couple of months before this, I would've been throttling Judas to hurry up and spit it all out. Patience is a virtue, or whatever they say, I guess.

"I got my first power when I was one when I'd touch people, you know?" he asks, and I nod quickly, thinking back to my own that could cause nosebleeds. "My parents knew that there was something wrong with me, and tried to keep me away from my big sister. She was already a sickly kid, and they didn't want me to taint her, and they made that point as nicely as they could." He laughs humorlessly at that, his eyes downturned and sad, his mouth forming a thin, pressed line. I listen though, glad to be the one not being questioned here, glad to hear his story instead of being interrogated for my own.

"So they kept me away from her as much as they could," Judas murmurs into the high collar of his sweatshirt, and I interject before I can help it.

"How much older than you was she?" I ask, eyebrows furrowing as I try to imagine a child barely older than him being forced away from her little brother.

"Eight years older," he answers, and I nod for him to continue. "It wasn't as hard as they expected to keep me away; if she was younger then, yeah, she'd have difficulty understanding. But she could sense that something was wrong with me, and took her distance from me.

"And then I turned five, that dreaded number." He cracks a tiny smile my way, but it's only full of hurt and a type of sorrow that has to make me look away in uncomfortableness. "She snuck into my room to wish me a happy birthday, found your mother standing above me, ready to take me." My eyes widen a little at that. Is this what she does? Curse children and then snatch them away on their fifth birthday when their powers have fully fledged and emerged? Or were we just special?

"She fought her off as much as she could, and when my parents finally heard the commotion, they came in, but she had already fled." Judas' voice becomes thick in his throat, like he's swallowing molasses, like it sticks to his esophagus and refuses to slide down until it's stolen his breath completely from him. He blinks a few times, chews on his bottom lip, eyes darting around the room, the smooth song transitioning into another to fill the silence as I wait for him to finish.

"I just wanted to hug my sister, you know?" His voice cracks, and I can't help but feel for him, even if it's just the tiniest bit. "It was innocent; I just wanted to thank her for saving me. But I had already fully developed my curse, and she just—just decayed right in front of me. Right in front of all of us."

The air hangs heavy in the room, thick and full of unwavering emotion. I had only learned how to comfort Ace in his emotions recently, and I wasn't sure if I could tack on handling someone else's emotions, too. So I sit there, stare out the bedroom door as Judas gathers himself as much as he can, glancing back over when I catch him wiping his face with the back of his sleeve. He clears his throat a little and sighs quietly, and before he picks back up, I stop him.

"You don't have to tell me this stuff, you know." It's as gentle as he can get from me, and I cringe a little at the way it comes out. He must understand me, somehow, without even having that much time to have known me in these past few weeks.

"I know," he chuckles, wiping at the corner of his eye with his index finger, his nail painted a chipped dark purple. "But I realized that we can never trust or understand each other if I'm always so closed off to you about my life. I know so much about yours, so I figured I could balance it out."

"You're a creep," is all I answer him with a little huff in my tone. Judas outright laughs at that and doesn't deny it. Just settles against the wall again, the faintest smile inching across his freckled cheeks, hands burrowed in his pockets.

"Why would they go to a witch to have a child when they already had one at home?" I blurt out, figured we could get back on topic as to hurry this all up. Too much vulnerability for my liking; it's awkward and weird, and what do you do when a guy starts crying after confessing he's killed his sister? Especially after he told you that you were a monster for doing the same with your family? I'm ready for this conversation to be wrapped up as quickly as possible, but I can't help my lingering curiosity.

"Greed, I guess you could call it." He shrugs, a look of deep thought passing over his face. "They just wanted one more, just wanted a healthy baby boy because of how sickly my sister was when she was born." His voice fades off toward the end of the sentence, and I fix him with a confused look as my eyebrow furrows.

"Is adopting that bad of an option?" I ask, grunting a little under my breath. Judas snorts a little at that and shrugs again.

"Black magic and witches over the adoption process, I guess." We both chuckle a little at that, the air in the room losing a bit of its earlier tension of emotions as we relax back into our seats. We sit in silence for a little while longer before another song comes on, this time with lyrics. I can't understand much of what they're saying, but the singer's voice is raspy, a gentle croon that makes the tight joints of my body relax until I find myself slumping a little lower in my seat.

"Your mother tried to come back and get me again, but I put my foot down and told her I wouldn't go. After that, we moved across the country, changed our names so nobody could track us and the suddenly missing daughter in our family portraits. And everything was good and well, or I thought it was, until I overheard my mom on the phone with dad." Judas's voice takes on a lower pitch, his lids falling until they're barely cracked open, a look I've never seen him sport gracing his face. It unnerves me a little, and my hackles rise instantly, readying myself for a fight I know I'll win.

"She told him that she was scared I would turn into you." His eyes slide over to mine at that, and I feel myself jolt a little in my seat. My face must hold a thousand questions, my eyes searching his for an answer that he barely gives me.

"We knew she had you; bragged all about how you killed your parents, how strong you were. She was hoping I'd be the same, and even though I wasn't, my actions still weren't enough for my mom." He shakes his head a little at that, dirty blond mane covering his eyes in the process until they're hidden. Judas pauses for another uncomfortably long time, before he tilts his head up, only the reflection of the glasses peeking through the curls of his hair.

"I snapped," he says quietly, his jaw set and firm as he clenches a few times until he can speak again. "Told her that I wasn't a monster, and all she could say was that I was, that I was just like you, that she should've killed me on my fifth birthday. So I became you." His words hang heavy in the air, and I don't know whether or not I want to stand up and strangle him or stay seated and listen to the rest of his story. I choose the latter though, but now with my guard up—to be referenced in his house as the monster parent killer, as if they knew my story. As if they had to endure the torture of verbal abuse and barrage as if they just weren't scared of their Frankenstein monster they chose to create because they just had to have one more kid.

"I held her body for so long." His voice cracks at that admission, head hung low again. "She was barely bones once my dad came home and saw what happened. I tried to go to him, explain what happened, and he let me because I had put my gloves back on at that point. But it was too late, you know?" Judas laughs humorlessly, tears starting to track his cheeks now as he leans his back against the wall, eyes cast up to the white ceiling, his bottom lip trembling.

"At that point, I realized that he was going to have the exact same doubts as my mom, that he'd never love me like how he promised he always would. So I took off my gloves and embraced him as tight as I could." His story ends on a dramatic finish, like it's something he's rehearsed entirely too many times. It's authentic, though, and I believe him, especially if the fresh tears that steadily fall are any proof of his confession. We sit in silence for a while as he tries to get himself together, sniffling a few times before he darts his eyes down to me.

"What's Priscilla like as a mom?" Judas asks, and I immediately roll my eyes up into my head. I startle a little when he laughs, forgetting that he can see me entirely without getting hurt. The realization is...nice, brings a little warmth to the bottom of my belly as I sink lower into my seat.

"She's not a mom at all," I shrug, trying to find the words to fit her, but are there any that can really capture the likeness of a person like her? "More like the handler to a weapon of mass destruction that she knows can never turn on her." I nod slowly at that, the imagery sinking in, as Judas hums under his breath before he cuts his eyes at me with a little grin.

"You're a weapon of mass destruction? You didn't feel all that destructive last time you pinned me," he teases, and the words make me scoff. I sit up a little in my seat, pointing at him as I narrow eyes that I keep forgetting he can see.

"Key words: I pinned you. Multiple times, might I add," I tell him, nodding my head in his direction as I can't help but let a small smile tug at the corners of my lips. The nerve of this guy challenging me like this while incriminating himself in the same sentence. I shake my head a little, huffing a silent chuckle under my breath as Judas relaxes against his bed until only his head is supported by the wall, the length of his body laid across the bed and hanging off the edge of it. He stares at me for a little while with a funny look on his face, as if he's contemplating, thinking, taking me all in as much as I'll allow.

"You're not too bad, Bright Eyes," Judas mutters, grinning wide enough that I can see that gap that I find myself starting to like the more I look at it. I scoff a little, rolling my eyes as I rest my ankle on my knee, propping my head in my hand as I look at him from under my lashes.

"Hmm, you could be better, Judas," I shrug to him, listening to his sudden loud laughter that drowns out that same music that seems to be on a loop. As we sit in here, in his room, chatting and making small talk, I realize that opening up really does have its benefits. Makes me want to strangle him a little less, but I can't say the urge completely goes away.

Judas offered to walk me home that night, and I let him. Not for my safety but because of his constant pushing about doing it. I think he just wants to talk more, and I allow him that for the time being. We walk slow, dragging our feet despite the freezing temperatures telling us to book it as quickly as we can. He bumps my shoulder once, and I knock him back hard enough that he stumbles just because I can. Judas chuckles once he regains his balance, hands shoved deep into his pockets as his hat-covered curls peek out against his eyebrows and forehead.

"Are you and that guy dating? Ace, right?" Judas asks quietly, a lilt to his voice that makes me shrug.

"No. I don't think so." Are we? He never even asked me out if we were. And how would Prissy handle it if we were dating? She already seemed upset about the relationship we've developed; I can't imagine the news would go over well for her. I frown at the thought of it, looking over to Judas whose mouth is set in a thin line.

"What's it to you, anyway?" I bump his shoulder again, gently this time and he lifts his shoulder a little, holding it up still as we walk to my house.

"Just nosy, is all," he mumbles, finally dropping his shoulder when I glance over at him. My glasses are back on for the time being; I don't trust myself to walk around outside without them in case someone unexpected comes into view. Judas gave me a funny look after we started walking, a mix between a frown and a scold, before he waved hello to his neighbor, who immediately looked at me. After that, the face went away, and he didn't say anything else.

We walk in silence for a while until my house comes into view, the driveway still thankfully empty. I let out a rush of breath that I hadn't realized I was holding, Judas turning his head slightly to look at me when the noise escaped my parted lips.

"I can walk myself from here," I tell Judas, turning to him as he smiles at me with a tilt of his head in my direction.

"Not gonna invite me inside for some tea?" he asks playfully, snickering when I lower my glasses to the bridge of my nose so that he can see my glare.

"Drink the shitty tea at your own house, Judas," I tell him, pushing my glasses back up before turning on my heel and walking away before he could say anything else. He huffs a laugh under his throat, snow crunching under his boot as he turns away from me.

"That's the first time you've said my name with no hostility in your voice, Bright Eyes." I hear Judas call out to me, a smile evident in his voice. It makes my shoulders rise up to my ears, and if it's from the cold wind whipping through my canals or the warmth that seeps through me from the fondness of his voice, I don't want to know.

"Go home, Judas," I snip out his name, waving him off from over my shoulder, hackles rising when he only lets out another boisterous laugh before it slowly starts to fade away from our mutual distance from each other. I make it the rest of the way to my home, fumbling with my keys in my pocket, cursing the cold for locking up my hands. When I finally get the door open, do I turn around, surprised to see Judas standing at the end of my street still. He only waves, and even from here, I can see the bright, wide, and blinding grin he loves to throw at me despite my scowl and slam of the door. Idiot.

Chapter 18

When I walk into the girls' bathroom, I don't expect to see Sophia there. I haven't spoken to her much since my first day, but she's always been polite whenever we ran into each other. When she looks up and catches me in the bathroom mirror, she smiles big, her gap shining through her plump brown lips as she finishes washing her hands.

"Well, well, well. If it isn't the girl who stole Ace from our friend group!" Sophia singsongs, flapping her hands to shake the water off. I don't know whether to prickle at her words or nod along in agreement. He has been extra clingy after his father died, and there's been talk about how he doesn't go out with his friends much anymore now. I can't be put to blame though; I want him off of my hip as much as everyone wants him on theirs.

"How are you guys doing, though? I haven't heard much from either of you, and I was hoping that y'all were okay." Her voice sounds sincere enough, and I tell myself to lower my hackles, at least a little. She never seemed to be the type that was possessive or mean, and I can only think that she's being genuine in her concern about his detachment from everyone else. I shrug at her, mirroring her position as she leans against the sink counter, crossing my arms.

"I'm fine. And he's alright, too, I guess," I answer her shortly. It's hard speaking on how another person is doing, in all honesty. Because looking at Ace? He looks like a mess. He doesn't cry much, but he's been very apathetic, which is still concerning in its own right. I know he's grieving, but it makes me question if his grieving process is healthy at all, and that's coming from me.

Sophia only chuckles a little under her breath, head resting on her shoulder as she takes me in with a small smile. She doesn't say anything for a long while, and I wonder if it's rude to up and walk away into one of the bathroom stalls. When I start to consider my options more and more, she finally speaks up, like she's been rolling the words around in her head in order to make sense of them when they spill out.

"Can I ask what's going on between you guys?" she implored, holding her hands up in defense when my eyebrow cocked in question. "I know it's not any of my business; I'm just curious!"

She tries to disarm me with one of those genuine-looking smiles, and it's hard to not be convinced when she looks like the embodiment of a cherub. Her cheeks are too round, and her eyes are too soft for me to want to snap at, but I keep my guard up anyway. I juggle around an answer in my head, start wondering if I should drop Ace because this is the second time this week that someone's asked if we had something going on between us. It was starting to irritate me more than I would like.

"We're just friends. Hanging out." The words feel like a strain trying to get out, like I'm regurgitating things Ace has been trying to drill into me since the day we first met. Friends.

That word felt so foreign in my vocabulary, like it was something that I would never truly know of. Prissy had made sure that I never made friends, especially when I was younger, and kept forgetting my glasses when I would sneak out to go to the playground. After enough children had gone missing, she made sure to beat it into me that friends would never be something that I would ever have.

"You sure it's not more than that?" Sophia asks me with a little grin, whipping out her phone as she cozies up next to me. I try to take a step away, but I'm cornered against the bathroom sink, and I can only make sure my disdainful frown is apparent. But she doesn't even look at me; just keeps scrolling on her phone until she finds what she's looking for, shoving the bright technology in my face.

"Because he's been posting you on his socials for like, the past two weeks now," she nearly squeals. I have to hold her hand to keep her still in her excitement and find my eyes bulging out of my head at what I see.

It's so many pictures of me under a username I had only seen in passing when Ace would show me things on his phone. Most of them, if not all, were off-guard photos when we would hang out. Me sitting on his couch watching a movie with him. Me sitting idly on the hood of his car, scrolling through my own phone. Me, smiling even, in his kitchen as I hold up our completed brain project. What the hell?

A lump suddenly settles in the base of my throat; panic starts to overwhelm my senses. How will Prissy feel about this? She never let me have any kind of social media presence because of these unspecified dangers that she refused to tell me. What would the consequences be? Who would find me? It wouldn't be hard to, with Ace tagging his location every goddamn picture. Will everything I have ever done catch up to me just because of a few off-guard photos? Will that incident in Arizona…?

I come crashing back down to reality when Sophia squeals again but takes her place back in front of me. Her grin seems to have widened despite the pure fear taking over my body and mind. She doesn't notice a thing and continues to blabber on as she waggles her thick eyebrows at me.

"Seems to me Ace thinks it's more than you're letting on, Areya," Sophia singsongs, but the sound of my own name only makes me cringe. If only she knew what connection this name had across the entire country, she wouldn't feel so comfortable asking me about my relationship status. I try to come back to reality when she suddenly loses her joy in one fell swoop, my eyebrows scrunching in confusion when she looks around the bathroom to make sure that we're really alone.

"Just be careful, okay?" she warns, voice a little quieter, making me lean in instinctively. "I always get so excited whenever Ace gets with someone new, but I've learned to not get my hopes up," she admits, looking back at her phone with an almost fond expression before meeting my gaze again. I shake my head in confusion, blinking a couple of times, looking at her expectantly to explain herself.

"Well, what does that mean?" I snap when she takes too long to answer. Sophia jumps a little in place, clutching her phone to her chest as she glances around the bathroom once more.

"He's just a little, hmm," she wonders aloud, looking off to the side in thought. "Possessive, than he originally lets on, you know?"

"I don't know," I say back almost instantly, making her laugh a little under her breath. She steps up and grabs me by my shoulders, her eyes sincere as she bounces between my glasses lens. I feel myself stiffen in place, and it takes everything in me not to step away and peel her hands off of me, but I don't move her in hopes of learning more about what she meant. I'll deal with it for now, but the moment she explains herself, I want her off of me.

"Just trust me, girl. I know he's pretty in the face and the stereotypical football star with a million girls flocking him. But there's a reason he's single," Sophia advises, squeezing my shoulders once before dropping her hands, but she doesn't take a step back. If anything, she leans in closer when a girl walks into the bathroom, heading straight for a stall, leaning in to whisper now.

"He's run off a few girlfriends in the past for being overbearing, and I don't want him to do the same with you. I really liked you from the moment I saw you, and would hate to lose another female friend just because he can be too much for someone." She sounds truthful, like it's actually a warning and not a demand to stay away from him. I stare at her for a long time, mulling her words over in my head, before I nod once.

Ace? Possessive? Honestly, it checks out. Judas calls him my guard dog for a reason, I supposed. I tongue my cheek for a few seconds, thinking about all the times Ace has gotten jealous when I couldn't give him my all attention, whenever he saw me talking to Judas. I could see where Sophia was coming from and only nodded when I realized that I hadn't said anything in a while.

"Thanks for telling me," I concur, straightening my back and taking a step away when the girl from the stall emerged to wash her hands. She gives me a once-over before speaking to Sophia, as I catch Sophia's wide eyes and low thumb jab in the girl's direction at the sink. Sophia mouthed something like 'ex' to me, and it all clicked when the girl snatched a few paper towels before looking at me once more.

"Listen to Sophia. I wish I would have," the girl advises me before shoving her trash in the little bin, making a quick exit out of the bathroom. We both watch her go, and I turn to Sophia with my eyebrows raised in surprise.

"Guess I'll heed your warnings, then." I nod to her, lugging my backpack up a little higher on my shoulder as I hum under my breath. "I'll talk to him about it today."

"What? You're gonna confront him about it?" Sophia gasps, stopping me with a hand out as I turn to leave. I give her a slightly confused look, resting my weight on my right leg, shrugging once I see that she's serious.

"Yeah?" I ask confusedly. "It's a bad habit that needs to be nipped in the bud. I won't tolerate it any longer." I nod to her, turning again before she can stop me. As I open the bathroom door, Sophia calls out as she digs around in her purse to pull out a tube of lip gloss.

"Well, good luck. But please leave my name out of it." She looks at me with big, round eyes that I can't help but chuckle at. I nod to her again, and she grins, turning to the mirror to apply the gloss. I watch her for a few seconds, wondering how differently my life would've been if I wasn't born wrong. If I had the opportunity to gossip in dirty bathrooms and have female friends and apply lip gloss without a care in the world.

"Will do," I affirm quietly before making my way out of the bathroom, trying to quell the frustration of circumstances that I was quickly growing tired of.

The rest of the day goes by pretty uneventfully, up until dismissal time, when I am suddenly swept up into a hug that I elbow my way out of. Unsurprisingly, it's Ace, as he's the only person in this school, maybe the whole world, who's comfortable enough to try to scare me like that. He huffs at the loss of breath before chuckling, spinning me around, and tries to duck down to kiss me when I evade him with a step back. Ace frowns, his hands instantly locking around my waist, restraining me from taking another step back. Before he can say anything, I quickly speak up.

"Why do you have so many pictures of me?" In your phone? On your social media? Without me ever realizing? There are too many branches for me to break off on, so I ask him the simplest way I can, my mouth pulled tight, my eyebrows drawn down in irritation. But Ace only laughs, squeezing my waist again in his hands as if the answer is as obvious as the sun shining.

"Why not?" he asks with a tilt of his head, curly fringe momentarily covering his eyes. "Besides, you should have some pictures of me too, since we go together now."

He gets a mischievous look in his eyes, and before I can stop him, he's pulling my phone from the back pocket of my jeans. I try to reach up to get it back from him as he clicks the phone on, uncaring of the other students who try to avoid our elbows flying as he raises my phone over his head. Slowly, his smile drops, his eyes scanning the screen as his top lip starts to slightly curl, his forehead creasing in agitation.

"What's this?" Ace asks, his voice suddenly dropping as he turns the screen to me. I stop trying to wring his neck in favor of reading the message that I hadn't seen come in beforehand.

Judas
12:49 pm
Hey gem. Wanna come over again today? I got some new vinyls in the mail ;)

I read the message and reread it a few more times, trying to understand why such an innocent thing has shifted Ace's mood so much in so little time. Before I can answer, Ace guides me into an empty hallway, desolate of any students or teachers, since everyone's racing against time to get home. I protest and send another elbow back into his rib, but he dodges it with a quickness that only makes me huff under my breath.

When the sound of students from outside the building dims, and it's just us two in the open wide space, Ace finally stops, spinning me around once more as if I weigh nothing. His eyes are lit aflame as he holds my phone with too tight of a grip, and I fear that the screen may break just from his hold.

"What's going on between you two?" he snaps, his form hunched over as if in intimidation. But the thought only makes me curl my lip in disgust as I snatch away from him with every fiber of my being, taking a few steps back to gain some space between us. My back is against a neon green locker, and I don't like the feeling of being cornered. When he acts like he's going to take another step forward, I fix him with a look that makes him pause.

"Why does it matter?" I snap at him, hiking my bag up higher on my shoulder, ready to flee because I cannot get caught with blood on my hands when exiting the school building. Would I hurt Ace, though? If it came down to it—could I really take off my glasses? Could I really beat him bloody, like I had done his father? Could I splinter myself from what I have learned of him and treat him like yet another job from Prissy?

If it came down to it, I fear I would have to.

"Because we're in a relationship, Areya, and I told you that that freak makes me uncomfortable, and you should stay away from him." The sound of him using my name makes me flinch back, a look of disgust overcoming my face. Was he already unlatching himself from me, or was he only sinking his being even deeper into my soul with every word?

"I don't have to listen to you, Ace. Besides, we're not together, never have been," I spit at him, teeth gritting as I go to stomp away from him, but pause when I remember Sophia's words from earlier.

"You're possessive, and it's your worst quality. You don't own me, and the thought that you would even consider trying to sink your claws into me makes me sick to have to look at you." I snap at him, finger pointed in his direction, but he seems lax, suddenly. Slouched and grinning, braces glinting in the low light of the hallway, his arms open and inviting, his head tilted to the side, antagonizing.

"It's not possessiveness if you're mine and I'm yours, right? It's equal footing, is it not, Bubbles?" Ace murmurs to me, taking a step toward me, and suddenly, his form doesn't seem so warm to fall into anymore. No, now it feels almost like a trap, like if I were to take another step forward, if I were to agree with his words, if I were to let him wrap his arms around me, I'd be forever plastered to him. Sunken into his very being, stuck together until he gets sick of me, as everyone always does.

"Screw you," I snarl between gritted teeth, stepping off before he can snatch me into his embrace. Ace calls my name a few times, his voice echoing in the quiet hallway, but he doesn't try to catch up to me. I don't look back, but I do flip him the bird over my shoulder with one hand, pulling out my phone to text an affirmative to Judas with the other.

"Bright Eyes," Judas smiles at me when he opens the door, wire-framed glasses glinting from the barely shining sun that peeks through gray clouds. "Oh, how I've missed you."

"Shut the hell up."

Chapter 19

As two weeks go by, conversation from Ace is scarce, and conversation from Judas is at an all-time high. Ace has texted me a few times, refusing to grovel but also desperate for me to just accept the fact that we are in a relationship despite the fact that he never formally asked me out. I wonder to myself often, would I have agreed? If he were to romance me like those in the cheesy romcoms he makes me watch when I go over to his house, would I have said yes? If he came to my house and asked Prissy for permission to take me out? Would she have agreed herself, or would she have made me kill him right then and there?

I try not to think about it much, nor do I try to think about the little part of me that kind of misses him. I know it's wrong, but I find comfort in being around someone like Judas, not because I necessarily like him, but because I don't know what to do with myself solitarily anymore. I had gotten so used to being alone, to making friends with my own voice, to hugging myself, and patting my own back when I was upset. Prissy only gave me company when she needed something from me or wanted to play a part in front of other people.

I had grown so used to, so comfortable, with my alone time that I hadn't realized that life could be better with someone else who didn't routinely beat you when you made even the slightest mistake. And I missed that, craved it even; the companionship, the bantering, the jokes, and the laughter with someone that I told myself annoyed me to no end.

"Prissy really does suck as a caretaker if she's never let you listen to Prince," Judas tells me as he crosses his room, pulling out another vinyl. I squint my eyes at him in confusion from where I lay across the foot of his bed, head propped up with my hand.

"Prince of what?" I ask him, to which he turns around quickly on his heel, his eyebrows screwed up in worry.

"Oh dear heavens, you're gonna make me cry from sadness for you," he whispers, hands clutching his heart in exaggerated sympathy. But I only huff with a roll of my eyes, flopping down to lay flat on my back as I stare up at his pale-colored ceiling.

"Shut up," I murmur, to which he softly chuckles under his breath.

As the song plays softly, a guitar strum loud amongst the other instruments, a masculine voice crooning out, strong, from the old music box, I'm suddenly overwhelmed with emotion. Was this what it was like to be a teenager? Sitting in some guy's house, listening to music from the eighties? With my glasses off and my ambitions lowered, my body relaxed, smiling?

"I wonder what life would've been like if Prissy hadn't cursed us," I whisper suddenly, figure that he can't hear me from over the music, but Judas' eyes snap over to mine instantly, where he lays next to me on his bed. He gives me a sad little smile, his rounded eyes downturned, his fiddling fingers pausing in their ministrations as he crosses his arms over his chest.

"Yeah, me too," he answers. "It's why I tried to carve out some normalcy after I had become—estranged." He pushes the words out, foreign in his mouth, unsure what to call independence after the murder of his parents.

"I'm jealous of you," I admit under my breath, eyes suddenly watery as the loneliness, the realization, the hurt, and the pain all come to the surface. Here, with Judas, I can spill everything about myself that I never could with Ace. Here, with Judas, I can take my glasses off without worry of ending his life with a single look. Here, with Judas, I can cry because he's too big of a crybaby himself to ever make fun of me for it.

"I don't wanna do this for the rest of my life, Judas," I admit to him, trying to rapidly blink away tears in the quietness of his house, the music still a soft lull in the background. "I don't want to keep killing people. I don't want these eyes. I want to be normal, Judas."

"Hey," Judas calls to me from only a foot away. "Look at me." He doesn't speak until I do, after I roughly wipe my eyes with the back of my hand, turning on my side to face him. He matches my position, his head pillowed on his arm, the other curled against his belly as if he were afraid to reach out and touch my own. (He should be, shouldn't he? Or has my belly grown soft, open, and inviting without the looming fear of an attack when caressed?)

"We're gonna get through this, okay?" he promises me, his smile soft and sweet, although I can't seem to match it with my own, mouth watery and trembling.

"How? She'll find me wherever I go. I can't be cured. I can't be normal," I whisper to him, my voice barely carrying over my own harsh breaths, a panic attack looming over the horizon. But Judas bites the bullet, reaching out to rest his hand on my side, heavy and warm, its pressure grounding me ever so slightly to even out my breathing. When I calm, I open my eyes that I hadn't realized I had squeezed shut to find Judas's pink-lipped smile soft and, inviting and reassuring.

"We'll figure it out," he tells me, sure and easy, as if he held all the answers to every single stupid question in the world.

Maybe it is because I miss the companionship; maybe it's because I miss Ace; maybe it is because I miss my relationship-not-relationship; maybe it is because Judas looks at me so deeply in the eye with no malice or hatred, nothing but pure adoration and honesty and something almost like—

Maybe that's why I lean in to kiss him. It's too early, too fast. I just stopped trying to kill him less than a month ago, but I miss it. I miss the press of someone else's mouth against mine, I miss the warmth of a body firm upon my own, I miss the way my head tilts, and my body goes slack, and the softness of someone else's mouth against mine.

Kissing Judas is nothing like kissing Ace. With Ace, he was always so domineering, always so commanding, pushing, and strong, and I liked it for the most part. But with Judas, kissing him is like being equal on a battleground. Maybe I shouldn't refer to kissing him with such hostile imagery, but I can think of nothing else but equity.

He pushes, and I pull, I tilt, and he follows, I gasp, and he whimpers. He holds me by the waist, and I scratch my hands into fluffy hair. His glasses knock against my nose, and I want to tell him to pull them off, but when I open my eyes to look at him, they're skewed on his face so cutely that I can't imagine him without them.

"We shouldn't be doing this," I tell him between kisses, breathless. "I barely know you. I was just trying to kill you."

"We shouldn't," he agrees, but he doesn't pull away; if anything, he pulls me in closer until we are slotted against each other. His bed dips under our weight, and his hands become so feverish that I have to push him away by the shoulders in order to gain a single intake of breath.

We stare at each other for a long while, silent, our chests rising and falling quickly before they steady themselves out. The song on the vinyl has slid into another one, one of a more upbeat kind of tempo, and its change whispers to me that I might have overstayed my welcome.

"We shouldn't have done that." Judas pulls away first, though, wiping his mouth with the back of his hand as he sits up against the wall of his room. When I said it, I meant it, but it was something about hearing him confirm my own words that stabbed through my chest, sharp, its pain never ending. Before I can respond back, my phone beeps with a message. I pat for it in the tangled-up sheets, tapping on the screen, my heart dropping at the message.

Prissy
7:42 pm
You have a job tonight. Come home now.

Judas must be able to read what kind of message I received because he draws himself away from me even farther than before. His eyes suddenly can't meet my own, and he starts fiddling with a loose string on his black sweatpants. I open and close my mouth a few times, wonder if I should ask him why we shouldn't have kissed, what his reasonings were because they had to have been different from mine. Wonder if I should tell him what Prissy said, if he should stay indoors tonight, if he would want to see me tomorrow with fresh blood on my hands.

But instead, I say nothing of the sort. Just stand up, pick up my glasses from his desk, and slide them over my eyes. I toe on my shoes and zip up my hoodie, glancing at him, still withdrawn on the bed.

"Bye, Judas." I hope you can enjoy your normalcy while I have to be the monster of the town, I say internally. I don't wait for him to respond back before I'm rushing my way out of his house into the icy night air that swallows me whole before I can even gain the chance to catch my breath.

Judas didn't invite me over to his house for a few days after I last saw him. I'm not sure if it's because of the kiss or because of the gruesome death that the news displayed the next morning of some local coffee shop owner. But when he does ask me to come over, something about the formal message sends rocks to the pit of my belly.

Judas
2:19 pm
Hey, Areya. Are you free to come over today? Please let me know.

I don't respond to his message as I find myself walking to his house, thankful that Prissy wasn't home so I wouldn't have to explain my whereabouts to her. The entire walk there though, my heart is in my throat. There's an uneasiness that lingers in the air, a tether connecting my chest to Judas', a line that pulls us closer and closer on shaky ground.

The sky is beginning to rumble. Clouds cluster around each other, darkening the sky until pitter-patter raindrops start to slide over my cheeks and behind my glasses. I blink away the wetness, hands curling and unfurling in my hoodie pocket, jaw clenched and tight in nerves.

Something's wrong. Something bad is going to happen and I won't be able to stop it if I don't know what I should be expecting. Should I turn around? Should I prepare myself with a weapon? I glance over to the lined-up stones in one of Judas' neighbors' yards, wondering if they'll notice if it goes missing, if its returned and still slightly bloody. I pick it up and shove it in my pocket; just to be safe, I try to convince myself.

I stand on his doorstep for longer than necessary, trying to swallow down the feeling that something just isn't right. But when no boogeymen jump at me, when no police swarm his house with handcuffs and a gun pointed to my head, do I finally knock on the door?

He opens it in only seconds, and I know to trust my gut feeling. He doesn't greet me in his usual warm way, doesn't begin our endless banter of insults and jabs and chuckles that we try to hide under our breaths. Instead, Judas stands there as stiff as some marble statue handcrafted by only one of the world's greatest artists.

His hair is as fluffy as I remember, a single curl resting on the middle of his forehead, a few other pieces framing his sharp and angled face. The freckles that splatter on his cheeks seem to blend in more with his complexion from the darkness of the sky, his pale pink lips looking almost blue in the dimness. He wears a loose linen shirt despite the breeze that blows past us into his home, his tattoos on display, his baggy pants wrinkling around his bare feet.

"Areya," he says formally, making bile rise in the back of my throat. Living with Prissy for the majority of my life, I know when danger is near. I sense it like one would when hunted; the hairs on the back of my neck stand, my heart races entirely too fast, and I can't get my breath to even out just right.

Fight, fight, fight. Prissy has always hated it when I tried to run, hated it even more when I froze in shock. But did she really? She would only hit me harder if I tried to fight back; used my fists thrown up in defense like ammunition, like a release, like a sigh of understanding that she only hit me this hard because I fought back. Do I fight? Do I run?

"Spit it the hell out already," I snap at him, body stock-still on the outside despite the way I internally shake all over. I can barely feel my toes in the coldness of the outside elements, terrified to take a step in, terrified that I might not ever come back out the same way I entered.

"Can you come inside first?" Judas says, which doesn't make me feel any better that something is amiss. He doesn't console me, doesn't try to make me feel better, doesn't reassure me that it's all in my head. I can't seem to let out the breath that I'm holding in, and instead suck in the air even deeper, the coldness of it shocking my system.

Not another person. I can't take another person doing something to hurt me when I finally start to understand them.

I step inside. One foot in front of the other, left, right, left. I keep my shoes on; no point in getting comfortable as we robotically climb the stairs to his room. I expect the SWAT team to burst through the windows at any moment now. I expect him to bash me over the head with the bat I spotted behind his door last week. I hope everything and nothing, willing my demise to at least come quick and easy.

"I have something I need to share with you," Judas confesses, his hands shoved into his pants pockets as he holds his chin high in the air, his gaze focused on me but simultaneously unseeing. It's like he looks straight through me, like if he doesn't focus on my physicality then the next words that spill from him won't sting me as harshly.

"I didn't wanna kill her," I blurt out before he can say anything else, my hands wringing against the other in front of me. "She was only twenty; she still had so much life to live, but Prissy—"

"We all have choices, Areya." He cuts me off, his voice monotonous. It makes me ache entirely, my legs suddenly feeling heavy as I try to take a step toward him, but he takes one back. I reach a hand out to him, confusion bleeding on my face. Did we not have an understanding? Did he not get who I was, who we are? We're the only two people in the world like this; he knows I never wanted to live a life like this, right?

"But I didn't wanna," I find the tears slipping from my eyes before I can stop them, a hiccup escaping my throat as I try to grab at it to stop the sound from spilling out. My nails dig into the flesh there, droplets of blood squeezing out from underneath my flesh as I try to calm my breathing. I want Judas to rest a hand on me again, like how he did last time. I want him to tell me it's okay, that we'll get through it, that he's the only one who understands me. But he doesn't. Just stands there, his mouth twisting as he averts his eyes from the crimson that slithers down the slope of my neck to messy the collar of my white shirt, stained.

"You need to turn yourself into the CIA," Judas says, his voice cold and devoid of any and all emotion. I can feel my stomach sink to the ground; my breath bolts from my lungs as I take an involuntary step back.

"Judas, you know I can't do that," I spit at him, eyes squinted as I looked at him as if he'd grown two heads in the last minute. Everything in here feels wrong; it feels so wrong; where's the music playing on his vinyl? Why does he have his gloves on around me? Why is he treating me like this? I'm not trying to kill him anymore; why is he looking at me as if I'm some attack dog that's off-leash, foaming at the mouth, poised to maim at any given second?

"And why not?" he fires back just as quickly, taking a hand out of his pocket as he points to me accusatorially. "Areya, this monster has you killing innocent people for no good reason."

"They are good reasons!" I yell back at him, spit flying from my mouth as I step to him quickly. It's my nature to intimidate, to strike fear in an enemy's heart. But he's no longer an enemy of mine anymore, is he?

"Oh yeah? If they're so good, then how come she doesn't let you know why you're taking away a human life?" Judas counters back at me, standing firm in the middle of his room, his arms crossed over his chest. He doesn't waver at my snarl, at my bite, and it makes me feel as if I stand on shaky, unknown ground for entirely too long.

"Because the weapon doesn't need to know the destruction it causes; it just needs to know where to fire," I tell him, sucking in a shaky breath as I suddenly feel dizzy. I turn on my heel to face away from him, both hands rubbing harshly on my temples as I try to gather myself.

"You're not a weapon, Areya!" Judas shouts at me, the loudest I've ever heard him speak, and makes me flinch as his shadow looms over my shoulder. "You're a person, too, just like her other kids."

Time seems to stop at that very moment. The rain seems to quiet for just a second; the house goes still, and my breathing stops. I straighten up from where I've curled around myself, temples suddenly soothing their ache as the pain instead sends straight to the entirety of my body. I don't think I could move my fingertips if I tried.

"Other kids?" I ask him slowly as I turn around to face him; his mouth suddenly pulled tight, his eyes downcast on his carpeted floor. "What are you talking about?"

Judas doesn't say anything for a long while; instead, he throws the right words around in his mouth until he finds something that he can spit out. My heart races the entire time, my palms sweating, my glasses sliding down the bridge of my nose from the perspiration.

"This isn't her first time doing this; poisoning kids with her witchcraft before they're even born, preying on parents who only want healthy children, using them for her own destruction," Judas says slow and carefully, his words even and precise as he uses his hands to walk me through what he tells me. But I don't get it. I don't.

"I don't understand," I whisper, hands shaking at my sides as my throat constricts, my words struggling to push up from inside of me. "That, that doesn't make sense—"

"She's a witch, one that's hundreds of years old, Areya. Just look." Judas says frustratedly, turning to his computer that sits on his desk. He types a few things on it as I follow behind him like some ghost haunting a graveyard, a simple floater that can only take in what surrounds them in this newly developed world.

Judas pushes the computer to me when he opens a file entitled PRO-JECT995-CASE23-MERCI. I don't understand what I'm looking at until he clicks on a picture that couldn't have been taken this century. It's Prissy, sitting there with two small children in her lap, one a boy and the other a girl. The boy wears a mask over his mouth, and the girl wears a similar cover over her hands. I shake my head in confusion, trying to understand what this could mean when Judas begins clicking on file after file.

"I've been working with the CIA for five years now, trying to track her down," he mumbles under his breath as he shows me another picture, this time a drawing of Prissy that is unmistakably her and two other children with various covers on their body parts. I'm so caught up in seeing so many variations of the woman who I thought was only my mother that Judas' confession of his affiliations hit me too late, makes my heart pang nonetheless.

"We think this goes back to the late seventeenth century, this pattern of her cursing children to do her bidding. She's only repeating the cycle and will continue to do so until she's caught and stopped," he tells me quietly, pushing the computer in my direction as he shows me another picture that looks to be in more recent years than the others.

Prissy sits there, seemingly posed for some family photo, as if the normalcy she tries to create will wash away the sins she has cursed these children with. There's another boy and girl beside her, both around the same age. The boy smiles brightly, his hands covered in thick gloves as he crosses them in his lap. He looks pleasant, his shiny brown hair and bright green eyes conveying the normalcy that Prissy so obviously wanted to create, if not for the girl on the other side of her. Her hair is red and fluffy, just like Judas', except that it seems to waterfall down her back to settle around her midsection. She looks miserable, her mouth set in a thin line, her eyes covered in blacked-out glasses, her hands balled into fists as she sits with her back straight and uncomfortable.

"I've seen her before," I whisper, covering my mouth with my hand in shock. I've found her red hair in nooks of my room, found her crying out to me in dreams, found her ghost haunting the hallways in what must've been her house originally. She was only a child.

"Priscilla killed her days before she turned nine because she rebelled against her. She killed the boy only a year later when he missed her too much," Judas comments monotonously, making bile rise in my throat. I have to swallow thickly as my eyes cloud with tears, suddenly feeling uneasy on my feet as I sway, grabbing onto the side of the desk tightly.

"But we," I swallow. "But she doesn't kill kids; said they're innocent, untainted—"

"Until they refuse to do her bidding," Judas cuts me off, leveling me with a look that screams how stupid and gullible I must be for believing anything that she could say. I feel warm tears sliding down my cheeks before I can register my eyes welling, wiping them away numbly with the tips of my fingers as I look up at him confusedly.

"Judas, I don't understand," I repeat to him, seemingly the only thing I can produce from my slowly closing throat.

"You have to turn yourself in, Areya. We have to protect the world from evils like her," Judas tells me, touches me for the first time since I came here, and holds my hands tightly in his. It doesn't feel the same when his gloves are on and my glasses are pushed up the bridge of my nose. I try to take a step back, body curling in on itself, but he holds onto me even tighter, his eyes wild and desperate.

"But she'll kill me," I whisper, my voice broken and hoarse as the realization comes crashing down entirely too fast, entirely too hard, on top of me. Prissy will kill me. She's done it before to children she's taken in, ruined, poisoned. If I didn't obey her, if I were to betray her in any way, she would kill me. Snuff me out as if I never mattered, replace me with another child, find another place to live, and continue the cycle until the end of time. She'll kill me.

I have always imagined what death was like whenever I took out a life. Would it be kind? Would it nurture? Would it hold? Would death grab onto me tightly and pull me down until my screams were overtaken by fire and flames? Would I see Ben Foster there?

"I won't let her," Judas whispers, but even he doesn't believe the words he utters from his quivering mouth. He doesn't stand a chance against her, especially if I can't even find the courage to raise my voice at her.

"I never wanted this, Judas. Any of this," I tell him as honestly as I can, a flash of all the people I've taken out overcoming my vision. My knees buckle, and Judas holds onto me even tighter, a promise to never let me fall as long as I hold onto him.

"But you have to do the right thing," he whispers to me, his voice dropping even further as he tilts his head to me, a secret shared between us. "If you don't, then I will," he promises, his eyes suddenly hardening as I reel away from him.

My heart drops to the pit of my belly, an array of emotions overcoming me. I straighten myself out as anger, always there, consistent, reliable anger floods to the forefront. I rip my hands from his own, my eyes wild with rage as I stand straighter, roughly wiping the tears off of my cheeks as I sneer at Judas.

"I hate you," I whisper before my voice crescendos. "I hate you!" I yell again as I shove him roughly in the chest. Judas stumbles back, his face going stony again like when he first opened his door for me. He doesn't try to fight back, stumbling into the wall that I back him into.

"I never wanted to be a killer. I never wanted to gut people, never wanted to slit throats, or wash blood out of shoelaces before I learned how to do basic math. I never wanted to kill mothers while their children watched." I couldn't seem to catch my breath as my body suddenly went limp at the confession. This time, he doesn't try to help me up, hold onto me like a lifeline, keep me afloat. Instead, he watches me, his nose turned up in the air, his eyes as cold as the rain that smacks against the windows.

Judas doesn't say anything for a long while as I sob, my hands fisted in my hair as I tear out chunk after chunk, my scalp throbbing from the vicious burn that I pay little mind to. He only waits until my sobs quiet ever so slightly before he steps forward.

"It doesn't matter. You know what you have to do," he states, voice devoid of all emotion. He doesn't say anything else as he steps around me, pattering out of his room as I yell at him over my shoulder.

"I hate you."

I don't see much of him when I collect myself enough to leave. Everything is a blur as I stumble down the steps out through the front door, tears wetting my face as they mix in with the rainwater. I don't think I have ever cried like this, not when I was born, not after I killed Kelly and Chad, not even when Prissy had beaten me black and blue. So why did I cry this hard when a boy I had known for only such a short amount of time betrayed me?

The house is empty when I come stumbling in. Prissy is still nowhere to be found, unaware of the threat that lingers over us. My mind skids to a halt at the thought of her, the only person who stood for me in this world, who showed me who she was from the very beginning, who made me believe that I was the most important thing to ever happen to her in her life.

How could she? How could I only be a simple cog in her machinery? For so long had she emphasized that I was the foundation of it all, that I mattered more than anything, that I was irreplaceable in the grander scheme of things. But now, to know that I wasn't the first, most likely won't be the last, it hurts more than her fists when they pound into my very flesh. How could she have done this time and time and time again to innocent children?

How many parents has she taken advantage of? Convinced their own children to kill them so that she could sink her claws into them?

Why...why was I not special enough to be the first? Was I at least the longest-lasting one? Had she kept me around all this time because she understood what she had to do, what lengths she had to go to keep me leashed, tethered? Did she love me, at least? Did she love me enough not to kill me before my ninth birthday because I no longer wanted this life?

Everything in front of me blurs as I stumble throughout the house, trying to make sense of everything that I have ever known. This house is not mine. This life is not mine. This story is not mine—simply a repeat offense made by a witch who wants to cleanse the world for whatever reason she'll never share with me.

So what's the point of any of this anymore? Of jumping from state to state because I got sloppy? Of killing people for a reason I'll never understand. Of getting physically ill from it? Of deriving pleasure from it when I think I'm only serving my due diligence? Am I bad? Have I always been bad—was I rotten before I even left my mother's womb? Do I even have the right to call her my mother?

A broken sob escapes me as I try to climb the steps, clutching at my head as the world around me spins entirely too fast for me to be able to keep up with it. I collapse against the railing, chest tightening, wondering—had Prissy chased her down these same steps when she killed her? The little redheaded girl; did Prissy knock her down, stomp her out, eliminate her, take her out like a mere bug beneath her shoe? Did she at least hold her tiny little lifeless body one last time when she took her last breath?

I have to clutch my stomach to keep the contents of my scarce breakfast down. It would be more stomach acid than anything; I don't remember the last time Prissy went to the store and cared enough to buy me ingredients, even if she wouldn't feed me herself.

The trek up the stairs is more effort than I expect it to be, and by the time I've reached the top step, my body collapses. I have to drag myself down the hall to reach my room, already knowing what I have to do.

I can't tell the CIA what sins I've committed, how many, how many state lines I've crossed, how many bodies I've hidden, how many I've left to rot in plain sight, how many times I've enjoyed the hunt.

But I also can't tell Prissy what our options are. She would only kill me for letting us get caught, for making that mistake in Arizona, for trusting someone that wasn't her, for getting sloppy. She'd snuff me out sooner than I'd have the chance to grovel for my mistakes, and as selfish as I am, I don't want to go by her hand.

So I decide to go by my own.

I stumble through my belongings pushed into the back of the closet of 'devices' I use when Prissy wants it messy. I can't hold back the bile this time at the thought of it, at the sight of flecks of blood that I couldn't fully scrub out. Pulling out some durable rope that I've used to strangle a woman before, I hold it in my shaking hands, my tears blocking my vision as I ask myself if this is the only option for me.

I can't go to jail. I can't betray Prissy. But I can't live like this anymore, either. So I do what I must.

I stumble over to the stool under the vanity, dropping to my knees as I realize that this was hers, too. I rest my forehead on it, sobbing uncontrollably as I apologize over and over to the little girl who just wanted to be good. To the little girl who was taken away from this world before she was even born through the curse that ran through her veins. She had eyes like mine; she must've been so strong, so much stronger than me. I ask her to lend me that same strength wherever her spirit lies.

I pull the bench from its resting spot until I stand underneath my fan. I can't see my hands in front of me from the tears that spill down my cheeks, my hands shaking the entire time as I knot the rope once, twice, until it forms a noose.

I look around the room once more, see that little girl and so many before her. See Kelly and Chad. See the woman in Arizona who just wanted to live out her life with her babies. See Ace crying on that football field after I snuffed out his only living parent. I took them away, all of them. It's only fair that I return the favor.

Placing the rope around my neck, I take in a deep, shuddering breath. I have to do this. To balance out the world, to cleanse away sins that I should've never committed, I have to do this. As I go to kick out the bench from beneath me, a soft, seemingly bored voice freezes me in my spot.

"Stop being dramatic, and get down from there already."

Chapter 20

"You know, I shouldn't have said anything and let you do it," Prissy says, leaning against the doorway of my room nonchalantly. She looks at her bubblegum pink nails, bored, before glancing up at me from under her thick lashes. "See how long you could last before you cried for me to save you."

At her words, I collapse with a sob, ripping the noose from around my throat as I go tumbling to the floor, the same floor that the little red-headed girl must've cried upon for countless nights. I can't seem to catch my breath, my throat closing, hiccuping sobs loud in the silent room as I gag from the sputtering coughs I can't seem to control. My head spins as I hear Prissy scoff under her breath at the sight of me, the spit trailing from my lips as I struggle to catch my breath.

"You're pathetic, Areya. Truly." Prissy sneers, pushing herself off of the doorway, finally marching into my room. She circles me like a vulture, all color drained from her eyes, seemingly black and unforgiving, where she looks down her nose at me. She kicks my flank softer than she ever has, as if a nudge to see if I'll look her in the eye when I beg for her forgiveness for trying to disarm her favorite weapon.

"I'm sorry, Prissy, I'm so—"

"Save it." She cuts me off sharply, makes me swallow my words with the venom that drips from her pink-painted mouth. She looks at me once more with such disgust in her eyes, her lips curled up, that I can only cower in fear that she may spit on me next. It wouldn't be the first time. "Get yourself cleaned up already. I can't stand the sight of you."

And with that, Prissy stomps out of my room as quickly as she enters it, with a huff and a few mumbled expletives said under her breath. I lay there as I hear her stomp down the steps, before she begins banging around in the kitchen. It's a signal that I better be up by the time she finishes fixing whatever monstrosity that she calls a meal and sitting with her at the dinner table.

With great effort, do I finally heave myself up into a sitting position. My limbs ache, a heaviness settling so deep into my bones that it takes all of my remaining strength to simply straighten out my arms. My tears never slow, but I can't focus on the way they blur my vision now. No, I have to stand up, shake away the stiffness that has made a home within my body, find it in me, somehow, the ability to put one foot in front of the other until I make my way downstairs to the dinner table.

Prissy doesn't acknowledge me when I come down, as she busies herself with scrambling eggs on too-high heat, but I don't dare correct her. The last time I did, she flung the still-scorching food at me and laughed when I screamed at the pain from it burning the sides of my face. Instead, I keep my lips sealed shut tightly, try to will away the tears that still leak slowly from my blurry eyes.

By the time she sets the plate of scrambled eggs and sliced-up strawberries in front of me, the tears have come to a slow stop, my cheeks still sticky in the tracks that they have left in their wake. She slides over a fork to me, her eyes never leaving my puffy face, as she searches around for answers that I do not have in me to share with her.

I eat slowly, my hands still trembling, gripping the fork entirely too tightly, but she doesn't say anything. She waits until I have finished my eggs and have moved onto the strawberries to stand and get me a bottle of water from the fridge. Then she hands it over to me silently, sitting before me once more as she rests her chin on her fists, her gaze pulling me apart with every passing second.

"Care to explain to me why you just tried to kill yourself?" Prissy asks finally, after I have guzzled down half of the water bottle, the cold a shock to my system that helps ground me ever so slightly. I mull over my options, what will become of me, of Judas, if I were to tell her the truth of the situation.

Should I prepare her for the inevitability of getting caught? Should I warn her that we have been watched since we moved here? That the CIA waits for us to either come crawling to them with our tails tucked between our legs or for them to tackle us where we stand and place a bullet in the back of our heads before we even have a chance to plead our case?

"I'm just tired," I say instead after a long stretch of silence. She doesn't believe me, which is obvious, but she pretends to care either way.

"Of what?" Her tone snappy, impatient, as if my simple reasoning will never make any kind of sense to her.

"Of living." I laugh humorlessly, my shoulders raising up to my ears as an almost delirious smile starts to form on my cheeks, my eyes watering once more. "Of having to be me."

"And what's wrong with you?" She bites, her teeth bared, her mouth all predator, and my exposed neck all prey. I can only shake my head at her, fisting my hair in my hands once more, feeling the already strained strands start to pull from their roots again as I explode at her.

"Priscilla, I am a monster!" I cry to her, eyes pleading for her to understand that no person was meant to live like this. Like some cooped-up attack dog that only ever gets to see the warm light of the sun when she shreds a so-called enemy to ribbons, like some handmade monster set loose upon an unsuspecting village, like some experiment, some non-human thing, like a bomb, packaged, armed to explode and take out everyone around her.

"You have turned me into a killer," I whisper the last word as if terrified someone would hear me, would bust down our doors and kill without question. She only reels back at the sight of me, her thin lips curled back in disgust as she points a manicured finger in my direction, the skin thin and wrinkled in the bright lighting of the kitchen.

"I did no such thing. You were a killer from the moment you were forced into this world." She spits the words back out at me as if disgust lines her tongue at the mere mention of my emergence into a body that has never fit me quite right. I have never talked back to her like this, had it beaten into me that whatever she said was the truth, that there was never any room to argue back. But I am so tired of everything that I cannot find it in me to be afraid at this moment, not when I was this close to jumping off of that stool with a noose around my neck.

"Because of your power. Because of what you did to me," I bark, pointing an accusatory finger in her direction that she smacks away. The sting is numbed by the anger that floods through me. I was meant to be normal, to be doted on, to be loved, to be soft, to be kind. I was not meant to be predacious and ugly and cruel and mean, and she did all of that to me by taking away the choice of what life I could have lived when she decided to curse me.

"What your selfish pricks you call parents asked me to do to you!" Prissy roars, her chair falling as she stands quickly to her feet, her finger now in my face. She pokes me roughly in the cheek, and I know better than to swat her away, but I don't cower in the presence of her fury, either. Instead, I curled my lip back, my eyes heating as I wished so desperately that my powers worked on her the same way they worked on regular humans.

"They were just vain!" I shout at her, my arms spread wide at my sides. "They just wanted a normal child! They didn't want this." I emphasize the last word with a flick of my hand over my body; my face, my eyes that glow an unnaturally eerie color that reflects into Prissy's own blue ones. She seems to puff up her chest for a second before she deflates, unnatural calmness blanketing her face as she rights her chair and sits back down across from me. Her demeanor makes every hair on my body stand, my mouth going dry as the room settles into eerie silence.

Is this it? Will this be my end, at the dinner table, in front of the fruit she so delicately cut for me? In front of the cold water bottle she had retrieved for me because it helps calm the body during panic attacks. Will she kill me with at least an ounce of love in her cold gaze? Will she hold my dying body with the nurturing hands only a mother could have?

"So you're ungrateful, is what I'm hearing," Prissy says softly, leaning back into her chair as she crosses her arms over her body. It feels like a setup, like an invitation to a battle I already know I won't win. So I deflate in my seat and eat a few slices of strawberry; their taste sour and bitter, my mouth numb. When I'm finished, I sit back in my seat, my eyelids heavy as I look at her with a pleading kind of stare that I know she loathes on me.

"I am just—just tired," I say slowly, sucking my bottom lip into my mouth before I lower my gaze to the table between us. "Can I go lay down now, mother?" I ask, trying to appeal to her in any way I can. But she only scoffs in disgust, snatching my cutlery away as she stomps over to the kitchen sink, throwing the glass inside without it ever shattering somehow.

"Gods, don't 'mother' me now. The sound of it coming from your mouth makes me sick." Prissy spits, her back to me as she flings ash-blond hair over her shoulder. She doesn't look at me as she begins to furiously scrub the dishes, muttering, "Just leave."

I do as I'm told without much fight, breathing in a sigh of relief when I reach the stairs, knowing that I live to see another day. I don't know if I'm thankful or resentful, jealous of the rotting bodies that get to lay peacefully, quietly, in the ground beneath us.

Life is cruel; I think to myself as the awful realization that I still have to go to school today settles in. Getting ready feels like a chore, my body stiff and locked up on me as I ignore the still-hanging rope on my fan. I'm not sure when the appropriate time would be for me to take it down, so I leave it there, still swinging somehow in the stale, rigid air of the room.

Prissy didn't come out of her room that morning, and I'm not sure why I expected her to. She was disgusted at the mere sight of me yesterday, but I still figured she would come down, give me some ominous warning about the day, and make herself coffee before stomping upstairs. I don't know why I still wanted to see her when she was willing to let me die yesterday.

But she wasn't actually willing, was she? She could've stood there while I jumped, laughing to herself at the sound of me choking, of my eyes bulging, of my body going limp. She could've turned around completely and only come back to collect my body before she began hunting for new children to curse.

But she didn't. In a way, her cruel and taunting words had saved my life. She had even fixed me a small, easily digestible meal afterward, gave me water, and helped me calm from my earlier panic attack. That meant she loved me, didn't it? Her care for me after my almost selfish act of taking away her best, her only, her favorite weapon? She loved me in her own way, and somehow, that was enough for me in the moment.

I couldn't bear eating anything, my stomach feeling heavy with lead from the previous night, but I still fixed Prissy her favorite breakfast: cinnamon French toast, hard-boiled eggs, salted potatoes, freshly brewed caramel coffee, two slices of maple bacon. She didn't get up when I finished, but after I left the house and got a few paces down the street, I looked over my shoulder and saw her sitting at the table, digging into her breakfast. The sight made my heart tighten in my chest at the thought that she waited for me to leave, that she was still disgusted by me.

I try to ignore the pang in my chest throughout the school day. Everything passes by in a blur, most of the classes coming to a slow as prom and graduation season approaches. The dance is in another week or so, and I'm sure I won't be able to make it either way. I'll most likely be dead by Prissy's hands or in jail by the CIA's hands. I've never really cared for prom anyway.

(I try to convince myself that it never really mattered, that a night where you spend so much money for just a few hours will never be worth it, but the books I snuck in under Prissy's nose always made it seem so glamorous. A little piece of me, a tiny little sliver, had the ache in my chest to go anyway, to avoid Judas, to hide away from Prissy, to show up on prom night with a simple dress from the little bit of money I had. I'll never be able to get that.)

I try not to let the realization bother me that I only have until Judas decides my time is up on making a decision before I am carted off, never to see the light of day again or buried among the soft soil of earth. My head is down as I walk through the halls, too caught up in my future and what will become of me when I have to come to a screeching halt at the sight of shoes planted right in front of me.

"Hey," Ace says, his voice quieter than I think I've ever heard it. I haven't seen him in days, maybe a week or so. Time seems to be slipping away from me these days, everything blurring together. I blink up at him, but he can't see it. He can only see the tilt of my head, the blacked-out lenses angling up in his direction, the set line my mouth is in.

"I don't have time for your games today, Ace." I snap at him, but even he knows that it doesn't hold the same malice that it used to. I'm tired. I'm tired and I'm angry and—and I am terrified. I don't know what will become of me, or Judas, or Prissy, or my entire world, and I cannot stand the thought of Ace finding out the ugly truth about me. I try to push past him, but he catches my elbow, his grip soft and gentle.

"No games," he says, his voice low. He looks around the hallway at the nosy gazes before pulling me to an emptier hallway. The lockers in this section are burnt orange, ugly, and loud, but he somehow fits amongst it all. Somehow makes, the colors look pretty against the brown of his skin, the flecks of gold in his eyes. He looks sincere, his gaze downturned, his mouth parted, his head slightly bowed.

"I'm sorry," Ace states plainly, and I can feel my entire body tensing up. I don't deserve his apologies; does he know what kind of monster stands in front of him right now? Does he know that the CIA has most likely seen him and heard him talking to me? Does he know that they will tell him who killed his father in cold blood? That he kissed that same girl only days after she washed her hands of his father's blood?

"Bubbles? Did you hear me?" Ace waves a large palm in front of my face, making me flinch in the process. His face softens at that, his hands falling slack to his sides. My shoulders are hiked up to my ears and I can feel the tears pricking my eyes already.

Does he know? Does he know? Does he know?

"I'm sorry, too. For being so shitty to you, Ace," I tell him softly, sure that this will be my last time speaking to him. Who knows when Judas will decide that my time is up? That the future of my fate rests in his hands?

It's ironic, though, isn't it? That I fear the moment that my time will be up, unfairly taken away by someone who is less than deserving. By someone who is greedy and following orders and just another puppet for someone else's bidding? Isn't it ironic? Isn't it funny?

"That's just your personality, Bubs," Ace says, making me break out from my own thoughts with a surprised chuckle. He smiles wide at that, his brackets colored red, his grin stretching across his face as he laughs, too.

"While I am sorry for having this personality," I start when our laughter dies and the bell rings for class again. "I do stand on the fact that you cannot own me just because you want to. I'm not an object." I say the last words slowly, unsure if I even believe myself.

To Prissy, I am her weapon. I am something meant to be owned, to be controlled, to be wielded. To Judas, I am a person with their own thoughts and feelings, with control over their own actions, with autonomy. With Ace—who am I? Was I ever meant to actually be someone more than the damaged goods that I came into this world as?

"I know," Ace says softly, nodding once as he presses his pink and brown lips together, licking at his bottom lip once. "And I'm sorry for that, truly, I am."

"Thank you, Ace," I say after a beat of silence, my words thick in my throat. I don't think anyone's ever apologized to me and meant it, especially not as sincerely as Ace did. He bows his head to me ever so slightly, as if in submission, as if remorseful of his actions, his words. I have to blink away the wetness of my eyes, looking away at the shuffling crowds of students hurrying to get to class.

"Would it be bad timing if I asked if you still wanted to go to the dance with me?" Ace says softly, so soft I could barely hear him over the conversations of other students. My body tenses at the words, my heartbeat jumping to my throat as I think about when he asked me to the dance the first initial time. How everything seemed so simple back then, how life didn't seem as complicated as it is now. And that said a lot.

"As friends?" I ask, my head tilted to the side as I look up at him, at the curls that shadow his eyes for only a second. Ace smiles again, but it's not as big as it usually is. His smile dimmed, a fraction of the sunshine rays he beams at me whenever I insult him or go to throw another punch at his head.

"As whatever you want us to be," Ace says slowly, carefully, dipping his chin once in confirmation. I stand there, digging the toe of my shoes into one of the cracks in the hallway floors, letting the question stew in my mind for entirely too long.

Did it even matter if we went as friends? Would I even be able to make it to the dance itself before I am either killed or jailed? Does it even matter, since he'll be heartbroken anyway, since I'll never understand what it's like to just be a high schooler going to their senior prom? Nothing matters, does it?

"I'll see," I say solemnly, already knowing my answer to his question. But Ace only chuckles under his breath, used to my usual dodgy antics. He checks his phone as it beeps before he begins turning on his heel. As he leaves, he tosses over his shoulder, "I'll pick you up Friday at seven, then, yeah?"

"Yeah—wait," I say, stomach sinking to the floor as Ace pauses a few steps away from me. "Did you say Friday? I thought the dance wasn't for another week."

"Yeah, a week ago, maybe." Ace scoffs at me playfully, pointing to the calendar on his phone that shows that today is Wednesday. How could time ever move that fast without me being able to catch up to it?

"But it's two days from now. You gotta dress, right? Do you need me to take you?" he asks, concern lacing his voice as he fully turns to me. My mouth opens and closes a few times, unsure of how to answer, if I had more time than I originally thought.

"No, it's okay. I'll get it myself," I finally manage to spit out, smiling ever so softly to him as I turn on my heel away from him. "See you then."

"See ya, Bubs."

Judas
2:19 pm

Hey Areya. I know this is a big decision, but have you come to terms with what you'll do yet? I can only hold off my contacts until Friday night. I'd rather give you to them than have them come to you and her. It won't be pretty if they do. Please make the right decision. The world needs you, too.

Bubbles

2:21

Ace. I've changed my mind. Can we go dress shopping tomorrow?

Ace

2:22

Whatever you want, bubs.

Chapter 21

Our school lets the seniors out three hours early to prepare for prom tonight. Ace meets me by my locker with a smile much dimmer than I am used to seeing on him, but a smile nonetheless. He walks me to his car silently, opening my door for me without question when I make my way around. I want to reject the gesture and tell him I'm not worthy of his kindness, but then I'd have to explain all of my sins to him. I don't think that's a conversation I'll ever be ready for.

The drive over to the shopping plaza is a quiet one between Ace and me. Although the tension isn't there anymore, it's not the same as it used to be just mere weeks ago. Ace holds on to the steering wheel a little tighter than necessary, his music a touch too loud, but I don't say anything. The pounding in my head from the beat feels like an impending punishment for all that I will endure after today. I should get used to the uncomfortableness, the fear. I'll be sitting in these sensations for the rest of my life if they do not put me to death sooner rather than later.

Ace pulls up to a department store, and I'm reminded of just how small this place is. Everything in the windows looks cheap and tacky, but most of the materials are better than anything I've ever worn while being with Prissy.

My mother would dress me up like a doll, I remember, before I murdered her. Even when my gaze made her uncomfortable, she'd sometimes find it in herself to use me as the little plaything she wanted. Never a daughter, really, just a mini version of herself that she could mold into her likeness. I always hated the dresses, the sparkles, the parading around as if I were less than human—an object to dress and play with.

But I find myself missing it: the little girl with olive skin, long curly hair, and too-steel-gray eyes that always went unblinking. Standing in front of the too-big mirrors in her bathroom, my hair pulled into Bantu knots, my dress a soft yellow, my Mary Janes polished, my stance poised. She was looking at me over my shoulder, her cheek nuzzled against mine, mesmerized by how much I looked like her on her first runway at just eight years old, my father looking over her shoulder at me fondly.

Father. I hadn't referred to them as my parents in so long, but there's something about knowing the inevitability of your future that makes the little things seem so trivial. If they were still my parents, the CIA wouldn't be hunting me right now if I hadn't chosen the witch over them. It's all my fault—it's always been my fault, hasn't it?

"Ready to go shopping?" Ace asks from beside me, where I've been standing in front of the window, staring at the toddler dress on display. Orange and bright and tacky, but childlike and full of love anyway. I nod wordlessly before I step inside.

We shop around quietly, for the most part, waving away annoyed workers who only come up to us because it is mandatory. There are a few other kids from school here, looking for last-minute things, side-eyeing me every time Ace holds out a dress for me. They look at me with such envy I wonder if my skin would start to sizzle away with every stare dipped in hatred. Ace pays them no mind.

"Do you know what you'd prefer?" Ace asks me, once we've walked around the store once already and I still haven't picked anything out. "In terms of style, or color, or length?"

"I'm not sure," I lie, my words soft under my breath. It feels hard to breathe, for some reason, to be surrounded by everything soft, everything I was never able to be. To be surrounded by what could've been me if I had stayed with my parents, if I hadn't let Prissy sway me, if I'd let them continue to treat me like the little doll they wanted.

I wonder how many dresses I would have had if they were still alive. Kelly had so many. Our house was so big, entirely too spacious for just two parents and a child. I remember hearing them rearrange one of her many closets while I was still in her womb to become the nursery for me when I would finally be born. I remember hearing her huff about how she'd have to cram her pageant dresses and runway outfits into the room on the other side of the house. I remember Chad telling her she wouldn't be able to fit them all in right now, anyway. I remember their laughter, how I felt as though I laughed alongside them when they both laid their hands over her belly.

"Something sparkly, maybe," I mumble, flashes of Kelly trying on luxurious outfits she'd been sent for my first birthday party, how lavish she wanted to look. Her skin was midnight dark and soft, a black dress short and puffy, accentuating her lithe curves. Chad kissed her gently as he noted how beautiful she looked.

The dress that Ace pulls from the rack is a sad comparison to the designer dress my mother wore in that memory, but it reminds me of her. It is pitch black, sparkly beads dotted along the edges of the dress, some already falling off from the cheap material. Its sleeves are puffy, stopping at the wrists, the neckline straight across the chest so that it's meant to fall off the shoulders. It stops just below the knee, the tulle fabric beneath it looking itchy and uncomfortable, but it is perfect, somehow, anyway.

Would it be cruel to want to be molded after the woman who birthed me, who I later killed? Is it cruel to want to look like her in my final moments, during the last time I could truly be happy? Is it cruel that I wish my hair were longer, that I took care of my curls the same way she did, so I could put them into Bantu knots like she always used to?

"You like this?" Ace asks quietly when he notices my silence. "It'll match my tux if you do. But if you don't want to match, that's cool, too."

I can hear the feigned nonchalance of his tone, the struggle not to come off so strongly as he used to in the past. I bite the inside of my cheek until it stings, nodding my head quickly as I take the dress from his hands.

"It's perfect," I whisper to him, my voice drowned out by the pop music blaring out over the speakers. I find my size as I finger through the racks, pulling it out and examining it once more in the fluorescent lights of the store. I try to bite back the pinpricks of tears threatening to cloud my vision. This could be the dress I'm arrested in. The dress that I am killed in, muddying it with my blood and my tears and my anger and regret. This final piece, something I've never been allowed since I've embraced my true powers, could be the final thing that I am seen in. And for just a moment, I'm okay with that.

Ace sits in one of the scratchy, stained chairs as I slide into a dressing room. It's messy, clothes strewn along the floor, the mirror dirty and covered in fingerprints. But I can't find it in me to care as I slip meticulously out of my own clothes. My phone buzzes in my hoodie pocket as I drop my clothes to the floor, but I can't look at it right now. I can't let the reality that looms over me shadow this moment; this moment that is finally, for once in my life, for me. About me. Not overshadowed by my famous parents or my witch mother.

No, this moment is for me. Something I've never been able to have in the entirety of my life, and goddammit, I deserve it.

Standing in my bra and panties, I stare at myself in the mirror. Slide my shades off ever so slowly and look at the entirety of me, laid bare, through too-gray eyes. Prissy once said they almost looked lifeless, so soft and shaded that the color almost bled into the whites of my sclera. Judas once called them pretty in their uniqueness, the rarity of being able to look at something so otherworldly without dying seconds later.

I hated them. Hated that they didn't look like Prissy's, or like Kelly's or Chad's. Hated that a key piece of my identity was altered because they couldn't be happy with a child that was less than perfect. Hated that they looked too evil to ever be human, to be normal, good. I wonder if I had been born regular if my eyes would be brown like my mother's or green like my father's.

"You need some help in there, Bubs?" Ace says quietly, startling me out of my own head. I shut my lids tightly in case he peeked his head in and saw me in the mirror—in case I paralyzed him to stone like some gorgon with unearthly eyes.

"No, I got it. Thanks," I say, clipped, my tone rushed and quiet. Ace only hums in acknowledgment, and I don't open my eyes again until I hear his footsteps pad away from the dressing room.

I let out a breath once I heard him sit down in the too-squeaky chairs, finding it in me to take the dress off the rack. It's cheap-looking, scragglier than anything Kelly would be caught dead in. But I find myself putting it on anyway, the process robotic and stiff as I unfurl my limbs to step into the dress. I pull it up slowly, watching how the midnight black of the dress seems to radiate the olive of my skin, a compliment that I didn't know was possible on my complexion.

I slide it up until it rests against my collarbone, pulling back to zip myself up. I should've asked Ace to do it, to feel his touch on my skin once more, but I know that that's selfish of me. I shouldn't let him get any closer, knowing that this would be my last night with him. So I struggle with my zipper by myself, huffing out a heavy breath once I'm finally settled.

My throat closes up at the realization that I look like Kelly standing here—a cheap imitation of her, but her nonetheless. I wonder if, should people look hard enough, they would find the missing child Vivienne McDowell—if they would see Kelly's sharp cheekbones and full lips in my features. I turn away from the mirror before it becomes too much, picking up and sliding on my glasses before I push back the curtain of the dressing room.

Ace is on his phone when I walk out, but once he hears my shuffling steps, he looks up and his face—it pains me to see the admiration there. To see something else I'm not ready to confront as his face falls so softly into the sweetest smile I think I've ever seen him muster.

"You are so beautiful, Areya," Ace says softly, standing up to see me in all of my glory. I can only bite my bottom lip to keep from crying at the guilt, at the weight that rests so heavy on my shoulders that I just want to collapse into the tiniest ball on the floor in front of him.

"So are you, Ace," I counter, stepping up onto the little platform in front of the wall-sized mirrors to admire myself. But it becomes overwhelming, seeing so much of a dead woman, that I watch Ace over my shoulder as he stands to the side of me.

"But I'm not dressed up?" he says, his mouth crooking up to the side in a smile, his head tilted at me. I can only muster up the tiniest, weakest little smile as I dip my chin to him, feeling more beautiful than I should.

"You don't have to be," I whisper to him, watching him watch me through the mirrors. He walks around me as if in admiration of what I look like, of how the slim curve of my shoulders are bared, more skin than I've ever allowed to be shown in my life. He notes the scars that Prissy has left and doesn't say anything about them, just watches me and watches me, as if to rip his eyes away would be an unforgivable offense.

And everything is going so well—well enough that I should already be prepared—for the inevitable, for the other shoe to drop, for every good thing that's ever happened to me to come crumbling down right before my very eyes. As I stare at myself in the mirror, Ace's presence gentle and steady beside me, I meet the eyes of another over my shoulder.

I look elegant in the silky material. I look normal despite the blacked-out glasses and the faint scars that should have paralyzed me years ago. I look beautiful and suddenly not when I find Judas standing there. He looks out of breath, his curls in disarray on his head, his steel-blue eyes wide and alert. I choke on my breath as he pauses at the sight of me: pretty and elegant, everything I'm not, everything I've always wished to be.

It's vulnerable, for some reason, seeing him see me like this. Like a child being caught playing dress-up in her mother's clothes, with too-red lipstick smudged over thin lips, with baggy dresses and too-big shoes falling from my tiny form. I've only ever been just a small girl, secretly, deep down, in my most intimate thoughts and wonders. To see this little girl so exposed by not only Ace but by the man who was working against me the whole time suddenly makes me feel naked.

Ace notices Judas behind us only a split second after I do, but his reaction is much quicker. I hadn't realized just how stiff I had gotten, how my breath caught so tightly in my throat. My hands grip the skirt of the dress so tightly I fear it may rip in my too-rough palms—I've always been too rough. Too strong, never girl enough, too much of a weapon, of something steel and strong and mighty, never just a girl.

"What do you want, freak?" Ace spits at Judas, tilting his chin up to him through the reflection of the mirror. But Judas only stares at me, his eyes round, his gloved hands (black and plain) trembling at his sides as he takes me in. He fiddles with his phone in one hand, the other twitching unsure beside him. He swallows when he meets my eyes, and I know he can't see me, but I look away. It's almost like he can see right through the lenses, with the way his face falls ever so slightly.

"I need to talk to you, Areya," Judas says, and it's a sting to hear my real name. This must be it. This must be the moment a raid comes swarming in on me, to arrest me, to drag me away in a dress too good for filth like me to ever step inside of.

"Alone," Judas tacks on when Ace doesn't move, finally looking to the other man. But Ace only crosses his arms over his chest, puffed out, his mouth pulled in such a severe frown, I feel like a small child being scolded by their father. I can't meet either of their eyes; the store is suddenly too small, and the dress is suddenly too tight. Off. I need it off. I can't breathe; I need it off.

Before either of them can say anything else, I find myself scurrying from the platform in front of the too-big mirrors. The mirrors that reflect every ugly thing inside of me, bleeding out through my pores, dirtying a dress I could only dream of wearing in another universe where I'm born normal, and my parents loved me no matter what I looked like. Where I'm just another eighteen-year-old girl getting ready to go to prom with a guy she's been seeing, with a guy she can look in the eye without killing him. Where I'm just normal and not on the verge of being arrested and most likely executed for killing close to a hundred people in such a short lifetime.

I try not to rip the dress as I tear myself out of it, my chest expanding too far and concaving too deeply with every forced breath. This isn't fair. This isn't fair. He shouldn't be here right now. I thought he would've at least given me until tonight when I inevitably stood Ace up and went to Judas with my hands already cuffed behind my back. He shouldn't be here right now when I'm not Areya Light but Vivienne McDowell, another spoiled nepo baby with too much money to spend, too big a smile to ever be dimmed, too much light to be so dark. He shouldn't be here.

"Areya, please," Judas says on the other side of the curtain, and it takes everything in me to control the shaking of my hands as I unzip my dress methodically, tensely. It's the same as when I come in after a gruesome kill: don't make a mess, take everything off swiftly but carefully, don't smudge the blood or gore on your face, fold the clothes neatly. I go about that routine until I am back dressed in my hoodie and leggings. The weather still has a bite of cold despite it being mid-May.

"Bright Eyes," Judas calls, desperate, making my heart pang in my chest at the softness of his voice. He hasn't called me that in what feels like forever. It stings just as much as it soothes the ache inside of my chest.

"At least check your phone, so you know what this is about," he pleads, so close to pushing back the curtain of the dressing room. I don't know why he hesitates—if it's Ace who holds him there, despite Ace being unusually quiet.

I swallow thickly as I pull my phone from my pocket, clicking it on to see three missed calls from Judas alone and a text message.

Judas
1:57 pm
Areya, please call me back immediately. This is about tonight. I think I found a way around this whole ordeal that can save all of us.

My heart drops as I read the message again and again and again until my eyes sting from their unblinking stare. A pang of anxiety fills my chest, the air around me suddenly too stiff and thick to breathe in, my hands shaking as I have to tightly grip my phone to keep it from falling from my hands.

What way? What is he talking about? Does he not know that there isn't some sort of way around this entire mess? That I will have to atone for my sins sooner rather than later? That it's my time to meet the other children Prissy hoarded and killed until they no longer served her?

I push back the curtain quickly, too harsh, always too rough in my grip. Judas stands there, wide-eyed and unblinking. Ace is still by the platform, his hands shoved in his pockets, his mouth set in a thin line, but I can see the way he grinds his teeth from here. I whisper to Judas so that Ace can't hear before stepping around him to stand next to Ace, the dress draped over my arm.

"I have to find shoes. And jewelry, too," I say stiffly, trying my best to seem as normal as possible, but even Ace can tell that something has set me off. He stares at me for a long while before looking at Judas, whose back is still to us, his shoulders hunched, his fists shaking. Ace looks at me once more with a question in his eyes but I only shake my head at him. Hesitantly, I reach my free hand out to his own, finding my grip to be clammy and shaking, but he grips it firmly, anyway.

He pulls me until Judas, who is still standing there, is far enough away from us. Then Judas rushes out into the stale air of the store, getting a few odd looks from shoppers. Ace watches him from over my head, his hand gripping mine tightly, as he slides the dress from my arm to his to let me shop around some more.

I pick out a plain pair of black flats, each with a fake diamond glued on top, and some costume jewelry that's too gaudy to be real. Ace doesn't say anything about it, nor about my shaking hands and clipped words, as we make our way to the register. I pay for it all in the cash I've accumulated behind Prissy's back, untraceable.

"Are you okay?" Ace asks once the dress is bagged alongside the jewelry and shoes as we make our way to his car. He opens the door for me again but doesn't close it until I look at him after buckling my seat belt.

"I'll be okay," I say instead of the truth, trying my best to not be too hopeful at the prospects of a future I had never imagined before. I give him a tight-lipped smile when he still doesn't close the door, to which he hesitantly does after a few beats of silence.

We drive home the same way: too quiet, stiff, something lingering in the air, heavy and unsaid. Ace doesn't ask me about what I said to Judas, and I don't offer up any information. The wall between us seems to get thicker and thicker the closer we get to my house. So thick that, by the time he pulls up, I'm surprised he says anything at all.

"I'll pick you up at seven, okay?" he says softly, as if the words pain him to even speak aloud. I nod, promising silently that this will be the last time I'll hurt him.

"Thank you for everything, Ace," I say softly, facing him in the passenger seat as I undo my seatbelt. I can feel the emotions welling up inside of my chest, and I can't help but reach forward and pull him into a hug. My arms are wrapped tight around his neck as I inhale his familiar scent of something sweet, something akin to cinnamon. Ace hesitates at my initiation of contact before he wraps his arms around me, tight, like he already knows that if he lets me go, I'll never return.

"It's no problem at all, Bubbles," he whispers into my hair, stroking my back softly as I hold him tight to me, memorizing the shape of him, sure that I'll never be able to see or feel or smell him again. I pull away when I've clung to him for entirely too long, pretending that my eyes don't well with tears. I gather my things wordlessly as Ace watches me, a small smile on his face. I hold my useless dress, shoes, and jewelry in my arms as I close the door, waving at him once through the window.

"Goodbye," I say to him, a sense of finality in my tone that he slightly furrows his brows at. But he only laughs, shaking his head at me as he puts his truck into drive.

"Yeah, I'll see you later, Bubs. Don't have me waiting!" he calls out as he pulls off, and I can only stand there and watch him leave. When he turns from my street, I finally step inside of the house, slipping quietly into my room to drop off my things despite the fact that I'm home alone right now.

But after tonight, hopefully, I won't have to be in this house for much longer.

Chapter 22

The walk to the abandoned playground is long but necessary for the time being. I don't know what I'm going into. If this was all some sort of trap set by Judas, if, the authorities would kill me right where I stand the moment I step foot onto the dried grass.

At the department store, I told Judas that I'd meet him here to talk about whatever was so pressing as long as he gave me until after the dance to turn myself in. He agreed, albeit hesitantly, and I hadn't heard from him since. I really hoped that it wasn't all a trick, a ploy, to get me here easier, without the fuss, if they already had Prissy. I hadn't heard from her all day, hadn't even seen her. I wonder if she was already starting to rot away in a ditch somewhere with a hole in her head.

The playground comes into view as I slow my steps down, suddenly feeling as though I couldn't breathe anymore. My chest tightens and my eyes water, my inhales too shaky and my exhales too quick. I have to slow my steps before I collapse, my vision in front of me blurry and shaky as I come to the realization that this could be the end for me right here.

But didn't I always crave my end? Easy and without so much pain that I could slip right into the afterlife without any scrapes or bruises? Didn't I always wish that there was a way to go out of this world easier than how I was brought in?

"You're okay," someone suddenly says beside me, making me whip my head to the right as I stumble away. "I got you." Judas. His voice is soft, his hair in less disarray than it was earlier. He doesn't have his gloves on as he holds me upright by my upper arms; his gaze is focused and steady as I start to hyperventilate.

"Am I going to die right now?" I ask him through a shaking hiccup, a cry breaking free from my mouth before I can swallow it back down. "Please, Judas, just let me know if I'm going to die in the next few moments. I don't want it to be a surprise. I'm tired of being scared; just let me know if I'm about to die."

I cling to him so tightly that he has to unfurl my hands from around his collar. He shushes me as I collapse onto him, my sobs too loud in the silence of the playground, the creaky swing set quiet for the first time since I've been here. I wait for the gun to press to the back of my head, for the whispering silence of Death to cradle me gently in its arms. But it never comes.

Judas ushers me to the swing set, still swaying despite the fact that there's no wind. He sets me down as gently as he can before he kneels in front of me. I let him reach up, slowly, unsure, to slip my glasses from my face. I must look a mess right now with my splotchy face and still running eyes, but he looks at me so kindly, as if my fate doesn't rest in his palms at the moment.

He cups my cheeks, wiping away the tears with his thumbs as he kneels before me, his skin touching mine, the feeling so unusual that I can't help myself from resting ever so softly against him.

"We have a way out of this," he says after a few minutes of silence when my breathing finally evens out. My body has gone stiff from the panic, and I can hear each and every bone creaking in protest when I finally straighten my back to sit up. I look down at him with my eyebrows furrowed, a pained expression taking over as I try to unravel his words.

"How? What does that even mean, Judas?" I ask quietly, voice bordering on defeat. I look down my nose at him, at how his cheeks have gone rosy, how the freckles across his nose seem to bleed into his complexion in the moonlit night.

Judas opens his mouth and closes it once, twice, trying to find his words. He bites at his bottom lip for a moment before looking up at me, his expression hard, serious. He lets go of my cheek, sliding his hands down until they find my own curled into my lap. He holds them firmly in his grip, my own sweaty and clammy, his cold and freezing, squeezing me with every passing second.

"It means I found a way for us to get away from everything," Judas says, pausing for a moment when I don't say anything. "From our powers. Prissy. The government. I found a way."

I find myself choking on the breath I struggle to inhale. It comes out shakily as I shake my head at him in confusion. A way out? That's impossible. If the CIA is waiting for me, how could I ever get away? If my powers have been intertwined into my very being since before I even left the womb, how is there any getting away from all of this?

And Prissy...there was never an escape from her. As much as I've thought about it, considered it, planned it—I could never get away from her. She was my mother, my owner, the hand constantly tugging at my leash. What would I even do once I got free? Run straight for the street, only to end up as roadkill, torn to pieces by something so much bigger than me, something that she tried to protect me from since I was born. Who am I without her? Would I even still exist if not under her thumb?

"I still don't understand you," I choke out, ripping my hands away from his own as I wipe them on my pants. I shoot up, startling Judas for a moment from how quickly I move. My legs feel restless, my heart hammering so quickly, I fear a ladder in my rib may break off and pierce the inside of my chest until it tears from my skin.

"Getting away from," I pause, motioning to the air around me, beyond me, my words thick as I try to fight the panic that builds inside of me. "That isn't even possible."

"I didn't think so either," Judas counters back just as quickly, standing from his kneeled position on the ground. He finds my faraway gaze, a mirror from when we first met, except this time, I don't tackle him or punch the swing set until my knuckles burst open red. Only this time does the sight of him calm me ever so slightly. My chest still feels too tight, but he holds my stare, his mouth set in a firm, unwavering line.

"But I found a way," Judas states surely, holding his hands out to me so that I can take them. But I can't; can only shake my head as I try to calm my racing heart, gesturing for him to continue speaking before I unravel right before his eyes.

"A witch in West Africa that I've been in contact with. She can heal us, and it'll be a way for us to have a fresh start." He pauses before tacking on, "Together."

I pause, my head reeling back in confusion as I just take him in. His baggy clothes and messy hair, his gap poking through pink lips, his glasses just slightly askew. His pleading gaze and open arms, waiting, ready for me to walk into, as if life were just that easy. He's always thought life was just that easy, though, hasn't he? That I could just stop killing people. That I could just stop being Prissy's weapon, that I could just choose my own fate and continue on with life without a care in the world.

Before I can stop it, a maniacal type of laughter bursts out of me. The sound is unheard of in my years of living, the distant memory of a time I've ever laughed this hard so far away that the picture of it is blurry in my mind. Judas' face sours ever so slightly, such a minuscule reaction that I would've missed it if Prissy hadn't trained me so well in studying people for so long.

"With what money?" I ask amidst the laughter, gripping my stomach as the escaped breaths inside of me press too roughly against my skin. "Prissy tracks everything that I have, so there's no way I'll be able to get it without her noticing and stopping me." And killing me is the last part that I don't say aloud, but he seems to understand my unspoken words anyway. My laughter dies with every word until I'm gritting my words through my teeth as if voicing these words out loud physically pains me. And they do.

Judas' face falls every so slightly. His nose twitches, his eyebrows turning down as if miffed at my laughter, as if his idea is something that is truly as laughable and unhinged as I come across at the moment. He huffs under his breath before crossing his arms over his chest and looking over to the deserted road beside us. No cars have passed by, which isn't unusual, but I still expect to see at least one black truck waiting around the corner to gun me down like the animal that I am.

"I have my own resources," Judas says after a long time, his tone hushed and snappy. He softens, though, when my face scrunches at him, my mouth turning up as I prepare to fire my missile at him.

Judas opens his arms to me, the illuming moonlight casting a halo around his blond hair, his eyes soft and his mouth agape.

"Please, just trust me," he counters when he realizes that his snappiness only raises my hackles more. "I've got it all figured out. All you have to do is say yes."

"And after that?" I shoot back, though, feeling cornered despite the open air. Has he lost his mind? Does he really think that a decision like this is so simple that all I have to do is say a single word, and everything will be better? Does he know that I've tried to simplify my life for years, and I've only ever made it more complicated when I tried to inflate myself as more than just a weapon? That I will only ever be an object used for mass destruction and nothing more?

"Then what?" I snap, flinging my arms around me wildly, feeling as unhinged as I must look at the moment. "We just get to ride off into the sunset, happily ever after? She'll never let me go." My words lose their bite with every word until they taper off into a whisper. Reality sets in, as it has so many times in the past whenever I've thought about escaping her.

Who will brush my hair when I've been good for so many weeks in a row? Who will help me wash the blood from my shoelaces when things get messier than expected? Who will cook for me when my panic attacks make my body akin to a statue, on the verge of teetering off a platform, ready to break into a million pieces?

"Then you have to get away from her before she finds out," Judas says slowly, his eyebrows turning down in concentration as he looks at me, his expression set and rigid. "Is she home right now?"

"No, but what does that have to do with anything?" I ask exasperatedly, the sudden rush of panic subsiding once more as I feel my body begin to stiffen once more. I collapse onto the swing behind me, swaying ever so slightly as I stare at the sand beneath my feet. I blink as I watch the tops of Judas' own feet press right against mine, looking up at him through wet lashes as he cups my chin in his cold grip. He holds my stare for a beat too long, and my heart drops before he even gets the words out, fearing what I know he's going to say just a moment too late.

"We leave now. Right now," Judas says quietly, his words hushed as he holds me steady in his grip. I feel my entire body lock up, my breaths pausing in the hollow of my throat as I tremble all over.

"That's impossible," I whisper back, mouth barely moving, eyes wide and unseeing. It's impossible, right? Hasn't it always been impossible to escape from her grip? Isn't that always what I've told myself? Isn't that what she told me when she found my bags packed once when I was younger and the money in her purse missing? Isn't that what happened after she beat me to the point of broken bones while she nursed me back to health in the same breath?

"Is it?" Judas rips me from my own thoughts, kneeling in front of me once more as he grips my cheeks in both of his hands to steady me. "You could go home, pack a bag right now, only the essentials, and we'll be on the road before she even comes home. I know some people who have connections. We can be out of the country by dawn."

He says it so surely that I almost believe him. That I almost let myself find the hope that I've buried deep inside of me so long ago. I shake my head, trying to pull away from his hold, but he only grips my face tighter, his eyes wide and pleading.

"Judas, I don't know," I whisper, feeling tears beginning to build behind my eyes, my face contorting, ugly, as I try to hold back a terrified sob from escaping my throat. Judas sighs, shaking his head at me, finally releasing me when my tears muddy his palms. He sits back on his knees in front of me, almost as if in worship, as if he is merely a beggar trying to convince me to give him a spare blessing.

"This is the only way for you," he says quietly, eyes far away as he looks past my head, as if watching someone from over my shoulder. The hairs on the back of my neck stand. "If not, the CIA will be at your door, if not at the dance, in front of everyone, airing out what you've done." His eyes slide to my own, such a muted blue that they seem unrecognizable in the moment. It unsettles something deep within me, so deep that I can't reach it if I tried. My breath catches in my throat.

"You don't want that, do you?" he asks, softening his words ever so slightly when the tears only spill over the apples of my cheeks in quick waves. I lean forward shakily, gripping his hands in mine as my bottom lip trembles uncontrollably.

"I want to be free," I whisper, something I've said to myself so many times in the dead of night when I was sure Prissy was asleep or out of the house. I've wanted to be free since the moment I gained consciousness within my mother's womb, since I was thrust into this cold world with people who were meant to love me. Since Prissy took me in and molded me not to be a person but a thing that she could dispose of any time she so pleased. I just want to be free.

"So come with me, then," Judas pleads, his hands gripping mine so tightly that the bite of his cold skin stings. I can't control my sob as I shake my head at him, drool spilling from my lips as I tremble all over, my mouth opening and closing, my throat empty of everything I want to say, the fear of letting it all out for once in my life.

"I'm scared," I finally confess, my eyes squeezed shut as I bow my head between us. But Judas doesn't let me curl into myself. He nudges my chin with our still clasped hands until I look at him through teary eyes, my breaths hiccuped and uncontrolled.

"I know you are. I am, too," he reassures me with the tiniest smile, tilting the corner of his mouth. "But we can't keep living in fear of her anymore. She can't keep having this control and power over us. It's time to get that power back. What do you say?"

Judas looks at me in a way that conveys that my answer will determine whether or not I make it out alive tonight with something as simple as a yes or no. Everything has always been so simple for him. Morality. The fate of a bad person in his hands. Leaving when necessary. I've always been too much of a coward to look at things through just a black-and-white lens.

"Just pack the essentials?" I whisper under my breath, holding onto his hands for dear life as if my answer will cause me to float away from him. Judas smiles ever so softly, as if I answered right, his eyes softening around the edges. He nods once, kissing the backs of my hands as if in thanks, as if my yes has saved him from some fate I'll never know.

"Just the essentials. I'll meet you back here in an hour," he says, standing to his full height as he pulls out his phone and begins typing furiously. He must be reaching out to those connections he said he has, readying our transport to wherever in West Africa. It all seems unreal.

In an hour, Ace will be on his way to pick me up for the dance. I'll already be long gone by then, it seems. In a way, I'm glad I won't have to see the way his heart breaks once he knows I chose Judas, my freedom, over him. But the reality sinks in that I won't ever be seeing him again. My gut churns at the thought of it, my tears finally slowing, but my body sways uneasily as I stand to my feet.

"Okay," I murmur under my breath, ready to start trekking back home, a home that was never really mine when Judas stops me with a hand on my shoulder.

"Are you sure?" he asks, eyebrows furrowed as he roams his gaze all over my face, tear-stained and puffy. "Because you have to be in this all the way, Bright Eyes. I don't need you to betray me because of your fear." He says seriously, turning me to face him when I try to look away. My bottom lip trembles in fear, in anxiety, in anticipation, but I bite it to keep it still. I hold my chin up, despite its wobbling, and look at him through teary lashes as surely as I can.

"I wouldn't. I'm sure about this," I state, despite the fact that I don't feel as sure as I would like to. Judas watches me for a few agonizing seconds, before he nods, head turned back to his phone as he releases me.

"Okay, then. Well, I'll go get a few things that I need, and then we meet back here at seven. Alright?" He glances up at me before holding the phone to his ear, the other side ringing faintly as I let the gravity of everything start to sink in. I nod, my entire body numb, as I turn away from him, the feeling of lead sitting heavy in my chest.

"Okay," I say one last time before I start my trek back home. I check my phone's time, which reads 5:56 pm. I don't know when Prissy will be home since when she's out all day, she usually doesn't come home from her "business" meetings until after nine. Ace should be picking me up at seven.

That means I have less than an hour to go home, pack, and meet Judas back here before anybody sees me. The walk back home from the park is a long one, which means I have even less time to get everything. I have to be fast. I have to be fast. I can't get caught. I can't be under her thumb anymore. I can't. It's time for me to finally be free for once in my life.

I have to be free, even if it's only for a moment.

Chapter 23

My breath is heavy and quick by the time I make it home, my legs screaming at me in protest from how hard I've pushed myself to make it back in time. The time reads 6:23 pm. I have to hurry if I don't want to run into Ace as I leave the house.

I rush upstairs, pulling out one of my many traveling bags that I've had to stuff my life into when Prissy and I have moved states. I know how to pack in a hurry, a skill I've developed over the years since being her weapon. Every time someone gets too close, or I make a mistake, or Prissy needs to leave at that very moment for whatever reason, I have to put my entire room into a few bags and boxes before she leaves me. I think thats why she never let me accumulate too many possessions, too much luggage to bear, too many things to have to keep up with.

In a way, I'm thankful for that because picking out the essentials is easy for me when I only have so many things. I throw in a few of my favorite pairs of pants and shirts, a couple of hoodies, two pairs of shoes, my phone charger, and a toothbrush. I ignore the glittering and sparkling black dress I just purchased earlier today, the shoes and jewelry matching it, pretend I don't feel its weight resting heavily on my shoulders every single time I pass it.

When I feel as though I've packed everything that I need, do I finally pause and look at my room—this room. It was never really mine, was it? Nothing about this life has ever been mine; I've only ever been a replacement for the replacement. A space holder for something that Prissy has been looking for for centuries, a stepping stone for some greater achievement that I'll never be worthy of knowing.

So, I do not say goodbye to this room, as its never been mine to have anyway. I turn on my heel, checking the time once more as I amble down the steps—6:36 pm. Knowing Ace, he's waiting by the door, ready to leave out at any minute now to pick me up promptly at seven. I have to get out of here.

My feet hit the last step, and as I turn toward the door, something makes me pause. The lights are still out, but there's a candle lit in the dining room that wasn't lit when I came home. It smells of lavender and honey, a scent I can't stand but one of Prissy's favorites. She only ever lights it when she's upset with me, to make me uncomfortable, to push me. I don't have to turn my head when she speaks.

"What do we have here?" Her voice is amused, a lilt to it that makes me aware of just how small I am compared to her. I am merely a mouse caught in her sharp claws, ready to puncture me when my screaming annoys her enough. My heart drops to the bottom of my stomach, and suddenly, the panic from before arises once again. I can't breathe. I can't move.

Why did I ever let myself ever dream? Hope that I could escape her? Foolish, I've always been so foolish to think that I would ever get to leave her without also leaving this mortal realm.

"Please, just let me go," I whisper, my voice cracking as my eyes well with tears. I can feel my bottom lip wobbling, my chest expanding too far out, my breaths uneven and heavy. Bile touches the back of my throat, and I have to swallow it back down, my fear alongside with it, but it doesn't go down as easily.

"I haven't even done anything yet, and you're already pleading?" Prissy pouts, demanding my attention when I stare at the door for too long. My only escape is gone; the distance to my only escape is so far away she'll have me dead on the floor before I even take another step toward it. I finally face her and find her sitting at the head of the dining room table, long and gray with a white cloth covering it, a single three-wick candle in the middle of the table. The curtains are drawn, making the space even darker, but my eyes adjust to her form either way.

She sits there, casually, so calm, as if she always knew that this day would come when I would leave her. Her hands are folded under her chin, her ash-blond hair tucked behind her ears, her glassy eyes almost as see through and clear as my own. I don't think I've ever looked more like her than in this moment, but the evilness that pervades her bright smile makes me pause. I've never been evil like that, have I? Despite my bloodied hands and my footsteps that have tracked through gore, I've never been as evil as her, have I? There's always been some slither of good, right?

Right? Aren't I redeemable, somehow? Aren't I worthy of another chance, despite the fact that I never gave extra chances to the people I hunted down as if they were mere bugs underneath my shoe? I'm still good, somehow, deep inside of me, right?

"Let's cut to the chase; you've been in contact with the boy," Prissy says, shrugging her shoulders, making me flinch at the minuscule movement, but she's always been a quick one. She narrows her eyes at me but doesn't move from her spot. Only jerks her chin toward me so that I stand on the other side of the table, my bag still slung over my shoulder, freedom still dripping from the tip of my tongue.

"Judas," I say his name in a rush of breath, realizing at this very moment that she must've known, somehow, all along.

"Yes, Judas. The name I gave him that night he betrayed me by choosing them over us." She spits the words out through her teeth as if they physically pain her to say. I try not to falter at the information that Judas is the name she gave him, much like Areya being the name that she gave me. So what was his real name? And why hadn't he ever told me? I shake my head to clear my fuzzy thoughts, focus on the situation in front of me, not the small details she throws out to unsteady me.

"He didn't betray you because he chose his actual family over a witch who had cursed him and another child," I say to her, my voice shaky, unsure of speaking back to her. I've never been able to do it since I was a child, in fear that she'd smack me so hard a few of my teeth would be knocked out from my jaw.

"Then what do you call me being here right now, then?" Prissy's smile unfurls like some Cheshire Cat, big and wide, as she wiggles her fingers in my direction. She's trying to throw me off kilter, trying to cast doubt in my mind so that the only person I'll ever trust depends on is her. I won't let her do that to me again. I can't. Not if I want to make it out of here alive and no longer be a weapon for her to use.

"I don't care anymore. I just want to leave. Please." My lip trembles on my plea as I let my bag fall from my shoulder. I clasp my hands together tightly in front of my face, my head bowing to her in submission. I won't fight if I don't have to. Please don't make me fight you, Priscilla. Please just let me go free.

"And go where Areya? What are you going to do without me?"

"Live," I say, my chin tilted up despite its trembling. "I am going to live, and read whatever books that I wish to. I am going to go out and make friends. I am going to be normal and have the ability to look those that I love in the eye and tell them just how much I love them. I am going to be Vivienne McDowell."

Silence hangs over the two of us for a few beats before Prissy bursts into a fit of laughter. It makes me startle, my hackles raised, my fists clenched beside me. She throws her head back, smacking at the table, the candle in the middle of it jolting ever so slightly. I tear my gaze away from the building flames when her cackles descend into barely muted chuckles.

"The missing kid from thirteen years ago, who also just so happens to be connected to almost a hundred murders across the entire United States? Don't make me laugh." She wipes away a stray tear, her grin wide and teasing. When her laughter finally subsides, the heaviness of the room weighs on both of us. There's a million things I could say to her right now, a million ways that this could go, none of the options looking to be in my favor whatsoever. I try again with begging.

"Please let me go."

"You are mine, Areya!" Prissy shouts so loudly, barely letting me get my words out before her voice rises. She slams her fists into the table, makes the candle in the middle jolt once more, and unsteadies it. I flinch, hands barely raising, forming ever so slowly into fists. Her eyes, pale cerulean and wide, narrow on my hands, her lip gritting back to show her teeth.

"Mine to use, mine to do whatever I please with. You are nothing but a dog on my leash, and the only way you'll ever leave me is if you hang yourself or I slit your throat myself." Her voice drips pure venom, a promise to follow through on her threat if I raise my fists any higher. Slowly, slowly, do I lower them, always the obedient mutt. That disarms her just a little, and she sits back into her seat, her arms folded across her chest as she curls her lip back in disgust at the mere sight of me.

"Why do you do this, Prissy?" I whisper when the silence has stretched on for too long, my voice wavering on a wet gasp. "Why do you keep damning children like this?"

Prissy only snorts, rolling her eyes into her head as she grumbles under her breath. She leans forward on the table once more, resting her cheek in her palm as if bored of this conversation, her body lax and annoyed. My own tense and trembling all over, rooted in place, ready to take off the moment I deem it safe enough to do so, which will never happen.

"Oh, he told you that, too, now did he?" She rolls her eyes once more, huffing petulantly as she turns her hands over, examining her nails as if bored with the conversation. "Anything to turn you against me," she grumbles beneath her breath.

"I was against you the day you cursed me," I say slowly, eyebrows turning down as I steady myself by clenching my hands around the top of the chairs in front of me. She could clear this table in seconds and be on me before I could even blink, and the fact that I dared stand so close to her shows that this was always a suicide mission.

"All of you children have always been so ungrateful, but I know you all can't help it. It's what she did to me, but God, it never gets easier." Prissy scoffs, leaning back in the chair as she begins to pick her nails. I give pause at her words, replaying them over and over again in my head as I try to digest what she's talking about.

She's never shared anything with me. Has told me time and time again that weapons were never meant to know why they're firing, just where to aim. After a while, I stopped asking her about...anything, really. About who she was, how she became a witch, and why she sent me on these missions for a reason I would never be able to know. I just assumed she'd kill me before ever revealing who she was. Maybe she'll just kill me after, anyway.

"What are you talking about?" I ask her slowly, expecting her to flip me off, to pounce any second now. But Prissy sits there, silent, staring at the dancing flames between us. Her mouth is set in a thin line, and the longer I look at her, the more her face seems to morph by the second. Old and tired, wrinkled beyond possibility, her eyes sunken and deep, her mouth creased into a thin line full of resentment and hatred. After another minute of silence, does she begin to speak.

"Centuries ago, when I was only a girl, taking care of the wealthy's children, I became extremely cocky. Arrogant of my skills to pacify a babe or to nurture a child to become strong and courageous, I got ahead of myself. I declared that I was better than any mortal or goddess when it came to motherhood without ever bearing a child myself. You can imagine how the goddess of motherhood felt when she heard my declaration." Prissy smiles without much humor, her eyes distant with every passing word.

"Her name was Leto, the goddess. She visited me nights later to bestow a curse upon me to live forever without ever being able to bear my own children, much less find the love from one." She pauses for a long time, opening and closing her mouth once, twice, again before she smiles humorlessly. I watch the way her eyes water ever so slightly, her lip trembling before she bites it to still its rapid movement. I've never seen her cry like this, emotional and open and vulnerable, and I have never been more sure that I am guaranteed to die by the end of the night if she is letting me see this side of her.

"I quickly was banished from my village, as the children could no longer stand to be near me. They cried and fought me every chance they could get, and things only got worse when a babe died because of me. Because I got so angry." She bites her lip once more; fists clenched where she rests them on top of the table, her nails digging into her pale skin.

"She loved me so much, and then—and then she would scream just at the sight of me, and she wouldn't stop." Her voice is pained as she looks down at her lap, almost as if reenacting the very scene in front of her once more, centuries later. "I shook her just once, and at the same time, a royal walked in. After that, I was driven out by my people.

"I wandered for so long, trying to find love, trying to bear children, trying to die. Nothing worked." Prissy shakes her head as a smile, a barely there smile, tilts up the corner of her mouth as if in remembrance.

"So I began practicing magic, anything to reverse her curse, and in the meantime, did I start to help people out with their own children. I blessed them, reversed illnesses, and made them stronger and healthier. And while I thought that this would help me find a purpose in my never-ending life, it only brought on such a bitterness that I couldn't spit from my mouth." Prissy's face morphs into one of such ugliness, such contempt, that I find myself rearing back when she finally looks up at me from under her lashes. I don't recognize her in this moment, clad in all black, the darkness of the room swallowing her up, everything except that hateful gaze illuminated by a single candle. She looks like the nightmare that she is.

"All of these people, all of these couples, never satisfied with just having a baby. Whether the baby was ill or had looks that they didn't like, they were never satisfied and would much rather take up a witch to change their baby than to love them no matter what." Prissy pauses, her fists slowly unclenching, her eyes softening as she takes all of me in. Her eyes roam my figure, from the hair she has always brushed to the hands that she always held whenever I was terrified.

"I thought love was supposed to be unconditional. It would've been for my child." She confesses so softly that just for a moment, for just a single slithering second, does my heart break for her. To have to walk this earth until the end of time, unable to do or find the one thing that you want and desire most in life. But it doesn't make sense to me.

"That doesn't explain why you curse them, Prissy," I say softly, snapping my mouth shut when her eyes quickly dart back to my own after wandering away. She sneers at me, the vulnerability that was shining through those tiny cracks going dark once more as she narrows her gaze.

"Why keep pouring love into those when you know you'll never receive it yourself?" she asks, her head tilted, greasy blond hair shadowing her face for a second. "So I used them, the children, to prove myself to Leto. Maybe she'd reverse the curse if she saw that I was doing good in the world."

"By beating your children?" I counter back wildly, leaning forward on where I rest my weight on the chair, incredulous. "By killing them when they no longer served your purpose?"

I think back on the little red headed girl, who was a decade my junior, and the boy that could not go on without her. I think about the loss being so great that he loved this girl who he must've seen as a sister, so much more than the mother that Prissy could never be to him. I think about the pain they both must've felt, being ripped away from the person who took them in, vowed to love them despite their differences, and snuffed them out the moment they could no longer serve her.

I think about all of those children over the years. I think about the first one she killed with such anger in her heart. I think about how I cannot let this go on any longer, even at the cost of my own life, even through the fear that pervades my very being.

"By ridding the world of evil," Prissy spits as if the answer were obvious this whole time. "Why do you think I sent you out there to kill people, Areya? For the fun of it? I'm taking out drug dealers. Rapists, pedophiles, burglars, unjust murderers, abusers, terrorists. I'm righting the world with the children who will never love me."

"Do you really think that that's what she wanted from you?" I ask incredulously, leaning forward as the words spill from my lips before I can swallow them back down. "What her end goal for you was? To kill god, know how many children, to use them and manipulate them, to show that you're some good guy? She's the goddess of motherhood!"

"Don't you raise your fucking voice at me!" Prissy screams at me, slamming her hands on the table so hard that it upturns the candle, the fire instantly alighting the cloth on the dining room table. I've always hated this table, this house. "I am your mother, Areya, and you will respect me!" She points at me, standing to her full height, which has never looked so big until now when the flame from the table lights up the wickedness that has always been in her eyes.

"You've never been my mother," I spit at her, the adrenaline of the moment lighting up my head, the thought that I need to leave this house before it burns down, fueling my words. "You've only ever been a witch that has ruined my life and countless others. I've always hated you."

Prissy's scream is so primal, so earth-shattering, and world-ending that when I finally open my eyes after her ear-splitting screech, she's already on me before I can even lift my fists.

Chapter 24

Prissy somehow clears the table in only a second, her hands around my throat as she leaps on me. I scream as we both go down, her weight pinning me to the floor as I thrash underneath her. She rests her weight on my hips, one knee pinning my arm down as she grits her teeth at me, her nails digging into my flesh, blood bubbling up from beneath my skin.

"Ungrateful!" she screams at me, leaning down until she can roar in my face. My breaths are shortening, black dots spotting my vision. I have to get out of here. I have to fight back, but I've always been conditioned to never fight back. She's my mother. I can't hit her, can I? But with the way she looks at me now, with such hatred and anger, I don't think she's ever truly loved me as a mother should.

With my free hand, I start to claw at her face, scratching up whatever flesh that I can to get her off of me, my throat. But she doesn't let up. Instead, she bears down even harder, crushing my windpipe until I wheeze beneath her, my eyes rolling up into my head.

With only a lick of regret, do I dig my thumb into her right eye, gritting my teeth at the feeling of it giving underneath my digit. Its softness makes a wet sound as I push even harder against it, waiting for the inevitable pop. Prissy screams, a banshee type of wail as she throws herself off of me, but not before delivering a backhand as she falls backward.

I barely feel the split of my lip from her ringed hand as I start to scramble backward. It's a sight I don't think either of us ever expected; the flamed tablecloth has touched the drapes that covered the closed window, almost the entirety of the dining room now on fire. Prissy kneeling only a few feet away from me, holding her eye as she screams profanities at me, the flame licking her pants from when she leaped across the table.

"Priscilla, don't make me do this! Please," I sob to her, crawling back on my hands as she begins to advance toward me once more. I hold up my hands to her, pleading, desperate, afraid of what will become of the both of us if I were to raise my fists to her for the first time ever in my life.

"I thought you were different," Prissy spits as she stumbles to her feet, the flame on her legs seemingly unnoticed by her. She merely shakes it off despite the fact that the fire only seems to swallow more of her body. She doesn't even look like she's in pain, only anger and hatred fueling her body as she takes another step toward me.

"I thought I finally had my perfect child, my perfect weapon. But you're a mistake just like the rest of them." She spits at me, throwing a punch that I should've dodged but take anyway. I let her punch me again and again until the pain becomes too great, and I knock my forehead against her own to subdue her. Prissy stumbles, shaking her head once as she falls to her knees, the flames now licking most of her body.

"I killed innocent people for you!" Her tears are swallowed by the heat, leaving burning trails in their wake as she claws at my ankles, trying to pull me toward her. I kick her off. I kick her again in the chin when she won't let go. She falls to the floor, her movement is sluggish now, her skin melting, dripping onto the floor, charred and smoky.

"The lady in Arizona? She was onto you." Prissy grits through her teeth, sitting up as she tries to make her way to me again. I shake my head at her, eyes wide and unseeing of her horrid face, only seeing pleading eyes and hidden faces, terrified of the real-life monster that had invaded their home.

"Had evidence against you. I had you take her out for your own good, and this is how you repay me? Selfish child." Prissy bites at me, clawing for me once more, but I reel my foot back and kick her so hard in the chest that she is sent back, flying into the flames of the dining room. It has touched the kitchen now and moves onto the living room, the stairs, and soon the front door. My only way out.

"Don't do this to me, Areya," Prissy calls when the flames have paralyzed her and when the eye I dug into melts down the apples of her cheeks. I can barely make out the person that she was, as she seems to morph into something entirely different, her face from hundreds of years ago. She looks so human, with brittle hair and a gaping mouth, pleading and so desperate to be saved, her ego and her arrogance getting the best of her once more.

I can only sit there, surrounded by the flames, chest a heavy mess, my neck and lip still bleeding from her hands. From hands that were supposed to love me and hold me and nurture me when my own mother didn't. From hands that have only ever brutalized me in the only way that she knew how to.

As I look at her, I realize that I have always loved her. I love my mother, and that statement doesn't feel as impactful in this moment, with her flesh dripping from her muscle from her tendons from her bones, with a face that morphs into old age and ugly, with a face that I do not match, but see every piece of myself in. I love her.

Despite it all, I love Prissy. She hurts me, and she uses me, but to the God above and below—I love her. She cries out for me, the marrow of the bones in her hand reaching for me in agony. She grits at me through it all. A demand to help her despite the fact that she'll throw me to the flames as soon as I hold onto her. That she'll pull me right back out the moment, I almost pass out from the smothering heat. That she'll nurse me back to health, hold me against her chest, tell me I'm worth the headache anyway.

But Prissy doesn't love me as much as I love her; she never has. But don't all dogs love their owners more than anyone in the world. Aren't their owners their entire world altogether? Are their owners, not both god and human, the beginning of all things, the ending of everything?

Her world is so much bigger than me. It always has been. I've only ever been another child, another name, another puppet, another rabid dog pulling at its leash for her. I've only ever been a stray that she buries out back when I snap at her too many times when the violence that overtook me in my forming years has hardened me to struggle with ever trusting a helping hand.

And yet, I love her. I love her enough to let the flames engulf me, too. We can go out from this world together, her soul old, mine still new, both so grossly tainted by our sins. But we'll be together, balanced, leveled this time. She'll love me as much as I love her.

I stand on shaky feet, reaching out for the extended hand that Prissy holds toward me before someone snatches me back. I gasp, crying out as I try to go to her, my mother, as her face melts from the fire, as the heat begins to engulf me too. But it's not letting me go, whatever force holds me back, and I cry for her as her eyes slip close and her arm weakens before falling at her sides.

"Bright Eyes, we have to go!" Someone screams at me, pulling me backward as I sob for her, for my mother that was never really mine, for a house that I never really fit in. I scratch at Judas, who is dragging me back toward the door, his thin arms suddenly strong around my middle as he coughs in my ear from the smoke overtaking the house. He snatches up my bag, somehow barely touched by the flames as he pulls me toward the door as my fight dies with every passing second.

Watching someone die is an intimate affair, I realize, as I watch the life sputter from Prissy's eyes, her gaping mouth. The moment isn't meant for me, for my teary eyes, or my selfishly trembling jaw. No, this moment was for her, as she gasped one last time, her voice hoarse, her throat burning with every gulp of ash dusting the air.

Watching someone die is more personal than anyone makes it out to be. It's close; Death lingering somewhere in the room, close enough to reach out and grab you, too, if you're not careful. I almost wasn't careful. It's harrowing, hearing their last choked cries and their eyes lose color with every second. Their hands holding onto the bleeding wound, holding onto your shaking hand, holding onto their newborn baby, holding onto Death's bony grip.

Watching someone die is as intimate as it is detached.

You go through the moment with cotton stuffed in your ears—"Areya, we're leaving now, okay? Do you hear me? We're leaving for good."

—You go through the moment with your vision blurred—the house burns so brightly, the roof caving in, a little redhead girl stares at me through the window as I watch the house through the rearview mirror.

—You go through the moment with your skin numbed over—burns cover my hands and my feet, but I don't feel the pain; Judas buckles my seatbelt for me, but his touch is distant; tears slide down my cheeks, but I haven't been able to feel my skin for what feels like ages now.

You watch them go and think; this must be how I'll go, too. Painful and slow and merciless as a crowd looks on, that I won't deserve the intimacy either, that I'll have to suffer, as do they. It's as withdrawn as passing by roadkill, knowing that Death will wrap you in its arms one day, too.

Judas shakes me until my head clears, my eyes still blurry, my mouth dry from the screams that I pulled from my throat. He's saying something to me, a phone shoved in my face with one hand as he uses the other to steer recklessly. I note the firetrucks speeding past us, concerned faces of people coming from their houses to see what the commotion is about. I take the phone wordlessly, my movement still stiff, my body still numb.

"Hello," I croak out, my voice scratchy, as another tear slides from my cheeks. I hear heavy breathing on the other side, and I don't think I can handle any more heartbreak tonight as Ace calls out my name desperately on the other side of the line.

"Areya!" he calls, almost relieved to hear me speaking. "Your house—your house is on fire. What's going on? Where are you?" I can hear him panting as if he had been running around and hear the firefighters and neighbors in the background calling out commands to stop the flames. Ace calls to someone in the back that I'm not in the house, but he doesn't sound relieved either way.

"Areya, where are you?" Ace demands once more when I have gone quiet on the other side of the line. I watch Judas speed down the streets, turning corners on two wheels to make his way out of Devils Lake, out of North Dakota, as quickly as he can. I can only hold on, my entire body locking up as more tears drip down the apples of my cheeks.

"I'm leaving, Ace," I manage quietly, my bottom lip trembling so hard that I have to bite down to quell it. Ace pauses for a long time, his breath sucking in quickly as the other side of the line goes eerily quiet. I can tell that Judas is listening, but he doesn't say anything; just keeps his eyes on the road as he navigates us onto the highway.

"Leaving? Areya, what are you talking about?" Ace pauses once more, and I can hear him swallowing thickly as he shuffles about, his voice suddenly dropping to a whisper. "You didn't do this to your mom, did you?"

And in reality, I didn't. She did all of this to herself, but a tiny slither of me, a piece that still sees her reaching out for me while the flames swallowed her, tells me that I did. I shake my head even though he can't see me, squeezing my eyes shut as I speak through my clenched teeth.

"I can't explain it right now. But I promise, in the future, I will," I tell him, sure of Judas' plan, of being healed, of becoming normal, of being reversed. We just have to give it time, the both of us.

"Areya, where are you?" Ace sounds frantic now as if he can tell that our conversation is on borrowed time. "I'll come pick you up, and we can talk about it. I'm sure it was an accident; the police will understand." His voice borders on pleading, and I can picture him pacing back and forth, hands in his hair as his eyes go wide with worry. I can't handle it; I can't handle seeing another person trying to reach out for me tonight, and I have to swallow down a sob as I clench my eyes shut.

"I have to go, Ace. I'm sorry," I whisper, pulling the phone away from me, but Ace calls my name once more, desperate.

"Areya." He starts, his voice dropping to unfamiliar territory. "Please don't go. You're the only person in this world who cares about me. Please." I already know what he's going to say, and I feel my chest squeezing in on itself at the very thought of it. Tears slip through my clenched lids as I shake my head, gripping the phone so tightly that I think I hear it crack in between my fingers.

"Ace, please don't," I whisper, pleading with everything in me for him to not hurt me so much with this goodbye.

"I think I'm in love with you, Areya," Ace confesses softly, and I can hear Judas suck in a breath. Everything goes silent for only a moment before I unleash such a gut-wrenching sob that my head goes light and fuzzy. Ace gasps quietly on the other side, but before he can say anything else, I chuck my phone from the window, hearing its distant crunch as it meets the asphalt.

I palm my face in my hands, my entire body lurching with every broken sob and cry I've held in for years now. Judas rubs at my back gently as he steers with one hand, his voice soft,

"It was for the best, Bright Eyes." But it doesn't comfort me as much as I wished it would have. "Everything will be okay after this. I promise you."

Judas sounds so sure of himself. Has always made everything out to be so simple. I'm not sure how I will survive him these next few weeks, months, maybe even years. But he will be the only person I'll be with, so I'll have to learn how. I just wonder how much being isolated with him will parallel being with Prissy.

About the Author

Laylah Jackson is a recent college graduate with a major in Psychology and a minor in English. While pursuing her master's, she still finds the time to write out every story and character that has crossed her mind. Despite her puppy fighting for her attention, she plans to continue her writing career by creating short stories, novels, and poetry. She is also a lover of music, having played piano for over a decade, along with four other instruments under her belt. When she isn't writing, she's crocheting, painting, having fun with her nieces, and cosplaying at conventions with her best friend.

Areya Light was made, not born, for power.

Cursed before birth and raised by a witch who sees her as nothing more than a weapon, Areya has never had control of her own life. With a single glance, she can kill - and that's exactly what she was created to do.

Now eighteen and hiding out in a remote North Dakota town, Areya begins to question everything she's been told. Stirred by the kindness of a local boy and haunted by the return of another cursed soul, she finds herself torn between the deadly path laid out for her and the fragile promise of freedom.

Will she remain the weapon she was shaped to be - or fight to reclaim her humanity?

www.ingramcontent.com/pod-product-compliance
Lightning Source LLC
Chambersburg PA
CBHW050304110726
47899CB00007B/2105